SOMEONE ELSE'S CONFLICT

SOMEONE ELSE'S CONFLICT

by
Alison Layland

HONNO MODERN FICTION

First published by Honno Press in 2014
'Ailsa Craig', Heol y Cawl, Dinas Powys, South Glamorgan, Wales,
CF64 4AH

1 2 3 4 5 6 7 8 9 10

The Author would like to stress that this is a work of fiction and no
resemblance to any actual individual or institution is intended or
implied.

A catalogue record for this book is available from the British Library.

Published with the financial support of the Welsh Books Council.

ISBN 978-1-909983-12-0
Cover design: Graham Preston
Text design: Elaine Sharples
Printed in Wales by Gomer Press

*In loving memory of
my father, David Howett*

ACKNOWLEDGEMENTS

I would like to thank all at Honno, especially Caroline Oakley, Janet Thomas and Helena Earnshaw, for their hard work in bringing this novel to publication.

Special thanks to my friends Elaine Walker and Martine Bailey for invaluable insight and support at all stages of writing this novel and beyond. Thanks also to Simon Rees for advice under the Literature Wales mentoring scheme, to the lovely Ty Newydd Writers' Centre and to Ann Stonehouse for all-round support and friendship, including providing me with a writing retreat at a critical stage. I am also grateful for the feedback and encouragement I received from Wendy Barker, James Layland, John Stonestreet, Kari Sperring, Heather Mitchell and Mary Perkins.

During my travels in the Balkans I met and talked to many people whose help was vital to my understanding, along with the chroniclers, in fact and in fiction, of the 1990s wars and their aftermath. I am grateful to them all, and to Zoran Stojanac for help with the Croatian language.

Thanks to barrister Richard Davenport and forensic investigator Paul Beeton for valuable advice on points of law and police procedures. Any errors in interpretation are mine.

And last, but never least, my heartfelt thanks to my family, especially my husband David, for everything.

Prologue

The boy wakes. It is still dark. The intermittent distant rumble is not a storm, or even a dream. He gets up and dresses quickly. The sporadic artillery fire is closer than he has ever heard it. Peering through the curtains, he is unsure whether the faint glow above the bare mountain ridge heralds approaching war or simply the sunrise. As he turns away, about to run to his parents' room, he hears a quiet but insistent tapping on the window. His friends beckon. More afraid of losing face than confronting the still-distant menace of what is approaching from beyond the mountain, he is soon out in the cold, pre-dawn twilight. He waves away their taunting – he is the youngest, and they accuse him of not wanting to come – and after a rapid whispered conference they head for the rise above the village, a perfect look-out. Their plan is to scan the road that winds down from the ridge and run back with details of the vehicles, the weapons, the number of men. Heroes valiantly raising the alert before diving for shelter with their families in the cellars. It is all too unreal, the more so for the constant TV reports, to be truly frightening.

But none of the boys can believe how fast they are. They are still watching the vehicles straggling over the ridge when the front of the small convoy is almost on them. And then the shelling begins. He watches, horrified, as a chunk is blasted from his neighbour's house, then another. He prays silently that no one is inside. Suddenly they are running back down, keeping to the trees, their planned warning redundant. He trips and the world comes up to meet him with a sickening crunch. It feels like only a few seconds that he lies winded, but it is too long. Although he is not seriously hurt, when he sits up and scans the slope below, it is empty. His friends have either given him up or are themselves too terrified to notice he is missing.

By the time he is on his feet and making his way cautiously through the sparse woods, the war has reached his village. Of course it actually reached them a while back. His best friend and his family, along with the other Croats, left months ago. Others, Serb refugees from Croat and Bosnian-held areas, have come here and taken over abandoned houses. Everyone has stories of relatives or friends elsewhere who have been killed, or horrifically injured, or lost their homes. The war is why he has not been out of the village, even to the next town, for a long while. And it has caused the constant lament and calls for retribution on the news, his parents' attempts to conceal their terror as they watch it all too obvious. Now it has come for him, too.

He picks his way carefully, as if a snapping twig beneath his feet could possibly be heard above the growing chaos below. There is no breeze but he keeps thinking he sees movement around him. He crouches immobile by a tree, watching the destruction unfold as the attackers move in. The returning fire, from the small unit installed to defend them together with men from the village, many of the villagers armed with little more than hunting rifles, does little to stop the onslaught. They were supposed to be safe now. This wasn't meant to happen. But it has; the Croats are moving in to reclaim their land. He is supposed to hate them for it. He has tried, but doesn't understand why his people claimed it in the first place. What does it matter?

Remember what happened in the Second World War, they tell him, never forget how the Ustaše killed tens of thousands of Serbs, lots of them children like you! But that was a different age, and try as he might cannot think of his friend's parents, or his teacher, whom he liked so much more than her replacement, as child-murderers. But now he watches smoke rise from another house. He tries to make out who is running desperately across the street, only to crumple – he shuts his eyes briefly. He desperately wants to reach the comfort of his family.

He wills his feet to carry him down the last of the slope, and creeps his way between the houses. As he reaches the corner with the main street, he crouches behind a parked car. He hopes it won't be hit and explode into flames. The smell of burning is all around him – he breathes it in, and with it, terror. The sound of the gunfire drums into him. There is shouting, women screaming, crying. He wonders if he can hear his mother or his sisters. He cannot tell. It is everyone. The whole village is on fire. There is shooting from windows – his neighbours, his father. Shooting from the street – the others. The shock of an explosion.

He wishes he'd been born a Croat so he could be somewhere else now. This thought shames him and he pushes it aside by trying to work out how he can cross the street to his house. But the shooting keeps him trapped and he crouches further into the shadows behind the car.

He hears the sound of running, peers out to see two men duck into a doorway across the street. The Enemy. One man raises a hand to shield his face. The boy realises the building beside him is ablaze. He cowers between it and the car, cringing in the heat, the noise, the dust. He closes his eyes, wishing he could close his ears, trembling for an age until the shooting and the explosions die down, flaring up again intermittently. He thinks again of the ragged convoy, cars heaped with belongings, leaving. He is not the hero who set off up the hill half an hour ago.

He hears snatches of the two soldiers' voices. Their words sound foreign. One stands, yells out to his comrades down the street. The boy understands him this time. Blood runs from a cut on the man's cheek. The other pulls him back down, muttering something in the foreign language. The boy forgets his fear in a moment of anger. He would spit if he dared. There is movement as the soldier with the bloody face rises again, runs a little way down the street. The boy slowly leans and risks looking out; the foreigner is watching his comrade, wary, ready to provide covering gunfire. The boy follows his gaze, turning his head as slowly as he can so the foreigner will not notice him. A defeated huddle cowers in the middle of the square; others are being herded in by more soldiers. It is not far, but it looks like another world. Buildings he once knew are belching flames and smoke from windows and doors. People he knows are helpless victims held motionless at gunpoint. He cannot see his mother or his little sisters, but thinks they must be there. Or dead. He wants to pray but the domed church is ablaze and the priest on his knees among the prisoners.

This is not real; he will wake up soon. He watches them pull a man forward. It is his father, shirt stained red. They beat him and kick him until he screams. They beat him until it is no longer his father. Until the body lies twitching on the ground. Until the whimpering stops. Then there is a shot. As the soldier who rubs shoulders with foreigners watches, mutters encouragement, as two men grab another of the subdued villagers, the boy turns away, shaking.

Through tears he looks up and sees the foreigner's rifle aimed at him. Why is this man here? This is not his conflict.

It is not the boy's conflict, it is not anyone's conflict any more, it is hell. The heat from the burning buildings is becoming unbearable. Motionless with fear, the boy stares at the foreigner. It is not the face he expects to see; it is an ordinary man's face. The eyes blazing with intensity, but otherwise unremarkable – dark hair, weathered skin, the shadow of a beard. Not a hideous face. Not a child-murderer's face. The foreigner moves slightly, breaking the moment, and the boy tenses. He does not want to die, not even now.

He realises the man is saying something. *Trči!* The boy hardly understands through the foreign accent and the crackling of the flames. He hears it again, more clearly. *Run!* The rifle twitches. Not to kill him, not this time, but to indicate the lane he has just come down. *Run, idiot, go!* The foreigner aims high, shoots. The whining ricochet from far above the boy's head snaps him from his paralysis and he obeys.

He runs.

Chapter 1

If he stayed on the bus, what difference would it make? He'd hardly been thinking when he chose to board this one. A sense of developing routine unnerved him. Jay shook his head, smiled a faint self-deprecating smile. The same route, but he could get off somewhere different. Somewhere less remote. He liked the sense of freedom he got from boarding a bus and buying a ticket to the end of the line, to leave himself free to choose where he ended up. This place had always looked good when he passed through. He put his hand on the rucksack beside him in readiness to get off. No rush; someone had stood and rung the bell.

The centre of the little Dales town of Holdwick looked more interesting than the impression its pretty but somnolent outskirts had given. The bus slowed at the edge of a central square – an elongated, irregular square, he told his inner pedant – lined by venerable stone buildings with ground floors housing a collection of neatly tended shop frontages, tea rooms and a pub. A small bustling market stood at its heart. He got up, swung the rucksack onto his back with an ease born of long practice, and braced himself – he'd noticed during the journey that this driver liked playing with his passengers. Having deprived the man of the satisfaction of seeing him so much as flinch as the bus jerked to a halt, he gave a cheery thanks and stepped down. Despite the inexorable advance of years he still prided himself in his agility, though preferred a test more worthy than mind games with a bus driver to prove it.

The fine autumn day had brought plenty of late-season tourists out to join the locals and the colourful market stalls were fairly busy on this Saturday afternoon. A stubborn awareness of the days of the week gave him structure in an otherwise unstructured life. As he passed the greengrocer's stall he caught the proprietor's eye with a smile. First things first; an enticing smell drew him to a fish-and-chip shop. He took a handful of change from his pocket and without counting saw that his bus ticket had consumed the fish – the mental image was an interesting one – leaving him with only enough for a bag of chips. Freedom and a limited diet. Fine. Hopefully that would be put right by the end of the afternoon.

His rucksack gave him anonymity in a town used to hikers and he sat on a bench near the market stall to eat, watching insignificant dramas of everyday life play out before him; concentrating on the activity at the stall. The burly, red-faced trader was pacing around the side of his display, occasionally pausing to adjust the artfully-arranged piles, nodding every now and again to a small team behind the stall, but mainly shouting out to the passers-by: 'Two pound f'r a po-ound!' 'Savoys fit for a king, love!' Jay assumed that cabbages had been a bargain at the warehouse that morning. The undiminished dark green pyramid indicated that Savoys obviously weren't top priority with most of the shoppers today, orbs fit for a king though they probably were.

Time for work. He wiped his fingers on the paper serviette and tucked it with the chip wrapper under the seat to dispose of later – this bench was too strategic to risk losing by going over to the bin – before producing a flute from a rucksack pocket. His colourful cotton scarf was soon spread carefully in front of his feet and his hat positioned neatly upside-down in the dead centre. A stage wasn't strictly necessary, but he liked the effect. He began to play. An audience started to gather, lingering at the safe distance people always left in these situations. He finished his tune, stood, made brief eye contact with a few in the scattered crowd – enough to intrigue them, not enough to intimidate – and began a story. The ideal tale for this situation, about the king's daughter who refused all her suitors, wasting away as she refused to eat until the right one came along. He had a store of exploits the unfortunate knights and princes performed to try and win her hand – some scary, some downright funny – which he could draw on or leave out as the attention of his audience demanded.

He watched with satisfaction as the dozen or so stragglers grew until he had quite a crowd – often, but by no means always, children dragging their parents over to watch. When he deemed the time was right, he brought in the peasant lad who, refusing to attempt any of the tasks set by the king, tricked his way into cooking the princess a meal. He had no treasure to offer, only the beautiful dark green, crinkly globe of a perfect cabbage from his father's croft, something the princess had tasted far too rarely among the overblown delicacies of court banquets. With the king's kitchens and herb gardens at his disposal, the lad cooked her a meal which in its simplicity was like nothing she'd ever been offered before. Unable to resist the hearty dish set before her, she ate and as she did so knew she'd found her future husband. As Jay came to the happy-ever-after, he glanced sidelong at the stall, smiling as if noticing its wares for the first time.

Ducking his head to acknowledge the scattered applause, he picked up his flute and started to play. One or two people wandered surreptitiously over to the stall. It was always a pleasure to observe the way they tried to look as if they were merely browsing while listening. Humble cabbages didn't make it easy; he would have preferred the greengrocer to have something exotic to shift like pomegranates, say, or coconuts, but he was adaptable and liked a challenge. Other stories, by no means all food-related (that would be too unsubtle), more music and soon his little crowd had grown, together with the greengrocer's supply of customers. Interested people attracted more people.

After about an hour, he pocketed his flute, gathered up the healthy pile of change and put his hat back on his head. He moved via the rubbish bin to join the customers around the stall, positioning himself at the end near the Savoys. The stallholder approached him with an open smile and served him in person. He chose a nice selection and delved into his pocket for some of the change he'd just collected.

'These are on me, mate,' the stallholder said, glancing at the crowd of shoppers and extending his hand.

'Thanks very much.'

As he shook the man's hand Jay showed just enough surprise to indicate he wasn't taking anything for granted but knew what he was doing.

'Don't suppose you fancy a final session?'

Jay shrugged in response as the greengrocer, who'd told him his name was Mike, glanced up at the sky. Dark clouds had been gathering as he performed.

'Best get going.' He, too, looked up at the storm clouds. 'Doesn't look promising.'

The greengrocer handed him the bag, and with it a fiver. 'Will you be here again?'

'Could well be.'

'We're here every Friday and Saturday.'

Jay thanked him and turned to go, surprised at the man's generosity. He often earned himself a meal this way, but tips were rare. Beyond the bench that had been his stage was an ethnic clothes stall, and he half-wondered whether to build on his good fortune by seeking to persuade them that the exotic atmospheres conjured by his performance had increased their trade, too. A swarthy young man was examining a rail of colourful shirts; Jay paused to work out if he was the owner or simply a potential customer. As he approached, the lad, younger than he'd looked from behind, turned. Jay stopped in his tracks. A translucence tinged the air at the edge of his vision. He fought the feeling down. The youth seemed to hesitate for an instant, watching him, before he turned and moved quickly off through the market. He soon disappeared from view among the shoppers.

Jay collected himself and walked over to the sandalwood-scented stall.

'Excuse me,' he said to the woman who was quite obviously the owner now he came to look, 'That lad in the leather jacket who was here just now. Do you know him?'

'Sorry, never seen him before.' She smiled. 'You're the street entertainer, right? I really enjoyed listening, between customers.'

'Thanks,' he smiled back. 'I think I'll be here again before too long.'

He left more abruptly than he'd intended, unable to resist heading in the direction the youth had taken. He knew he'd already lost track of him and told himself his story-heightened senses had overplayed the resemblance anyway. Normality began to settle around him. After scanning the streets for a few moments, he shrugged it off as uncanny but impossible and went in search of a newsagent's to buy

11

some pipe tobacco. A snatch of overheard conversation in the shop confirmed that storms were on the way, borne out by the gathering clouds, so his next move would be to find somewhere to spend the night before the rain arrived.

Marilyn sat down on the bench the busker had vacated and went through her bag again, trying to be systematic about it while not attracting attention. She checked every pocket – jacket, jeans – even though she knew her purse was not in any of them. The *Keep calm and...* range of mugs and teatowels in the window of a nearby gift shop attracted her attention. *Keep calm and kill buskers.* She'd been glad she'd stopped to listen, but the magic was soon supplanted by the nagging suggestion that perhaps the guy had an accomplice and did this routinely. At least being unable to find her purse meant she hadn't thrown him any change; that would have added insult to injury. The clouds that had been gathering all day finally conspired to hide the sun as a fleeting image came to her mind of the teenager standing nearby in the small audience. She clearly remembered his sharp features softened by a dark floppy fringe, with a stud earring just visible. Her annoyance transferred to herself. Why suspect him just because he was a youth? It wasn't so long since she'd been that age. Or was it the hint of a foreign accent in his 'Excuse me', as a boisterous child had jostled him against her? He'd been friendly enough to apologise, and returned her accepting smile with one of his own. It was obvious he'd been as entranced as she was by the performance, not some thief alert for a mark. No, just because she felt a residual resentment at having to spend the morning in the spare workshop at Matt's craft centre, with no inkling of when her own place would be ready, didn't mean she had to go pointing the finger indiscriminately.

It wasn't as if she had anything too important in the purse – just enough cash, a few receipts and only one card, which she'd phone and cancel as soon as she was certain. What really riled her was the inconvenience and blush-inducing embarrassment of it – Mike the greengrocer's patronising show of understanding as he offered to keep the bag of goods behind the stall until she, the scatty woman, sorted herself out. And the fact that if she did want to claim them she'd either have to go back and borrow from Matt, or waste the good part of an hour, and half a gallon of petrol, going home and back. The first was unbearable and the second impossible – she had an appointment at four with a new outlet for her pottery, and reporting the theft was a priority for the little time she had left.

She was fortunate to catch an officer in at the police station, and while she was describing the purse, its contents and where she'd last seen it, her annoyance and frustration grew as it occurred to her that her fuel tank was low and she now had no money or card to fill it. She gave a brief description of the youth – purely as a possible witness, she told her conscience – and left as quickly as she could, as if by setting off sooner she could reach her destination before the petrol tank ran dry. It didn't work. The gauge was too low for common sense and she ended up phoning to rearrange the appointment for Monday and going straight home to raid the freezer.

Why had he run? He hadn't run, Vinko's pride told him, he'd walked away. Had no choice, after being so reckless. Reckless? The woman had her patchwork bag hanging open, purse on full view – an opportunity, and he'd have been a fool to let it go. Better a sparrow in your hand than a pigeon on the branch. The kind of wisdom peddled by the storyteller – he hadn't understood every word, but the stories held him all the same. And the music…the tunes had got to him, kind of familiar. What had been reckless was allowing himself to be held there, lingering when he should have been long gone. But since he *had* lingered, after the woman with the patchwork bag had safely moved on and the busker was packing up to go, he should have stopped to talk to him. Something had held him back like a physical barrier. Perhaps it might have been different if he hadn't overheard the conversation at the market stall which suggested the man would be back.

The square was still busy though the sky was duller, the air muggy and threatening. Eager to salvage something more than a day out in much pleasanter surroundings than the city he was living in for now – he refused to think of that as anything other than temporary – he spent a few moments watching the steadily dwindling crowds. People on days out, perhaps less wary of their possessions than they normally would be. He wasn't particularly proud of the way he got his pocket money, but it didn't bother him too much. These people would happily put coins in tins rattled for the orphans of war, so wasn't he simply cutting out the middleman, saving them the trouble of nagging their consciences to part with a few pennies? Enabling them to help a little without having to worry about the blanket nationality of *Illegal* to colour their judgement? He hated the drudgery of his job at the factory and knew they paid him half what they should, but he also knew he was in no position to complain or do anything about it. It barely covered the rent of his room in a run-down shared house and only just bought him enough to live, so he felt entitled to make a little extra until he could find a way of getting citizenship. Get himself a proper job, train to do something

14

worthwhile. If he ever did. His mother had been forced to stay on in Germany when the refugees drifted home, had never registered his birth, and ever since he'd been old enough to wonder about these things he'd never known where it left him. As far as he knew he wasn't legally entitled to be anywhere. He supposed you could buy anything if you had the means, including the right to exist.

He hung around for a few more minutes, vigilant; this wasn't as easy as he'd hoped. People may be less wary, but he was unsure of his ground, had to keep an additional part of his awareness alert for others whose territory he might be invading. Eventually he decided to content himself with the sparrow he'd already caught. Locked in a cubicle in the public toilets, away from prying eyes, he removed the cash. He had no use for cards, and in any case he never intended to take that much. On his way back to the square he dropped the emptied purse onto a low wall as deftly as he'd taken it. As he walked towards the bus stop he saw the woman heading for the car park. He hoped she'd see the purse.

The bus finally carried him away and a calm began to settle over him. He'd be back, just as the busker had said he'd be back. It briefly occurred to him that it was something they had in common: elusiveness, the ability to disappear at any time if they chose. He wondered when the time would come to make that choice, and move on. His mother had always said he should come here to find his grandparents, his family. He had the address, but had always held back from following it up. The only other family he'd had contact with had let him down. Dumped him here, then disappeared. Why should they be any different? But something in him knew that he would not move on until he'd at least tried.

Dusk was drawing down, brought on early by the heavy clouds, as the bus pulled in to Keighley where he had to get off and change. Or simply get off, he thought, if he was going to pay that call. He wandered along the soulless concourse, a chill wind blowing fast-food wrappers to the cacophonous accompaniment of rolling drink cans and the distant rumble of traffic. He looked at the numbers and names on the buses he passed, thinking that most were still as unfamiliar to him as the places of the faraway home he'd never known but had heard so much about. And there it was again, that nagging reminder. It had to be done; the longer he delayed, the worse it would be. But it was getting late, not the kind of time to make an unexpected social call. There was always the morning; he lingered long enough to let the next Bradford bus leave, telling himself he merely fancied a change of scene for the night and could see how he felt in the morning.

The premature twilight had turned dark, the weird light accentuated by the jaded orange glow of the streetlights. The heavens opened as an extraordinary flash illuminated the early Saturday-night revellers dashing for cover. Neither the rain nor the explosive rumble that followed interrupted the studied cool of Vinko's stride as he looked in his own time for shelter. He found a shop doorway at the top of a sloping street which offered a reasonable view of what promised to be a fine show. He briefly wondered if he'd be enjoying this as much if he'd experienced the same things his father had – but he'd never know so it didn't matter. He took his phone from the pocket of his charity-shop leather jacket and quickly texted Ravi to say he wouldn't be out with them that night, giving no reason and hoping his housemate would think he'd picked up a girl. The next lightning flash coincided perfectly with the moment he pressed Send. He grinned to himself as he leaned against the side of the plate-glass entranceway to watch the bonus entertainment, a prelude to his planned take-away followed by a few drinks and a good night's clubbing.

Chapter 2

Lightning slashed deep cuts across the bruised sky. The intervals between the flashing and the growling response grew smaller as Marilyn sat by the window. The angry colours were incredible – sometimes dark purple blue, sometimes pink, sometimes even green – like the end of the world. Like nothing she'd ever seen. She was trying to capture the mood with her camera, experimenting with different exposures to distract her attention from the innate fear she was unable to suppress. She'd had enough now and longed for it to end so she could move away from the window. Silly, she knew, but while she stayed in one place and kept her eye on it, she felt safe. Who knew what it would do while her back was turned?

As she watched, she felt as if the anvil-head stormclouds were as enchanted by this moorland Yorkshire paradise as she was. They lingered for an age, before hurling a particularly fierce shaft that shook the land round about. She tensed, wondering what damage it had done, to her house or her neighbours'. Had anyone been hurt? The storm finally decided enough was enough and skulked off down the valley, still grumbling angrily, defiant flashes like cheeky tongues darting as it faded. Drumming rain was left in its wake, new rivulets decorating the yard and surfaces of the outbuildings in ways she hadn't seen before, each drop conjuring a dancing fairy to celebrate the clearing of the air.

Her tension finally lifting, she stood but lingered at the window. The unnatural storm-twilight had given way to a translucent dusk, the heavy rainclouds tinged at the horizon with a friendlier pink where the sunset tried to reach through with its customary nightly farewell. Ashamed at her irrational fear during the past hour, she was glad no one had been there to see her. It wasn't as if she'd been in any real danger, here in a thick-walled stone house that had stood for centuries. She knew she had a tendency to over-react, but prided herself in getting on with things matter-of-factly as soon as she caught herself doing it. An expedition across the clutter of the darkened living room to the light switch yielded nothing but a futile click. She sighed; the storm had left her a little something to remember it by after all. Guided by the warm glow from the fireplace, she lit a candle from the mantelpiece and decided on an early night. Despite her best intentions, lingering fear shifted her focus away from the candlelight's warm heart to the shadows it attracted around its edges – hovering threats, undefined beasties watching.

Further down the dale, a small tent crouched like a wary animal in the corner of a field. Its occupant stirred and poked his head through the door. The rain now pattered on the canvas to a lighter, more natural rhythm and the refreshed air was a relief. As Jay sat and watched the black clouds disappearing up the valley, the hints of rosy sunset emerging from beneath echoed the lifting of his spirits. The apocalyptic storm had awoken his familiar terror, and he was only just beginning to feel the oppressive darkness drain away. This one had been exceptionally bad – the hollow-rumbling thunder getting beneath his skin and stirring his deepest fears, the lightning threatening to rip the canvas walls and tear him apart. He realised he was still shaking, but at least there was no sign of the boy. Glancing around as if it still wasn't too late for him to appear, Jay almost broke into a grin. He checked himself, keen to keep control.

You can't run forever.

The words flashed back into his mind and he concentrated on convincing himself he hadn't heard anyone else saying them. The insistent notion that had come to him amid the bedlam of the storm had been his own and no one else's. He glanced around more nervously this time, relief at the sight of the empty field turning to uneasy anger. Hadn't he earned the right to be left alone by now? And yes, he'd had a change of heart during the last hour and would enjoy keeping to it. He couldn't run forever; it was time to start thinking of a life that didn't involve a succession of journeys monotonous in their empty promises. Time to settle down, maybe; make his way south over the next few days, take possession of his house, find some meaningful work. Or stay round here? Why not? It seemed a nice place.

He shrugged. Early days. Perhaps making definite plans was too big a change too soon. The idea was enough; with the intention in place, he was satisfied he'd know the right thing when he found it. Performing on the streets to indifferent audiences, convincing suspicious householders of his skills and integrity as a handyman, would soon be things of the past. And he'd say goodbye to Dan. That raised a hollow fear, but he insisted. He breathed deeply, distracted himself by taking out his pipe and filling it from the tobacco pouch. His hands were shaky. Only the storm. The aftermath of holding himself tense for over an hour. He inhaled the first lungful of welcome smoke. Yes, Dan would have to go. But perhaps not yet. *You can't.* The tobacco comfort began to pervade. *Run forever.* No, but one step at a time, hey?

The rain slowed and uneasy patches of clear sky began to appear. The promise of sunset was already fading to dusk, and the clouds crowding back in, as he got out his stove and took his plastic container in search of water. It wasn't an ideal pitch, but his search had been cut short by the need to erect the tent before the storm hit. He felt a sense of purpose far beyond the immediate act of preparing supper. You didn't need a plan to have a sense of purpose, after all.

Marilyn fell asleep to a waterfall of heavy rain, and was awoken in the night by a persistent rumble. The storm must have returned, insistent on having the last word. In the hush that followed she lay, willing herself not to need to go downstairs through the ghostly living room to the ground-floor bathroom. For once willpower worked; dawn was seeking entrance through the curtains when she opened bleary eyes. She got up and looked out. Everything was still; no wind, no rain, friendly white clouds in a blue sky.

She glanced to her left and saw that the world had changed.

Opening the window and leaning out, she stared, wishing the scene before her wasn't there. The barn seemed to be groaning beneath the weight of the hillside which had slid down and tried to sit on it. The woodpile and the makings of her new kiln behind it were buried, as was her carefully-tended vegetable garden; the straggly trees up the hillside were a tangle of limbs reaching through the heap of soil and stones, like drowning sailors pleading for rescue. A larger tree was split, limbs scorched, one half leaning on the barn at a crazy angle. Like a dream, she recalled the rumble she'd heard in the night.

She dressed quickly and went downstairs, pausing to curse as the light switch on the landing refused to obey. Putting the big old-fashioned kettle on the hotplate, she felt more than her usual self-sufficient satisfaction. A spring-fed water supply and solid fuel Rayburn meant she still had at least a few home comforts.

Putting her coat on, she stepped out. It was a beautiful, clear morning, the weather seeking to offer her an apology for the previous day's antics. Not an apology she felt she could accept right then. Genghis materialised from behind her and meowed loudly for breakfast.

'You'll have to wait.'

Leaving the cat for a moment, she walked warily over to the barn as if the landslide were about to come alive and bite her. It almost had. Another twenty metres this way and it could have been the house. At least her room was at the front, but she wondered how much good that would have done her. She told herself she had enough on her plate worrying about the scene before her, without wasting energy on what-ifs.

Having finally made the decision to stay and live out here, she'd been beginning to allow herself to feel some satisfaction in what she'd achieved. And now the vegetable garden she'd carefully prepared and planted out with a few winter crops would need digging out rather than digging over. She'd cleared out the barn, burned the rubbish and made a careful pile of salvageable materials behind the growing woodpile. Woodpile, useful rubbish, vegetables, garden shed and, most importantly, the outbuilding where her kiln was going to be housed – all were now little more than an interesting challenge for archaeologists of the future to scratch their heads over. Not to mention the car. After clearing the barn she'd given the ageing jeep shelter from the elements in the hope it would thank her with improved reliability.

She scrambled over the heap of earth and stones spilling down in front of the building and, unable to shift the doors, peered through a gap in the venerable timbers. The interior was dimly lit by dappled light from a hole in the roof, where the fallen tree had sent a scorched branch through the slates and the rafters, as if trying to grab her car. She couldn't see whether or not it was dented, but told herself, trying to stay calm, that it would still be driveable. Once she'd shifted a tree. Once she'd dug out a pile of rubble larger than herself to free the doors.

She went back in before the kettle boiled dry, shutting the door firmly on the nightmare. Sitting with hands wrapped round a mug of strong coffee and staring into space, she wondered if this was all a sign, trying to tell her this decision had not been a good one and she should go down into Holdwick to live sensibly. She reminded herself forcefully that she wasn't superstitious. Everything was in place, the builders were about to start on the work of converting the barn to a workshop, and this time she wasn't going to give up on her dream. Or accept favours from Matt a moment longer than she had to.

No point sitting brooding, either. She glanced at her watch. Early, but not too unreasonable to be phoning the neighbours, see if their electricity had also been affected and if they had any news of when it would be back on. She picked up the phone and the dead absence of dialling tone felt tangible. It was a long trudge in any direction until she could get a mobile signal, and over a mile to the Harringtons'. But moping would do her no good. She yanked on her boots, almost snapping the laces in anger and frustration, and set off to make contact with the world.

A short way down the lane she rounded a bend and saw a figure approaching. There weren't too many hikers at this time of year, the summer stream dying down to an autumn trickle. It wasn't yet half-past eight, but she'd observed that walkers often made an early start. This one seemed especially keen; he must have set off in darkness as the nearest bed-and-breakfast or campsite were almost five miles distant. Although he had the copious rucksack and sensible outdoor jacket of a long-distance hiker, he didn't radiate the sense of condescending earnestness that many of them did, especially the older ones like him. His practical gear looked well-worn and lived-in, the overall effect brightened by a colourful cotton scarf at his neck, and he gave her a friendly smile as they neared one another. As he did so, she recognised him as the busker from the day before.

'Morning. Didn't I see you in Holdwick yesterday? Telling stories?'

'That's me. I'm flattered you remember.'

His modesty seemed genuine. Genuine? She'd see about that! It might not be wise to accuse him outright, but she'd never forgive herself if she didn't say something.

'Um…there was something I wanted to ask you.'

'Me?'

'My purse got nicked while I was watching.' She looked him in the eye. 'You didn't happen to, you know, *notice* anything, did you?'

'I'm afraid not. It sounds silly but I get in the zone and… Hell, I'm sorry if anything I did or said… Did you lose much?'

His confusion sounded as real as his apology. Common sense had already intervened to tell her if he had an accomplice they'd most likely be travelling together.

'Not really. Don't worry. I shouldn't even have mentioned it.'

'No harm in asking.'

'Anyway.' She was feeling embarrassed now. 'I don't think

it'll affect you, but there's been a landslide back there. Where the track ends and it becomes a path.'

'Is the way blocked?'

'I don't think so. It was a bit higher up and the trees caught the worst of it.' Not to mention her barn. 'But I just thought I'd mention it.'

'Thanks, much appreciated.' He removed a battered leather fisherman's cap that was more in keeping with the scarf than the hiker's jacket, and ran a hand through dark curls. She noticed a hint of salt-and-pepper at his temples before he replaced the cap, frowning slightly as if coming to some decision. 'Do you need any help?'

'Help?'

He shrugged. 'I'm guessing you must live nearby. I just wondered – landslide, that storm last night…'

She suddenly wished she hadn't said anything. It reminded her how isolated she was.

'No, everything's…fine, thanks. I've got to see my neighbours, down the lane here, about something, that's all.'

He nodded. 'Good-oh. I'll be on my way then. Thanks for the warning.'

He raised a hand to his hat in an old-fashioned salute.

As she continued on her way, she wished she'd locked her door. She glanced over her shoulder a few times before he disappeared from view; if he did likewise she didn't catch him.

Dorothy Harrington invited her in for a cup of tea. The roar of a generator drowned out the usual farmyard sounds.

'Richard drove down to the phone box earlier. The electricity board said it'll probably take a couple of days or more to get it back. You'd be amazed how widespread this storm's been, love. They said there's a central fault and a fair few lines down in the county. It's no surprise that a remote

25

area like ours is low on their list of priorities, though you can imagine Richard gave 'em what for.'

Marilyn smiled as Dorothy continued. The telephone, true to form, looked set to take even longer to restore.

'He told them about you as well, love. They said they'll happily divert our calls to our mobiles and pay the bills.' They both laughed and tutted at the absurdity – neither of them had a signal at home. 'Do you want me to run you to the phone box now?'

'That'd be great, thanks. I could do with phoning Alan.' On her walk down she'd planned to ask, cajole, even beg the builders to start early – finding a way to scrape together the extra to pay him to work today, a Sunday, if he was willing – so they could get the devastation cleared and start almost on schedule the following week.

Over a mug of tea, she told Dorothy about the landslip, playing it down, emphasising her relief that it wasn't worse. Dorothy promised that Richard would come over and see what he could do to help as soon as he could, but he'd already gone out. 'I did ask him to call by to see you before he went, but he thought old Mrs Horton might need him more. She's 82 and on her own as you know. Sorry, love.'

'That makes perfect sense. I'm fine.'

As they went out to the car to drive to the phone box, her neighbour paused and leaned towards her confidentially.

'I forgot to mention…we had a fellow here earlier asking if we had any work. A bit early in the day if you ask me – goodness knows where he popped up from. He looked harmless enough, if a bit eccentric. He hasn't been up your way? Forties, fifties, big rucksack, funny hat?'

'I passed him on my way down. He was heading off over the moors towards Annerdale.' Marilyn had no reason to doubt he'd be well on his way by now, and wanted to reassure her neighbour, who found it difficult enough as it was to come to terms with a young woman living on her own out here. She appreciated her willingness to help, but bristled at fuss. 'I'm sure he was harmless.'

All thoughts of power cuts and suspicious strangers were eclipsed on the way back from the phone box. Alan had apologised profusely, but that was little comfort. Not only was he unable to start clearing the mess today, but he'd have to delay starting on the barn itself. One of his customers on the edge of town had suffered a direct lightning hit to their house causing structural damage, and he was sure she'd understand that it had to take priority... She did understand but it didn't make her feel any better.

She had the presence of mind to borrow a sturdy shovel in case hers was buried, and allowed Dorothy to drive her up the lane to her house. She even summoned the grace to receive her sympathy with a show of gratitude as she got out of the car at her gate, but insisted there was nothing further to be done. She'd manage.

Diverted from her purpose only long enough to change into her oldest work clothes and plait her hair to keep it firmly out of her way, she took up the shovel and set to work. After a few minutes she began to feel daunted. She paused, but thought of the jeep, her link with the world, stuck inside, and kept going. Whenever she stopped to wheelbarrow the debris to a disused corner of the yard to deal with later, she noticed how much more she ached. Each time, she allowed herself no more than a minute's pause. She had to be able to get out, see people, show them she was reliable, not some airy-fairy artist who crumbled at the first sign of a crisis. The breaks became more frequent and her digging – work she would never admit she was not cut out for – slowed, her breathing increasingly ragged as the pile of earth and stones appeared to grow rather than shrink beneath her ineffectual onslaught.

'Hello again.'

Marilyn jumped, annoyed both by her involuntary display of weakness and by the interruption. She had hardly given her morning's encounter another thought, but knew who it was without turning.

'I haven't got time to stop.' She heaved one more shovelful into the barrow to prove her point before turning to face him, wiping her brow with a grimy hand. 'What are you doing here?'

It came out more sharply than she'd intended, but he seemed unconcerned.

'I followed the path up there and paused to admire the view from the shoulder of the hill.' He waved a hand. 'Looks bad. I know you said you were OK but I wondered if you wanted some help after all.'

'I'm fine. Thank you,' she added as an afterthought.

'I'm not trying to be patronising. Think about it. Teamwork. One of us digs' – patronising or not, she knew which one he meant – 'while the other wheels it away. We'd get the doors free in half the time.'

'I'm afraid I couldn't afford to pay you much.'

'Who said anything about paying?'

'Mrs Harrington down the lane said you'd been asking for work.'

He rolled his eyes. 'No secrets in an area like this, eh? I don't want payment – it's not very often I come across a damsel in distress. Good to be able to help. Though a spot of grub later wouldn't go amiss.'

She relented. 'You're right; I guess it'd be easier with two. I don't want to hold you up too long, though. It's quite a way over the moors before you get to Annerdale, and the days are getting shorter.'

He looked back towards the barn. 'Are you sure it's safe to move much of this? We don't want to make things worse.'

She was grudgingly impressed by his forethought.

'Why don't we go and have a look?'

He shrugged off his rucksack, left it outside the porch and they climbed the hillside through the trees behind the house.

'It all looks so different.'

She gazed across the devastation. The tips of small trees poked through the heap of soil that thickened as it slumped towards the bottom. A hedge with a low wall running at its foot disappeared into one side of the slide and re-emerged on the other. She wondered how many of those stones were now littering her vegetable garden. The worst threat was the lightning-struck tree that was leaning at a crazy angle, still attached to the roots in the ground, but for how long? A huddle of sheep munched unconcerned on the far side of the fall. She felt strangely distant herself, as if she'd wake up soon.

'I don't think there's any danger of a second slip,' he said. 'The soil looks pretty thin up there and it looks as if all that was going to move has done.'

Marilyn wondered how much either of them really knew, but saw no real reason not to agree. She saw no real reason to refuse his offer, either, though the idea of a stranger working uninvited in her yard unnerved her. As they scrambled back down, she hoped he'd clear the barn doors quickly and leave. Turning towards the house to fetch a hot drink and a slice of the fruit cake she'd made yesterday, she apologised to him for the lack of bacon or sausages – she wasn't one for cooked breakfasts herself and didn't have a lot in. He waved away her concerns, saying with an easy smile that he'd be grateful for whatever she had. It made her feel guilty for doubting him, but didn't stop her wishing he'd gone straight to make a start on the digging instead of following her to the house. He waited in the porch as she removed her boots then bent to do the same. Marilyn hovered in the inner doorway watching him.

'Sorry,' he said as he straightened up, 'you ought to know who it is you're inviting in.' She'd been intending to take the mug and cake out to him. 'Jay Spinney.'

She took his proffered hand and shook it.

'Good to meet you.' The introduction did nothing to lessen her reluctance to let him in. 'So is that J as in short for something, or your full name?' she added, to fill the space in the porch.

'You intending to write me a note of thanks?' He grinned. 'Hmm, Jason, you mean? Jonathan, Justin? Actually, it's simply Jay. The woodland watchdog, they call us; *garrulus glandarius*, magpie's cousin…'

She couldn't help returning his smile. 'I'm Marilyn.' She finally stepped aside. 'Come in, then. Tea or coffee?'

'Coffee, please. As strong as you can make it.'

'A man after my own heart,' she said, and immediately regretted the familiarity.

She filled the kettle and put it to boil as he removed his coat in the warmth of the Rayburn.

'Water supply OK, then?' he asked.

Marilyn nodded. 'The spring's not in the path of the landslip, thank goodness.'

'At least you don't have to fetch your water in buckets. But do tell me if there's anything else I can do for you while I'm here.'

'I can manage, thanks.'

'Oh. Right. Of course. I'll just finish freeing your barn door and be on my way. I suppose your husband'll be back later.'

'I said I'll be fine.'

She felt more exposed than the bare soil of the hillside.

'Well, things could be worse,' he mused as she brought to the table two mugs, the coffee pot and the fruit cake.

'Forgive me, but why do people always say that?' she said as she sat down, poured the coffee and handed him a mug. 'Whatever life throws at you, there'll always be someone telling you things could be worse.'

'Ouch. Yeah, I've always wondered myself why it's supposed to make you feel better – sorry.'

He picked up his mug and took a sip, studying it appreciatively before setting it on the table. She felt a flash of pride; it was one of hers.

'Sorry myself if I sounded ratty.'

'Understandable.'

He smiled and she began to relax.

'What brings you round here?'

'Just a whim. Well, I lived for a while in Keighley when I was younger; used to like coming out to the Dales. So I'm spending some time revisiting these parts.'

She nodded, offered him the plate of cake. He took a piece and they ate in silence. There was a long moment where she felt she should say something, but couldn't think of a word. She noticed his free hand playing with the end of the colourful scarf around his neck.

'That's a nice scarf.' Although she meant it, she immediately felt embarrassingly girly. He grinned as if he'd read her mind.

'Thanks. I'm settling into it. Got it at a craft fair in Bath last year. The old one was like a rag; high time it went. I

31

always wear one, you know, like some guys identify who they are with a tie. You know where in the world the convention of wearing a tie originated?' She shook her head. 'Go on, have a guess.'

'Well, from the way you ask, it's obviously not from the fashions of the English court.'

'True enough. Though I'm sure English high society helped to establish it. But back in the 17th century, when I guess they were all still wearing lace collars, the army of the French king, Louis – the 14th, I think – called on a regiment of mercenaries. Those guys identified themselves with distinctive red scarves. They must have done all right because people eventually came to adopt scarf-wearing as a Good Thing. *Hrvati*, the foreigners called themselves.' The *h* was a strong sound, deep in his throat. 'The French couldn't get to grips with that so it came out as *cravat*, and it came to be used for the scarves rather than the people. We can't really handle that *h* either, so we call them Croats.'

'I never knew that.' She smiled. 'Cravats from Croatia.'

'*Hrvatska.*'

They laughed as he got her to try and pronounce it.

'Have you got connections?' she asked.

'With Croatia?' He paused. 'I…I used to know someone. I've travelled. Got all sorts of connections.'

The way he spoke backed him up. Marilyn realised she hadn't been able to place his accent. His rich voice had the trace of northern that a childhood in Keighley would have given him, but no more; he clearly enjoyed pronouncing foreign words, but wasn't a foreigner himself. He sounded like a man who'd travelled, hints of vowel sounds and expressions picked up like mementoes of places he'd known.

Before she could ask any more, Jay brushed the crumbs from his fingers and went to put his mug and plate neatly by the sink, something Matt would never have thought to do.

'Best crack on with that digging,' he said with a smile. 'No rest for the wicked.'

Chapter 3

Vinko awoke, damp, shivering and stiff, in the scant shelter of the bridge under which he'd taken shelter in the small hours. The creeping dawn light was as grey as he imagined his face to be, but at least the rain had stopped. Wishing he'd had the guts to go to his grandparents' house the previous evening, he decided the moment had passed. Another time. He'd come back another time. Cursing the whole situation, he wandered back to the bus station, hoping the thin wind would take some of the damp from his clothes, and used the stainless steel handwashing facilities in the gents' to freshen up. One of those automatic things where you didn't get enough water and had only lukewarm blown air to dry with. No soap, of course. He triggered the contraption a few times in an unsuccessful attempt to warm and dry himself through, and peered to comb his hair and brush down his tatty leather jacket in the blurred reflection of the stainless steel. Better than nothing.

Slightly revived, he told himself he'd been crazy to even consider coming here, and roamed the stands until he found the stop for the bus back to Bradford. He studied the timetable and looked around the deserted aisles, the occasional voice and the revving of a solitary bus echoing round to emphasise the emptiness. He looked again at the timetable and realised it was Sunday. Just missed one – ages to go. He trudged over to the newspaper stand, open for trade despite the lack of traffic. He bought a chocolate bar, a drink, tobacco and a packet of mints and as he paid found himself asking in his heavily accented English the way to Fairview Terrace. He'd never spoken the name out loud before, and felt as if the few people scattered around the bus station had stopped to stare.

There wasn't a soul in sight but Vinko felt just as conspicuous as he stood at the end of Fairview Terrace, having walked slowly and taken a roundabout route to kill time. He was no stranger to killing time. He studied the twin rows of identical stone houses, smaller but much neater and better cared for than the house he shared back in Bradford. Headscarf-sized gardens, yards, a few of them untidy but mainly well-kept and well-swept, windows and front doors vying for attention with a variety of colours – people making their mark because they wanted to be here. He stared for a while, plucking up the courage to walk on and find number 52, trying but failing to imagine the hero Ivan Pranjić growing up here. Vinko had never seen the farms and fields his father should have grown up in, the farms and fields he'd fought and died to safeguard – for his son and all the other sons. He wondered if he ever would see them now.

He looked up the street, counting in his mind to locate 52. He wondered why his grandparents had chosen to come here in the first place. Why had he? He still couldn't answer that one. He almost turned away. But he was here now; he steeled himself, pausing only briefly at the small wooden gate, went up to the door and knocked. It was opened by a young blonde woman, only a few years older than he was. Vinko's heart started thumping. Could this be a cousin no one had told him about? Family?

'I… I look for Boris and Anja Pranjić?' He disgusted himself with how small and pathetic his voice sounded.

'Sorry, love, Mr and Mrs Pranjick moved a few months ago.'

–yitch. It's Pran-yitch, not –jick. But he didn't say it out loud. He never did. His irritability faded as he registered that this girl meant nothing to him.

'Can you say me where are they?'

The girl pulled her towelling robe tighter and looked cautiously at him. He realised how early it still was. She broke into a smile. 'Yeah, course. Wait there. No, you look froz. You may as well come in a mo' while I fetch you't address. Kettle's just boiled, I'll get you a coffee if you like.'

'Thanks.'

He was reluctant to enter the house, but welcomed the warmth. He sat down, out of place on the neat cream easy chair.

'You come far?' She put the steaming mug on a coaster on the coffee table in front of him. 'Where d'you live, like?'

'Holdwick.' He said the first name that came into his head. 'It's not far, for seeing my friends the Pranjić family.'

She nodded, sitting on a sofa opposite him. 'Don't worry, they're not a million miles away. Moved out Oakthwaite way, they did. Don't blame 'em, nice area that. I'd like Gaz and meself to get a place somewhere like that one day, though I doubt he'll ever shape hisself enough for that. Came into money, the Pranjicks, a few months ago, like I said. A right fortune it wa' by all accounts, though they kept close about it, wouldn't say how they came by it. We all reckon they must've won t' lottery, didn't want the publicity or summat. Don't blame 'em. Right vultures, the press. Anyway me mum lives a few doors down and Gaz 'n me like it here, so when it went on t' market we thought better t' devil you know an' here we are.'

Vinko nodded wordlessly, understanding the gist if not every word.

'Nice people, the Pranjicks,' she continued. 'Well Anja were, any road; I never saw too much of him. I remember old Anja when I were a kid – seemed quite old even then, she did, though she must only be seventy-odd now – always had a sweetie for you. She sometimes took us into t' woods an' all, in that patterned headscarf of hers, to look for mushrooms – she knew what were fit to eat an' what-ave-you, learned it in t' old country, she'd say, though if we brought owt back me Mum'd always chuck it in t' bin saying you couldn't be sure, wharever t' old country had to say. Though I s'pose you know all that yourself.'

'No, I don't,' he said. 'I visit the first time today.'

'You'll like 'em,' she said decisively. 'They'll make you welcome. Think she missed havin' family around, old Anja. Daughter 'ud visit but she were a bit of a sourfaced... Sorry, no offence like, but any road, her kids 'ud never come out an' play wi' us when she were there. Think there were a son, too, but summat happened when he were younger, before my time, like. He—'

'Who's that yer got down there, Nicky?' An irritable male voice drifted down the stairs.

'Lad come askin' after t' Pranjicks. What d'you say your name wa', love?'

'Vinko,' he said and regretted it.

'Vinko here's a friend o't family and—'

'Didn't you tell him they're not here no more?'

He heard heavy footsteps on the stairs.

'I'm just getting him t' address now.' She went over to a sideboard and rummaged in a drawer.

37

'Aye well, gerrit quick an' mek me some brekky. Got a mouth like t' bottom of a budgie's cage an' me belly thinks me throat's been cut.'

A man dressed in boxers and a grubby T-shirt walked into the room. Vinko tensed. 'Sort o' time d'you call this? Bit early i'nt it? Respectable folks should be sleepin' it off.' He coughed harshly. 'Like I were tryin' to do. Got a fag, Nicks?'

She threw him a packet, turned back to her scribbling. 'Offer one to our guest, then.'

Vinko shook his head. He was ready for one, but didn't want to stay the length of time it would take to smoke it. He put his mug, barely touched, back down on the table and stood, looking over to where the young woman was folding a piece of paper.

'You excuse,' he said to the man. 'I don't make no trouble. I'll go now.'

'Wait on, love, you sure you don't want some bacon an' eggs? I'm just doin' 'im some anyroad.'

'No,' he said quickly. 'Thank you,' he added.

'Bet he'd rather have soddin garlic sausage or sour kraut or summat.'

'Gaz, honestly! Sorry 'bout that, love. Anyroad, here's the address.' She handed him the paper and showed him to the door. 'I hope you find 'em, an' when you do, remember me to 'em. Nicola Radcliffe, Ellie Radcliffe's lass, Anja'll know me.'

'I tell them. Thank you. Bye.'

'Good luck, love.'

As she closed the door, he heard the man's growl: 'What the fuck d'you let *him* in here for? Best change t' bloody locks now.'

Vinko shoved his hands into his pockets and walked away.

Chapter 4

'Your carriage awaits, madam.'

Jay doffed his hat theatrically and Marilyn felt slightly silly as she got into the jeep and turned the key, simply to feel the comfort of the engine running. The afternoon was already well-advanced; freeing the barn doors had only been a start. Before they could move the car or do anything more, they'd had to make the tree safe. She'd watched, heart in her mouth, as he cut through the branch from the top of a ladder and they lowered it slowly through the hole in the roof. He'd waved away her embarrassment that she hadn't got round to learning how to use the chainsaw, wielding it expertly and insisting he was glad to do whatever it took to help. After a late lunch of hot soup, they'd managed to coax the car with its erratic electrics into life and she could now bring it safely into the open.

Relieved, she turned off the engine and got out. The roof was dented and scratched, and she ran her hand over it. She shrugged. 'I suppose it adds character.'

'It's out and working, no real harm done ... Sorry, that's a bit like the old "could be worse", isn't it?'

'I didn't mean to sound ungrateful. It's…a relief. Thank you for all your help.'

He offered to chop the branch up as a substitute for her buried woodpile.

'Don't feel you have to. I'll run you back to Holdwick if you like. You should be able to find somewhere to stay, but you'll not get there on foot before it gets dark.'

'Much appreciated.'

He started to gather up the tools he'd been using, pausing to stick out a hand as some scattered drops of rain fell. He looked across at her.

'You know you were talking earlier about your builders not coming for a while?'

'Mm-hm…' She could imagine where this was heading and was already trying to think of excuses.

'I'll be honest with you. I haven't had any steady work for a while. Don't get me wrong; I'm not about to starve or anything but, well, I've enjoyed today, and…if I can make myself useful till they start, perhaps…?'

He looked slightly embarrassed and she wondered, not for the first time, what his circumstances were. Her mind raced but no excuses came. It would certainly speed things up, and in any case, even if she managed to find someone else to finish clearing the yard, she had no guarantee that she could trust them any more than this man, who at least came with the character reference of a day's willing work.

'Let me think about it. I suppose I'd have had to pay Alan extra anyway, what with all this.'

'The price isn't an issue, don't worry on that count. I know I can do a good job in preparation for the experts, and it'd be satisfying to be working on something worthwhile.'

'I'm not promising anything, but…' The rain was getting heavier. 'Step in for a moment.'

He joined her in the porch, dragging his rucksack in behind him.

'Listen, I've got quite a bit of food in the fridge and freezer that's only going to go off.'

'And you need me to dig a hole to keep the stuff cool underground?'

He grinned and she smiled back.

'I think you've done enough digging. I mean I could use some of it up by cooking you a meal. To say thanks.'

'Hey, that'd be amazing, cheers. I've even got some supplies I could contribute.'

He opened the top flap of his rucksack and produced the carrier she'd seen him get at the market.

'*Then* I'll run you to Holdwick.'

'OK. Or, well, could you just show me a field where I could pitch my tent? Save you having to drive.'

'It's no trouble,' she said, waving a hand at the glass roof of the porch, where the initial drumming had increased to an insistent tattoo. 'You can hardly call this camping weather.'

'I'm used to it.'

She realised how tactless she'd been, assuming he could afford bed and breakfast in town, and rushed to cover up for herself.

'You know, I…I could just about clear enough space for you to sleep in the spare room for tonight. It's a bit of a tip though. I haven't got round to sorting it out yet; I…' She stopped herself talking, realising the words were spilling out to hide her incredulity at the offer she'd just heard herself make.

'Don't worry about that,' he said as if reading her mind. 'You don't have to.'

'I mean it.'

'The barn's cleared now. That's more my usual style.'

Looking at him, she could believe it.

'We don't know it's safe, and there's a great big hole in the roof,' she said, 'You'd get soaked.'

'There's plenty of space away from the hole. I could even put the tent up in there. Whatever. You're on your own here, aren't you?'

She shrugged; no point trying to deny the obvious.

'The barn'll do me fine, really.'

'I can't just chuck you out in the rain.'

'Well…' He hesitated, but not for long. 'If you insist.'

As she showed him the spare room she realised clearing enough space would be harder than she'd thought; there was hardly room to fit his rucksack in. The bed frame and its mattress were leaned against the wall to make room for boxes of her stock.

'I'm intending to set up my workshop in the barn. This is my store till I do,' she said, annoyed with herself for feeling the need to justify anything.

'You make pottery?' He picked up a piece from a nearby box. One of her favourite wall plaques, a stylised landscape in blues, purples and greens.

'I do. Until I get the barn sorted I'm having to work somewhere else. It's not ideal, but I need to get established – supply enough stuff to local shops in time for Christmas, then get going properly for next year's tourist season. So it's what I've got to do.' She sighed. 'It'll all just take a bit longer now.'

'You haven't been here long?'

'Several years. Just not on my own. My partner, Matt, and I split up early this summer.'

'Oh. Sorry.'

'Nothing for you to apologise about. We did up an old mill in Holdwick, ran a craft centre there. Since we split he's been converting the top floor to a flat. I stayed here.' She stared, unseeing, into the jumble of boxes in the spare room. 'Well, in a manner of speaking. Actually, I went off to Ireland for a while. Stayed with a friend from college who's living the good life in the wilds of Donegal. She runs a pottery, too, so it was a chance to get some experience working with someone else. It was great for a while. Exchanging ideas, all that. But I began to feel I was overstaying my welcome. She never said anything; I dare say she'd be mortified to hear me say it, but…it felt right to come back. You can't run away for ever.'

She looked up, caught him frowning.

'You know about running away, too, then?' she ventured.

'Figuratively, you mean?' She felt a sudden unease that the question had even occurred to him. 'I believe it's part of the human condition.' He shrugged, laughed softly and ran an appreciative hand over the plaque before passing it to her carefully. 'Now then, you'd better tell me where you want these boxes.'

He'd got the two of them moving before she found her voice to press him further. By the time they'd finished, the small landing was crowded but there was a space in the bedroom big enough for one person to sleep in.

'We can bring cushions up from the chairs, later, and I'll get you a spare duvet.'

'Thanks, but my sleeping bag's all I need.'

After sorting out candles and lamps before it got fully dark, she packed him off to the bathroom with some old clothes Matt had left behind. She insisted Jay gave her his things to wash, despite his protests that she shouldn't feel obliged.

She'd left his two sets of scruffy clothes to soak and was contemplating the contents of the fridge when she heard the low hum of an engine approaching. Out in the rain her neighbour, Richard Harrington, appraised the landslide and its effects and was most apologetic about being unable to come and help sooner.

'I see you've managed admirably, though,' he said, nodding towards the jeep.

43

'It wasn't as bad as it looked.' She found herself somehow unwilling to mention the help she'd had, or reveal to Richard her impulsiveness in inviting a stranger to stay the night. If there was a wrong impression to get, he'd probably get it. 'The car started, thank goodness, so I've got a lifeline. There's still a lot of work to do though.'

Despite the rain and deepening dusk, he insisted they walked up the hillside to inspect the slip. He knew this land far better than she or Jay did and she was reassured when he confirmed their verdict that it was probably safe from further movement.

'Dot said to tell you you're welcome to come over and stay with us while the electric's off, love.'

'Thanks, but I'll be fine. I've got far too much to do; I should stay here. There's the cat to think of as well.'

'I'm afraid I can't really come up and help you for a few days. I promised to take Dot over to her mother's tomorrow. She's not well. Tom'll be keeping an eye on the farm, so we'll be away till the end of the week. I could drop her off and come back, though, and—'

'Don't feel you have do anything of the sort. I can manage. If the phone's still off next weekend I'll pop down and see you so you know I'm still here.'

'I have to admire your independence, love.' He laughed, but sounded relieved.

She watched his tail lights disappear down the lane through the trees, went indoors and began to think about cooking. Her guest eventually emerged from the bathroom in a cloud of steam, Matt's clothes looking slightly big on him. He appeared to have made a real effort.

'Sorry to have been so long. Dozed off.' He grinned sheepishly and with brushed damp hair, neatly-trimmed beard and clean face seemed quite at home. He glanced over to his own clothes in the sink. 'It occurred to me, your washing machine won't be working. I can't believe you made an offer like that.'

'I've been thinking the same thing myself.'

She left him with instructions to prepare the vegetables he'd brought and went to enjoy the luxury of a hot bath. A short time later she returned to a scene of candlelit domesticity, the table laid, a row of clothes strung up and steaming above the Rayburn, the occasional spitting hiss as a drip hit the hob, lidded pans bubbling away. A bottle of wine was open on the table; she was looking at it as Jay came through from lighting the living room fire.

'Hope you don't mind,' he said, waving a hand towards her wine rack. 'I know as a dinner guest I should've brought something, but...' he gave her another of his disarming smiles, 'I wasn't sure where the nearest off-licence was. I'll make up for it tomorrow.'

'Um, don't worry, I'd have opened one anyway,' she lied as he picked up the bottle and poured two glasses with a flourish.

'Here's to good old-fashioned hospitality,' he said, raising a glass.

She chinked hers against it and as she sipped heard heavy rain battering against the window. A wind had risen. She felt vindicated; she'd never have forgiven herself for turning anyone out on a night like this. She went to the stove and gave the casserole a final stir.

'I really appreciate this,' he said as he sat to the table. 'You don't want to know how long it is since I had a hot bath. And a square meal, let alone a dinner half as good as this.'

'You haven't tasted it yet.' She brought the pot over to the table.

'A proper roof over my head,' he continued, 'and a pretty woman for company.'

'Less of the sweet talk,' she said, turning back to drain the vegetables and put them in serving dishes he'd left to warm with two plates.

'Only being appreciative.' He grinned. 'But I'd better shut up or you'll have me out in that barn before you can say *garrulus glandarius*.'

'I'm not likely to do either of those. What did you say that meant?'

'Posh name for the jay.'

She laughed. 'Suits you.'

'Garrulous? That's why I remember it.'

He reached out and took the plate she handed him, put it down quickly and shook his hands dramatically. 'Ouch – hot.'

As she watched him begin to attack the food on his plate – there was no other way to think of it – she wondered just who it was she'd taken in.

'What were your plans? Before…this.'

'I don't usually do plans,' he said as if that answered everything, before devoting his full attention to his long-awaited square meal.

She watched Genghis make his cautious way round the edge of the kitchen, drawn through to the living room by the warmth of the fire. He eventually settled in its warm glow, tucking paws and tail in neatly but keeping his head alert, like a ship about to set sail across the rug. Marilyn thought that if the cat could accept the presence of this man in the house, perhaps she should put away her doubts. They ate in a not-uncomfortable silence. Jay wolfed his plate clear in no time and glanced at her, eyebrows raised, hand already on its way to the pot.

'Help yourself to more.'

He made short work of a second helping, sitting back satisfied as she finished her first.

'Thanks for all this, Polly,' he said as she topped up their wine glasses.

'Marilyn.'

'Polly originally comes from Mary, did you know that? Mary – or Marilyn – became Molly became Polly. I think it suits you.'

'Makes me sound like an old woman.'

He drank. 'Age is the product of one thing alone – the time that's gone by from when you were born to the present. I don't see that what people call you has anything to do with it.'

Chapter 5

Vinko walked quickly along litter-strewn streets towards the house he currently called home, hands shoved in his pockets. After a couple of hours in his room catching up on some sleep, he intended to take himself off to the multiplex where he'd slide in for free under cover of a rowdy group, beneath notice of the ticket collectors. He'd often lose himself in the cathartic bombardment of sight and sound offered by an action film. It was especially appealing today. He felt on edge. Angry with himself. Whatever his grandparents' new address meant, he should have gone to see them. He wasn't scared of the meeting, of course he wasn't, merely angry with himself for being over-cautious.

He rounded a corner and came within view of the house. A silver car he hadn't seen for months was parked alongside the kerb. He wasn't sure if he wanted to see it now. Fairly certain he wouldn't have been noticed, he paused, then made himself continue walking. Didn't he want answers? He'd done enough putting-off this weekend. The windows were tinted and he peered in vain as he approached, checking involuntarily for the knife in his pocket. His uncle, Mihal Novak, had always been as good to him as he could have expected, but nothing was certain; it paid to be alert. The driver's window swished down as he approached and an arm beckoned him over to the passenger door. Vinko walked resolutely up to the driver's side. He wanted answers, but he'd do this on his own terms. Novak greeted him in Croatian and Vinko replied courteously enough in the same language, standing close to the car with his hands still shoved into his pockets.

'Haven't seen you for a while,' Vinko said.

'Sorry about that. I've been busy. I tried to call but you weren't answering.'

'My phone died. I got a new one.'

'You didn't think to give me your number?'

'I texted it. Didn't you get it?'

He knew Novak would recognise the lie for what it was.

'You'd better give it to me now.'

Vinko rattled off a set of random digits – he'd felt abandoned; this time he'd be in control of any communication. A petty victory, but any victory at all was a rare treat.

'Where've you been?' he asked as his uncle entered the number.

'It's not important. I'm here now, aren't I?'

'I assumed you'd gone. Done your bit for me and left me to it.'

'That's why you changed your number – sulking, hey?'

'I'm not some little kid,' Vinko muttered.

'Look, there's absolutely no reason why I should justify myself to you, but an old friend called. Important job, needed my help. OK?'

'You're obviously a very unselfish man. Always off helping people.'

Novak gave no indication he'd noticed the irony in Vinko's voice. 'I'll make it up to you. Go and smarten yourself up. We'll have a meal, then we can go back to mine for some beers and a film.'

Vinko didn't argue. A free meal was enticing and his uncle's DVD collection was at least as good as what was usually on offer at the cinema. The house itself was nothing special, but better than anywhere he'd ever lived. On the few occasions he'd been he'd found it a decent enough place to spend an evening.

'I'll be right back.'

The restaurant was half-empty, a few lunch-time parties lingering, not yet time for the early evening sitting, and Vinko made a conscious effort not to feel out of place. He tucked into his steak greedily, glancing occasionally at the man he'd once thought of as his saviour. Mihal Novak had found them in Dresden and offered to help. He'd been too late for Vinko's mother, but had eventually arranged for him to come to England, even getting him a job and a place to live. It wasn't much of a job, not much of a place to live, but last year he'd welcomed both as a new start.

'Have you seen them yet?'

Vinko knew without asking who he meant.

'It was the wrong address.'

'Can't you get anything right?' A flash of anger Vinko had seen before briefly crossed Novak's face. 'What do you mean, the wrong address?'

'They moved. The woman who lives there now—'

'What woman?'

'I don't know; the woman who lives there. She said they moved a few months ago. How come you didn't tell me?'

'I didn't know, did I?' His tone added, do you think I'm stupid? 'Why would I? I'm not in touch with them anymore; their precious daughter divorced me, remember? So, did this woman give you the new address?' Vinko nodded. 'Where are they living now?'

'Some place I'd never heard of. I can't remember and it's in my other pocket, sorry.' He patted the jeans he'd changed into, to emphasise the point. In fact it was next to his phone

50

in the inside pocket of his jacket, but he chose not to pass it on just yet.

'I take it you didn't go?'

'Not yet.'

'Why not?'

'It was only this morning. I'll go when I'm ready.' Something inside him had always kept him away, as if preserving the dream until reality crept in to spoil it. The new address prolonged the respite. 'Look, it doesn't matter. Whether or not they accept me you don't need to feel responsible. I can look after myself.'

'That's perfectly obvious, my boy.' His smile seemed forced. 'Did she say why they'd moved?' Vinko sensed a reason behind the question, and chewed a mouthful of steak instead of replying. Novak stared at him for a moment. 'Well? Did she mention any...change in their circumstances?'

'Why should she? Why would she even know?'

His uncle nodded slowly. 'I hope it's not too late.'

'Too late?'

'Vinko, lad, there's something I haven't been telling you. My mistake. I thought it best not to affect the way you were with them. But you're taking so long. What's the problem? Don't you want to see your family? Anyway, this changes it.'

'What does?'

'Someone I know, someone who knew your family, tells me there's some money of his that may have come their way. Money they shouldn't have. I'd like you to help me find out, and if it's true, help me get it back for my friend. You'd be rewarded.'

Vinko concentrated on his last few chips, then speared the final piece of meat. As he chewed he tried to settle his thoughts, knowing Novak was watching his every move.

The dream was shattering, here, now, before he'd even met them.

'How?' he said eventually. 'What could I do? I haven't been near them yet.'

He took an inelegant gulp of red wine and listened as Novak suggested he find a way – how was entirely up to him – to lay his hands on the relevant bank account details, and he and his contacts would do the rest. Vinko would get a generous share. He remained noncommittal. Apart from his uncle, whom he didn't particularly like despite his wining, dining and home entertainment system, they were the only family Vinko had. If he was to meet them, he wanted to get to know them properly, not start by stealing from them.

'They're not the dream family you want them to be.' It was as if Novak could read his mind. 'And anyway, they need never know your part in it.'

Vinko stared at his empty plate, fingers drumming on his thigh.

'Don't you want a chance to earn some real money? Think of all the stuff you've done before. This is easy in comparison. You're not even stealing – this money isn't theirs.'

'Why can't you do it?'

'How thick *are* you?' His tone was low, in keeping with the surroundings, but menacing enough to make Vinko tense. 'How many times do I have to say? They won't let me near.'

'Sorry. But what if I don't want to get involved?'

Novak leaned back, composure restored. 'Then you take your chance.'

The nature of the man's smile told Vinko that 'chance' meant more than whether or not he got to know his grandparents, whether or not he eventually saw any share of the money. He wanted to leave.

Outside, he thanked his uncle for the meal but claimed tiredness after a sleepless night as an excuse for going straight home. They drove back in silence and it seemed an age before they came to Vinko's street.

'Go and see your grandparents,' his uncle said as he pulled over to the kerb, 'and let me know how you get on.'

Vinko had his hand on the door catch but Novak stopped him. 'Check your phone for me, will you?'

Vinko got it out reluctantly.

'Any messages?' His uncle gripped his arm, looked at the empty inbox. 'I think you've made a mistake with your number, my boy.'

Vinko muttered an excuse as he gave him the correct one. He waited impatiently, fingers tapping restlessly, for the test call to come through.

'No need to apologise,' said Novak cheerfully. 'I like your thinking. You know, Vinko, I've enjoyed getting to know you. Now I'm looking forward to working with you.'

Chapter 6

Marilyn insisted they left the washing up until morning and they settled down in front of the living room fire. Jay produced a pipe and a tooled leather pouch.

'Do you mind?' he asked.

'What's in there?'

'Just tobacco.'

She surprised herself by believing him. 'Go ahead. I don't mind at all. Most of it'll go up the chimney anyway.'

She watched him intent on the job of filling the smooth wooden bowl, collecting up every crumb of spilt tobacco.

'You don't see many of those these days. Surely cigs are easier?'

He rolled his eyes theatrically. 'Commonplace. Anyway, you can't beat this.' He crumbled a flake of tobacco between his fingers and held it out for her to smell. 'If you're going to do a job do it well, I say.'

He produced a Zippo from the pouch and disappeared momentarily in a cloud of fragrant smoke. She breathed in luxuriously, suppressing one of the rare moments of regret she'd felt since giving up. Something else she'd determined to change about her life when she and Matt split up.

'If I ever did settle it would probably be somewhere like this,' said Jay out of the blue. 'Woods, trees. A mighty forest. The kind of forest travellers get lost in. For days. Wandering round and round, trees looking the same, each clearing a relief until you realise there are more trees the

54

other side of it… Until you come to one with a house. A house not unlike this one. Like the house the children came to.'

'The children?'

'In the story.'

Story? After a day in which her world, or the Stoneleigh part of it, had literally been turned upside down, not even the idea of listening to a man she hardly knew telling stories in her own living room seemed strange. It was good not to have to think for a while. Let him do the talking.

'They'd been walking for days.' He waved the pipe in a gesture that encompassed days, weeks, months. 'They'd lost everything – homes, friends, families – just the three of them left there were, two boys and a girl. They'd also lost their pursuers. Outrun them, outwitted them. Outraged them. And now they were free. They didn't want freedom; they wanted to go home. But their homes no longer existed, so freedom was their only choice. They had no food, it was cold. Then they came to a house in a clearing. They were afraid; they'd learned to fear everyone they didn't know. But where else could they go? The oldest boy knocked, and an old woman answered.

'"Come in, I've been waiting for you."

'She invited them in to the warm fire and fed them with a hot, wholesome broth. As the younger two were falling asleep in the cosy cupboard bed at the side of the room, the oldest boy asked: "How did you know about us?"

'"The forest told me. If you hadn't arrived I'd have come to find you."

'She led him to join the others under the warm blankets. As he drifted off to sleep he half-opened his eyes and thought he saw a huge raven circling the room before it flew out through the window. He called out to the old woman once in his fear but there was no answer and sleep soon overtook him.

'The next day the children were allowed to rest, but after that the old woman had them working for her. The youngest boy swept the house, the girl gathered and prepared the food, the oldest boy tended the pigs and collected firewood. The old woman slept by day as they worked, but every afternoon she woke up, looked over the work they'd done and gave them a hearty meal from the ingredients the girl had prepared. Every night they ate the food she gave them and fell asleep straight away afterwards in the cosy bed, grateful for the new home she'd given them. Sometimes, the oldest boy thought he saw the raven leaving the room, or returning before dawn, but mostly he was too tired to give it a second thought, and by morning he'd forget. One day, the oldest boy looked at the girl as he fed the fire while she sat spinning.

'"What were we sad about when we came here?"

'"I don't remember." She looked at the youngest boy who was polishing the old woman's shoes. "Do you remember feeling sad?"

'The little boy shook his head. He couldn't remember a time they hadn't lived in the cottage in the woods. The girl realised she only had a few vague pictures in her head of her home, and after a few days those had gone too. They continued, strangely content. The oldest boy couldn't remain content for long. He wanted to know who he was. He tried and tried to remember why they were there, why they had been sad, but it was no use. The others began to get annoyed with him for fretting. He never dared ask the woman they had come to know as Grandmother.

'One day, he was collecting firewood and he cut his hand on a thorn. He saw his own blood drip onto a leaf. He

56

looked up and saw the black and white flash of a magpie watching him. The bird spoke and the boy nearly dropped his bundle of sticks in surprise.

'"What's the matter, young man?"

'"We're happy here, Grandmother looks after us, but I don't know who I am anymore."

'And the magpie said, "She wants children. She wants to keep you here as her own. She'll care for you, but she'll never let you remember in case you decide to leave."

'"I want to go back. I want to remember."

'"Your memories will bring you sadness. Are you sure?" said the magpie.

'"I want to be myself," said the boy.

'The magpie told him not to eat the food the old woman gave him. He would have to leave that very night – he would have no choice, as the old woman would know. She was at her most dangerous in her raven-winged night, but if the boy waited until morning she would trap him.

'The boy's cut began to scab over and as the blood dried the magpie's voice became a bird's screech as it flapped off. The boy ran back to the cottage and called the girl and the youngest boy to him. But to his dismay, he couldn't remember what the magpie had told him. Soon he had forgotten what kind of bird had spoken, if it had happened at all. The girl huffed and went back to her spinning, and the little boy went out to dig some potatoes for their meal, singing to himself. The older boy was sad; not the deep sadness they'd been running from, but regret that he couldn't remember something beautiful, and his friends wouldn't help him remember.

'That evening he caught the cut on his hand as he was feeding the fire and he watched a bead of blood well up. He felt lightheaded.

"'I don't want any supper tonight, thank you," he told the old woman. "I'm not feeling well."

'She peered at him. "Did anything happen while you were out?"

"'Nothing," he said, and she seemed to believe him.

'He went to bed and she brought him a bowl of steaming broth. "You must try and eat something to keep your strength up."

'He nodded and put the bowl to his lips, but only pretended to drink. "It's too hot. I'll drink it once it's cooled."

'The old woman bustled off to watch over the other two and he rolled over and tipped the contents between the bed and the wall. When she came back he feigned a wan smile. "Thank you. I feel much better now."

'But he felt worse. He tried to sleep, but was plagued by images of houses burning, people he loved whom he knew were no longer there. He felt a deep sadness and had an urge to leave; he worried at the cut on his hand to keep himself awake. He tried to hold back his tears in case the old woman heard, and was grateful when the other two came to bed and he eventually heard the beating of wings that he feared but was waiting for.

'When all was quiet he got up, pulled his coat around him, tiptoed to the door and went out, easing the door closed behind him. He heard a croak and the beating of wings. As a black raven bore down on him, he scratched at his cut and drew a drop of blood. In a flash of black-and-white, the magpie darted into the path of the raven. He watched, terrified, as the two birds tore into one another in a storm of feathers.

"'Go!" screeched the magpie.

'Back at the house, the youngest boy awoke with the

58

dawn. He felt a small sticky patch on the blanket. He lifted his finger and saw in the pale light that it was blood. As he looked at the stain on his finger he heard snatches of wings beating, birds screeching, footsteps running. Somehow he knew it was his friend; he wanted desperately to go with him. He shook his sister awake and told her of the birds and the empty space beside them.

'"Don't be stupid. Go back to sleep or Grandmother will hear you."

'He dozed for a while and by the time it was fully light he hardly remembered the dream of the birds. The old woman gave them their breakfast porridge by the fire and the two of them set about their chores. The younger boy went out to fetch firewood – hadn't that always been his job? Who else had ever been there to do it? – and as he reached the edge of the garden he saw a black-and-white shape motionless on the ground. He rubbed a red patch that had appeared on his finger overnight and as he reached out to touch the dead magpie he thought he caught a glimpse of a boy running through the trees. At the same time he felt a hand on his shoulder and started in fear.

'"Come back to the house, little one," said the old woman. "You need your coat or you'll catch your death of cold."

'By the time he went out again there was nothing there. The youngest boy never lost the red patch on his finger where the drop of blood had stained it. If he rubbed it he'd catch a glimpse of a magpie in another place that somehow felt like home, and see the face of a half-remembered friend in his mind's eye. He didn't understand these images, and they felt like the saddest things he knew, but he was glad he had that red patch on his finger.'

A candle sputtered and flickered rapidly before settling again to a steady flame. Jay moved to put a log on the fire, raising a shower of tiny sparks.

'What a sad story,' Marilyn said. 'Where did he go, the older boy? He must have been so lonely.'

'Brought it on himself. Imagine refusing a gift like that. The chance to forget all your troubles.'

'Gift? She had them imprisoned.'

'Wasn't it better than sadness and loneliness? I tell you, it was a gift. Crafty things, magpies. They'll steal anything, even when it means nothing to them.'

'That magpie sacrificed its life to help the boy remember who he really was.'

'Perhaps he'd have been better off if it hadn't. Perhaps the magpie was simply jealous. I would be... The gift of forgetting all the bad stuff in your life.' He rubbed his index finger absently with the tip of his other; shrugged. 'Perhaps not. Perhaps you'd just end up making the same mistakes over and over again.'

'Anything in particular?'

He looked away and busied himself firing up new life in his pipe bowl. His silence suggested she'd gone too far.

'I like the way you told it.'

It was an over-obvious olive branch but he glanced up, clearly willing to accept it. He relaxed visibly, smiled.

'The odd jobs pay better when I can get them, but the stories – busking – are way more fun. It's a question of balance.'

He blew a smoke ring, let it hover and speared it with a thin stream of smoke.

'Your turn.'

'You're joking? You're the performer; I'm happy to listen.'

'Everyone's got performance in them somewhere. I'm guessing yours is in your work.'

She smiled. 'Nice concept. Ceramics as Performance – discuss.'

'From what I've seen you do it well. Have you got any more you can show me?'

She got up and held a candle to illuminate a lamp base she was proud of, organic curves intended to catch the light. 'It's better when the bulb's working, of course.'

'Adaptation – the key to life. Put this power cut experience into making a chandelier next time.' He grinned. 'Actually it's lovely as it is. You've got a real talent.'

'It's not my best.'

'What is?'

She shrugged. 'Depends on my mood. Most of the time I don't think I've made it yet.'

'A good place to be.'

'Would be if I could feel more inspired at the moment. I need to be more settled.'

'Make sure you don't lose the edge.'

'I know what you mean, but there's a difference between edge and being all over the place. It doesn't help that my temporary workshop is at the craft centre, so I feel as if I'm still beholden to Matt.'

'Your ex, right?'

She nodded.

'Is he creative, too?'

She shook her head. 'The kind of performance he understands is economic. We established the place mainly to sell my stuff, and other people's on commission. Subletting spare space to others. It was doing quite well. Still is – he's carried on running it. He was the one with the business head – or so he liked to tell me. I didn't argue. We met at college; I was the artist, he was doing business studies. Anyway, when we split up we agreed I'd keep this place on – it was originally my parents' holiday cottage, but that's another story – and he'd continue with the craft centre. I still get a bit of money from my share.' She frowned. 'In theory. I haven't seen anything for a while – I'm using a spare workshop there till I get my own place sorted, which is worth far more than anything I'd get from a share in the business.'

'Sounds reasonable enough. You mentioned selling through other shops…'

'Yes, it's coming on all right. I just feel like inspiration's a bit elusive at the moment.'

'If you're doing OK as you are, and managing to keep producing, why worry? Inspiration for what?'

She shrugged. 'I don't feel like I'm making a difference. People seem to like it, and I'm proud of what I do, of course I am, but sometimes I can't help asking myself what's it all for.'

He laughed quietly. 'Does anyone – anything – truly make a *difference*? You obviously love this place, this landscape, and that comes across. So you're sharing it with others. Isn't bringing beautiful things into a grey world difference enough?'

Perhaps it was the wine, but Marilyn felt herself cautiously warming to the man. There was no hint of mockery or irony in what he said, and though she knew he could simply be trying to flatter her, she decided to relax and simply enjoy Jay's company for what it was. She brought a few more pieces to show him.

Eventually she looked at her watch. 'It feels later than it is. I'm tired, sorry – awake half last night with that storm. I think I'll turn in now. Feel free to stay here by the fire as long as you like.'

'I'm knackered myself, to put it politely.' He glanced towards the stairs. 'Are you sure you don't mind me staying?'

'You're welcome to the barn if you'd prefer,' she said. 'Seriously, Jay, I'm grateful for your help. It's the least I can do.'

As she passed the closed door of the spare room a few minutes later she thought again how little she knew about this man who was staying under her roof. Where he was from, whether he really lived like he'd said and if so, what had led him to it. He'd told her next to nothing, but then she'd hardly asked. At least he hadn't tried anything on; it surprised her to realise how safe she felt despite this stranger in her house. She shut her own door firmly and drew the curtains on the mess outside. As she drifted off to sleep she almost forgot about the damage to the barn as a wave of optimism turned her present circumstances from an insurmountable obstacle to a temporary challenge.

Jay huddled restless in his sleeping bag, surrounded by the clutter of the room. He'd had a phase of sleeping well recently, even weathered a thunderstorm relatively unscathed – surely he should be able to get a good night's sleep indoors? His mind kept turning to the young woman in the next room, and he wished she were either a long way away – or even closer.

He rolled over and rummaged in his rucksack for his book and clip-on light, but managed no more than a few sentences. He regretted choosing *Crime and Punishment* – he was enjoying it on one level but Raskolnikov unsettled him far too deeply. He considered getting up and browsing Polly's shelves for an alternative, but settled for his CD player and headphones. The music, a compilation made by a friend he'd met at a drop-in centre where he'd spent some time volunteering, was pushed into the background by the unease that came in waves. He thought again of the young

lad at Holdwick market place. Told himself to forget it. So
he reminded him a bit of Ivan. And? All sorts of people
looked vaguely like all sorts of other people. But hadn't the
lad stared at him before he turned away? Of course, he told
himself firmly, wouldn't you be staring in his shoes?
Wouldn't you be wondering what the old git's looking at?
But…no buts. And definitely no resemblance.

He glances up and feels the world shift as he sees the boy
standing by the door. There isn't enough space for him in
the cluttered room but he always finds a way in when he
wants to.

'I thought you weren't coming back,' Jay says. He keeps
his voice quiet, despite the overwhelming dread that grips
him. He wonders why he always tries to deceive the boy
with outward calm. This one cannot be deceived.

The boy says nothing.

'You promised me you wouldn't come again. After last
year.'

The boy still says nothing but Jay can tell he is thinking
that such promises are meaningless. Any promise that can't
be kept is meaningless. The boy walks away and Jay follows
him. He has no choice. His familiar terror that he won't be
able to find his way back is heightened by the hope that this
time he might have something to come back for. He realises
with sickening certainty that this is why the boy has
returned.

He passes the silent carcases of empty houses, walls
pockmarked with bullet holes, here and there the gaping
wound of shellfire, rafters like ribs. All with the life bled from
them, from the houses, from the hamlets and villages they
used to be part of. He wonders how much, if any, of it was his

doing. It doesn't matter what he did, which of these sad ruins is the testimony – he was there, and when he comes back he is responsible for it all. Things are always the same; it doesn't get any less with time. He feels his feet sink into the rutted lane with the weight of crushing responsibility, adding to the chaos caused by neglect and the old passing of military vehicles.

With the harsh cawing of the crows in the trees above him, he continues until he reaches the village and recognises the corner where he took up his position. The burning buildings that surrounded him then are still here, surprisingly intact despite the ubiquitous pockmarks, their windows blackened holes. The smoke has gone, though in places the line between the remains of the ruined buildings and the rubble-strewn street is indistinct. There is silence. He feels the boy watching him. He thinks he sees movement from the alley the boy fled down. He hurries away, unable to face the accusation in his eyes. But perhaps that's what he should do, face it. Ashamed, he slows, turns.

A dog emerges and pads towards him, from the building with the bloodstain on the wall, hunger and menace in its attitude. It sees him and bares its teeth. He grabs a piece of wood from a broken table – he won't touch the gun he is carrying for the sake of a mangy dog. They face one another over the rubble and the scattered dispossessed belongings, and he hears the crackling gunfire echoing. Then laughter. The echoes scare him; the laughter scares him more.

He is on the square now. The laughter came from a wizened old man who sits by the shattered stump of the monument and watches him with piercing eyes. He stops, glances back to see the dog slinking away. Smothered by the cloying smell of burning, now old and damp, watched by the eye sockets of the ghostly shops and houses, he tries to force his feet to move, to run. When he looks again the old man's face is vacant, unseeing, lost. It is not a face that could have produced laughter. The old man is looking at a space just beyond him. He turns his head and his stomach lurches as he sees the square is no longer empty. One white-shirted arm is flung out from the heap of bodies as if in casual repose, the skeletal corpse-face flung back and staring at him with empty eyes.

'I didn't do this!' he yells, turning and looking round wildly for someone other than the old man to hear him.

'You were here,' the grey, dead face says quietly from beneath his feet.

He turns away.

'You let it happen,' says the old man.

He closes his eyes to shut them out. When he looks again the square is empty except for the boy watching him from where the old man had sat. It is menacingly quiet. Suddenly he is running, pulling himself away from the absurdity of it all, away from that place. Zora is waiting for him where the dirt track runs into overgrown, neglected fields. He can't shake the smell of old burning and decay, it is on him, it is part of him. It is also on her. They are the same.

She beckons. He stands facing her, refusing to approach.

'Come to me. Let me comfort you. Let me make it right.'

'No.' It should be so easy, but every word is leaden. 'Please go. Leave me in peace.'

She reaches out her hand.

'I can help you. Come to me, Šojka.'

'I'm not Šojka!'

He pushes her away from him, turns and stumbles away across the rutted, muddy fields.

Chapter 7

The tentative autumn sun through the curtains was grey as Marilyn woke to the prospect of having someone to share breakfast with. She vaguely remembered waking once, but had gone straight back to a better night's sleep than she'd had for a long time. Looking out of the window as she opened the curtains, she tried to ignore the sight of the landslide. The night's rain had left, leaving a grey and blustery day.

The spare room door was ajar as she edged her way between the boxes on the landing. She glanced in, trying not to intrude. The space they'd cleared the previous evening was empty, his sleeping bag neatly rolled and stowed to one side. She listened for sounds from downstairs; Jay didn't seem the sort to be shy of looking in cupboards to find what he wanted. She ought to mind that, but didn't. The smell of coffee proved her theory. Downstairs, she found the place looking tidier than it had since she'd got back from Ireland. Genghis's food bowl was half-empty, indicating he'd been fed, and he favoured her with a sleepy glance from where he was curled in front of the fire. Which had been lit. Still in Matt's old jumper and jeans, Jay had his back to her at the kitchen sink, finishing last night's washing up.

'Morning,' he said, turning to her with a smile like the sun struggling to break through clouds. As if recalling a dream, she remembered it was the sound of his voice that had woken her in the night.

'Thanks for all this,' she said, waving a hand over the room. 'You didn't have to, honestly.'

'All part of the service. Hope you don't feel I'm interfering.'

'Not at all.'

She poured them both a coffee and he joined her at the table, drying his hands on a teatowel.

'I didn't sleep well. Eventually decided I might as well put the time to good use.'

'I thought I heard you shout out in the night.'

His expression clouded again. 'Did you?'

It was out before she could stop herself: 'What does "shoiker" mean?'

'Shoiker?'

She nodded, regretting her intrusion. He was still wringing the teatowel, though his hands must have been long dry. He paused, began to fold it.

'You know, one of these days I'll really get myself into trouble, rambling in my sleep like that! What on earth else did I say?'

'I'm sorry, I shouldn't have mentioned it. But your voice was raised, and... That was all I heard, honestly. You just said something like "I'm not shoiker," loudly. It intrigued me, that's all.'

'Sorry if I disturbed you. It's coming back to me now you say it.' He leaned back and hung the teatowel on the rail of the Rayburn. 'It meant "jay". My name. In another language.'

'So why would you say you *weren't* Shoiker?'

'Search me.'

He stood and went over to the sink to finish off the pots. 'You know what dreams are like. Weird.' Still with his back to her, he scrubbed vigorously and upended a pan on the draining board. When he turned, teatowel back in hand

68

like a security blanket, it was as if the dream and its darkness had melted away like a wisp of morning mist.

'Time for me to get you some breakfast,' he said, breezily. 'Tell me what you want and where it is. We ought to get moving – haven't you got an important appointment this morning?'

'It's a shop I know, Jay. They might sell my stuff. Hardly an exam or a major job interview.'

He grinned. 'Whatever. But *I've* got work to be doing.'

'Work out there; it doesn't include you waiting on me hand and foot. Aren't you supposed to be the guest here? Sit down, drink your coffee and I'll see to breakfast.'

He seemed restless, edgy, and it occurred to her that his offer might have more to do with keeping himself busy than doing her any favours. She wondered briefly about the wisdom of leaving him here while she went to Skipton, and tried to think of a plausible excuse for locking the door while he worked outside. Nothing occurred to her that didn't involve offending him, and in any case she thought that getting into locked houses could easily be one of his many talents. Chiding herself for overreacting, she recalled how the previous night had passed without incident and she'd actually enjoyed his company. By the time he'd finished several slices of toast and jam as quickly as the Rayburn could brown them, she had decided to trust him.

She quickly changed and he helped her to the car with one of the boxes from the landing. They decided it wouldn't be worth him patching up the hole in the barn roof, as the whole thing was to be replaced, and he should concentrate on finishing clearing the yard.

'OK, see you then. I'll be back by lunchtime at the latest.'

She moved towards the car, but he called her; she paused and looked back.

'The joys of country living, hey? Don't you lock up round here?'

He sounded genuinely surprised, and she hoped her cheeks weren't reddening.

'Oh, I…won't there be things you need inside?'

He shrugged. 'The tools are all out here, aren't they? Leave me a biscuit or two, perhaps. Apart from that, I've got my baccy in here,' he patted his jacket pocket, 'and I can drink from the stream there, if I need to.'

She locked the door as he suggested.

Marilyn's meeting at the shop went well. Despite having played it down to Jay, it was important to her, and she felt buoyed up on the way home, deciding as she drove through Holdwick to call on Matt to update him. Nevertheless, as she parked the car and walked over to Barton Mill, she found herself wishing Jay was there. She shook her head, annoyed that she still felt anything around Matt, as well as for thinking that a near stranger like Jay would make any difference. Inside the building, she made her way past the ground-floor units and up the solid stone stairs to the shop that had once been partly hers.

The traditional brass bell rang out, and the familiar board creaked as if to warn of her presence. When they'd taken over the place they'd hardly believed that such thick, heavy floorboards could move, but the mill had its voices like any other building. The clanging faded into a background of atmospheric music. Marilyn recognised it and briefly wondered whether to ask for the CD back as she made her way between the shelves towards the empty counter, plucking up courage. The items on sale were the same but different. She let her eyes linger on the homely colours of a stoneware bowl. One of hers. She swallowed her resentment together with her nerves.

The storeroom door was ajar. Voices floated through to the shop, the sound of boxes being moved. A woman laughing. Matt teasing. Dust was in the air, in her nose, catching in the back of her throat. Like the early days. Marilyn coughed.

'Customer,' Matt muttered to the other, then in a raised voice: 'Be with you right away.'

His footsteps approached from the depths of the storeroom. She leaned on the counter, stood tall, leaned again, hating herself for feeling nervous.

'Marilyn. To what do we owe the pleasure?'

'I'd like a quick word. With you.'

She glanced pointedly towards the storeroom. She had nothing against Lucy and grudgingly liked her, despite everything, but didn't particularly want her there.

'Fancy coming up to the flat for a coffee?'

Not like him to be so tactful; Lucy must be having a positive effect. He called through to the back that he'd be gone for a short while and she followed him out.

The top floor of the small mill made a lovely flat and she felt an insane surge of jealousy as she thought of their plans for it. Plans that would now benefit someone else, while much of the fruit of her labours lay under a heap of soil.

'No need for coffee; I won't stay long.'

'Ah, just wanted a nosy?'

She bristled. 'I wouldn't be here at all if my phone was working.'

He waved her to a seat and looked round. 'We've nearly finished, though you wouldn't believe it with all this mess.'

There were a couple of boxes in a corner, one unpainted wall with some paint cans and dust sheets. Otherwise the place looked good, and she felt as if he was mocking her inability to be in a room for more than half an hour without filling it with clutter.

'I just thought I'd better let you know – that storm Saturday night? It's caused a few problems.'

'Hence no phone.'

'And still no electricity, plus it caused a landslip against the barn.'

'Sorry to hear it. Any structural damage?'

'A bit to the barn; nothing that wasn't going to be rebuilt anyway. But that's not why I'm here. I came to say that Alan won't be able to start this week as planned.'

'Saw him in the pub last night. He told me he'd spoken to you and you didn't seem happy. He's started on the Grants' place, hasn't he? You've got to admit, Lynnie, he's bound to give them priority. It's their home, they've got three young kids—'

'Did I say I was complaining? And I've asked you to stop calling me that.'

'Sorry on both counts.' He held his hands up and she wondered how she'd ever found the familiar gesture and accompanying expression anything other than patronising.

'I just wanted to say I'll probably be needing the spare workshop a bit longer than we planned.'

'Hm. We could do with letting it out before too long. We'd hoped it'd be free in the next couple of months. But I do understand the position you're in.'

'I'll be leaving it in a far better state than when I came. It was a wreck.'

'Merely cosmetic.'

'A wreck and you know it. And don't forget it's in lieu of my share in the business.'

Matt laughed. 'How much do you think we're making

here? If it was a market rent it'd already take months of your "share" to balance it out. Of course I wouldn't dream of asking for money, seeing as it's you, but... I'm sure you know where I'm coming from.'

Only too well; he never tired of reminding her what a favour he was doing her.

'Listen, Lynnie – Marilyn – since Alan told me the news I've been thinking. What have you told the insurance? Could you get them to cough up some rent for the extra period?'

'I haven't mentioned it as such,' she said.

'"As such". You haven't contacted them, have you? I'd have thought even you—'

'We've been too busy clearing the yard and getting the car out – no phone, remember? – and I had an appointment this morning. I'm going over to the brokers' now. I wanted to update you first. And...make sure it was all right for me to stay on at the unit a bit longer.'

'If you say so. Good luck, then. So who's "we"?'

'What? Oh, I've had a friend over to help me.'

'Anyone I know?'

'No.' She smiled and stood. 'Right, I'll be off. Thanks for being OK about me staying on.'

'And for reminding you about the insurance.'

For once his smug insistence on having the last word didn't bother her. As she left she thought that, rent aside, the insurance might enable her to give Jay a decent wage. Perhaps she wouldn't even need Matt's mate Alan at all.

Chapter 8

The hole in the roof was still bothering him. Try as he might to ignore it, it was there. Even if he concentrated determinedly on the view, the solid stone house across the yard with its pretty but neglected garden, the dwindling pile of rubble at his feet, it was still there, seared into his imagination like a brand. Every piece of damaged, broken timber pointing accusations through the grey-skied hole. He wished he'd insisted on patching it up. As soon as she'd gone he'd even got the ladder back out and checked the rest of the roof in random places. It seemed fine. Those builders were deceiving her, suggesting work that didn't need doing, for extra money. He wouldn't deceive her. Not about that. Not about…

He forced himself to concentrate. A few more shovelfuls and he'd be ready to take the barrow with another load of debris to the pile. Past the gap in the barn wall with its glimpse of the hole in the roof. He kept shovelling. Soil was overflowing. Go. More shovelling. You weren't going to think about it. He picked up the handles and the creaky wheel was part comforting, part menace. He breathed deeply and headed up the yard to the pile. Wonder what she'll want to do with all that soil? Better. Don't think…He should insist, sooner rather than later, patch it up. The hole in the roof. Don't think about it. He glanced up and his heart lurched as he saw the boy sitting on the stone wall between the yard and the fields beyond. The drystone wall that was just like the drystone walls from back then. He put the barrow down, stared hard at its contents. Don't be stupid, a drystone wall is a drystone wall. The land around is totally different. Can't you smell it? Hear it? Different. He tipped the barrow. As the crunching slithering of soil and gravel stopped he glanced nervously at the base of the wall. Stop it. There's nothing there, only trees, grass and a bit of dying bracken. And looked up. The boy was still watching.

'There's nothing for you here, can't you see? You might as well go. Leave me.'

He forced himself to turn his back, grabbed the barrow and made for the barn and the next load. No good. Need a rest. Getting old. If only that was all. The bench against the side wall of the house beckoned. He sat and filled his pipe as purposefully as he could with shaking hands. Just need a break, that's all. Scary: had he spoken out loud just then? He had before, in the night, that was for sure. Šojka. So why hadn't he taken her cue, told her... Told her what? he thought irritably, what for? Why tell her? Because she seems like someone who'll listen? What makes you think...? He drew deeply on his pipe, looking up as the boy jumped from the wall and turned away. And him – what was that about last night? Christ, he was giving the little bastard stories now. That's right, off you go into the woods. The cheery birdsong harmonised with the breeze-rustled leaves. Where were the ravens when you needed them?

He made himself put the pipe aside and went back to work. She trusted him to do a good job, better do one. Or? Why not walk away? He'd laid it on a bit; yes, earning something decent would be good, but he managed. With no responsibilities it was amazing what you could get by on. But something regular. Nice change. Or even... *You can't run forever.* And – come on, admit it – she was worth getting to know. Pretty, too, though he suspected she wasn't confident of that. Which was nice in itself. It was refreshing to meet someone who didn't eye him with distrust all the time, even if he deserved it – hell, she wasn't even going to lock the door this morning! Apart from their first meeting – hadn't she as good as blamed him for losing something? Only natural. Even though it could have been anyone in that crowd.

The sound of a vehicle crunching up the track made him tense up. He instinctively turned to face it, irrational fear giving the air around him a harsh glare. Her car. He made himself breathe deeply and deliberately unclenched his fingers muscle by muscle from the handle of the shovel. With a dirty hand he wiped sweat from his brow that wasn't only from exertion, and thought what a sight he must look. That sort of thing didn't usually bother him unduly, but he used his forearm, hopefully less muddy, to wipe again.

She was smiling and waving something as she got out of the car.

'Hey, you've been busy, well done! Look at this!'

A shiny purse with a giant cat's face motif. Was it supposed to mean something? He recalled the pickpocket incident but she was talking fifteen-to-the-dozen before he had chance to comment.

'The police left a message on my mobile say it had been handed in, so I called to collect it, seeing as I was over that way. The money's gone – there wasn't much anyway – but nothing else, not even my card, though I'd cancelled it anyway so it'll still be a load of hassle. But someone handed it in! Restores your faith, doesn't it?'

He frowned, nodded, amazed that the handing-in could so easily cancel out the fact of it being nicked in the first place. He could do with sharing in some of that optimism.

'Nice one.' Feeling calmer now, he stuck the shovel in

the dirt pile and walked over to the car. 'How d'you get on at that shop?'

'Great, thanks. They like my things and it looks like the sort of place that could shift plenty, too. It'll mean a lot of work, but it's wonderful news.'

'Congratulations.' He spread his muddy hands. 'Forgive me if I don't…shake your hand.'

Had he really been going to say 'give you a hug'? She frowned and he was telling himself no, of course she couldn't read his mind, when she said, 'So that's all the good news. It's downhill from there, I'm afraid.'

'Problems?'

She shrugged. 'Trivial, I guess. Shouldn't complain. Come in and I'll tell you over lunch.'

He wiped his hands on his jeans, followed her in and sat at the kitchen table as she made a plate of sandwiches and told him about her visit to Matt – he noticed how the man still seemed to bother her, though she insisted he meant nothing – and then the insurance broker's.

'Of course Matt's hoping I can pay him some rent from it. A legitimate claim, seeing as it'll be longer before I get my own place. And I want to be able to pay you properly, so we can get on with it – if you agree. I just want all this done, so I can get myself established.'

'So do you think they'll accept the claim?'

'The broker was helpful enough, but…'

She shook her head, biting her lip.

'Don't tell me. "Act of God",' he said and noticed her looking across as if wondering how someone like him knew about the technicalities of insurance. 'You can argue it, you know.'

'I know. But it could take ages, and whatever happens there'll be a huge excess to pay.'

He tutted in sympathy. She placed the sandwiches and two plates on the table and sat opposite him. He helped himself as she indicated and began eating, watching her stare at her plate. He was surprised and nonplussed to see she was fighting tears.

'It seemed such a good idea. But it seems I'll have to wait after all. I can do it, of course I can; I really shouldn't be complaining, but I just know Matt's going to make things difficult. I'm going to say something I regret and lose that place, and then… Well, it'll just be back to square one.' She shook her head. 'It's stupid, but on my way to the broker's I'd even got to thinking I might not need a loan. I can't really afford it; there's no way I'll be making much to start with. I did a business plan – on Matt's advice, of course – to get the loan offer in the first place, but that's all up the spout now because of the delay. I probably won't even get anything, and then…' The tears got the better of her; she tried to sniff them back. 'I'm sorry. Don't know what's got into me. I think I'm just tired.'

'Steady on.' He fished in his pocket and produced a grubby tissue, looked at it, and sheepishly put it back, hoping she hadn't noticed.

'Thought that counts,' she muttered, looking at his hands. He'd forgotten to wash them. She got up and grabbed a piece of kitchen towel to wipe her eyes and blow her nose.

'Nothing's changed,' he said. 'No need to worry; I'll still stay and get on with as much as I can till your guy's ready to start.'

'You don't understand; thinking about it in the cold light of day, I'm not even sure I could afford to pay you at all. You ought to think about going to find some decent work.'

'I said don't worry about it. Call it a loan. And…and,

well, if you have trouble with the bank, I could…I could probably contribute a bit myself.'

'You?'

'Yeah. Help you get on your feet. A kind of investment; I like what you do.'

'But—'

'We can talk about it. After this afternoon's work.'

With a smile, he got up to belatedly wash his hands.

Chapter 9

Another unfamiliar house and another bout of nerves. Vinko had been on an early shift and, the previous day's meeting with Novak still nagging like a wasp in his head, had made himself come before he changed his mind. Whatever happened here, he wouldn't be any worse off. He walked up the drive. The angry insect buzz of a lawnmower reached him from the next-door garden, someone making the most of the failing light and the gap in the changeable autumn weather. A woven-wood fence and a line of shrubs saved him from the neighbours' suspicious looks.

He knocked at the door, waited, nearly walked away, tried the bell. The thumping of his heart almost drowned the sound of footsteps approaching from within. He heard the noises of someone fumbling with a lock, and a grey-haired woman with a friendly, lined face opened the door as far as the safety chain allowed.

'Hello,' he said before his nerve left him. 'Anja Pranjić?'

She nodded.

'I'm your grandson,' he said in his own language.

She stared at him in silence.

'Your grandson,' he repeated, 'Vinko.'

'Ivan's son?' Her eyes widened and the hand that wasn't clutching the door went to her cheek.

'I'm sorry I surprised you,' he said.

She stared a moment longer, then unhitched the chain and opened the door wide.

'Come in, *srećo moja.*'

His grandmother drew him in, closed the door and held him in her arms. He returned her embrace awkwardly. He hadn't known what to expect, but certainly not the feel of warm arms enfolding him, or the endearment he hadn't heard since his mother died.

She released him and led him through into a homely sitting room full of chintz, heavy old furniture, ornaments and pictures.

'Your mother wrote to us, told us she was expecting Ivan's baby. So long ago.' She looked as if she was on the verge of tears. 'And now here you are!'

He nodded, surprised by his own emotion. 'I didn't know if I should come.'

'Of course you should.' She moved as if to embrace him again, but he stood impassive. She hesitated, embarrassed, and motioned him to sit, joining him on the sofa. 'And how is your mother?'

'She died. A couple of years ago.'

'I'm sorry.' Anja looked saddened. 'We never met her. I tried to find her. Boris said to let the past lie, but I went myself, as soon as it seemed safe to go. It was heartbreaking. The family house, where your great-aunt lived, where your father went to make his home – nothing but charred, overgrown ruins. The village fared better than some in the area, but it was totally changed. Some of the old people had moved back, and a few newcomers, but much of the place was empty. Abandoned. No one knew where you'd gone.' His language, their language, had sounded rusty with her to begin with, but was now beginning to run more freely, like an old machine newly oiled and coaxed back to life. 'But what about you, Vinko? You had other family?'

He shook his head. 'I managed.'

'Where have you been living?'

81

He could hear her other, unspoken, question: Why didn't you come to us?

'My mother went to Germany after the war. I was born there. I came to England a year or so ago. I got a lift but it wasn't easy.'

A forty-eight hour journey boarded up in a cramped, stuffy compartment at the back of a furniture lorry with two others, relieved that he hadn't needed the faked identity card.

'You're all right now?'

He nodded. There was an uneasy silence.

'Listen, I ought to tell you. Before your grandfather gets back. He doesn't like mention of the old country. He hardly refers to it at all. Living in the past is what caused it all, he says. Lost your father to us.'

'I know. My mother told me.'

'What did she tell you?'

'That…that my father went back to Croatia on his own.' His eyes were on the ground; he couldn't meet hers. 'Because you and Grandfather wouldn't take him.' He looked up. 'I'm sorry. She told me she'd written to you…must be the letter you got…she said you had a right to know. About me. About what happened to my father. She gave me your address, too.' He was careful not to mention Novak. 'The old one. The girl who lives there now gave me this one. She sends her greetings. I'm sorry, I can't remember her name.'

'Young Nicky Radcliffe?'

He nodded, uninterested. That episode was past. 'Where is he now? Grandfather?'

'He's gone to see a neighbour about something. He's well-liked round here, you know.'

She seemed eager to persuade Vinko of it, but he'd make his own mind up, like he'd always had to.

'I'll go and put the kettle on,' she said. 'Make us a cup of tea. We usually have dinner around seven; I hope you'll stay.'

She bustled into the kitchen, leaving Vinko to look round the trinkets and photos on the sideboard. He couldn't help weighing up the value of the smaller ornaments, or noticing two ten-pound notes beneath a glass paperweight. But he held back. Glancing around, he opened the top drawer a crack. Nothing but an assortment of mats and cloths. He quickly tried the rest of the drawers. No bank papers. He had never expected it to be that easy, and it was more of a relief than a disappointment; he still wasn't sure that was the reason he had come. He studied the photographs instead – a black and white wedding photo, presumably of Anja and Boris. A couple of portraits of a woman he thought must be the 'sourface' Nicola Radcliffe had mentioned – his aunt, Novak's ex-wife, smiling now for the camera. A boy and a girl at various ages, he guessed his cousins, the most recent a similar age to himself. None of them included Novak, which was not surprising. Vinko was saddened, however, to see no sign of his father, not even as a boy. He sat back down, wondering whether he should have come. Presently he heard the back door open.

'Boris, we've got a visitor. Wait, let me tell you…'

Footsteps sounded and the connecting door was pulled closed. He heard muffled voices, hers hushed, his deeper and louder. Vinko considered trying to listen through the closed door or slipping away out the front. He decided the first would be too risky and the second pointless. Inertia won and he sat looking across at the pictures that didn't include his father. The voices in the kitchen got more insistent, more heated, and he heard movement, braced himself for the door to burst open. Instead he heard the back door slam and heavy footsteps down the side of the house and out along the drive. He looked through the window and saw a stocky, balding figure in a blue anorak striding down the road.

Anja stood by the kitchen door looking apologetic.

'He had to go out again; he'll be back to meet you later,' she said as she put a tray with tea and cakes on the table. 'A friend of his—'

'I know. He doesn't want me here. It's all right, I'll go before he gets back.'

'You won't!' she said. 'Only if you want to,' she added more gently. 'This is my house too. I'll not have him turn you away so soon after I've met you.'

Her tears were welling up again and he felt embarrassed. He looked over to the sideboard.

'Is he the reason why there are no pictures of my father?'

Anja nodded. 'Shall I show you the letter your mother sent?' she asked as if by way of apology.

She disappeared upstairs and he heard the shuffling of things being moved. She returned with a yellowing envelope, the 52 Fairview Terrace address in hurried scrawl across the front and a German stamp and postmark. She removed the letter carefully and passed it to him. It was in the same hastily scribbled hand, apologising that his father had never written; he'd always intended to, and to visit them when the war was over. His mother told of their marriage, and how sorry she was to inform them of Ivan's death soon after in the fighting. She told them she'd fled to Germany with the help of a neighbour and would write again when the baby was born. It seemed she never had, and he wondered what Anja had thought for the last seventeen years. He was surprised to find his hand trembling and glanced at his

84

grandmother. She was staring at the letter she must know by heart, shaking her head slowly.

'If only he'd never gone.'

Vinko shifted uneasily. 'Are those photos?'

She handed two pictures to him. A copy of one his mother had shown him many times, the two of them on their wedding day. His father in combat gear, his mother in a pretty flowered dress. Circumstances hadn't allowed a traditional wedding. He looked long at them, his father's expression one of joyful pride and his mother staring at the camera as if resenting having to take her eyes off her new husband. The other was also a copy of one his mother had treasured; he remembered her crying when she lost it. She used to cry a lot. The photo showed his father 'looking like a real hero' as she'd said, together with his closest friend, grinning and posing for the camera. He stared hard at the two young men, dragging his eyes away from his father to the other. As he looked, Vinko realised why the busker in Holdwick had held his attention so strongly.

'That one particularly irritated Boris,' Anja was saying. 'Though I know my Ivan would have loved me to see the two of them looking so happy.'

'You knew Šojka?'

Anja frowned momentarily then smiled. 'So that's what they called him, is it? Yes; they were at school together. You heard about him, then?'

'A little. I found it amazing that a foreigner fought for us in the war. He must have been special.'

'That's not what your grandfather would say.' She glanced towards the window. 'Not what he said when he turned up on our doorstep last year, either.'

'Šojka was here? He's alive? Can you introduce me to him?'

She shook her head. 'We don't know where he is now, though I'm fairly sure he doesn't live locally. In any case, Boris told him never to darken our door again.' She took Vinko's hand, gripped it tightly. 'I don't think he knew about you or he'd have asked after you. I never got a chance to ask him about your mother either, with all Boris's cursing and threats.'

She sighed again and gazed over towards the family photographs, seeing ones that should have been there. 'I always liked him, even though Ivan might not have gone, might not have listened so hard to my sister's obsessions, if they hadn't encouraged each other. But whatever his faults, I wish he'd stood up to Boris last year and stayed. Maybe he could see I still partly blamed him.' She shrugged. 'Perhaps he'll come back one day, though I doubt it.'

Vinko stared at the cooling cup of tea and uneaten buns. He reached out and took one, heedless of the crumbs he dropped on her sofa as he ate. An echo drifted into his head of a tune he'd heard the day before, like one of the songs his mother had sung to light up his troubled childhood. He looked again at the photograph he was still holding. If only he'd had the guts to talk to the man last week. Why? It was probably a complete stranger, and if not, what did any of it matter? He put the photo down as if it was contaminated and swallowed the last mouthful of cake with difficulty.

'I'm sorry,' he said suddenly in English. 'I go.'

'No! Please.' Her grip on his arm was tight, insistent, and he sat back.

He enjoyed listening to her talking about Ivan as a boy, and nodded politely as she mentioned others in the family. He paid particular attention as Anja told him about his aunt, Vesna, wondering if he'd learn anything about her marriage to Mihal Novak. Anja merely said they'd divorced. Vinko tried to keep his voice casual as he asked why.

'From what she told us, there was no one reason. Things just got steadily worse. He was often away on business, sometimes for weeks, leaving her with the kids. He ran a small transport company, though we weren't convinced everything they carried was strictly legal. And when he was at home, he was…not an easy man to live with. Worse when he drank. Towards the end, we believed – though Vesna never said – he'd threatened her with violence. Even hit her. Though we were never sure.' She looked sad and angry. 'Divorce is never good, especially not when children are involved, but I'm not ashamed to say I was relieved.'

It was also a relief of sorts when the back door opened and they both looked round. Boris came noisily through to the living room.

'So you're still here? Come and shake your granddad's hand, then.'

Vinko obeyed and could smell drink on the man's breath as he approached.

'It is an honour to meet you, sir,' he said in the language his grandmother had led him to associate with these surroundings.

'We'll have none of that here. English it is in this house. You can speak English?'

'Yes. Though I like more to talk my own language if I can. With my family.'

'Well you can't. Not in my house.'

'Boris—'

He cut Anja short. 'I daresay I've forgotten every word I ever knew – I chose to, like I chose to make a new life here – and I'll not have you two whispering behind my back. So if you're going to stay…'

Vinko looked at Anja, saw the plea in her eyes. 'If this you want.'

'Aye. That's what I want.'

He sat down in an armchair. Vinko perched on a dining chair at the edge of the room, shy about returning to Anja's side on the sofa. She rose and picked up a magazine from the coffee table together with the letter and photos she'd hastily concealed beneath it when her husband arrived.

'I'll just go and make a start on the dinner.'

'Hide 'em away well, love.' Boris laughed to himself as she left the room. 'Thinks I'll chuck 'em on t' fire one day.'

Vinko flashed him a look but kept silent.

'So what brings you here? Spinney found you, did he? Been talking to you?'

'I don't know who is…Spinney.'

'Do I look like I were born yesterday? If he's sent you here for us to see you right 'cause you claim to be our Ivan's kid, he can think again.' He pronounced it eye-van, which got Vinko's hackles up. He focused on this legitimate annoyance to keep from betraying himself by asking Boris too eagerly, too soon, to clarify what he meant by 'see you right'.

'I don't know who or what you talk about.'

'Now look here—'

'He doesn't, Boris,' said Anja, coming through from the kitchen. 'He didn't even know Jay was still alive. And of course Vinko's who he says he is. Haven't you got eyes in your head?'

'That's as may be. And I suppose seeing as how you're here you can stay for a while. Anja says she's invited you to have dinner with us.' He looked from his wife to Vinko. 'But don't go asking for owt else, eh?'

'I'm sure he's got no intention of asking for anything,' she said, calmly. Not directly, Vinko thought.

'Aye, well, I'm just saving him the trouble.'

Chapter 10

Marilyn got up, added a log to the fire and sat back down, watching the smoke from Jay's pipe drift towards the chimney and mingle with that from the flames in a comfortable silence. She assumed it was comfortable, at any rate; she must be mad, but she felt comfortable. She had no idea what he was thinking.

Eventually she plucked up the courage to ask him how someone living in hedgerows and barns, scraping a living from street entertainment and odd-jobbing, had enough money to be offering her a loan. She immediately regretted being so direct, but he smiled as if being offended wasn't an option.

'Zora was beautiful,' he said, in the same once-upon-a-time tone that had won her over yesterday, 'but in trouble. She was living in a remote house on the fringe of a war zone. She'd left the relative security of the city and gone to live in her family's crumbling house in the area where she felt she belonged. She'd taken in refugees who'd fled from villages disrupted by the conflict. And the local militia leader was her lover. This man was strong but cruel, respected and feared.

'Our heroine held a small fortune abroad – part inheritance, part savings smuggled out – and wanted it to help them rebuild their lives when the war was over. Her man, cold, battle-hardened, found out about it and wanted to use it there and then, not only to get supplies to help make sure they won the war, but to avenge his people by causing as much death and destruction as possible.'

He leaned forward and prodded the fire with the poker, sending a dramatic shower of sparks spiralling up the chimney.

'So, while her lover was away fighting, she confided in a young soldier she'd grown fond of. He'd been injured and was still too unwell to fight, but recovered enough to travel. She knew her lover, the militia leader, would eventually bully her into handing the money over and asked this young man to take it away, to keep it safe in a new account until things had settled down. There would be risks and she told him how much he could keep for himself as his reward. They both knew the dangers she was facing, too, and she told him that if she died he was to keep it all. She didn't want it to be used for evil.'

He glanced at her as if to check she was still with him.

'I knew that man, once. That was how I came to be custodian of a substantial sum of money. She died, tragically, shortly after her young friend left, and the money became his in accordance with her wishes. He bought a house but couldn't bear to keep it so he made me custodian; eventually signed it over to me and said I could do what I liked with it. I lived there briefly, but it didn't seem right, somehow. For reasons of my own I took to the road after a couple of years, putting the house to let with an agent. There was enough profit from the rent to pay back what I'd always considered to be more an unofficial loan than a windfall. Once I'd done so, with a respectable amount of interest, I contacted her family and handed the money over to them. But the house is still there, rent still coming in – and now I've found a good home for the surplus.'

He looked at her.

'That's…a great story.'

'But.' His eyes twinkled in the firelight. 'You don't believe I have a house in Hampshire, do you?'

She laughed. 'Whether I do or not, it's not the house that's the problem.'

'Good. Because it's true. You can't argue with bricks and mortar. I could take you there now.'

She sipped her drink. 'It's the gorgeous wealthy heiress leaving her fortune to a hapless young soldier that's a touch less credible.'

'When you put it like that…'

'So?' She waited, but Jay simply smiled, drew on his pipe, exhaled luxuriously.

'All right,' she said, 'let's say I ask no questions and take it on trust that you've got a house. What's the real reason you come to be wandering the country apparently aimlessly, and how do you really make your living?'

'The second part first: it's as you've seen. Straight up. I don't earn much but I don't need much. And, whether or not you choose to believe me, since last year I've been getting a reasonable income from the house.'

'What happened last year?'

'Like I said, I'd finally saved up enough to find our heroine's family and give them their small fortune.' She couldn't help shaking her head. 'Believe what you will. Truth can be stranger than fiction. What is true is that I've finished paying off what I borrowed to buy the house, so the income's mine now, see? Well, yours for a while, if you'll accept it.'

'I'll accept it when I know the truth about where it's come from. So, back to the first part of my question – how come you're on the road if you've got a perfectly good house?'

'Tenancy agreements. You get a long-term tenant in, it's a pig of a job getting them out.' He grinned in a way that suggested he knew she felt like shaking him. 'OK, OK. Not merely tenants – lifestyle decision, pure and simple. Well, if I'm honest, not entirely my own. My late father sowed the seeds.'

'You're going to tell me you've got Romany blood.'

He picked up his wine glass and studied it as if it were a crystal ball.

'Not as far as I know. We moved around a lot, but it was pretty mundane – not caravans but cars and Pickford's. Dad was ambitious in his own sweet way and thought nothing of upping sticks on a regular basis for new starts and "business opportunities" that became tediously routine in their frequency. It was better when Mum was alive; she stayed put with us more or less every other move, and made him commute. But then…then she died. Car accident.' He paused and ran a hand through his hair. 'It…it was about the time my sister went off to college. A few years later, the summer I was seventeen, I spent the holidays abroad with a mate. Dad said I should stay and help him with the business he was trying to get off the ground at the time. I wanted nothing to do with it. So I get home late August and find my key no longer fits the door. He'd left an address, on the other side of the country, and passed on the message through my sister: "If the cocky little bastard wants his independence, he's welcome to it." No hard feelings, did I understand; he wasn't one to shirk on his responsibilities and I was welcome to join him when I was ready.'

He finished his wine and topped up both of their glasses.

'I never saw him or spoke to him again.' He said it as if that was an achievement to be proud of. 'I spent my A Level year dossing on a series of mates' floors. Mainly Ivan's. He was…he was my best mate, the one I'd been on holiday with, when it all started.' He paused, long enough for her to wonder if 'it all' was more than merely a restless lifestyle, and whether his friend, whose name he'd pronounced in the foreign way, *ee-van*, could have anything to do with the mysterious inheritance. He continued before she had chance to ask. 'I had a tent, of course, and used it whenever the weather was good enough – I'm not one to impose, as I tried to tell you.' He glanced across the room and she half-expected him to go and get his bag. 'I suppose you don't believe any of that either?'

'It sounds… extreme. Are you implying I shouldn't believe you?'

'Up to you. You asked for explanations.'

His manner suggested denial of all responsibility for tall tales and truth-stretching – it was she who'd made him do it.

'Why won't you just tell me?'

He shrugged. 'The way I look at it, if you think a story's obscure, you should take it as a compliment.'

'Oh, really?'

'It means the person telling it is crediting you with enough intelligence to work it out.' She shook her head. 'Whatever… I can honestly tell you the money I'm offering you is mine to give. There's nothing dodgy about it.'

'And, as an intelligent person, I can take your word about that, can I?'

It came out more harshly than she'd intended. He sat forward, his expression more serious than she'd yet seen it. 'I've told you as much as I tell anyone. More. Just think on this. If I were a scammer, would I be offering to give instead of take? You've said yourself you probably won't be able to pay me for a while – not that I'm complaining. Just saying.' He got up, crouched by the fire and tapped his pipe into the grate. 'If it was dirty money I was trying to lose, I'd

93

hardly call repairing a barn in the middle of nowhere a viable money-laundering scheme.'

'But—'

'Wouldn't your average confidence trickster behave in a way…in a way that would actually inspire *confidence*?'

He sat back down, picked up his wine glass and drank deeply.

'Jay, I'm sorry if I've hurt your feelings. I don't want to sound ungrateful. But surely you can understand.'

'Of course I do! I just thought for a while there…oh, never mind what I thought.'

He drained the glass, put it heavily on the table beside him. The silence was now definitely not comfortable. Her head was foggy with questions, with doubts. But she didn't have the words to put voice to any of them. She felt him watching her, looked across.

'Penny for them,' he ventured.

She shook her head. 'I honestly don't know what I'm thinking.'

'My offer still stands – the other one, where I get up this instant, pack my bag, walk away and leave you in peace.'

A gust of wind blew a rattle of rain against the window.

'Don't be silly.'

'It's the most serious I've been all day.'

She believed he meant it, and also knew it was not what she wanted.

'I'll get on up to bed; leave you to your thoughts.'

He was on his feet wishing her goodnight, giving her no chance to object. As she listened to his feet on the stairs, the door softly closing, faint rustlings as he prepared his makeshift bed, she wondered whether the spare room had been such a good idea. He could obviously look after himself; she had no reason to feel sorry for him. He'd never once asked her to. But had he been playing her like he played his audiences? Was he doing so now? Perhaps he was right, perhaps she should be asking him to sleep outside. They were supposed to be working on the barn floor the next day, so that would soon be out of the question, but he seemed to enjoy telling her he was fine with his tent.

She remembered his obsession with that hole in the roof he'd spent the afternoon patching up. For a few moments there had been something strange, distracted about his manner when she'd arrived home that morning. As if something had happened while she was away. Staring into the flames, she shook her head. Must have been listening to too many stories.

Chapter 11

The next morning, Marilyn sent Jay off to the builders' merchant to pick up supplies and hire some equipment while she stayed to make the preparations at home. He knew what he needed and she'd be more use clearing the few remaining bits from the barn than going along for the ride. She briefly wondered whether she'd ever see her car again, but told herself a decision to trust someone involved more than words. He wouldn't get far in any case. She smiled to herself as she shifted half-empty sacks and an assortment of gardening equipment out of the barn to clear the floor.

He was back before she had time to begin worrying, the old jeep groaning under the weight of the hired trailer. They spent the morning excavating the soil floor with a mini-digger. He began by teaching her how to operate it, freeing him to do the heavier work on the ground. She became aware of how well they worked together, often even anticipating one another's movements. Jay took charge, but in a way that didn't make her instantly want to contradict him, and listened to her suggestions with a respect Matt had rarely shown her, not latterly at least.

It was warm work, and when the autumn sun broke through the steely clouds, a touch of gold glinting in the iron grey, Jay paused to remove his jumper. His T-shirt rucked up slightly and she thought she glimpsed a scar on his side before he pulled it back down. He glanced over and caught her watching him.

96

'I…I thought I'd go and make us a drink,' she said. 'Shall I take that in out of the way?'

He passed the jumper over to her with a smile. A warm feeling suffused her, but she stopped the train of thought in its tracks by asking, awkwardly, whether he wanted tea or cordial and walking briskly in to the kitchen.

When she came out with two mugs of tea he stopped work and joined her on the rickety bench against the front wall of the house. It creaked as he sat down.

'This could do with a bit of work,' he said. 'Couple of rotten bits need patching up, a brace or two on the wobbliest joints. I'll add it to the list of jobs if you like – it's not as if we're short of timber.'

'That'd be great, thanks.'

They sat gazing out through the trees, the song of the curlews bubbling up into the sky over the moors beyond.

'This is an amazing place to live,' he said.

'I still stop regularly and think how lucky I am. Sorry about my little outburst yesterday. At least I've got a week off from my other job to enjoy it.'

'Your other job?'

'A friend of mine runs a pub – small hotel, really – in the next dale. I help out behind the bar; at least it's something regular until I get established. Though it's only temporary – Sue's doing me a favour, really. I bet she'll be happy not to have to pay my wages this week. All the more reason to make sure I get my own business going sooner rather than later.'

'You will. I can see you've got determination. And self-respect.' He was suddenly serious. 'If you don't respect yourself, who knows where it might lead?' Wondering how to reply, she watched him staring towards the horizon. He picked up his tea mug and drained it in a couple of gulps. 'Just listen to me! What do I know?'

He stood abruptly and reached for her mug to take into the kitchen with his own. On his way back out he paused on the doorstep.

'See, no self-respect. Or respect of any kind. I forgot to take my muddy boots off.'

'It doesn't—'

'I'll learn. Listen, I want to thank you, Polly.'

'I should be thanking *you* for all you're doing.'

'No, I mean it. Thank you for…for trusting me.'

'I—'

'It means a lot to me.'

He moved past her and she tried to think of a reply as she followed.

'Now then,' he said with a grin and a theatrical clap of his hands, 'where were we?'

They worked hard, the chuntering of the digger limiting conversation to planning the next move and the give-and-take of instructions in the welcome pauses. He was a man on a mission, she thought as they worked. They stopped only for a brief lunch and a mid-afternoon cup of tea, determined to have the digger ready to take back and exchange for a concrete mixer the following day. By the end of the afternoon, shortly before their self-imposed deadline of the first signs of dusk, they had the floor excavated and much of the soil at the back cleared.

'There,' he said as they stood back and surveyed the gutted space. 'It's amazing what you can achieve when it matters.'

'Matters?'

He turned to her. 'Oh, you know. Job satisfaction. Didn't mean anything by it.'

'I…I didn't think for a second that you did.'

They stood looking at one another for an awkward

moment and she hoped the flush she felt on her face was the result of the afternoon's work and fresh air.

'It'll be getting dark soon,' she said. 'We should be thinking about getting cleaned up and making some dinner.'

'Why don't we go out?'

'We could...' She hesitated.

'I'll pay; I know you're strapped. Oh, hang on, you said you had a freezer full to deal with. Sorry, bad idea.'

She shook her head, smiling. 'That was just me trying to impress. I'm not that efficient. A few bits but nothing that goes together. Should've done more of a shop when I was out yesterday. My head was all over the place, sorry.'

'That settles it. Where's good nearby – this place where you work?'

'What day is it?'

'Tuesday,' he said without hesitation. She was mildly surprised he kept track.

'She doesn't do food on Mondays or Tuesdays at this time of year. There's one over the moors does. A bit of a drive, but I've always fancied trying it.'

'Sounds good.' He grinned, gestured towards the car. 'I really liked getting behind the wheel this morning. I hadn't driven for ages before that. Can I offer to be your chauffeur for the evening?'

It wasn't a pub she'd ever been to; Matt had never fancied it. It was surprisingly busy for the time of year, but they managed to find a quiet corner. She felt good in her favourite flowing skirt, with her hair loose, freed from the plaits she braided whenever she was working. Jay had called them 'sweet' and she was fairly sure from his tone that it was a compliment.

The beer was excellent and the food plain but good. As they ate she told Jay more about her plans and listened to some anecdotes from his nomadic life. He insisted on paying for them both and she watched him at the bar, chatting easily with the barman, looking over to their table every now and again and catching her eye. He was wearing the clothes they'd washed on the first night, a cotton shirt and cargo trousers – plenty of useful pockets for his travels, she thought. He'd laughed when she'd apologised for being unable to iron them as the electricity was off, and she smiled now as she thought how the creases actually suited him. She noticed he paid with plastic and commented on it when he returned with last drinks for the road.

'I don't always carry pockets of change around,' he said. 'Could give the wrong impression, especially on a first date.'

She felt a little tug of surprise. 'Is that what this is?'

'If you're happy about it, I'm honoured. If I've misunderstood I apologise – I'd be quite happy to think of the investment I want to make in your pottery venture and call it a business dinner.'

'I think I prefer the first option.'

She wasn't sure if he was serious, but was happy to play along for a while and see where it led. Their hands touched as he passed her drink over. He took hers, leaned across the table and brought her fingers to his lips in an old-fashioned gesture. Marilyn laughed gently, but savoured the tingle that his touch sent through her. She looked at their hands, fingers lightly intertwined, on the table in front of them. His long fingers looked used to work, unadorned but for a small gold band on his little finger that seemed to have grown there. He noticed her looking.

'I just saw it and liked it. It doesn't mean anything.' His expression was serious. 'I've never been married, and believe

100

me when I say I'm not one of those rover types with a no-strings-attached woman in every town.' He relaxed. 'I mean, honestly, who in their right mind would have the likes of me?'

'Are you doubting my sanity?' she teased.

'I didn't mean—'

'I know. You must have had a serious relationship or two.'

He nodded. 'But I'm a man. I don't talk about things like that. Seriously, there was someone once, yes, but it was a long time ago. Things didn't work out. My fault mainly, I can see that now. I'm older and wiser. Well, older.'

'And no better at selling yourself, obviously.' She smiled. 'Was that when you were still living in that house of yours?'

'In Winchester? Yes.'

She picked up her glass and drank. 'Is that where you're from originally?'

He grinned. 'I knew you weren't listening to a word I've said. I've never lived in one place long enough to call myself "from" anywhere.' He shrugged. 'The opposite. I think I liked the fact that Winchester was somewhere I had even less connection with than anywhere else. I don't really do connections, as you may have gathered. I send my sister a Christmas card every year; I doubt she wants it but it's become tradition. And that's it.'

'Really?'

'I haven't seen her for years; she moves around, works for a hotel chain so it's been hell tracking her down at times. It's obviously in the blood. She's married now, though, so at least that means they stay put a bit longer. Not that I've ever met the guy. Haven't seen her for years.'

'Doesn't that make you sad?'

'Not really. Suits us both. She thinks I'm an irresponsible waste of skin and I…I don't care to be thought of in those terms.'

'There you go, over-selling yourself again.'

'I have an e-mail address so Cath can let me know if anything important happens, though it's rare she gets in touch and even rarer that I seek out a library with a computer. Especially since I didn't turn up to Dad's funeral. I just couldn't face it. It was ten years ago, and I was still… in a bad place.'

'What—'

'No excuses; if I'm honest I'm not even sure I could have faced it now. All those people I used to know. Having to pretend… Anyway, that's it for contact.'

And that's it for explanations, Marilyn thought as he brushed aside another interjection: 'I reckon if she gets an annual card from me with a postmark that isn't a prison one she knows I'm safe and reasonably well. Duty done. So what about you? Haven't you got family you could've asked to help you out?'

'I'm as likely to do that as you are,' she said. 'I don't want any more lectures about "getting a proper job." But I must say I do better than you at keeping in touch.'

'Granted; most people do.'

'Mum and Phil, my stepdad, moved to the south of France a couple of years ago. We phone and I go over when I can afford it – you can imagine how often that is. Dad's in London. We may see each other more often now Matt's out of my life; they never got on. Likewise, Laurie, my brother. We're quite different, but we get together once in a while. Hopefully you'll meet one day. You'd be good for him.'

'Me?'

'He needs shaking out of unbearable conventionality from time to time.'

Jay grinned. 'So, while we're on the subject of real life… *Are* you going to let me help you out? Financially, I mean?' She

102

hesitated. 'It honestly has come from saving up rents. OK, I originally bought that house by using money I probably shouldn't have. But I've paid back every penny I owed.'

She raised her eyebrows. 'That was said with feeling.'

'Just…years of having a great big debt hanging over me. Paying it back bit by bit. It's been good to be free of it, is all.'

He fished his pipe and tobacco from his pocket, and began the fiddly business of packing the bowl. Marilyn watched him. She'd never really believed he was trying to swindle her, but it had crossed her mind that he might be on the run from something. She dismissed that idea whenever she thought of him performing publicly in the marketplace, and she wondered now if it was himself he was trying to hide from.

Sensing she'd never get anywhere by pushing, she stopped herself from asking by suggesting they went to finish their drinks outside so he could enjoy his pipe. The autumn evening wasn't cold and she savoured the enhanced flavour of the beer in the night air, breathing in the soft, nutty fragrance of his smoke as it floated away. They watched occasional car headlights wind their way down from the lonely moorland road to get swallowed up in the valley below where she knew, but couldn't see, that a village nestled.

'Where does that road go?' he asked.

'Across the moors to Holdwick. The track past my house turns into a footpath and crosses it over there somewhere.'

'I'd like to explore the moors more while I'm here.' She felt a slight jolt at the suggestion of not-being-here his words implied. 'I've got this thing about finding places that aren't really on the map.'

'Like deserted villages, you mean?'

'Sometimes. Not even that. Just…signs that someone's been there but isn't around anymore.'

'I don't know of anything like that nearby.'

'Yet.'

He smiled in the light from the pub sign above them and without warning leaned over, arm round her shoulder, and kissed her. She put her hand on his neck and held him there for a lingering moment, until the door behind them opened, spilling out light and a gaggle of noisy people.

As he drove them home, wisps of stories grew between them like the sparse patches of mist that gathered in hollows and hovered in ambush on apparently random patches of moorland. They reached the end of the lane through the trees, and saw a light.

'Looks like there's someone at the house.' His voice was harsh and he looked tense in the glow from the dashboard. 'Were you expecting anyone?'

'No. Strange, I never get visitors unannounced. Unless it's Richard Harrington back early. I doubt it, though. He's got a key but he'd never let himself in uninvited.'

Jay turned the car slowly into the yard and killed the lights. There was no sign of life, simply the yellow light spilling from the kitchen window and pooling out to lap at the doors of the barn. It reflected dimly from sweat on his brow.

'We'd best go and check it out,' he said. He released his white-knuckled grip on the wheel to turn the key and cut the engine.

'*You* aren't expecting anyone, are you?' she asked quietly.

He shot her a look of pained innocence. 'Of course not. Let's go.'

He insisted on entering first, grabbing the axe as he

passed the woodpile, and opened the door as soon as she unlocked it. The kitchen was empty. Motioning her roughly to stay by the door, he made his way in silence through to the darkened living room. Marilyn obeyed, paralysed by the same kind of fear that had engulfed her as she watched the storm. She glanced over to the microwave, her eyes drawn by the clock flashing. *0:32*. Surely it wasn't that late? The blinking figures ticked on: *0:33*. And then the relief washed over her together with a fit of laughter as she realised.

'Jay, it's OK, come back!'

He appeared immediately in the doorway.

'Ssh! What …?'

'It looks like we've got the electricity back.' She indicated the flashing green digits. 'About half an hour ago, it seems. That's why the light's on.'

He glanced around. 'What the fuck d'you leave it on for?'

'I kept flicking the switch out of habit,' she replied, taken aback by his tone. 'Must have left it in the on position.'

He relaxed suddenly, broke into a smile. 'And you refuse to believe some of the things *I* tell you? Electricity blokes working at this time of night?'

He looked at the axe in his grip as if wondering how it had got there, walked over to the porch and put it back in place.

'I'm sorry. Really I am. I…I overreacted. You must think—'

'I don't think anything.'

He looked even more worried that he'd upset her than he had about the threat of intruders in the house. She gave him a reassuring smile as she put the kettle on. He came to her, put a tentative arm around her and she relaxed into his embrace. It wasn't only the electricity; she felt as if she'd got *him* back from somewhere, too.

She made hot chocolate while he coaxed the fire in the living room to a blaze. They lit candles and switched out the lights because it still felt right that way. He told her a story in the fireglow. As they went upstairs, by candlelight as if that had become tradition, Jay paused outside the door of the spare room.

'Your place or mine?' he said with a smile.

She stopped short, one foot hovering over the top step, lost for a reply.

'Sorry, that was…' He looked at his feet. 'I shouldn't have said that.'

'It's not… You took me by surprise. It… it's a bit soon. I hardly know you. No, it's not you.' She laughed self-consciously. 'I mean – I swore I'd give myself time. You know, after Matt. At least a year, I said.'

'What's a year between friends?' His laugh sounded equally forced. 'Don't feel you have to explain. *Mea culpa.*' He turned to go into his room, paused and looked back at her. 'Night night, then. Sweet dreams.'

'You too.'

She stared at the closed door for a moment. Going to her own room was an effort, but she told herself it was for the best. She realised she hadn't even thanked him for a lovely evening. Too late now. He'd know. And if he didn't… Well, in that case they didn't understand each other as much as she liked to think. She should be pleased; she'd done the sensible thing for once in her life. But *was* it sensible? What if she drove him away? If that drove him away, let him go.

Slivers of moonlight found their way round the curtains and she lay chasing sleep in the pale light. The after-image of his expression as he'd shut the door wouldn't leave her – disappointment, but more; a hint of loneliness that mirrored her own. Her eyes followed over and over again the same fine ceiling cracks she'd traced during endless nights alone. She turned over. She'd got used to it now. Hadn't she?

Eventually, not sure if she'd dozed or not, she gave in to the need to go to the bathroom. She forced herself not to look at his door as she passed and crept down the stairs, the living room familiar in the fireglow and the bathroom welcoming in the glimmer of the candle she'd left burning out of habit and now thought she'd always prefer to the harsh electric bulb. On the way back upstairs she couldn't help noticing a faint light showing beneath the spare room door. Before she knew it she was knocking softly.

'Come in.'

Jay was sitting up against the wall in his sleeping bag among the clutter, holding a paperback with a clip-on book light.

'I saw you had a light on. I realised I hadn't even thanked you. I really enjoyed this evening.'

He grinned. 'Me too. My pleasure. I mean that.'

She nodded. 'Aren't you cold?'

'Not in this sleeping bag. I don't carry much but I make sure what I do have is good quality.'

'You're leaning against a freezing cold wall.'

He shrugged his naked shoulders. 'I don't want to go spoiling myself with too much luxury. It'll be winter before long. It's surprising how soon—'

'You weren't thinking of moving on just yet?'

He frowned. 'I wasn't... I'm sorry, I overstepped the mark earlier, didn't I? I'd understand, you only have to say.'

'You haven't overstepped anything, Jay.'

'You're not angry with me?'

'Of course not. Why would I be?'

'Do you think I'd be daft enough to remind you?' He

reached over and drew a shirt round his shoulders. 'You shouldn't have mentioned the cold. Standing there with the door open and a draught coming up the stairs.'

'Sorry.' Her hand moved to pull her robe tighter. 'Anyway I'd better be off now, let you get some sleep.'

'I don't think I'll be sleeping just yet.'

'Me neither.' She smiled, looked at the floor, met his eye. 'So why don't we go where there's a bit more room?'

Jay moved as if to get up, paused. 'It... it sounds inviting. But, Polly, I don't want to do anything either of us will regret.'

'No...of course not.'

She stood, deflated, staring at the way the faint light brought out one side of his face in sharp relief, leaving the other in shadow. There was a seriousness about him that contrasted totally with their earlier lightheartedness. The moment hovered between them as she began to wonder if he was one of those men who, on getting close to what they wanted, were no longer interested.

As she was about to leave, he grinned briefly and scrambled up, taking her in his arms and kissing her. She returned his embrace and felt a flood of relief mingling with her desire, somehow aware that it hadn't been arrogance or indifference or even respect that had held him back. It had been fear.

As if scared herself that one of them would have a change of heart she held him tight, running a hand down the smooth skin of his back beneath the fabric of his shirt. As he pressed against her she drew away momentarily, catching the soft gleam of his eyes in the halflight and smiling. She led them through to her bedroom, pausing to open the curtains and let the moonlight in to bathe the bed that a short time ago had seemed such a lonely place.

'I still don't think you boys should have come.'

Zora's enigmatic smile belies her words. Even before they set off she protested that they should postpone their visit, and has continued to do so; tensions in the area where she now lives could soon boil over and become really dangerous. Yet she has done everything she could to speed their journey, to make them welcome. Guiltily, he studies her for a few moments in silence, even more beautiful than he remembered from last year, with her legs drawn up luxuriously beneath her in the sagging chair and the firelight glinting in her hair. This corner of the room is all the more homely for the air of neglect that pervades the rest of the house.

That will soon change. She has only just moved here from the capital, after all, and with their help will soon transform the run-down farm back into the home it used to be. Her spiritual home, she says. He is sure Ivan feels the same as she does, even though it is also his first visit to this place – they are family, after all. As for himself, he realises, with a sadness like nothing he has felt before, that he doesn't have a spiritual home. Throwing all his energy into helping repair, clean and awaken the sleeping house, adding a layer of the habitable to the spiritual, he is more than ready to believe her when she says he is young yet and he will know when he finds it. That may be true, but he senses it is something she has always known, that she had no need to discover, and it makes him feel inferior.

And now she has told them they shouldn't be there. Her smile seems just for him and he is reassured that she is speaking from concern. She looks at him in a way that makes it perfectly clear she does not want them gone.

The sound of the front door opening echoes down the hall. Zora frowns.

'I didn't expect him tonight.'

He and Ivan exchange a glance.

A formidable-looking man enters the room and he shivers as he is touched by the fresh, cold night air that accompanies the newcomer. The intense jealousy he feels as Zora rises to greet their visitor, embracing him warmly and kissing him on both cheeks, is irrational but real. The same goes for the fear he feels under the hostile, disapproving gaze. His grasp of the language is insufficient to understand the man's question and Zora's rapid reply, which adds to his disquiet.

'I was telling him my nephew and his friend have come to stay,' she tells them. 'This is my good friend Lek.'

Without knowing why, he is fully aware that the man is more than a good friend. Lek's face is expressionless as she presents them. She introduces him as Šojka, the name she gave him when they first came last year, saying it sounds so much nicer in their language, suits him so much better, than Džej. He agreed willingly; from the moment they first met she has made him feel older, interesting, an exotic foreigner – someone more special than he really is. But now, though his expression does not change, Lek's eyes bore into him, unequivocally conveying that being named for a bird is something to be despised. It is a challenge.

Unsure of the etiquette, they stand to shake Lek's hand. He makes himself look straight into the man's eyes and ensures his handshake is hard and strong. It is a challenge he accepts.

'You are welcome here,' Lek says, glancing possessively at Zora, 'but you will soon wish you had not come.'

The nature of his smile makes it clear he is in deadly earnest.

110

Chapter 12

The orange-tinged dawn was clearing to a dirty daylight by the time Vinko headed back to the corner shop, his collar turned up against the drizzle. He was grateful it had only just started and he'd managed to do most of the round in cold but clear air. When the weather was right, if he had to choose he might even say he preferred the paper round to his main job at the factory, though he hated both. On mornings like this he would simply think of the extra money through a haze of embarrassment and regret at the impulse that had made him respond to the card in the window a few weeks ago. The other paper rounds were the territory of boys who seemed half his age or less – he couldn't remember ever feeling that childish. Their initial phase of mocking his accent had by now settled into a respectful distance, and he was happy to keep it that way.

As he rounded the last corner his heart sank as he saw the silver car parked across the road. Giving his uncle a minimal wave he disappeared into the shop to hand over the empty bag and the reflective vest, trying to stall for time by engaging Mr Choudhury in conversation as he bought his tobacco. Today, the shopkeeper was more interested in the customers and getting his own small children off to school on time than chatting to an oversized paper boy.

He lingered in front of the magazine rack gathering his thoughts. Two calls from Novak in as many days had been ignored, but now he had to make some kind of decision. He desperately wanted to feel he belonged somewhere, but although he'd warmed to Anja, Boris had eyed him with suspicion from start to finish and he couldn't imagine them ever offering him a way in. It would be a while before he could face going back. Now he had to deal with Novak's insistence. Whatever he felt about the family that should be his, he had no taste for the job he'd been given, either. Then again, if Novak paid him well, he would have no need to depend on anyone. Anyone at all. After a few moments he reminded himself that if he stood for much longer by shelves of headlines that meant nothing to him, he'd miss his bus to work. He steeled himself and stepped out onto the street.

Novak grinned as he crossed the road to the car.

'Going up in the world, are you?' He nodded towards the shop.

'I can't stop or I'll miss my bus.'

His uncle gestured towards the passenger door and Vinko reluctantly accepted the offer of a lift.

'So, have you seen them yet?'

'I went, yes.'

'And?'

'Nothing you'd be interested in.'

Novak turned out onto the main road and put his foot down, swearing as he dodged to avoid two young girls crossing the road.

'Watch it,' Vinko muttered, gripping the edge of his seat. 'We'll get stuck in traffic whatever you do. No need to kill anyone.'

'Since when have you been able to drive? Shut it.' He slammed his brakes on within inches of the last car in the tailback. 'So, bore me. What did you talk about?'

'Nothing. My father. The past. All right? I didn't tell them I knew you, where I live, where I work, so you've no need to worry on that account.'

'Did you find anything out about the money?'

'I looked in a few drawers. Found nothing. No one said, "Hello Vinko, so lovely to see you, now can we give you a tidy sum to set you up in life?" And I didn't ask. One thing I don't do is beg.'

'That's exactly what you will be doing if you don't start showing some respect. Listen, son, you were in trouble when you came to me. The way you're talking anyone would think you're squeaky clean. We both know you're not. I've helped you, set you up here, and now it's your turn. Not even a favour – I've said you'll get your share. My friend's getting impatient. I need to be able to tell him something.'

'Tell him I don't want to know!'

The traffic lights were on red and Vinko moved to get out. The central locking clicked on.

'Not so fast. I've got some information might help you. Someone my friend would really like to see. If you could track him down for us… Play your cards right and not only will you get yourself a decent financial reward, but he could also help you with old Boris Pranjić. It's a long shot, but… We're ninety-nine per cent certain he's the one who gave them the money, so we think he must be living somewhere in the area. He was a friend of your father's. I was told to ask if you knew him.'

'I don't know anyone.'

'Then you can help us to look.'

The traffic started moving and they drove the rest of the way in silence. Novak stopped the car a little way down the road from the factory. The expensive glow of the dashboard clock told Vinko he was early.

'So,' his uncle said as he offered him a cigarette. '*Do* you know Jay Spinney, by any chance?'

'No.' He lit up and inhaled deeply to avoid looking at Novak. 'What makes you think I would?'

'Like I said, he knew your father. You'd think he might have wanted to get to know his mate's lad. Do something for you. But that was down to me in the end, wasn't it?' He sighed dramatically. Vinko stared through the windscreen. Much as he hated to admit it, it was true. Novak had been there when no one else was. But that didn't mean he had to trust the man.

'Look, what's going on? Who is this "friend" of yours? If he even exists.'

Novak gripped his wrist so hard it hurt and pushed the glowing tip of the cigarette to within a centimetre of his face. 'Like I said, boy, time you started showing some respect, right? Let's just say he's called Lek. That's all you need to know – and if you don't buck your ideas up you'd better hope you never meet. He's been inside till recently so he needs the money. And he has a strong suspicion our friend Spinney might have had a hand in putting him away, so you'll understand he's also got personal reasons for wanting a reunion. Enough information for you?'

Novak released Vinko's arm, took a drag of his cigarette and produced a photo from his pocket. Vinko was fairly sure it was the same man he'd seen in the picture Anja Pranjić had shown him a few days ago. Young, with short wavy hair and a clean-shaven face – Vinko still couldn't be certain it *was* the busker he'd seen in Holdwick. He shook his head. Novak stowed it away. 'Keep your eyes and ears open.'

'I'm not promising anything,' Vinko muttered.

'I know you won't let me down. You've got a phone; use it. Let us know the moment you find anything out.'

He released the lock, smiling unpleasantly as Vinko made his escape.

Chapter 13

'Did you have a good day?'

As Jay got into the car and she set off towards home, Marilyn wondered if her voice betrayed the fact that she'd missed him. It was Friday afternoon and, with the barn's concrete floor laid and hardening, she'd spent the best part of the day at the craft centre workshop while Jay had returned to the marketplace. He leaned over and gave her a quick hello kiss and she realised how much having him around had come to mean to her. It was just under a week since he'd appeared, even then getting on with his digging as if he'd always belonged there, but it seemed more like a month. They'd achieved a lot; Alan still couldn't tell her when he'd be ready to turn his attention to her barn, and she was seriously beginning to wonder if she needed or wanted him to. She liked having Jay around.

'Mike Greene was pleased to see me – I honestly wondered if he'd remember me. You know, I think I saw one or two shoppers from last week and I'd swear even *they* remembered me.'

He sounded boyish in his pleasure at the recognition.

'That's great. You're already claiming that territory as your own.'

The silence surprised her like something tangible. She gave him a moment then glanced at him. 'Jay? I said—'

'Yeah, I could be a regular. That'd be good.' He stared at the road ahead. 'Anyway, I can get to know the bus routes, go a bit further afield.'

'You don't want people getting too familiar with your stories, do you?' she said, trying to understand his sudden change in mood.

'I've got quite a repertoire, and I'm always putting new stuff together.'

'Sorry, I didn't mean—'

'I know you didn't. It's me.'

'What? Was there something wrong in Holdwick?'

'No, it was good. I like it round here.'

'So what's bothering you?' she insisted.

'What the–?'

A car overtook them in a ridiculously tight spot as another appeared round a bend. Marilyn had to brake hard, as did the approaching car. Jay swore at the receding tailgate of the overtaker then grinned at Marilyn in relief. The previous moment had gone and, as her pulse slowed from the adrenalin of the incident, she realised she was glad she'd been saved from pushing it with him. There was no point; he'd told her little more about his life before they met than she'd learned in the first couple of days – there were fleeting moments when he seemed to want to, but he always backed off, covering his momentary weakness with flippancy. It was probably for the best; she was enjoying their growing intimacy but was wary of getting too attached. He would leave, sooner or later. It was bound to happen and she would handle that when the time came.

'Nice one,' he was saying. 'You handled that well. Good job, too – I don't want anything happening to my gracious employer.'

She smiled. His teasing reassured her – that lighthearted banter that kept it all at arm's length. A working partnership, a friendship. Sex. She had even become used

116

to his occasional brief mood changes. They never lasted and certainly never implied any blame of her.

'I don't want to feel I'm tying you down,' she found herself saying later, over dinner. 'I could manage. You know…if ever you felt you needed to get away for a while.'

'What makes you say that? I've got a job to finish.'

'I was just wondering,' she ventured. 'I know how much you love the freedom of life on the road. Something I said earlier, about establishing yourself a pitch…it seemed to get at you. I'd hate you to think I'm trying to commit you to anything you don't want. I'm not.'

He finished his mouthful and grinned.

'I don't even know myself what got into me. If anything did.'

'I mean it. I really appreciate the work you're doing, and…I like having you around, but, you know, I don't want either of us to feel any ties.'

He reached over and helped himself to another potato. 'Sounds serious. Is this a kind way of trying to tell me something? Young Matt changed his tune, suggested a reconciliation?'

'No!' It was out before she noticed his hint of a smile and mischievous eyes. She tried to rescue herself. 'Carry on like that, though, and I might.'

She watched him eat, wondering if, despite her best efforts, she was allowing herself to get too attached.

'Are you going back tomorrow?' she asked, to stop herself thinking. 'To Holdwick market?'

'See? There you are trying to get rid of me and I've only been under your feet for a week.' This time she saw the gleam in his eye and smiled without rising to the bait. He shrugged. 'Why not? I think Mike would like me to. I know the bus times now.'

'Take the car if you like.'

'Thanks, but I don't like to think of you stranded, with the phone still off and all.'

'Don't remind me. But I'm not going anywhere tomorrow. You know what I've got on.'

She'd made a start at tackling the piles of boxes in the spare room. The clutter had seemed to multiply and the landing was now almost impassable. Letters, souvenirs and photos kept surfacing, demanding her attention and surrounding her with nostalgia, before a decision had to be made between ruthlessness or putting back in a box for posterity. She'd hoped that with an objective helper, one who clearly wasn't used to being surrounded with cupboards and shelves for hoarding, she might end up with more space in her house. But although Jay had seemed interested enough in sharing her memories, he insisted that saying goodbye to a phase of her life and starting a new one was something she had to do for herself.

'That settles it. I'll clear off tomorrow, and in my absence you'll have that room emptied and ready to paint, with all your equipment ready to set up in the barn the minute we get it finished.'

'You make it sound easy.'

'Isn't it?' He got up, cleared their plates and took them to the sink. 'It's surprisingly easy,' he said over the sound of running water.

They spent the early evening making a further attempt on the landing and clearing more space in the spare room. Jay had moved into her room and spent every night there since the previous Tuesday, but he was a restless sleeper. He said he wanted that small space of his own so he could leave her bed to avoid disturbing her – although the couple of times he had she'd sensed him go.

118

'Do you honestly only have what you carry around with you?' she asked him as she shook open another black bin bag.

'More or less.'

'Nothing in that house of yours?'

'It's let unfurnished. Walls and a roof. I do have a small store in one of those lock-and-go places nearby, though it's hardly worth the rent for the few bits I keep there.'

'What kind of bits?'

'Papers, photos, a couple of old favourite toys.' He shrugged, waved an arm towards the room. 'Like that lot of yours only less of it.'

'A lock-up store. Don't you feel…rootless?'

'Yes, I do.'

'You sound like you think that's a good thing. I can't imagine the reality of it. Scary.'

He laughed. 'Totally scary – imagine the size of rucksack you'd need to cart all that clutter of yours around. Seriously, though,' he looked over at her with a smile and she knew what was coming. 'It reminds me of a story.'

'That's tonight's entertainment sorted out, then.'

'Once, an acorn got carried out of a forest onto the edge of a great plain. It took the sapling a little longer than its contemporaries to flourish without shelter from the winds, the frosts, the harsh sun. And the thinner soil of the plains, without the rich leaf mould of the forest floor, meant it had to send its roots out further to look for nourishment. But that made it strong, and once it began to grow there was no need to compete with its brothers, sisters and cousins in the forest for food and light. It grew, knowing one day it would raise a host of little saplings and spread the forest out over the plain. Trees don't have feet but they understand time; they don't think in days or miles but in generations.

'For now, the beautiful oak was proud to be different, content in its solitary magnificence. And in the shade of its boughs in summer, a young man and woman courted and fell in love. Their clan was nomadic, wandering the plains with the seasons and settling for a while wherever they found food and water. Now the two lovers sat in the shade of the mighty oak and listened to the whispering of the leaves.

'"I don't want to leave this wonderful tree," said the girl. "I'm tired of always roaming from place to place. We can stay and make ourselves a home in the shade of this beautiful oak."

'She claimed it was the tree who gave her the idea, though I suspect she chose to think that because she was a little scared of her own thoughts.

'The girl got her way and when the clan moved on a small group stayed behind. And so a little village grew up around the tree. The people flourished over the years. They had plenty of food, they traded with the nomads; when they were threatened they were able to defend themselves on the raised hillock beyond the edge of the forest. And they had time. No longer did they have to roam the plains, hunting and foraging, but they stayed in one place and grew what they needed, with more time to devote to the arts, sciences and love – the good things in life.

'Over centuries, the people came to revere the tree as their true founder. It stood, the magnificent centrepiece of a spacious garden before the palace of what had become a sizeable town. They left plenty of room for the rain to soak its roots and for the ground to provide nourishment. They developed special food, which they poured around it. As a result the grass there was richer and greener than any other grass; the flowers that grew there were rare and more colourful than any other flowers.

'The people had a special ceremony every autumn, to thank the tree. In the prime of its life, when its magnificence matched the power and influence of the city, the tree produced an acorn for every man, woman and child. The acorns were gathered and distributed, and the people would keep them in special shrines in their houses for protection until the next autumn.

'But trees get old like any living thing. Over the years the oak produced fewer acorns. At first they stopped giving them to children; to receive your autumn acorn became a sign of coming-of-age. Eventually the ageing tree produced so few acorns that the people held annual games, and competitions of the arts, beneath its branches to find the most worthy to receive the talismans. They believed this was the tree's way of telling them they had to be strong and wise.

'As time went by, and the tree grew older, there were only enough acorns for the strongest, no longer the wise, to receive one. Competition became so fierce that they would fight to the death. The blood that was shed beneath the tree appeared to revive it, and the people took to feeding it with human blood all year round. They used the blood of their enemies but in time, as the tree aged further, that was not enough. They began to make human sacrifices. And because they'd come to set greater store by strength than by wisdom, they believed that the whispering of the leaves on the few remaining living boughs told them this was the right thing to do.

'But Arno, the gardener's assistant, a small boy who would never be strong enough to be a warrior and win an acorn, knew that a tree could not want blood. He helped his master to give the tree its gory food. He cleared away the fallen leaves so that the bright green grass and beautiful

121

flowers could flourish and remind the people that despite the tree's ageing appearance, it remained the protector of their city. The boy would pause in his work and listen to the breeze in the leaves. He didn't hear words but he understood that the oak knew it would not live forever, despite being fed blood, despite all the nurture the people of the city heaped on it. A tree should produce saplings to carry on its life. And there were no saplings because the acorns were all given away as annual prizes to the greatest warriors.

'As autumn drew near, the boy would peer up into the remaining living branches, foreboding creeping over him. He hated autumn. It was his job to climb the tree before the games to gather the acorns. If so much as a twig snapped while he was climbing, it would be an omen and he would be taken as the next human sacrifice. But year on year the tree had protected him, keeping its remaining twigs and branches intact to save the boy's life. This year, his last before he came of age, before he became too big to climb the tree, was especially terrifying. There were only two acorns on the tree, growing along the most fragile-looking branch. These were to be given to the king and queen; they in turn would give bountiful prizes to the winners of the games as the losers shed their blood to feed the oak's roots.

'Arno understood the rustling of the leaves, and knew it pained the tree to see all this being done in its name. A few nights before his ceremonial climb, he crept past the tree's guards, who had become complacent – no one, not the greatest warrior, not even the smallest squirrel, would dare approach the tree in those days. He began to climb. His affinity with the tree, and the tree's desire to help him in his purpose, meant he could keep the rustling of his climb quieter than the whispering of the withering autumn leaves and the creaking of the ancient branches. He plucked the two acorns, hid them in his pocket and scrambled down. He slipped past the sleeping guards and ran.

'He escaped deep, deep into the woods, taking his acorns with him. He found a clearing in the densest part of the forest where no one would find him, and planted the acorns where there was enough light and mulch for them to grow, but where the trees gave them shelter and hid them from discovery. He was too afraid to go back; he stayed to nurture his saplings and live the life of a hermit.

'News eventually reached the hermit from the kingdom which had once had a magic tree. He heard how the tree's last two acorns had been lost, and the king and queen had retreated to their private stronghold to cocoon themselves against the disaster that would surely befall them. When all was still well the following autumn, but the tree had produced no acorns at all, they emerged, declaring that the oak had outlived its usefulness. They cut it down and used the wood to make a beautiful carved panel that would adorn the great hall of the palace forever. That autumn there were no vicious games, there was no bloodshed, but a great bonfire marked the ultimate sacrifice – the stump of the tree itself.

'Arno the hermit was glad to hear the games had ceased, but sad at the news of his friend, the oak. He sat for a while beneath his two burgeoning trees, listening to the whisper of the breeze in their spring-green leaves and remembering their venerable father. He knew they would never be as mighty or as magnificent as the great oak, living as they did among the other trees of the forest. But they would be beautiful and they would pass on a part of the great tree in their acorns and saplings and that was how it should be.'

The glowing wood on the fire settled into itself noisily as it burned away. Marilyn felt almost guilty as she broke the moment and moved forward to feed the flames with another log. She sat cross-legged on the hearthrug and he came to sit beside her.

'What is it you're trying to tell me?' she asked eventually.

He shrugged. 'You said you thought the idea of rootlessness was scary. Look what happens when people become attached to places and things. When they start giving them symbols.'

'Being attached doesn't need to mean blood sacrifices.'

'So I've heard,' he said.

'You're saying it's wrong to want to belong?'

'Not wrong. Just that…it scares me.'

He fell silent. She sensed he was willing her to ask more. 'Scares you why?'

He shrugged. 'I respect those who feel it, that attachment to a particular place, and so I sympathise with them. And I've supported some. People feel the need to defend their territory, and who am I to argue just because I've never truly felt it myself, deep down? It's real, that need – but, like religious faith, I can't say I genuinely understand it. Though believe me, I've tried. Even convinced myself for a while.'

He looked away, running a hand through his hair, before meeting her eyes again. 'If any one set of people had a God-given right – well, as I don't believe in God, let's say an inherent, indisputable right – to a particular place, then why would others feel they have that right, too, and claim the same space? Who's right and who's wrong? At the end of the day people just want to get on with their lives. What does it matter what the environment they do that in is *called*?'

'It matters if those "others" are trying to impose a different way of life, especially one that leaves people worse off.'

He shrugged. 'Of course. I love the richness of different cultures and I'd like to think I respect the ones I encounter. I just wish they didn't so often seem to be mutually exclusive. You know, I'm not talking about simply being meek and mild and letting anything happen. If you believe in something enough you should defend it. But a lot of the time it doesn't really appear to be about that. It becomes a great mass identity that can blind people and drown out personal responsibility. And that's when it becomes dangerous, especially if some madman comes along, takes it and feeds on it to gain power. The identity becomes the cause and people lose sight of individuals – themselves or anyone else.'

'Are you referring to any cause in particular?'

He smiled and looked away again, shaking his head slightly.

'I'm generalising as much as any extreme nationalist, aren't I? Just being naïve and idealistic. Too much time spent on my own.'

He put an arm round her shoulder and drew her close.

'I can't explain. Some stories have answers. Others... others are just there to think about.'

The truck screeches to a sudden halt and he is aware of the crackle and roar of gunfire ahead. He steadies himself and releases his grip on the side of the flatbed. Lifting his rifle he glances warily into the trees, looks ahead to the abandoned house beyond where the other lorry is stopped. As he looks wildly around, he hears the word 'ambush' several times. Zasjeda. He is amazed by the kind of vocabulary he has learned in their language, then by how he can think such a banal thought at a time like this.

'Keep down!'

He ducks his head below the side, putting out a hand to steady himself as the truck is thrown into reverse. There is angry shouting and it stops. The other truck is stuck somehow and they cannot abandon their comrades. A storm of noise and the whining hiss of bullets surrounds him. The focus of the attack is on the truck in front, but it is terrifying enough from where they are. He is fairly certain they have not yet reached their destination. He is not even sure which side of the self-declared border they are on, though they have stormed their way through a number of roadblocks. But whoever is in that cover, they are hostile, and this, this is not training, it is real.

He sees a figure weaving towards them through the trees, then fall as he is shot down. Ivan raises a triumphant fist and Lek claps him on the shoulder like a proud father. It is moments like this that Šojka feels like the foreigner he is. Lek sees him watching, glares at him with his usual contempt. He returns the older man's stare unflinching before turning away and firing at a movement in the trees. This is not what he came to live here for, but doubtless none of them actually wants it like this. He will do his share.

The attack becomes more intermittent until the air is blissfully silent. No one trusts their enemy to have gone, but when the truck manoeuvres to turn round, Lek leans forward to the cab and shouts angrily at the driver to stay where they are. The vehicle ahead remains motionless, smoke drifting up from the engine. They roll nervously towards it. Several of the men are injured. Amazingly, no one in his own party is seriously hurt. They hurry to fetch the wounded, in a frenzy of activity so they can get away before the enemy return. He helps lift, support, carry, sickened by the blood, torn flesh and the sounds of agony. One of them does not move at all.

They set off on the overcrowded truck, pressed together like the crowds at the matches his father used to take him to when he was a boy. It is less claustrophobic at the back, but the raised tailgate presses painfully into his side and he hopes it is securely latched. He feels exposed. The moans of the wounded are almost worse than the sounds of battle, making him feel guilty for even noticing his discomfort. He wonders how the injured men will manage on the crowded truck during the half-hour journey back, and allows himself to admit relief that he is separated from the huddle of those tending them and won't have to face putting his first-aid training into practice. He concentrates on keeping watch from the back of the truck. Ivan is doing the same from the side, and gives him the thumbs-up sign. His friend's grin seems incongruous but he echoes the gesture.

A burst of acceleration shoves him against the unforgiving tailgate and he hears the chatter of gunfire above his own cursing. He looks up and on the scrubby hillside sees a small makeshift emplacement. Only two of them. He gets them in his sights as well as he can. Despite the bouncing of the truck he has the sensation of seeing them unnaturally clearly. There are more than two now. The nearest is aiming straight back at him. He tries to compensate for the movement of the truck; it is impossible but he fires anyway, telling himself that it's them or him. In a moment of panicked confusion the kickback seems ridiculously exaggerated. This notion is shoved aside by the awareness of an overwhelming pain in his side. He is no longer bracing himself against the tailgate but borne up by the men next to him. Momentarily immobilised, he thinks please don't let me fall out before succumbing and finding himself on the bed of the truck peering, bewildered, at the jumble of legs around him.

His body has curled around the pain and he is vaguely aware of being moved. His overwhelming feeling is shame that he has been taken in his first real sortie. As the commotion – he is not sure if it is the world or inside his own head – dies down, he hears the whimpering of a wounded man. He rolls his head and sees a man cowering, his face unrecognisable beneath blood from a head wound. Overcome by a surge of pain, Šojka shouts out, then tries to suppress it, tries to appear stoical as he realises they are examining and binding the wound in his side. Someone passes him a water bottle. He reaches clumsily but can't grasp it; Ivan holds it to his lips. It hurts to drink but he gulps greedily. He pushes the bottle towards the man at his side, but it is snatched away.

'One of them. We need to conserve it. We can deal with him when we get back.' Ivan looks almost apologetic. 'But you; are you—'

'We can't just leave him to suffer,' he tries to say.

'Our men are suffering.' Ivan waves a hand over their own wounded men. 'You are.'

His friend shrugs and he can't argue as all his energy is consumed by the pain. Ivan tells him his wound isn't so bad, he'll survive, and it seems as if his friend believes it, that he's not just muttering empty reassurance. But he knows what it is like to wish you were dead, as half an hour more of this nightmare journey stretches before him and every second is intolerable. He notices the way some of the others are looking at the prisoner and thinks he, too, would be better off dead. Ivan holds a different bottle to his lips. He thinks even the rakija can't touch this, but gulps greedily. He imagines it leaking out of the wound and wishes he could stop his mind from working.

Ivan grins and asks couldn't he have thought of an easier way to get out of the fighting. The last thing he remembers is trying to make himself smile back.

128

Chapter 14

Holdwick marketplace was fairly quiet as yet, but it was still relatively early. Jay brought his first story to a close and paused to savour the moment. The pleasure he got from recognising a couple of the faces and knowing they had stopped to listen again outweighed any of his lingering doubts. A movement caught his eye.

'What d'yer think yer doin?' A burly, leather-jacketed man with a guitar case strode up, gesturing over his shoulder for Jay to move. 'This is my usual place.'

'Is it?' he replied calmly. 'I didn't realise. Seeing as you weren't here yesterday. Or last week.' He glanced over to the stall. 'Seeing as Mike asked me to come back.'

'Acts like he owns the place but he's got nowt to do wi' it.' The man stepped nearer, a head taller than Jay, who stood unmoving.

'Asked you to move on before now, has he?'

'Now look 'ere.' The busker jabbed the air with his guitar case like a weapon, alcohol-laden breath steaming in front of him. His aggression told Jay he'd guessed correctly. 'You're doin nobbut yakkin anyway. People want proper music. Songs they know, like.'

Jay nodded, imagining the jaded repertoire. 'Perhaps we could work together,' he said, safe in the knowledge his offer would never be accepted. 'Some kind of accompaniment. It'd be good to work with a guitarist.'

'I don't work wi' your sort.' He moved a menacing step closer. 'Now fuck off.'

Jay saw the shove coming and fended it off. In a single, smooth action he had the guitar case on the floor and had gripped both the man's wrists hard. He stared unflinching into his adversary's eyes. 'We can settle this however you like,' he said quietly, 'but I don't think a scrap's good for anyone's business, do you?' He glanced over and saw Mike serving a customer. 'Me, I'd be happy to move on if it came to it. But I get the impression you want to come back here again – so you don't want to cause trouble, right?' He felt an almost imperceptible tension and tightened his grip even more. The slight relaxation as the man yielded broke the moment and Jay smiled. 'So if you'll excuse me, I've got some yakking to do.'

The busker bent to pick up his guitar case. 'Fuckin nutter,' he muttered as he strode off. Jay took a deep breath, picked up his flute and quickly began a lively tune to recapture his audience's attention and distract his own.

A short while later Mike brought him a coffee. 'Sorry about that, mate. Bit of a rush on there. I was going to come over as soon as I'd done, give you a bit of support, like. Can't be doing with him – he stinks and his playing's crap.' They exchanged a knowing smile. 'He can be a nasty piece of work, can Ferris, though – we're lucky he decided not to push it today.'

Jay nodded, sipping at his coffee in an attempt to dissolve the lingering tension inside, choosing not to remark that luck hadn't come into it.

'If there's any more trouble I'll stand by you, don't you worry,' the market trader continued. 'I like what you do. You bring a breath of fresh air to the place.'

He returned to the stall as Jay turned back to his listeners. He prepared himself to wander the winding paths his stories and music led him down, to let them carry him a safe distance from the encounter, the memory of the previous night's conversation and the persistent whisper of *hypocrite* in his head.

A sizeable audience had gathered when he caught another glimpse of leather jacket among them. His heart sank, though he didn't falter. He glanced down at his hat. Quite a collection already, and Mike's stall was nicely busy. This time he'd walk away. When he looked up again the people had shifted and he realised this was not the same leather jacket – equally worn and tatty, but the wearer was smaller and slighter. Jay's relief was jolted by another rush of adrenalin as he registered that it was the youth who had caught his attention the previous week. And what of it? A number of his listeners had returned; why should this lad be any different? Trying to pretend he hadn't noticed the young man mouthing the words to the tune he'd just played, he made himself tell a long, involved story as if nothing had happened – nothing *had* happened, after all – a story with a lot of laughs, a lot of action and a happy ending. By the time he'd finished there was no sign of the lad.

Jay gathered up his hat and told his audience he'd probably be back after lunch, though he knew most of them wouldn't, and went over to tell Mike the same, before setting off towards the baker's to buy a sandwich. As he passed a shop window full of phones he thought absently that they even had a shop dedicated to the gadgets in a place like this. At least it was an independent – he'd seen it before but until then assumed that Dog & Bone was a pet shop. It gave him an idea and he stopped walking. If he was starting to get his life sorted… Her phone was off. But that wouldn't be forever. He was inside the shop before he could talk himself out of it.

He bought the cheapest model they had and a pay-as-you-go sim card for the provider the young assistant told him gave the best coverage in the area. She offered to set it up for him. As she showed him how to use the basic functions, he felt slightly ridiculous about being so out of touch. The feeling annoyed him; until then he'd always had a proud disdain for the ubiquitous gadgets. Apart from his sporadic visits to libraries to check for e-mails from his sister and search for news on the Internet, there'd been no one he needed or wanted to keep in touch with.

He left the shop trying to memorise his new number, and finally headed for the baker's.

'Excuse me.'

Jay paused and looked round, somehow not surprised to see the dark-haired youth in the scuffed leather jacket.

'I...I like your stories. And the music.'

'Thank you.' He smiled warily. 'I noticed you listening.'

'I know some from the tunes. I have surprise hearing them here.' He was looking at Jay intently. 'You...you are Šojka?'

The question sounded more inevitable than surprising.

'Once upon a time,' he said. Šojka was another place, another age. 'Jay Spinney, pleased to meet you.'

He swallowed as he held out his hand. The youth shook it.

'Vinko Pranjić.' His eyes were shining and his grip on Jay's hand was tight.

'*Drago mi je*,' Jay replied automatically, triggering an excited torrent from Vinko. He caught a few snatches, including the word for 'father' – so his notion of a resemblance to Ivan the previous week had been correct – before losing track completely. 'Whoa, Vinko, slow down. It's been a long time since I heard or spoke your language. I'm afraid you've left me behind.'

'But you are Šojka.' Half statement, half question, to match the mix of pleasure and sudden disappointment in Vinko's expression.

'*Stranac.* The foreigner.'

'The foreigner who was one of us.'

Jay's feelings were also mixed as he regarded the lad who, now he knew, looked so like Ivan in his expressions, his gestures. He felt a real pleasure at discovering that his friend had a son, and remembered the growing closeness between Ivan and one of Zora's refugees. He assumed that must be Vinko's mother; he could still picture her face and tried to remember her name. The memory, shared with a real person in the clear light of day, brought on strangeness, and he was deeply afraid, both of the inevitable disillusionment he would represent to the lad, and of what the meeting might awaken – like removing a bandage too soon from a wound not yet properly healed. He wished he could simply walk away.

'Listen,' he said, looking round the busy market square, 'I'm sure we've got a lot to talk about. Let's have some lunch.'

Vinko looked like he needed feeding up. As they walked across the square to an inviting pub and settled in a corner, he postponed any more difficult topics of conversation by finding a solution to the communication barrier. Vinko seemed unsure of himself speaking English, though he could understand Jay well enough. He'd grown up speaking Croatian with his mother and some of her friends, and German with the rest of the world. Jay found in turn that as Vinko slowed down and he really tuned in, his understanding came back more readily than he'd ever have expected. He could even envisage himself speaking it again without too much problem. For now they settled on each of them using their own language, or a strange mixture of the two. Just like the early days with Zora. He shook his head at himself. No. Not like those days at all.

He went to the bar and ordered two shandies and two steak pie lunches. As he returned to the table, drinks in hand, Vinko gave him a broad smile. Jay's pleasure at meeting him returned and eclipsed his doubts. They chinked glasses, drank.

'I can't believe you've suddenly appeared after all these years.'

Vinko frowned. 'So you did try to find me?'

'Find you?' He shook his head. 'Why would I? I didn't even know I should be looking. How old are you?'

'Seventeen.'

'See – you were born after I left Croatia. How could I know you existed?'

'You didn't hear news?'

'I heard your father was killed. But not until a long time after it happened, and that's all I heard.'

'*I* heard you died with him.'

It was an accusation. Jay shook his head.

'I had to leave.'

'Why?'

He shook his head again.

'But you did know my mother?'

'A little.' Assuming it was her. 'Do you have a picture of her?'

Vinko smiled . 'Of course.'

He immediately produced a battered photo from inside his jacket. Jay smiled. 'Marta. How is she? Where's she living now?'

'She died. Nearly two years ago.'

'I'm sorry to hear it.' Eyes lowered, he handed Vinko his photo back.

'It's in the past.' He shrugged. 'I was upset then. I'm all right now. She was ill. She wasn't happy.'

'I'm sorry,' he repeated, taking a drink to mask the inadequacy of his response. Vinko smiled hesitantly, as if to suggest the subject was dealt with, waiting for Jay to speak again. He obliged. 'So what brings you here looking for me?'

'Not looking. Chance.'

'We're hundreds of miles away from the place that links us. That's some chance.'

Vinko shrugged. 'You grew up not far from here, I think. So did my father. I suppose that's why I came to England. Why did I come to Holdwick? Chance, and then…I like coming here. It's not like the city. I think…' He looked slightly embarrassed, fingers drumming lightly on the edge of the table. 'I think it's the kind of place I imagine home to be.' Jay nodded. 'And one time, I see a man I haven't seen here before, playing music from home, telling stories from home – though he chooses to change them…'

'Stories evolve and grow, to suit the time and place, and the person telling them.' Jay leaned back in his chair. 'Like the one about Šojka Stranac, the hero who died in the fighting by his best friend's side.'

Vinko was looking at him intently. Jay wished he hadn't said that, and willed the lad not to ask more. A waitress approached the table with their food and Jay felt as if he'd been rescued. As they ate, he asked Vinko about his life, partly to ward off any further talk about himself. After Ivan died, Vinko's mother had gone to Germany with some distant cousin. He didn't say much about their lives, only that he'd come to England shortly after she died; someone he'd met in Dresden had suggested it and offered to get him over. The same contact had got him an underpaid job in a sweatshop factory and a dingy bedsit in Bradford, not too far from where his father's family had lived. Vinko spoke as dispassionately about all this as he had about his mother's ill health and death, but Jay could sense the emotion simmering underneath.

'I want to learn to do something well.' He fixed Jay with a stare. 'I want my life to be worth something!'

Jay felt inadequate. 'I'm sure—'

'I'm sorry,' Vinko said with a sudden smile. 'I'm all right.'

He admired the flashes of good humour illuminating the pride in Vinko's dark eyes. The lad's positive attitude sparked in him an overwhelming desire to take him under his wing, offer him some kind of security. He stopped himself short. They'd only just met. And there was Polly – his heart leapt a little as he thought of her. He had to keep reminding himself there was another person in his life to consider now. But there was something definite he could, and knew he should, do for Vinko.

'I'm glad you introduced yourself,' he said. 'You see, I…' He fell silent. 'How did you recognise me?' he heard himself asking instead.

'I first saw you last week, here, but – you'll think this is mad – I didn't recognise you until afterwards. My mother used to have an old photo of my father and you. I saw the same picture last week when I went to visit my grandparents. I think, though I didn't know then, that it must have been seeing you here that made me go. I was never sure that I should.'

'Why not?'

Vinko lowered his eyes.

'My life hasn't been good,' he muttered. 'I'm not a grandson they can be proud of.'

'They *said* that?'

'Of course not! My grandmother welcomed me. But also…I'd always known, my mother told me, that they disowned my father, you know?'

Jay nodded; he knew only too well. One of the experiences he and Ivan had shared.

'They didn't want him to go,' Vinko continued. 'They didn't believe he should get involved.'

'Weren't they proved right in the end?'

'No! How can you say that?'

His eyes flashed with a passion Jay remembered feeling.

'We didn't make much difference, did we?' Hurt a few more people, caused a bit more destruction. 'I understand them now, though at the time I felt like you do. I guess it hurt them that he threw away the chance they gave him. They'd come here in the early sixties because they wanted safety and a better life for their family – not so different, I dare say, to the reasons why your mother went to Dresden.' Vinko glared at him angrily. Jay cut off his protest before he had chance to speak. 'So you went to see them. How did you get on?'

Vinko stared at the table in front of him, shifting edgily in his seat.

'*He* was just like I imagined,' he said eventually. Jay gave a crooked smile of sympathy. 'I think you know. Anja was lovely, though. She shouldn't put up with him like that.'

'I think he's got a better side.' Jay thought as he said it that guilt must be making him feel charitable. 'People like you and me just don't get to see it.'

Vinko nodded. 'Anja said you'd been to visit them last year and he didn't make you welcome.'

This was it. The moment Jay had feared. He was surprised Vinko hadn't challenged him before now. 'She told you about that? What did she say?'

137

'That Boris turned you away almost as soon as you arrived. I think she would have liked the chance to talk to you.'

'I mean about the reason I went to visit them.'

Vinko shrugged, still staring at the table. 'She didn't mention a reason.'

At least that explained why he wasn't angry. 'The money?'

'What money?' Vinko's eyes flicked up, but he dropped his gaze just as quickly. 'The woman who lives in their old house – the address I had – said they'd come into money a few months ago, that was why they moved. But I never thought any more of it. Neither of them mentioned it to me.'

Jay felt his anger rising, glanced round the busy pub and forced himself to keep his voice steady. '"A few months ago" was when I called on them, Vinko. It was your aunt – sorry, great-aunt – Zora's money. At least some of it should be yours. They didn't *tell* you?'

Vinko shook his head, frowning, as he picked up his drink. 'What do you mean, should be mine?'

'She wanted it to go to Ivan. I can prove that. And you're his son.' Jay put his head in his hands. 'I wish we'd met earlier.'

'You think it's too late?'

'No.' He looked up; Vinko was watching him eagerly. 'Probably not. You'd have to talk to them. I'd go with you. If you want me to.'

'You would?'

'It's my fault I haven't got it here to give you right now. Of course I would.'

'When?'

'Any time. This afternoon if you like.' Vinko looked worried. 'Sorry, you probably want to leave it a bit. See if they offer you anything of their own accord.'

'No, it's not that.' He smiled and his doubts seemed to have vanished. 'Yes, why not this afternoon?'

Chapter 15

Jay gave Vinko what he hoped was an encouraging smile as they walked up the drive. He looked at the house: an unremarkable semi. The Pranjićs would consider it a step up in the world from Fairview Terrace, but they hadn't gone over the top with their windfall. There would be money left. Anja opened the door to them and despite himself Jay felt a genuine warmth towards her.

'Hello, Mrs Pranjić. It's good to see you again.' He held out his hand. 'You remember me, Jay, don't you?'

'Of course I do.'

She shook his hand and returned his smile after a momentary pause.

'And I understand you've met Vinko.'

Her smile broadened. As Vinko stepped forward to give his grandmother a brief hug, Jay felt glad he'd persuaded Vinko to give Anja the benefit of the doubt, to begin with at least. Her smile faded and she looked nervous, but she agreed to let them in.

'Nice house,' Jay said. Let her wonder whether he meant anything by it.

'Thank you,' she replied, revealing nothing. 'I'm sorry, but Boris isn't here this afternoon,' she added as she showed them through to the living room. Presumably the apology was for show; she must have a pretty good idea that neither he nor Vinko would be sorry about the old man's absence. 'He's gone over to Vesna's to help fit some cupboards.'

'How is she? Where's she living these days?'

'On the outskirts of Bradford. She and the kids kept the house when they divorced.'

Jay nodded, unsure whether he was expected to show sympathy or relief when he had no idea what kind of a man Vesna's husband had been. He glanced at Vinko, whose face was expressionless.

'Sit yourselves down,' she said. 'Wait here a moment. I'll make some tea.'

'Can I give you a hand?'

She seemed as surprised at the offer as Polly had when he'd first gone there. It was easy to be helpful in someone else's kitchen when you didn't have the drudgery of your own to concern you.

'Don't worry yourself about that, love. You make yourselves at home.'

He'd have liked a quiet chat, but didn't insist. As they waited he went over to the sideboard and studied the pictures, sensing Vinko watching him. No sign of Ivan; he could imagine how that made the lad feel.

'Vesna doesn't seem to have changed much.'

He wondered as he spoke why he'd said it; he knew she wouldn't mean much, if anything, to Vinko. None of these photos would. He looked in the sideboard mirror and caught sight of the lad behind him, sitting stiffly on the dralon sofa, gazing at his hands. A movement behind Vinko's shoulder caught Jay's eye and his heart skipped a beat. The boy was standing by the window, watching him. Why here, now? Wasn't Jay doing the right thing? He closed his eyes, breathed deeply. When he opened them and turned from the mirror, he and Vinko were alone in the room.

Anja came through with a tray and set it down on the coffee table. She poured three cups of tea from a china teapot.

'So you do know Jay,' she said as she passed Vinko his. The accusation in her voice was accentuated by a slight rattle of the cup in the saucer as her hand shook.

'I…not when I talked you last week,' he said. 'I…I…say hello to him the first time today morning. I…'

'Speak your own language, Vinko,' said Jay. 'If that's all right with you, Mrs Pranjić? It's an awkward enough situation as it is.'

She raised an eyebrow, but nodded. 'So you met today. That's quite a coincidence.'

She spoke the language more slowly and deliberately than Vinko did and Jay could understand her well. The suspicion in her voice was plain in any language.

'They happen,' Jay said as he took the cup of tea and a biscuit from the plate she offered him, balancing it awkwardly on the saucer. 'Coincidences.'

'It's true,' Vinko continued. 'I'd seen him before today, in Holdwick, but didn't realise who he was till you showed me that photo. Even then I wasn't sure.'

'So, as he says, he came and introduced himself to me. You can imagine what a surprise *that* was. Now then.' Jay put his cup down and leaned forward, waiting for Anja to sit before going on, hoping the pause would help him keep his anger in check. 'If we want to talk about not telling the truth – isn't there something you forgot to tell Vinko last week?'

She fiddled with the teacup in her lap and spoke without looking at him. 'Boris and I…we wanted to discuss it first.'

'And didn't you think to tell *me* when I was here that Ivan had a son? Don't you think it would have made quite a difference?'

'We didn't know about him.'

'Didn't know?'

'His mother mentioned she was expecting when she wrote to tell us…the bad news about Ivan. But she never wrote back.'

'You never even told me that much.'

'What difference would it have made, Jay?'

'Apart from the fact that Ivan was my friend, you know what difference it would have made. Practically. I showed you Zora's will, didn't I?'

Her eyes darted from Vinko to Jay. 'I'm sorry, but I'm not sure we should be talking—'

'Tell Vinko the main reason I was here.'

She glanced nervously towards the kitchen. Vinko had told Jay about the heated discussion between her and Boris the week before, when he'd thought they were merely arguing about whether or not to make him welcome. 'There…there was an inheritance,' she said to her grandson now. 'My family was quite wealthy, before the war, before Tito. I thought the money had been lost long ago. But it turned out my sister – your mother told you about Zora?' Vinko nodded. 'Zora had it in an account abroad. I don't know how or why, but she gave a substantial amount to Jay in the nineties, to keep safe till the conflict was over. He came last year to sign it over to us.'

'It wasn't as simple as that, was it?' Jay took the biscuit from his saucer and crunched it, swallowed. 'Not that simple at all.'

'I'm Zora's closest living relative,' she said, defensively.

'I'll save you the embarrassment. I told Vinko before we came about the will.'

He had no idea what Vinko made of it all – the lad had simply listened impassively. Of the two sisters, Zora had considered herself the sole heir because their family had disapproved of Anja marrying Boris and leaving the

143

country. In turn, when she'd entrusted the account details to Jay, she had also given him a letter stating that if and when she died, Ivan was the only family member she wanted to inherit it. If the conflict meant that Ivan died before he could claim it, Jay should keep it.

'We only had your word about that,' said Anja.

Jay willed himself to stay calm. 'My word and a legal document.'

'Which was probably a fake.'

'I can prove it. But surely you can see that Vinko has a claim to at least some of it?' He glanced apologetically at the lad. 'Surely you'd agree he needs it?'

'We offered to help him in other ways. We talked over dinner, didn't we, Vinko? We…' She fidgeted with her teacup again, looked at Jay. 'He's only young. We wanted to make sure he wouldn't just pour the money down the drain, that he wasn't after it for anything…' she reddened, '…for anything criminal.' Jay could almost hear Boris persuading her. She looked uncomfortably at Vinko. 'We've been discussing it, of course we have, and we were going to offer to share it equally between you and Vesna in our own will.'

That sounded more like Anja herself speaking, but Jay shook his head nevertheless. 'He needs it now.'

He looked round with the others as they heard a car pull up. 'Is that Boris?'

Anja had the best view through the window from where she was sitting; she nodded.

'Good. I'd hate to be accused of plotting behind anyone's back.' Jay flashed Vinko a smile, as much to give himself confidence as anything.

'I might have guessed,' said Boris as Anja called him through to the sitting room. He looked from Jay to Vinko, and finally to his wife. 'Didn't I say Spinney would be behind all this?'

Jay stood and approached Boris, offered his hand. He wasn't really surprised when the older man refused to shake it.

'How long have you been here? It's a good job we got things finished sooner than expected at Vesna's, isn't it?'

'If that means we can get things finished sooner than expected here, then yes,' said Jay. He realised why Anja had refused his offer of help making the tea. She must have phoned her husband.

'How long have you been spying on us?' Boris glared at him.

'Spying on you?'

'Thought you'd make sure I was out? Thought you could terrorise my wife into giving you what you want?'

'Boris, calm down, please.' Anja rose, gestured to her husband and reached for the teapot. 'Sit down and let me get you some tea.'

'I'll not drink with these two!'

Anja hovered nervously.

'I'd hate you to go thirsty,' said Jay. 'Hear me out for a few minutes and we'll leave you to have your tea in peace.'

'You stay out of this, Spinney. We owe you nowt and—'

'True, you owe *me* nothing. I'm a reasonable man. All I'm asking is that you agree to give Vinko what's rightfully his.'

'Rightfully his! The pair of you turn up here, claiming he's a grandson of ours and expecting me to shell out, just like that?' His attention turned to Vinko. 'Prove to me you can be a worthy member of this family, lad, and I'll think about treating you like one!'

'You're not giving him much of a chance to do that, are you, Boris?' Jay dug his fingernails into his palms to keep his voice calm.

145

'I'll not have you come here and talk to me like—'

'Like what? Reasonably?'

'Call that reasonable?'

'Just shut up and listen!'

He was surprised and relieved when Anja intervened by motioning to both of them to sit down.

'I'm sorry,' he said to her, returning to his chair. Boris said nothing as he joined his wife on the sofa. 'I don't want things to get nasty. But I made a mistake last year; I was never sure I was doing the right thing.'

'You wouldn't know the right thing if it—'

'*I said shut up and listen!*' He glared at Boris. 'Knowing about Vinko has changed everything. Made me realise I was wrong to have gone against Zora's wishes and handed the money over to you. All I'm asking now is that you give the lad the share he's entitled to.'

'Who the hell do you think you are?' Boris made to rise but Anja put a restraining hand on his shoulder. 'What percentage is he offering you, eh?'

Jay merely laughed. 'For fuck's sake, Boris, why would I have given it you in the first place if *I* wanted anything? I'm here for Vinko.' He looked steadily into the older man's eyes. 'And for Ivan.'

'Get out!' Boris stood this time and Jay rose to face him. 'You're lucky I didn't take you to court last year for stealing what was ours and holding on to it for so long. My wife persuaded me to let it drop then, and she'd probably want me to do the same now. Be careful, Spinney, or I might change my mind.'

Jay breathed deeply. 'Empty words, Boris. I haven't done anything wrong and you know it. I'd have been entitled to keep the money then, and Vinko's entitled to it now.'

'And how do you intend to prove that, eh?'

He shrugged. 'I assume that means you've destroyed the will.'

'You guessed right, lad.' Boris ignored Anja's sharp look. 'You haven't got a leg to stand on.'

'It's a good job I wasn't daft enough to hand you the original over, isn't it? I'd just have hoped that you'd see fit to help your grandson make a decent life for himself without the need for all this.'

Anja moved to stand by her husband. 'Boris, we can talk about it. We'd agreed, hadn't we—'

'We'd agreed nowt.' He looked at Vinko. 'Nothing. Understand? *Ništa*. Now get out, both of you!'

Vinko got to his feet awkwardly.

'Jay will help me,' he said to Boris.

He went to his grandmother and grasped her hand briefly before moving to the door. As Jay made to join him he caught another glimpse of the boy by the window and wondered if he'd actually been there, watching him, throughout. Watching the situation descend to such a messy argument.

'Listen, I'm sorry if I sounded a bit—'

'Get out!'

Jay tensed, looked past him and gave Anja a brief smile. 'I'll call round again in a couple of days. When we've all had time to…' He shrugged. 'Thanks for the tea, Mrs Pranjić.'

The restrained slam of the door followed them down the drive. Vinko paused to roll and light a cigarette before they set off towards the town centre.

'I'm sorry,' Jay said.

'You did what you could. I know you're trying to help. I've lived without it for this long.'

'I meant I'm sorry because I've probably messed up any chance you might have had of friendship with them.'

'I would never be friends with *him*.'

Jay was taken aback by his intensity. 'Anja lets him get away with it. I find that almost as hard to take.'

Vinko shrugged and walked on in silence, eyes on the pavement ahead of him.

'Anyway, I'll be in touch,' Jay said as they neared the centre of Keighley. 'Have you got a phone?'

'Of course.'

Jay smiled, handed his new gadget over. 'Stick your number in this for me. And take mine while you're at it.'

Vinko halted and Jay watched him tapping the numbers in with practised ease. Even to his inexperienced eye he could see the lad's was far more sophisticated than the simple model he'd just bought himself.

'Cool phone,' he remarked.

Vinko passed Jay's mobile back sullenly and set off walking. He strode to catch up, wondering how a remark intended to put him at his ease could have offended him.

'I saved up,' he snapped as Jay drew level. He recognised the lie, remembering he'd first seen him standing next to Polly when her purse went missing, but decided not to push him further. It was hardly surprising, given the lad's circumstances, and he merely hoped for now that it was only petty theft and he wasn't involved in anything more serious.

They reached the bus station and Vinko followed him to the Holdwick stop, watching over his shoulder as he examined the timetable.

'What time is it?' Jay asked. He'd given up bothering with watches and clocks years ago.

Vinko scarcely lifted his sleeve, but it was enough for Jay to notice that the watch was more flashy than he'd have expected, too. This time he hardly registered it, or the lad's defensiveness, as he swore in his frustration at missing the last bus.

'Why don't you come home with me?' asked Vinko cheerfully, his annoyance forgotten as quickly as it had flared.

Jay nodded, forcing a smile back. 'Thanks.'

He wanted to get to know the lad better, and in any case he stood next to no chance of hitching in a place like that, at that time of day. As they made their way to the Bradford stop he recalled what he and Polly had been talking about the previous night and hoped he'd managed to convince her that he had no intention of leaving, at least before he'd finished the job.

'You are living in Holdwick?'

Surprised by Vinko's halting, accented English after an afternoon of hearing the fluency of his own language, Jay had no ready answer. 'For now,' he said.

'You are… You have a wife?'

'No. Not yet,' he added to soften the abruptness.

'But you love a woman.'

Jay smiled. 'I've got a girlfriend.'

Vinko grinned back as if he somehow knew he was the first person Jay had told.

'I think you did want to see her now.'

'Never mind. Is there anyone waiting for you?'

Vinko shook his head. 'There are girls, sometimes. But it is not love. I am hoping always.'

The bus rattled in, saving Jay from having to think of a suitably profound reply.

'So why English all of a sudden?' he asked as they pulled away.

Vinko shrugged. 'I need practising. You help me. You are helping with the money, I think you will help that I am

149

staying here, making the good life. I must learn gooder –
best – English.'

'Better,' he corrected. 'I'll do what I can.'

He glanced round, saw they might be overheard, and
decided against saying anything right then about Vinko
promising to live within his means before he helped him
any further.

'You will phone her?'

'Who?'

'Your girlfriend.'

Jay shook his head ruefully. 'Her phone's off – not
working.' He didn't want to admit he didn't even have her
number. 'I hope she'll understand.'

He tried not to think how bad he was feeling about it
and wondered if he should have splashed out on a taxi.
How had he let it get so late? He tried to look on the bright
side, telling himself he should be relieved at the
postponement. He'd have to tell her about meeting Vinko
and dreaded the further explanations that would lead to.
He came to the conclusion that perhaps some situations
just didn't have a bright side.

Chapter 16

Vinko's place was much as Jay had expected. The decaying house, once-garish paint flaking from windows that were more filler than wood, was the end of a terrace reached via a small patch of willowherb, bindweed and scattered rubbish from an overflowing bin. As Vinko opened the door and they stepped over a collection of flyers, Jay saw a dark hallway lined with textured wallpaper held in place by layers of uneven paint. The smell, a combination of damp house, spicy frying, cigarette smoke and unemptied bins, was familiar to him. He'd known plenty of similar places – the pads of temporary acquaintances, squats shared or bagged for himself. Vinko's room was on the second floor and he led the way towards the sort of creaky stairs it was always a relief to climb without a foot sinking through.

'That you, Vin?' a voice drifted to them on a tinny wave of bhangra music from the shared kitchen.

'Yeah,' he called from the first step. 'I come talk soon.'

He took another step.

'Hang on, we've got a message for ya.'

Vinko sighed and headed for the kitchen. Jay followed. The room was a mess of heaped dishes in the sink, all manner of packets and tins on every filthy surface – Jay knew from experience most would be almost empty – and a table piled with advertising leaflets, empty take-away cartons and overflowing ashtrays. The soles of his shoes clung stickily to the worn lino. Three men, two fairly smart Asian lads about Vinko's age and a white guy with greying hair and a face that looked prematurely lined, were sitting round the table with mugs in front of them, recently-cleared dinner plates pushed to one side. They all looked past Vinko at Jay with a mixture of curiosity and suspicion.

'Hi,' said Vinko without introducing him. 'What message is there?'

'You had a visitor,' said one of the younger lads. 'That bloody fella again. Novak. Said he was waitin' to hear from ya.' Vinko shrugged. 'Just bloody talk to him will ya, Vin? So you don't want to know him – then phone him up an' tell him. And while you're at it you can tell him to piss off an' stop botherin' us, yeah?'

'I did tell to him I'll ring him,' Vinko said irritably.

'Whatever. So who's your friend?'

'Dan,' Jay said, 'Dan Freeman.'

'He is…he plays music…' Vinko glanced at Jay.

'Busker,' he said helpfully.

'I know him longtime. He needs a place to stay. I say he can sleep on my room floor.'

'Busker eh? You could give us some home entertainment,' said the trio's spokesman, making exaggerated dancing movements with his arms. 'Sing for your supper.'

The three of them laughed, not entirely pleasantly. Jay grinned. 'You never know your luck.'

The lad shrugged, looked at his housemates in turn. 'He looks harmless enough, don't he? You do what you like in your own room, Vin mate.' He winked and the others chortled. 'I'm not the landlord.'

'I *like* that you will clean those.' Vinko waved irritably towards the sink. 'I'm wanting to cook food for my friend.'

Amidst general laughter, which Jay might have been tempted to join in under other circumstances, Vinko strode to the door.

'Don't worry, I'm not as fussy as he'd have you believe,' Jay said with a wink over his shoulder as he followed him. 'See you, lads.'

'They are animals,' Vinko muttered on the way upstairs. 'I don't want to live like that. You don't think I am like that, please.'

His room bore out his words. The uncluttered floor had a threadbare but colourful cotton rug, the washbasin with its cracked tiled surround and the mirror above it were clean, curtains moved gently in the breeze from an open window. Vinko hung up his jacket behind the door and gestured for Jay to sit on the neatly made bed. He bent to pick up the kettle from a tray on the floor and Jay noticed the mugs beside it were clean and tidily arranged. As Vinko filled the kettle at the washbasin, he looked around at the walls. There was a framed photo of Marta and Ivan; it felt strange to see the image of his friend in this new context. There were also a couple of large posters, a fantasy cityscape and a Salvador Dalí, but it was the drawings that were the most striking. Lots of drawings – faces, buildings, strange hybrid animals, all in bold pencil strokes, depicted in varying degrees of abstraction. There was an open sketch pad on the table beneath the dormer window.

'These yours?'

Vinko nodded. 'They hide…' he waved a hand, 'ugly walls.'

There were plenty of damp stains and cracks still showing, but they seemed not to matter beneath the magical papering-over. Jay reached out to press a curling corner back in place on its wad of blu-tack.

'They're amazing.'

'Thank you. I told you I wanted to do something worthwhile with my life.'

He'd slipped back into his own language as if practising English no longer mattered in the privacy of his own space.

'That one's my home.' He pointed at a drawing of an intricate stone folly of a building, with a shadowy figure that could have been partner, child or self-portrait, the whole perfectly placed within an intricate geometric border. There was a darkness to the beauty of the scene, something about the impossibility of telling whether it was day or night, that Jay found intriguing. 'I'll find it one day.'

'I hope you do.'

Vinko made two coffees and sat on the room's only wooden chair. He rolled and lit a cigarette and offered Jay the tobacco. He shook his head, took out his pipe instead and sat back comfortably across the bed as he filled it.

'Why Dan Freeman?' asked Vinko.

'What?' Jay looked at him in surprise. 'Where did you hear that?'

'That was what you told them you were called.'

'Did I?' He laughed to cover his unease. 'Force of habit. I tell people my real name when I think they need to know. Sometimes that's immediately, sometimes... never.'

'You don't have to worry about that crowd.' Vinko smiled. 'They live like pigs but they're my friends.'

'I could see that. It was more...that visitor they've been getting. And your nervous look as they mentioned him. Who is it?'

'It doesn't matter.' He picked up his mug and tried to sip the too-hot coffee. 'Someone I met. A deal. I was drunk. Don't want to get involved. It's not important.'

Jay lit the pipe. 'What kind of deal?'

'Nothing. Selling things. I don't earn much, I always need extra.' He glared defensively at Jay as if it were his fault.

'Shouldn't you do as your friend says, phone him and tell him you're not interested?'

Vinko flicked ash into the ashtray in an agitated gesture.

'I have and I'll tell him again.' He picked up his mug and blew across it so he could drink. 'If he doesn't go away I can always disappear – find somewhere else. You help me, Šojka, you help me to be a proper person here – then I won't have to do things like that.'

Jay stayed silent, feeling as guiltily helpless at this display of faith as he had at the first mention of Šojka the war hero. Vinko crushed his cigarette out and stood.

'I have to go to the shop for food. Are you coming?'

'Why don't we eat out? I don't want to spend all evening washing up to make space in that kitchen.'

'You don't have to – you're my guest.' The lad looked wounded.

'Watching you wash up, then.' Jay grinned. Vinko continued scowling. 'That was meant to be a joke.'

He nodded with a wary smile.

Over a meal for which Vinko insisted on paying his share, and a number of drinks afterwards, Jay found himself telling the lad tales from his restless life, more than anything else to avoid the subject he knew the lad was burning to hear about. But when Vinko asked directly about Ivan, he felt he had to try. He deserved to hear about his father.

'He was like the brother I never had. An older sister doesn't count. We'd always moved around a lot and I'd never fitted in, never found close friends. The butt of people's jokes, the outsider.' He looked at Vinko guiltily. He'd have had it far worse. 'I got so's I could look after myself and kept my own company most of the time. Sounds daft but I never really realised I'd been lonely, never thought any of it bothered me till I met your dad. Ivan and I clicked from the start.' So far, so straightforward. 'He was fun to be with, we shared books, music… We were both into the sort of stuff you'd get laughed at for liking. And walking. We often took ourselves off, walking and camping together. We felt a deep connection to the countryside. Better, closer than anyone else. Of course – we were young.' He reminded himself Vinko still was. 'What I mean is, Ivan believed passionately in everything he did. And he was keen on politics, which is more than I was – I've always been too much of a dreamer – and I learned a lot from him. Most of all, he always felt a strong connection to his roots. Again very different from me. We'd always moved around. I didn't have any. With Ivan I liked having somewhere special I could feel an attachment to, even if it was…kind of borrowed. At first. Not later. Definitely more than that later. So anyway, it suited my sense of adventure to go with him when he visited Croatia.'

'That was why you went? Adventure?'

The critical tone of his voice made Jay look away. He picked up his glass and drank.

'The first visit, perhaps. A holiday, to stay with your great-aunt, Zora. I loved it there and wanted to go back. But the second time was more than mere curiosity. It was the year we finished school, 1990. We'd seen the wave of change across Eastern Europe, the demos, the air of revolution, the fall of the Berlin wall. I guess you heard something about it, from your mum?' Vinko nodded. 'We'd watched it all happening on TV and, well, if something similar was going to happen in Yugoslavia, we wanted to be there, to be part of something big. So we both planned a gap year, and…' He paused; if Vinko was unfamiliar with the concept of a gap year he didn't show it. 'Even as young,

156

idealistic lads, we knew it wasn't as simple as an enthusiastic crowd waving *šahovnica* flags and having a great big party on Zagreb's Jelačić Square. But we had no idea it would get as bad as it did. No one did. Though…in the end there was no question of us not getting involved.'

'You adopted our country?'

So like Ivan – "our country" when, as far as Jay knew, Vinko had never even had the chance to set foot there.

'You could say that.'

He swallowed. It was getting harder.

'Could? You mean you didn't really?'

'No, no. I did. Zora, she…she said there'd be chaos, and yes, there was talk of civil war – some said it was inevitable, others that it couldn't possibly happen. She suggested we waited before going. But we were determined and she didn't try for long to dissuade us. She even made special arrangements for us. She'd moved permanently to her old family home by then, in Dalmatia. She'd got herself a transfer from Zagreb to the university in Zadar because, well, things were getting uncertain, and if she was going to be stuck anywhere she wanted to be there, at what she thought of as her home, rather than anywhere else. She told us the train would be hopeless – we'd have to go through Knin and that would be…difficult, even then. By road, too. There were roadblocks in parts of Dalmatia; that was how it started. So she arranged for us to come by boat from Trieste. Imagine that. Talk about adventure!

'That should have been it; we should have known, but we talked each other up. Even then, at first Ivan and I were disappointed; we thought it (whatever "it" was) would all be happening in Zagreb. But as it turned out, we were in the thick of things. The Krajina, the area the Serbs were claiming as an independent region, was only a few miles east of us. There was trouble; even then people who'd lived side by side, been friends for years, began to suspect and even hate one another.

'People, Croats, were forced from their homes in the Krajina region and Serb families were driven out of Zadar. Zora used to get mad at us: "Look, people are leaving and you two idiots decide to *come*." But we knew she was pleased we were there and, well, deep down I guess we thought it'd be no more than a bit of unrest before…before things settled down. At first the worst of the trouble – we watched it every night on the news – was happening far away, in the east, Vukovar. It didn't involve us. We were just there because we couldn't leave Zora alone in that house, in that volatile region. Weren't we? That was all. But of course we got involved.'

The flood of words dried up and the noise of the crowded pub swirled in to fill the silence. The air around him felt increasingly bright and strange and he closed his eyes to ward it off. He wondered how he'd got this far.

'What happened then?'

'The war happened,' he muttered.

'But what—'

'Enough!' He looked up and for a moment saw Ivan sitting across from him, all reproach and contempt. He rubbed his eyes and it was a young lad dying to hear about his father. 'I'm sorry. Another time, all right?'

His voice didn't come out as conciliatory as he'd intended. Vinko stood abruptly.

'I go outside for smoking.'

Jay took out his own tobacco and slowly began to fill his pipe, watching Vinko disappear into the pub's Saturday night crowd. Best give them both a few moments' breathing space. Perhaps now would be his opportunity to walk away.

He shifted in his seat as if to rise, but sat back, shaking his head at his own cowardice. He let his mind wander for a while. Realising he was beginning to think through a haze of alcohol, he tried to count back how many they'd had, coming to the conclusion this was the fourth. Which meant it was probably the fifth. Too many, whichever way he counted. He attempted to convince himself his head was perfectly clear and his legs were steady as he picked up their half-empty glasses and elbowed his way towards the door.

Outside the air was fresh, but though he breathed deeply, greedily, he found the orange light of the city street and occasional swish of passing cars oppressive. A crowd of drunken lads approached; their incoherent shouts to a similar gang across the road made him tense up. They passed without even noticing him. There was no sign of Vinko. Jay was surprised at the strength of the momentary concern he felt for him. He saw a covered passageway set aside for smokers and went over to look up it. A slight figure was sitting alone by an upturned-barrel table at the far end and he wove his way between noisy groups of people towards him, relieved. As he approached Vinko was tucking something away in his pocket. He looked up guiltily as he registered Jay's presence. Jay glanced back over his shoulder, trying to remember whether he'd seen anyone Vinko could have been meeting.

'I…I usually see my mates on a Saturday night.' Vinko glanced down at his pocket. 'I was just texting to tell them I won't be there.' Jay nodded, relieved it had only been a phone he'd seen. 'So they don't hang around waiting for no reason, you know?'

'There's no need to spoil your Saturday night on my account. Go and join them if you want. I can sort myself out.'

Vinko shook his head and rolled a cigarette. There were no spare seats; Jay passed him his drink and took a draught of his own before leaning against the wall and lighting his pipe. When Vinko finally looked up, his expression was hostile.

'You blame him, don't you?'

'Blame who?'

'My dad.'

'I never said—'

'You don't have to say. You hate the fact that you had anything to do with that war and you blame my dad that you were there.'

'For fuck's sake, Vinko!' His voice echoed round the alleyway and he expected the other drinkers to fall silent, though in fact not a single person turned to look. 'If I blame anyone, it's myself.'

'So why won't you tell me more?'

'It's not a question of blaming anyone.'

'There's always blame.'

Jay stared hard at a crack in the render over Vinko's shoulder. He imagined the wall as a cliff face, the crack his escape route.

'How did my dad die?'

The accusation had faded; it was as simple as it was possible for such a question to be.

'I wasn't there by then. He was shot in action during Operation Storm.'

'You weren't there.' Vinko was glaring, angry again. 'Why weren't you there?'

He inhaled deeply. 'I got injured,' he said slowly. 'I came back here before the war ended.'

True. Except for the missing parts.

'What happened?'

'What I said.'

'But—'

'Please stop going on about it!' His voice was harsh, as defence turned to anger. Like it usually did. He wasn't being fair to Vinko but he didn't feel fair. Life wasn't fair. 'I'll tell you when I'm ready. If I'm ever ready. Can't you understand? It's in the past. Our lives – mine and yours – have moved on. Understood?'

'You—'

'Understood?'

Vinko glowered at him.

'I want to be your friend. Help you. Now. Nothing to do with then. Stop going on about the past, stop… Stop seeing me as anything other than a…a concerned mate, or I'm out. On the road. Off into the sunset. Leave you to as many shady deals as you want to get involved in!'

'I told you I don't!'

'I'm sorry, I…I shouldn't have said that.'

Vinko stared at his hands, one curled round his glass, the other drumming in front of him on the table. 'I'm sorry, too.'

Jay suppressed an impulse to move over and put a fatherly arm round his shoulders. Vinko stubbed out his cigarette and drained his pint. Jay realised his own was empty.

'Want another?'

'Yes.' He glanced down the alley towards the street. 'No, it's late. We ought to go back.'

Jay had no idea of the time, but it didn't feel late. Not for a Saturday night.

'You sure?'

'Did you mean it when you said you'd help me?'

'Of course.'

'Then perhaps it's better to talk at home, Šojka.'

'Jay. We'll get on a whole lot better if you start using my proper name.'

He grinned and was relieved when Vinko smiled back, much of his anger and disappointment dissipated.

On the way Vinko called at a mini-market to buy tobacco. As he came out, hunched against the drizzle, Jay looked at the bulge in his pocket.

'What's that?'

'Whisky. Only a half-bottle. I thought—'

'Half bottle or not, how can you afford that, on top of fags and all we've just spent? You told me what you earned hardly covered rent and food.'

'You told *me* not to ask questions.'

He began to walk away. Jay stopped him.

'Not while you're with me, you don't,' he said. 'You want your life to be worth something, remember? Value yourself.'

He handed him a ten-pound note and sent him back in, watching through the window to make sure he paid this time.

They filled the neat, strangely homely room with smoke and the whisky bottle fuelled their plans. Any doubts Jay still had were dispelled as he rose from arranging a makeshift bed of blanket and cushions on the floor and saw Vinko watching him.

'I'm sorry, Jay. For earlier. I'm glad you're here.'

Vinko put a tentative hand on his shoulder then clung to him as if he were Ivan himself come back to life.

He lay staring at the orange glow penetrating the thin curtains that billowed against the open window. The waves of light made the pictures on the walls appear even more surreal. He tried to shut out Vinko's stifled sobs. Twice he had asked if he was all right.

162

'I am OK. Thank you, Jay. I sleep now.'

He wondered what caused Vinko's tears. Was it the reminder of the father he'd never known? Eventually the lad fell silent, the deepening and slowing of his breathing revealing that he had found sleep at last. Jay felt guilty at not telling him more. But he'd never been able to talk about it. Never. He hadn't even been able to say much to Polly. His heart tightened as he thought of her. He wished he was back at Stoneleigh and could talk to her now. No – perhaps it was a good thing he missed that bus; perhaps he needed time away. It wouldn't do to get too involved. And he never talked to anyone; not in that way. There was never anyone to talk to. Which was good – with two people in as many weeks now he'd proved he wasn't up to the job of talking. A man of action, then. He wasn't too good at that either. There he was, about to leave Polly's barn unfinished – only for a couple of days, and he'd do his best to let her know, but even so – and who knew how far he'd get with sorting Vinko out. But he was determined to try.

Vinko had almost pleaded with him to set off on their planned trip first thing the next morning, and despite Jay's protests that now wasn't a particularly good time for him, something – guilt, or a sense of responsibility – had made him agree. He tried not to ask himself why, but the question crept in regardless. Of course it wasn't purely altruism. If at all. Helping Vinko was about his own freedom. He'd thought he was free after giving Zora's inheritance back, but now he knew he had not been. His peace of mind, his life, couldn't be bought back that cheaply. Perhaps he still wouldn't be free after seeing Vinko right. But he had to hope, or he might as well give up now. The alcohol blurred his thoughts and he turned over and tried to sleep.

A beeping announced the appearance of a glow in a corner of the room. He knew he shouldn't, but fighting off guilt was something he'd got good at. He only stared at the screen of Vinko's phone for a second before checking the inbox. There were two new texts waiting, both from sender MN. Knowing he'd be found out, already preparing his excuses – 'I'm new to this mobile business, thought it was mine' – he looked.

What's your problem? Get in touch said the latest arrival in Croatian.

The previous one was also unopened but received earlier in the evening, at around the time he'd found Vinko outside the pub.

Good work. Where is he now?

Glad he'd interrupted him, Jay hoped they'd be able to talk about whatever it was Vinko seemed to have got mixed up in. It could wait until morning – the peaceful breathing from the narrow bed was not something to be disturbed. The phone revealed nothing else; as far as he could discover with his limited knowledge, the other folders – Outbox, Sent – were empty. Vinko was obviously a good housekeeper. He wished he knew how to mark the incoming messages unread. Vinko would probably be annoyed, and justifiably so; disturbing their fragile peace with an argument first thing in the morning was not something he relished. He quickly deleted the messages into oblivion, put the phone back in its corner and went back to his attempt to lull himself to sleep to the steady waves of the lad's peaceful breathing.

He opens his eyes again as he senses a familiar presence. The boy is sitting on the end of Vinko's bed looking down at him.

'You've found me here too, have you?'

The boy says nothing, merely turns his head to look at Ivan's son. Vinko turns over noisily in his sleep.

'Leave his dreams alone,' Jay says under his breath. 'He had nothing to do with any of it, you hear?'

The boy turns his attention back to Jay.

The truck driver stops and leaves him to walk the last couple of miles to the place he has come to think of as home. He wonders if he will ever feel that as well as thinking it, and is shocked by the realisation that he doesn't already. The truck rattles away down the damaged road and it feels good to be free of the merciless jolting. The engine noise fades and he becomes momentarily aware of the sporadic sound of distant shelling in the hills behind them, before shutting it out like an ordinary town dweller ignores the constant hum of traffic. It is hard to imagine there is anything left worth attacking and he wonders when they will come this way, hungrily looking for more. Zora is confident the house is safe now, and the extended family of refugees seem to share her optimism – they have stayed, after all – but he is not too sure he does.

He no longer thinks too hard. Since his injury and fevered weeks of recovery he has felt different. Though the wound was not directly life-threatening, the infection was serious and left him feeling as if he did die and someone else is now acting through him, as unreal as the stories Zora would tell him and he would then continue in his head to while away the agonising hours of his lucid periods. His feelings and reactions, including the sense of comradeship and family, are more intense, but he is sometimes conscious of being on the outside, aware of himself experiencing them.

He hears a heavy vehicle approaching and instinctively ducks into the scrubby undergrowth before it comes into view.

His gun has been an added burden in the heat, but he feels safer with it. The armoured truck turns out to be one of theirs, but is past by the time the adrenalin rush of fear subsides. He hears others approaching and waits, concealed, for them to pass. Nothing is certain here. Even walking down a road. There were no road blocks in this area last time he was here, but it has been a while. His senses send feelers out around every bend. It is a relief of sorts to turn up the stony track and know that anyone who passes is likely to be friendly.

One more hillock to go and he is relieved not to see a pall of smoke. Relieved, too, as he crests the rise in the land and does not see an empty, blackened shell. The fields of a working farm are a rare sight in a place where most have done the sensible thing and fled for safety. Or stayed and been killed.

The newly reopened wound in his side nags, the hastily-rebound bandage chafing. His weakness, which eventually got the better of him so he could no longer hide the pain, means he has been allowed some time to rest and recuperate here before it is back, back to the constant fear of being hurt, seeing others being hurt. The fear of his own actions inflicting that on someone else. He never voices that last one, doubting it is a fear the others share or would understand. It stays inside, eating at him like the infection in his side had. He's getting over that, isn't he?

Zora isn't expecting him. Her surprise makes the homecoming even sweeter. She embraces him and her touch makes his dusty, war-weary world seem momentarily brighter. He leans his head on her shoulder, wondering if he will ever be able to leave again.

She dispels his guilt with a kiss and a few words.

'You did well. I've heard things are going well. Don't be ashamed you've had to come back. They weren't sure you should go at all, you know.' For all he feels different now, her smile can still melt him. 'But you showed them.'

She means 'us' – he knows she'd shared the opinion. He went back before he should, not only because he couldn't watch Ivan leaving another time without him. He'd gone to prove himself. To her, as they both know. He smiles, telling her even Lek might be beginning to respect him – he's allowed him back now after all. But none of it is making him feel as good as it should. Not even when she says he must be fearless.

He shakes his head. 'No. You don't stop feeling fear. You just get used to it.'

Despite the absence of Lek and the others, he is surprised when she invites him to her that night. He can't refuse. He shouldn't be there but it's where he wants to be.

Fear isn't the only thing you get used to.

Chapter 17

Marilyn woke to an empty bed. As she realised that the space beside her was cold and empty, she wondered if he'd been suffering his night terrors again and crept out of their bed to his sleeping bag in the spare room. But as she came fully awake she recalled the growing foreboding of the previous evening's endless wait. On her way downstairs she glanced into the spare room, still vainly hoping to see the huddled shape of his sleeping bag. There was certainly more space after her clearout, but no one had been there. The armchair downstairs that had become his was also untouched. She'd told herself throughout not to get attached, but the hollow emptiness of absence hurt nevertheless.

Over breakfast she listened to the showers pattering occasionally against the windows as she relived the previous evening's drive to the end of the lane to meet him off the bus, recalling the way her heart leapt as the wide-spaced headlights rounded the corner, the bright rectangles of the steamy windows brash and out of place in the dark countryside. Eagerly anticipating his pleasure and surprise as he saw her and realised he didn't have to face the long walk to the cottage, she'd felt an intense wave of disappointment as the bus didn't even slow. She'd driven to Holdwick, searched the emptying, orange-lit market square and scanned the road on the way back for the eerie movement of the reflective strip on his jacket in her headlights.

Now, in the clear light of morning, the recollection reawakened her growing concern, which she fended off with indignation and practicalities. If he didn't come back she'd have to find someone to continue the building work. A good job it was a Sunday, allowing her to postpone the difficult decisions until a more reasonable time to be phoning round. She glanced frequently towards the kitchen window over her breakfast toast and coffee. A sudden rattle sparked a hope of his hand on the latch, until she realised it was the cat flap. Genghis made a noisy entrance, his demands for food like a strident reproach.

'You know there'll be a good reason for it,' she told the cat, trying to convince herself of it as she rose to feed him and go about her morning routine.

As she crossed the living room she paused in front of the pictures. Two matching frames she'd found during the big clearout yesterday. She'd returned the souvenirs of a holiday in Tuscany with Matt to the album, so she could use the frames for the pictures Jay had brought. *The Rock Sequence*, he'd called them with a laugh. A couple of days ago they'd allowed themselves a break and set off to explore the moors. She could still feel the freshness of the wind, the earthy peat beneath their feet, the expanse of blue-grey sky keeping guard. The rocky outcrop showed no signs of habitation despite its fort-like appearance, but they drank in its atmosphere all the same, taking photos of one another. Textures, shapes, light, shadow, skyline. He'd surprised her on Friday by having the *Sequence* developed while he was out and presenting the pictures to her before she even realised the film had gone from her camera. Matt had bought her a digital camera and sulked when she continued using her old one. She took Jay's lack of comment as tacit agreement – a roll of film concentrated your mind and imagination, as did

169

the black-and-white. Whatever the reason – perhaps it was simply the remembered magic of the moment – these pictures were special and she'd enjoyed picking out her favourites, one of each of them, and fitting them in the frames. Carefully positioning them on top of the bookcase, where they'd felt right. Yesterday. And today? What if he didn't come back? Then they'd be there as a memory of the fleeting time they'd enjoyed together.

Reminding herself to be careful how *together* she thought of them, she tried to convince herself there'd be a perfectly rational explanation for his absence. Anyway, if he'd gone for good he'd have taken his rucksack. She went upstairs and checked, as if it might have grown feet and tiptoed out to join him in the night. It was lying open, still occupying the corner of her bedroom that it had claimed as if it had always belonged there. Like its owner. Without thinking she knelt down and lifted up the canvas skin that held together the viscera of a life on the road. She had a moment of doubt, imagining him appearing in the door behind her demanding what did she think she was doing – she almost hoped – but smiled as she saw the cover of a book. Whenever she went to someone's house she loved browsing the shelves, comparing, recognition alternating with curiosity and unasked questions. Jay had done the same in her house and that was all she was doing now. It looked like there was little else in the rucksack anyway; his washbag was in her bathroom and his clothes were in a pile on the nearby chair. She distracted herself by taking Matt's jumper and jeans from the pile ready to return, but was drawn inevitably back to Jay's backpack. She convinced herself she simply wanted to feel closer to him; in any case, he'd left the bag open and she had no doubt that anything truly private would be with him, in his pockets.

The novel, *Crime and Punishment,* was well-thumbed. She frowned slightly as she noted the pencilled price from a charity shop and read the blurb, wondering how much it meant to him before savouring the memory of the night she'd first seen him reading it. The bookmark was a dog-eared photo of an attractive terraced house. Old mellow brick, but otherwise impossible to locate. On the back, in Jay's handwriting, the simple word *Home?* Probably the house he'd mentioned. The question mark seemed poignant. She tucked it back in its place. The clip-on reading light was there, half a dozen CDs with a portable player and ear buds, and a Landranger map of the area. A small fold-away gas stove lodged in a lightweight pan, a plastic mug and plate, a container of instant coffee and a couple of packs of dried food, a compact first-aid kit and a water bottle. Beneath that was a pair of open-toed sandals; she wondered if he noticed the difference in summer when it came to wearing the sandals and carrying the heavier boots. Practical, and comfortingly ordinary if she disregarded the fact that this was his life. She took out one of the CDs, attracted by the cover, a medieval-looking woodcut of a fairytale town, and filled the house with strange and mysterious but somehow familiar music, at once ancient and modern, as she washed up and got ready for the day.

She remembered a couple of particularly heavy boxes of rubbish in the spare room, which she'd been intending to leave for Jay to carry out, an opportunity for him to indulge his self-image of the gallant knight errant. She decided now to make the effort herself, dividing up the contents if she had to. Having manoeuvred the two boxes down the narrow stairs and out through the rarely-used front door, she lifted the tarpaulin she'd used to cover the bonfire, placed the new boxes on the pile and weighted the tarp carefully back in place with stones. The wind was only light, but she didn't want any of her past escaping to litter the future.

She stood back and looked at the heap. Jay had had a point; sorting through it all had been something to do for herself, but she'd looked forward to him being there so they could set light to the bonfire together. The unlit pile now seemed like a symbol of her faith in his return. Smiling at her own exaggerated notion, and insisting to herself that his return meant nothing more than rewarding her faith in him as a reliable man who wouldn't leave the building job half-done, she imagined them watching the flames, wine glasses in hand, eyes following the clouds of tiny sparks rising into the night sky to join the stars. Backs freezing, faces burning. She'd describe to him the alchemic processes in the kiln she was increasingly desperate to get going; he'd tell her an equally magical fire story.

On her way back to the house, she glanced over at the barn. It looked forlorn, awaiting attention, and she wondered when it would get it. Perhaps the contents of Jay's rucksack, which until now she'd considered a kind of insurance policy guaranteeing his return, were disposable and he'd done a disappearing act after all. She'd wait another day – she had plenty to be getting on within her temporary workshop at Matt's – and then decide what to do. All kinds of notions crowded their way into her imagination; perhaps he'd got into some kind of trouble. Perhaps he was visiting one of that string of women whose existence he'd denied – a scenario she'd used before in a vain attempt to curb the growth of her feelings. She liked to think she knew loneliness when she saw it, but the idea continued to niggle and in her moments of doubt she was glad of it. Surely he could at least have let her know where he was? Her indignation at the fact he'd failed to do so was immediately superseded by the realisation that her phone was off and he might well be trying. She really wanted to believe in his goodness, that he wouldn't let her down, but despite their growing closeness, she didn't really know him at all.

On her way back into the house she gathered some logs from the porch to lay a fire. A vivid image of Jay in the living room flashed into her mind, and it reminded her of the night they'd come home to find the electricity was unexpectedly back. That had been eclipsed in her memory by what happened later that night, but now she felt a lingering trace of unease. What *would* he have done if someone had been there? She busied herself with newspaper and kindling, chiding herself for her negative thoughts. He'd merely been nervous; protective of his new-found temporary home, of her. Home? She certainly felt he belonged here, for the time being at least. Perhaps she should be worried about that, too. It had all happened so fast. Matt had swept her off her feet once, and look where that had left her. But this was different. Or so she'd thought. She wasn't so sure now.

After the daily ritual of trying the phone – still dead – she drove down the lane to within mobile signal, to call Sue and make sure the pub could manage without her for a second week off. Thinking of her empty house, she half hoped she'd be needed, but Sue assured her everything was fine. Once again she wondered how long she'd have a job there now the tourist season was over. To stop herself asking outright she began to tell her friend about the new man in her life.

'So what does he do?'

'He's a storyteller.'

'I mean for a living.'

'Yeah, that's it. Street entertainment, busking.'

'You *are* joking?'

'No. He does make a kind of living from it. Odd jobs, too. He hasn't always done that – just made a conscious decision to leave the rat race behind, you know?'

'Oh my god, Marilyn, you haven't found yourself a bloke who's more of a dreamer than *you* are? Are you sure you can trust him not to wander off when the wind changes?'

'Of course,' she said, her own certainty suddenly repaired and shored up by her friend's doubt.

'Listen, why don't you come over? Steve's off on a climbing weekend, but bring Gypsy Jay anyway.'

Marilyn laughed. 'Much as I'd love to introduce you, I'm afraid he's had to go off for the weekend too.'

'Girly afternoon it is, then.'

As she drove over to the Mason's Arms, Marilyn wished Jay was in the car with her, but was determined not to brood. She'd give him another day before she got either worried or annoyed. There could be any number of places he'd had to go; letting her know would be awkward to say the least. A day away would do her good, get things in perspective.

She'd timed it well; the Sunday lunch rush was slowing as she arrived. Marilyn pitched in to help until it was quiet enough to leave to the staff, and she and Sue went out for a walk. She enjoyed catching up on the gossip – it was amazing how much could happen in a couple of weeks. In turn she told her friend about the recent storm disaster and the progress they'd made since. She tried to ignore today's absence and concentrate on the optimism she'd been feeling, more positive than she'd felt since a long time before Jay appeared on the scene. Sue seemed impressed by the help he'd given her, and eventually even stopped teasing her about his unconventional lifestyle. Simply telling her friend about him made it all seem more real, more reliable, and as Marilyn drove home, enjoying a moment of satisfaction as Jay's atmospheric music matched the rhythm of the wipers, she was sure he'd be waiting for her when she got back to Stoneleigh.

He wasn't.

Chapter 18

The English countryside flashed by. Rolling fields, clumped trees, roads and canals with their cars and boats, houses isolated or huddled in villages, the spire of a church standing guard. Occasionally Jay even caught a glimpse of people. Perhaps it was the speed, but it was rare he saw people, as if they were hiding from this speeding monster. Buildings, objects, fields – snippets of lives that he knew nothing about and never would. The detachment made him feel good to be back on the move after all. Wasn't this where he belonged? Not here, this train, this table, but the freedom of transience. He thought of his bag, his life, left behind at Stoneleigh. He shook his head at the ghost of his reflection in the window. Come on, this never really felt right. Simply less wrong, when there was always the promise of something else round the corner. He suddenly felt glad his bag was at Polly's; it meant he was sure to go back, whatever else happened. He couldn't run away this time, and he was ashamed he'd even thought about it. However briefly.

He glanced at Vinko across the table, gazing out as if entranced by the landscape, the far horizon rolling gently by and the nearer view streaking to a blur or separating into blinking snapshots. He wondered what it was the lad had got himself involved in. After a flash of anger he'd actually seemed relieved when Jay confessed about eavesdropping on his messages. As if he'd have done the same, or as if he now had something on his new friend that he could use if

Jay tried to criticise him. Perhaps that was mere projecting; it was Jay himself who needed that kind of defence.

Whoever this Novak was, he was asking Vinko to do something he didn't want to do; he'd been evasive, saying only that he'd failed to meet someone the previous night. Vinko had again seemed eager for Jay to make this journey to Winchester as soon as he could, and had jumped at the chance to come along to get away for a day or two. He said he'd never been on a train before, but Jay suspected that wasn't all; hopefully he'd tell him what it was about when he was ready. Or not. Perhaps the man would get the message and lose interest.

Jay didn't think too hard about why he was doing all this. He rarely questioned why he did anything these days. He didn't always like the answer. The only reason for doing so now was to have some idea of what to tell Polly. When he got in touch with her. He was about to get his phone out, think of how to track down a number for her, when Vinko looked round. With his fleeting half-smile, Jay was as struck as he had been when they first met at the resemblance to Ivan.

'I can see why you enjoy travelling,' Vinko said.

'Enjoy?' Jay shrugged. 'It's just what I do.'

Vinko turned from the window and leaned on the table between them.

'How do I know I can trust you?' His voice was matter-of-fact; he could have been suggesting they went for a coffee. Jay was taken aback. Trust as in did he mean him harm? That was easy – no. Or, more likely, could he rely on him? Not so easy.

'What do you mean?'

'What do you want from me?'

'Nothing.' The first. Easy.

Vinko shook his head. 'Everybody wants something.'

'I just want to help. I told you this wasn't a good time for me. I didn't have to come now – I hope that tells you something.'

He got no response; Vinko was looking past him, tensing visibly, and he heard the connecting doors of the carriage opening. Jay looked round and saw the ticket inspector, recalling the lad's earlier nervousness at the station. He had turned back to stare out of the window, hunched into the seat as if trying to make himself invisible.

'There's no need to worry,' Jay said, digging into his pocket, 'I've got the tickets.'

'I've got no ID,' Vinko muttered. 'I should have told you.'

'You don't need anything like that.'

'He won't ask for ID?'

Jay shook his head and held the tickets up for the inspector as he passed. Vinko forced a smile as the man nodded to him.

'See?'

The man moved quickly on down the half-empty carriage. Vinko started to roll a cigarette. Jay reminded him he couldn't smoke on the train and he put it away reluctantly. He looked briefly like a small boy.

'It reminded me of a bad experience I had.'

'What happened?'

'I tried to go on a journey.' He glanced round, taking in the few scattered passengers towards the other end of the carriage, who wouldn't understand the language they were speaking even if they could hear. 'I have been on a train before. Once. Ran away. I was ten, eleven. Had the crazy idea of going to Croatia, where I could *be* someone. But I didn't get far.' He paused, looked down at his restless hands, turned again to stare out of the window. 'I had no ID, hardly any money, nothing. I managed to dodge the ticket guy, but got as far as the first border and realised I knew nothing. Thought I knew but I didn't. Nothing about where I was or how to get anywhere if I was nobody. I was nobody because my mother had done it like that, told no one about me, couldn't even send me to school, because I was all she had and she was terrified they'd take me away. So I left the train at the last place before the border and went straight back to her. Never explained where I'd been, never tried again. I realised she was all I had, too. She and her friends in the…house where we lived. Where she worked.'

He was still turned towards the window, fingers tapping restlessly on his knee.

'Didn't any of them tell anyone about you? Try and help you both?'

'Of course not. They were in the same position as she was. Don't get me wrong, they did their best. My mother and my "aunties" took it in turns to look after me. Gave me what I needed, taught me stuff, reading and the like. I was allowed out sometimes, had one or two mates. I was happy most of the time.' He turned. 'What kid wouldn't be happy, not having to go to school?'

Jay echoed his sudden smile uncomfortably.

'*I* wasn't! The other kids were jealous I didn't have to go and I was jealous of them because they did. Always wondering what I was missing. You said you know what it's like to be an outsider.' He turned back to the window. 'There was a special section in the library, in our language, collected for refugees – my mates never knew I went there or my life wouldn't have been worth living. But I always wanted to know things. Mum liked it when I told her

179

things I'd read.' He paused. 'I was often the only one she'd listen to. When things were black. Sometimes even I couldn't reach her.'

'Weren't you—?'

'That was just how it was.'

'Why didn't she go back?'

'She couldn't, could she? As I got older, I knew she was controlled. The people who ran the house, they kept her there. She had no money of her own. They'd taken her passport. And she was totally dependent on stuff. Smack. That was another thing I realised – she said it was her comfort, the only time she felt happy. But I know they got her dependent. Another form of control, wasn't it?' He seemed to shrink into himself. 'I hated it when she died, but her life wasn't much better.'

He turned and looked at Jay intensely, challenging him to judge.

'I don't understand... I thought there were all sorts of facilities for refugees. Why did she end up there?'

'I don't know, do I? I think she spent some time at a centre towards the end of the war and it was pretty grim. Till someone she knew offered her this *opportunity*.' He spat the word. 'When you've got nothing people offer you all sorts of things. You're going to end up somewhere decent, get away, get a job. They'll make sure you and your kid when it's born will be OK. And when you've *really* got nothing you believe them. Mum said if Zora's place hadn't burned down it would've been different. After my dad was killed, it would've been somewhere she could have stayed at least long enough to get herself together... She loved that place. And the woman who took her in. Where she met my father. But it did burn down.' He shrugged. 'And she had nothing.'

Not for the first time Jay wondered what would have happened if he'd stayed. He shook his head. What made him think he could have done anything?

'Do you know what happened? The front line was miles away. How come the house was destroyed?'

Vinko looked at him wryly. 'You're the man with the questions this morning, aren't you?'

'I—'

'I don't mind. Not that I know much. But I know what Mum thought, though she hardly ever talked about it. I think Zora and her husband had some violent rows. Literally violent. I suppose you knew?'

Jay barely managed to nod. Vinko continued.

'He assaulted people, my mother included – I'm not sure she ever told me that, but I knew. One time he came back from the fighting and something had happened. It was particularly bad. He ended up setting fire to the house. People probably thought it was war damage, later. Zora got away, I think they all did, but there was no house and my mother never saw her again.'

Jay felt hollow. When he eventually found his voice, it sounded surprisingly normal. 'You're saying it was Lek destroyed the place?'

Vinko was silent for a moment. 'Lek?'

'Zora's lover. I don't think they were married.'

Vinko stared at him. 'Yeah, right. My Mum just called him "that bastard" or the like – the few times she mentioned it and I could get what she was on about. It was mainly a case of looking at the few photos she had – that was how I recognised you. And talking about Dad – Zora – the house, like a safe place despite everything. She used to smile. It scared me – as if the only time she'd been happy was in the middle of a war. But then she'd close up. Most of the time she'd get mad at me

181

for even asking. I didn't ask much anyway. I'm probably guessing most of what I've told you. Sorry.'

'Don't apologise. I should be doing that. I don't know what I can say.'

'What is there to say?' He shook his head. 'I told you yesterday: I don't mind, it's done and gone. And you said yourself, it's all in the past.'

'So how come you ended up here?'

Vinko turned back to the window, got his tobacco out of his jacket pocket, remembered he couldn't smoke, put it back. Jay waited. 'There were things you wouldn't talk about last night. I've had enough talking.' He smiled. 'I'll tell you when I'm ready. *If* I'm ready.'

It stung all the more for being an echo of his own words.

'You still haven't told me why I should trust you.' Any trace of humour had gone from Vinko's expression. He seemed to have closed himself off as he glanced around the half-empty carriage. 'Or this guy you said you'd take me to see.'

'You don't have to see anyone. I said my agent might know someone who specialises in immigration. You asked. I might be able to get you an appointment, though I'm not promising anything.'

'I've told you now. How it was. I don't have to go and see anyone. You do the talking for me.'

Jay shook his head. 'It'll have to come from you. Facts, Vinko.' The lad shrugged. 'Or did you really only come for the ride?'

'I don't know.'

They travelled on in silence. Jay wished he knew what to say. He wanted to talk. About anything, not prying, not a desperate attempt to make up for years of absence in just a few hours. Talk about anything, the scenery, ask him what music he liked, whatever. And talk to stop himself thinking about what he'd heard. He told himself the fire couldn't have been his fault. They'd argued about all kinds of things. And it might not even have been as Vinko said; the lad had suggested as much himself. Even if it had been because of him, that didn't necessarily make it his fault, did it? 'There's always blame.' The train slowed, came to a standstill. Typical Sunday service. He saw a movement in a nearby copse of trees. The boy, watching him. He breathed deeply.

'Vinko?'

'Uh-huh?'

He turned, his expression open, but Jay's mind was blank.

'I... Nothing.'

'Why are we stopped?'

'It happens sometimes. It'll move soon.'

They waited.

'Why don't you tell me one of your stories?'

'What?'

'Like in the marketplace. Why not?'

They exchanged a smile and the relief was as good as any talking. But Jay tried in vain to find the words, any words, a key to unlock the gate to his well-trodden escape route. He was saved by the ringtone of Vinko's phone, which seemed to announce the train lurching into movement. Vinko looked across apologetically, glanced at the screen and edged out of his seat as he answered. He made for the connecting door speaking quietly. 'Hello? ... No, nothing ... I haven't heard a word from you. Really. But it doesn't matter. I was mistaken and anyway I've changed my mind—' The door swished shut on his voice.

Jay stared after him for a while before reminding himself he had an important call of his own to make. He hoped he'd be able to find the right words.

Chapter 19

Marilyn found it hard to concentrate the following morning, even though her temporary workshop was at the back of the craft centre, which meant she was cut off from any comings and goings. She was on edge, listening for a knock on the door. Even though that usually meant Matt, and she knew it was highly unlikely that Jay would just appear here, the irrational hope persisted. She was missing him, waiting for him to return, and not only because she'd have a thing or two to say to him about leaving her in the lurch.

It was almost lunchtime when she finished applying the glaze to a batch of mugs and left them to dry. They would keep their final appearance secret until they'd dried and been fired, but that was part of the magic. She was pleased with her morning's work; the warm feeling of inspiration Jay had kindled in her continued to smoulder despite his absence.

Following her clearout she had a bag of things for Matt, including the clothes she'd lent Jay, and before settling down to her sandwiches she decided to get the visit over with. Although her own situation had taken a turn for the better during the past week, she still felt the same mix of nostalgia and jealousy as she entered the shop. Lucy looked fully at home behind the counter, with her wavy hennaed hair, nose stud, butterfly tattoo on the back of her hand and floaty blouse that was a bit flimsy for the time of year despite the efforts of the portable gas fire Marilyn could smell above the shop's air of patchouli. The woman Matt had left her for gave her a friendly smile and didn't seem at all perturbed at seeing Marilyn. She silently wished them well, despite herself. Lucy phoned up to the flat and told her Matt said to go up.

'He's just doing some accounts. We were having a big stocktake when you came last week, you know? I think he was also going to look at the figures on that spare workshop. Between you and me, we're doing OK and as far as I'm concerned I think you should stay as long as you need to, yeah? I mean, seeing as your place was damaged in that storm – something like that's no fun, is it?'

She smiled as if to add *no hard feelings?* to her flow of questions. Marilyn smiled back and was surprised how easy it was. She was also surprised at how calm she felt as Matt let her in and offered her a coffee.

'No thanks, I won't stay long.'

She noticed that the room hadn't changed much; the pile of decorating materials was still in the corner. She felt a flush of self-satisfaction at the amount she and Jay had got done on the barn in the same time.

'Did you get anywhere with the insurance?' Matt asked.

'These things take time. Still no phone. I was going to pop across and check it out later.' She walked over to the window and gazed down on the car park. 'Anyway, whether or not I can get payment for this, we're doing well with the preliminary work at Stoneleigh. A good start so when I can get Alan, or whoever else, going it shouldn't take too long. Unless we get finished ourselves in the meantime, that is.'

'That friend you mentioned still around to help you, then?' he said, obviously trying, but failing, to keep his voice neutral.

'Yeah, we've got quite a lot done,' she said non-committally. She turned to face him in the ensuing pause.

185

'Anyway, I've been having a clearout. Found some stuff of yours.'

She handed two large carrier bags over and watched him rummaging through.

'There's nothing here that couldn't have waited.'

'It's OK, it needed doing.'

He smiled as he held up a hand-knitted, multicoloured jumper. 'The one your gran knitted me. Hadn't thought about it in years. Till...till I met this guy in the builders' merchant last Tuesday.' He waved his hand towards the pile of decorating materials. 'Needed a new roller. Time flies. It's been a week now; can't believe I haven't used it yet.' He looked back at the jumper. 'So I guessed right – the stuff he was hiring was for your place?'

'No secrets in a small town like this.' She laughed as the phrase reminded her of the first conversation she'd had with Jay.

'Seemed nice enough. Not that we spoke; just that hello-sorry-to-keep-you-waiting kind of thing at the counter. How do you two know each other?'

'We met.' She shrugged. 'Around. He...called by on the off chance last week just after the storm. On a walking holiday in the area. Saw my problem, decided to make it a building holiday instead.' She laughed awkwardly; gestured to the jumper. 'His own clothes were wet.'

'No probs. Well, I hope it works out.'

'You're assuming rather a lot, aren't you?'

'No need to be so defensive. I could have meant the work on the barn. I take it that means you're not an item?'

'He's a good friend.'

'Whatever. Would that be him I saw busking on Saturday?'

She nodded. 'We've concreted the floor, needed to give

186

it time to dry. I had to sort my stuff out and he came to town.'

'You've done the floor already?'

'Only the base.'

'Impressive nevertheless – you're certainly getting on with it. That lad I saw him with helping you too?'

'What lad?'

'Obviously not. Teenager, dark hair? They were crossing the square, looked like they were heading for the Black Bull. Don't worry, I wasn't eavesdropping. Couldn't anyway; I think they were talking some foreign language.'

'Wouldn't surprise me. Jay's travelled,' she said, distracted by the memory of the youth she'd accused of stealing her purse and the attempt to convince herself this was someone else. 'I don't know anything about any lad; must just be someone he bumped into.'

'Must be. Listen, did you say Jay? That reminds me, I've got a message for you – got a phone call the other day.'

'You weren't going to tell me?' The strength of her feelings made her snap it out.

'Give us a chance. I'd have called down at the workshop if I'd known you were there.' He held his hands up in that characteristic gesture of mock innocence she'd once have found humorous. 'Yesterday, Sunday morning of all times, this guy phones saying he's trying to get hold of you, can't get through, must have the wrong number for Stoneleigh, could I give it to him? I told him you were ex-directory so, no, I couldn't, and in any case your phone was down. So, cool as you like, he asks if I could perhaps give him your mobile number instead?' Matt laughed as if it were the most ridiculous request in the world. 'Needless to say I told him if you'd wanted him to have your mobile number presumably you'd have given it to him. I did the right thing, didn't I?'

She sighed. There had been a series of nuisance calls shortly after she'd come back to Stoneleigh from Ireland, so she'd changed the number and had her listing made private. Even so. 'Did you have to be so obstructive?'

'Your phone's been off anyway – what difference would it have made? I'm telling you now.'

'So did you get his number?' she prompted.

Matt plucked a piece of paper with a mobile number from a noticeboard by the desk. He frowned as he passed it to her. 'Strange thing is, he said it was Jay, claimed you'd be expecting him. I assume it's that friend of yours. So how come—'

'Thanks, Matt.' Marilyn took the paper from him calmly, determined not to betray her perplexity. She also wanted to ask if he'd said anything else, but didn't want to reveal that she knew nothing about where he'd gone. 'Well, I'd better be getting back. Pots won't fire themselves.'

'Look, is everything OK?'

'Of course.' As if she'd tell him if it wasn't.

'I just want to say…this guy had better be all right, is all. Seriously, I hope things work out – you deserve a bit of a break, Lynnie.'

'Thanks.'

She got up to go. For Matt to say something like that was as good as an apology for the way he'd treated her. He went with her to the door and clapped her on her shoulder; she turned and gave him a brief hug.

She made herself wait until she was back in the workshop with the door closed behind her before whisking the scrap of paper from her pocket and dialling. She got the standard network answering service and her eager anticipation plunged into negativity. What was he up to? Why had he disappeared? Who was he with? She left a brief message, trying her best to sound matter-of-fact.

On her way home later that afternoon, Marilyn stopped at the last possible moment to try the number again before she lost signal. The recorded message politely informing her that the person she'd called was not available made her feel like throwing her phone out of the car window.

Passing the farm, she noticed the Harringtons were back; she called in to let Dorothy know she was fine, but didn't stop long. Her own place was deserted. Marilyn parked the car and looked into the barn; it seemed worse now than it had before the storm. There was still a long way to go; the new floor with its ugly concrete over the damp-proof membrane made the place look soulless even though she knew the underfloor heating and stone flags would be in place eventually, and the window openings knocked into the walls gave the building a derelict air. She thought of what Jay had said about sleeping in barns the day they first met and wondered where he was now. She instinctively drew her phone from her pocket as if the strength of her feelings were enough to give her a signal.

She was in the porch contemplating the contents of her freezer, wondering what she could make to cheer herself up, when an unaccustomed sound reached her from inside the house. Dropping the freezer lid with a whump that sent Genghis skittering through to the comfort of the kitchen before her, she rushed to the phone.

'Polly?'

The sound of his voice made her realise how futile any attempts to convince herself she wasn't missing him had been.

'Good to hear you.'

'Got your message, thanks. I'm sorry I couldn't get in touch before. And I'm so glad you got mine. I wondered if you would – that Matt's a difficult one, isn't he?'

'Can be. So what's going on? Where'd you get to?'

'Last Saturday…I met an old friend. Well, an old friend's son. So I missed the bus home Saturday night, and then… I'll explain when I see you.'

'And when's that likely to be?'

'Tomorrow, hopefully. Wednesday at the latest. Listen, Pol, he needed my help; I had to… I'll explain…'

She wanted to fill the silence by reminding him he was supposed to be helping *her*, but told herself not to be so self-centred.

'Where are you now?'

'Winchester. Where my house and stuff are. I *will* explain,' he said for the third time. 'It's a long story. Too long for now. Please trust me. I'll be back as soon as I can. I've got a confession to make.'

'Confession?'

'I… I soon realised how much I'm missing you.'

She smiled with relief, savouring the moment, then realised he couldn't see a smile down the phone. 'Me too.'

'I feel really bad about just disappearing. I know we've got loads to be doing. You OK?'

She told him she'd been at the workshop, playing down the annoyance and frustration she'd been feeling.

'You can't believe how relieved I am,' he said. 'To speak to you. That you understand.'

'I can't say as I do, Jay. But I'm glad to speak to you too. You'd better be back soon, though, or that bag of yours is going on the bonfire with my old stuff.'

'You wouldn't.' As he laughed she heard the muffled sound of a door down the line, a male voice in the background. 'Look, I'd better go. I'll tell you all about it when I see you. Only a day or two, yeah?'

'I hope so. Thanks for ringing, anyway.'

'My pleasure. It's lovely to hear you. See you soon, Polly.'

And he was gone. She wished he'd said more, hoped she hadn't sounded too distant. As the warmth kindled by his voice faded, she found herself wondering, if it was so important for him to help his friend's son, whether that 'friend' was a woman. She told herself firmly that even if it was, it was in the past. But why so evasive? She tried to convince herself that if he were being evasive he wouldn't have phoned at all.

She spent the evening distracting herself by phoning her mother, father, brother. Each time, she played down the storm damage so that she didn't have to mention the help she'd had in overcoming it. If she'd felt apprehensive about the right way to present Jay to them before, anticipating the disapproval-laden questioning and inevitable need to justify herself, his absence and inadequate explanation made it ten times worse. She came to feel that perhaps the disapproval wasn't only from outside, and it was herself she was justifying things to. It made her frustration all the more intense.

Yet as she went upstairs for an early night, she found the rucksack in the corner of her bedroom oddly reassuring.

Chapter 20

Two days later Marilyn was trying to rescue her kitchen garden. The sound of tyres approaching over the rough surface of the lane gave her a good excuse to pause in the Sisyphean task. It didn't sound like either the post van or the Harringtons' four-wheel drive, and Jay had phoned that morning to say he'd call when he got to Skipton; she'd promised to collect him. She wiped her hands on her jeans and walked down to the yard to see who it was. There were two strangers in the car and she felt slightly embarrassed to be staring as they pulled up. The passenger door opened and a middle-aged, friendly-looking man in a waxed jacket got out, followed by a smart younger woman in a green suede winter coat who'd been driving.

'Marilyn Dexter?' the man asked.

She nodded.

'That's quite a lane you've got there. You get stuck much in winter?'

He had a homely local accent and manner that put her at her ease.

'Not as much as you'd think.' She gave him a reserved smile. 'What can I do for you?'

He produced a card from his jacket pocket. 'Detective Sergeant Chris Terry. I wonder if we could ask you a few questions, in connection with a murder case over in Keighley.'

'Murder?' Marilyn felt a deep fear creep through her, though she had no idea what he was talking about.

'We're following a few leads, that's all. It's a small detail but at the moment we've got very little to go on, and any information helps.'

She examined the ID he proffered and handed it back to him. Like when a patrol car came up behind her on the road, their mere presence was making her feel irrationally guilty.

'This is DC Kate Taylor.' He nodded to his colleague who flashed her ID dutifully. In an attempt to steady herself, Marilyn reached out for it to take a closer look, earning herself a flash of irritation from the woman.

'You'd better come in,' she said. The kitchen table was cluttered with her breakfast things so she showed them through to the living room.

'Coffee or tea?' she asked despite herself.

'We'll be fine, thanks,' DS Terry said. 'I hope we won't keep you long.'

He sat in the chair that had become Jay's.

'So,' he said, 'an elderly couple, Boris and Anja Pranjić, were murdered on Monday night, at their home in the Oakthwaite area of Keighley. Have you heard anything about it?'

She shook her head, wishing she'd taken more of an interest in the news.

'It was a break-in. They were shot.' Marilyn shuddered, and thought of the number of times she'd forgotten to lock her door. 'At the moment the most likely scenario is an interrupted burglary, but we have reasons to believe there may be more to it than that.'

'Sounds horrid. But what has it got to do with me?'

'You had your purse stolen recently, didn't you?'

'Yes.' She frowned. 'It was nothing serious. They took the cash and dumped the purse. I got it back, minus the money of course.'

'I believe you suspected someone? Got a description?'

'I can't be sure the lad I noticed, the description I gave, was actually the thief.' She remembered the guilt she'd felt at suspecting him. She hated the thought that she might have literally rubbed shoulders with a murderer, but there was a huge difference between stealing a purse and murder, and if he was nothing to do with it she didn't want to say anything that might get him into more serious trouble.

'Could you confirm your description? Do you have anything to add?'

'It was nearly two weeks ago. I'm not sure. What's he got to do with your investigation?'

'We got fingerprints off your purse and credit card. They match a set of prints found on furniture in the Pranjić' living room. There's no indication that Monday night's intruders went in there, but obviously we want to know who he is, what he knows. Especially since there's another lead – Mr and Mrs Pranjić moved house a few months ago. The woman who lives at their old address tells us a young man, whom she describes as "suspicious-looking", turned up at the house a week last Sunday looking for them. When she asked him – purely making conversation, she says – he said he lived in Holdwick. Nicola Radcliffe's description matches yours quite well.'

Marilyn reluctantly repeated the vague recollection she had, answering the detective's prompting – white, late teens, medium height and build, worn leather jacket, dark hair, an ear stud. Nothing particularly useful. After she'd remembered all she could there was a pause as the detective jotted it all down.

'Can you remember anything else about him?'

She thought for a moment.

'He had a foreign accent.'

'He spoke to you?' The detective glanced at his colleague. 'What did he say?'

'Nothing, really. We got jostled; he apologised. "Excuse me," I think were the exact words. He had a friendly smile. That struck me because he seemed a bit... serious, edgy somehow, the rest of the time. But of course I could be imagining that. You know, because I got my purse stolen. And now this.'

'Any idea what kind of foreign accent?'

'From two words?' She shook her head. 'Sorry, no.'

'Could it have been Eastern European? Balkan?'

'It could have been anything; sorry.'

He made some more notes, which she found increasingly unnerving.

'What were you doing when the theft occurred?'

She felt slightly relieved at a question she could answer. 'Watching a busker. He was telling stories and playing music.'

'A teenager watching a storyteller? Do you think there was any chance they knew one another? Working together, perhaps?'

'No, he had nothing to do with it.'

'You sound certain.'

'Oh, I...I know Jay. The busker.' She laughed nervously. 'Can you believe the same thing crossed my mind and I actually accused him of it? I could tell he didn't know what I was talking about.'

The detective nodded. 'Did you see where either of them went afterwards?'

'The young lad went off into the market as far as I remember. Jay stopped to chat with a nearby stallholder. After that I was too busy fretting about my purse to notice, I'm afraid.'

'You say you know the busker – Jay, did you say? How well?'

'We've become friends.'

'How long have you known him?'

This new line of questioning got her back up. 'A few weeks. Is this relevant? Is he involved with the case?'

As she spoke, she remembered what Matt had said about seeing Jay with someone last Saturday. She pushed the thought back down.

'Everything's relevant at this stage. But for now...' The detective smiled and seemed to back off a little. 'Can I just ask if he's ever mentioned anything else about the incident?'

'Not really, no. When I got the purse back he was pleased for me. That's all.'

'Has he ever mentioned anyone called Vinko? Have you heard the name, from him or anyone else?'

She shook her head, wondering what the friend's son was called. But she could honestly say she'd never heard the name.

The detective seemed satisfied for the time being. He asked Jay's full name and contact details, with a raised eyebrow she thought was quite unnecessary when she said she didn't know his address or phone number. She agreed to ask him to talk to them, next time she saw him.

'I don't think that lad's got anything to do with any murder,' she said as they were leaving. 'He didn't seem the type.'

'I've seen a fair few criminals with friendly smiles,' the policeman answered with a wry grin.

Marilyn felt lightheaded with relief as she watched the car bump down the lane. Her feelings veered wildly. One minute she wondered if she'd said too much, and the next she wondered why she'd been so evasive. Common sense told her if Jay had nothing to hide it didn't matter what the police knew, but her instincts had told her to be cautious. She knew so little, and the last thing she wanted to do was inadvertently cause trouble by saying the wrong thing. She'd gone far enough and she hadn't lied. Let him do the rest. She hadn't done anything wrong. As she waited for his call and the relief that would come from seeing him again, she told herself that once he'd had the chance to explain, everything would be all right and she'd wonder what on earth she'd been worrying about.

Chapter 21

It was dark by the time the bus pulled up and Marilyn felt a moment of doubt, remembering the previous Saturday when she'd waited and he wasn't there. But the sight of a familiar figure stepping down from the bus lifted her spirits. Jay looked round hesitantly and broke into a broad smile as he saw her and hurried over. Any intentions she'd been nurturing of keeping a sensible distance vanished as he hugged her. Even the faint dusty smell of his jacket was familiar and comforting. The warmth of his embrace and kiss suggested he felt the same way.

'I'm so glad to see you, Polly,' he said quietly as he stood back. 'I kept having daft moments of worrying you wouldn't be here.'

She laughed, trying not to smile inanely.

'Come on, let's get home. I'm parked over there.' She glanced round. 'You're on your own?'

'Of course.'

'That friend of yours?'

'I'd like you to meet before long, sure I would, but he could only manage a few days off work.'

She thought that sounded promising. It was going to be all right.

'In any case, I wouldn't just turn up on your doorstep with a stranger – I'd have asked you before bringing him.' He laughed. 'I'm learning, see?'

As they drove home, and she gave him an account of what she'd been doing, she sensed they were both holding any serious conversation back until later. She managed to keep her reproach about the lack of building progress lighthearted, but he was full of apology and regret all the same.

'I'll explain,' he said, echoing the previous day's phone call. 'It's a bit complicated, you know?'

'Sure. Let's eat first, then you can tell me all about… What did you say he was called?'

'Sorry, thought you knew. Vinko. He's Croatian.'

Alarm bells rang and Marilyn fell silent, concentrating on the road ahead. She'd spent the afternoon trawling the local news sites online for anything she could find. The murdered couple were described as 'from former Yugoslavia'. Other than that, there was little more than she already knew. In a clip, Nicola Radcliffe appeared to be enjoying her fifteen minutes of fame, and her exaggerated performance together with a glimpse of her uncouth husband had been almost enough in itself to convince Marilyn of the young foreigner Vinko's lily-white innocence. She reminded herself again that none of it meant he necessarily had anything to do with any crime. And of course it could be a common name where Jay's friend came from. For all she knew, even in Holdwick there might be one or two other Vinkos going about perfectly ordinary lives.

Back at the house, Jay walked in as if he'd never been away, hung his coat and hat on the row of pegs by the door and paused to savour the homely smell that filled the kitchen.

'I made us a winter stew. Even managed to salvage one or two bits from the veggie garden.'

'Well done.' He grinned and busied himself setting the table, then went through to the living room to light the fire.

She followed him a few moments later and saw him kneeling in front of the hearth, looking up at the photos as he waited for the flames to catch.

'You framed them.'

He smiled as he looked round at her, but she paused before returning the favour.

'There were one or two moments when I nearly unframed them again. Especially before you rang, when I hadn't a clue where the hell you'd got to. Whether you were coming back.'

Her voice had more of an edge than she'd intended. He stood, frowning, the early flames of the fire ticking behind him as it caught.

'You didn't really think I'd just upped and disappeared, did you?'

'I didn't know what to think.'

He glanced towards the stairs, his expression brightening. 'You had my bag as hostage.'

'How did I know you'd consider the ransom worth paying?'

'Surely you know me better than to believe I'd—'

'Jay, there are times I feel like I don't know you at all.'

She looked at him, studying the familiar lines round his eyes, the dark, hint-of-silver curls framing a face that held the same mix as ever of mischief and past cares. She tried to see if the cares were showing through more than the last time she'd seen him, but in truth he didn't seem any different.

'I admit you don't know everything *about* me—'

'I hardly know anything!'

'But you know who I am.' He tapped his breast, suddenly serious. 'In here. Whatever I tell you, please try and think of the me you allowed into your life the last couple of weeks.'

His hands were on her shoulders and there was a plea in his eyes that suggested any hopes of trivial explanations and everything being all right were futile.

'That's who I *want* to believe in,' she said.

'But you don't.'

'I didn't say that.'

'Polly, what's changed?'

'Oh, come on, Jay. Let's start with you disappearing without warning. With a mysterious "friend's son" I've been hearing things about.'

'What things? What do you mean?'

'"I'll explain," to quote a man I know. Come on, let's eat.'

They went through to the kitchen and busied themselves serving the dinner, even chinking wine glasses before they ate. She felt as if they were both trying to preserve a fragile sense of normality, this scene of sharing a meal together, as they had when things had been new, slightly strange, but straightforward. As always between them, the silence seemed companionable. She made herself break it.

'I think we've both got some explaining to do.'

He nodded. 'What is it you've heard? About Vinko?'

'I had a visit from the police this morning.'

'The police?'

She took a deep breath. 'Jay, have you heard of a couple called Boris and Anja, um, Pranitch, I think it was?'

'Pranjić?' He stopped, his fork halfway to his mouth. 'Yes. Yes, I know them. You remember I told you once about my old friend Ivan? That's his mum and dad. Vinko, who I've been with these last few days – that's his son. Their grandson.'

She stared at the candle flame as if trying to draw strength from it. 'How well did you know them?'

'Not very. I hadn't seen them for over twenty years till last year. Hang on, what do you mean, "did"?'

'I'm afraid I've got some bad news for you, Jay. They…
they're dead. There was a break-in. Murdered…bodged
burglary, probably. The police aren't sure yet. I'm sorry.'

She wished she'd found a better way of saying it.
Obviously moved, he swore quietly, stared at the table in
front of him, then ate a forkful of stew as if he needed
something to do. After a long, heavy pause he looked across
at her. 'Sorry. It's just so difficult to believe. What else did
they say? What brought them to you?'

She told him about the visit. After a brief, incredulous
laugh when she mentioned Vinko saying he lived in
Holdwick, his expression got gradually colder and harder.
As she came to an end, he turned on her.

'You ratted on him? For nicking a few *pence*? You didn't
even know it was him! What did you go accusing him to
the police for?'

She returned his angry stare.

'I wasn't accusing,' she said, indignant. 'I reported the
theft; that's natural isn't it? I… I didn't think it would come
to anything.'

'Didn't think! You even accused me, didn't you?'

'Calm down. No, of course I didn't. The opposite. I told
them—'

'I mean when we first met.'

'I didn't know you then.'

'You said earlier you don't know me now!'

'I'm sorry.'

His head was down and he was eating as if it were the
last meal he was ever going to get. His behaviour hurt her
and she could only hope it was fuelled by shock at the news.

'But,' she continued, 'but you're implying that it *was*
him. And you know him. So I wasn't far wrong, was I?' He
looked up at her, his face unreadable. 'He stole from me,

Jay. What was I supposed to do? Find him, take him aside and listen to his bloody life story?'

He almost smiled, then sighed, relaxing slightly.

'I'm sorry,' she said again. 'If I'd known, I—'

'No, I'm the one should apologise.' He ran a hand through his hair. 'I'm sorry I took it out on you, Pol. Forgive me. It's a lot to take in. Anja. Boris. Dead. But I'm an idiot – I've been dying to see you. Whatever's happened – particularly given what's happened – the last thing I want is to argue.' She nodded, fighting back sudden tears. 'Listen, I only met him last Saturday. We've never "worked" together. I wouldn't do anything like that; you must know—'

'You seem to think I know a lot,' she said, and their eyes met, discharging the tension.

'So… I guess it's about time I told you who he is and where he fits into my life.' She nodded again.

'It's a long story.' He put his knife and fork down neatly on his empty plate and reached over to clear hers away.

'Leave the plates. No procrastinating.'

She gestured through to the living room. As they rose from the table he hugged her; she sensed a strange mix of reassurance and fear. He went to sit in his fireside chair and started to fill his pipe.

'I'm worried about him,' he announced. 'Even more so now.'

'Stop rambling. Tell me straight. So he's your mate Ivan's son. Why can't he be doing all this worrying?'

'Ivan? He died, must be eighteen years ago. Before Vinko was even born. That's just it, see. He's on his own, Vinko. *Completely* on his own given what I've just heard. Except— Sorry, right…' He looked at her apologetically. 'This is difficult.'

'Go on.'

Jay nodded and cleared his throat as if about to make a speech. She wondered if she should offer to get them a drink.

'Vinko came up and introduced himself to me last Saturday,' he said, delaying the decision for her. 'Said he'd seen me busking and recognised me from a photo his mother had. I believe him. I think. He needs my help to get back some money he's owed. And I've got to help him – for one thing because it's my fault he's owed it. Don't get me wrong, that's not why he came to me. I don't think he even knew till I told him.'

He glanced across as if checking she was still with him.

'He… I just felt for him. I want to make things right. You'd understand if you met him. He's got his problems but I'm sure he's a good lad deep down. I went off with him and then…then I missed the last bus home. I hoped you'd understand that I couldn't phone you, although I… Listen, the reason we went off goes a lot further back. It's hard to know where to begin…'

He studied the worn fabric of his trousers, put his filled pipe down and placed the leather tobacco pouch on the arm of the chair, resting his hand on it and fiddling with the fastener. 'So. Begin at the beginning.'

Much of what he told her, about his friend's Yugoslav family and the two of them going to Croatia, she'd heard in fragments of stories before. This time the fragments came together. And this time, she realised she was actually starting to believe him.

'Listen, you remember the wealthy heiress I mentioned?' Marilyn nodded, though she certainly hadn't believed that one. 'There was a bit of poetic licence and exaggeration, but that was Ivan's aunt Zora.'

Jay paused and Marilyn studied him in the soft firelight.

'Really. The house in the country – that was hers. Dalmatia. It had been her family home. Her parents were killed in the second world war by the Ustaše – the fascists. You ever heard of Jasenovac?' Marilyn shook her head. 'It was a concentration camp. Political prisoners like Zora and Anja's parents were supposed to fare better than the Serbs, Gypsies and Jews who were sent there to be killed but… they died anyway. Zora was a baby and Anja only a small child, and they'd been sent away to live with relatives for safety; they only learned what really happened as they grew up. Anja reacted like most people would, by staying out of trouble and eventually moving abroad, but Zora…it fired her up. Shortly before we went, she reclaimed her family's house and land, which had been confiscated but because of where it was had stood deserted for years. She had money, too. She kept it abroad, and added to it over the years. For when she needed it. When she could do something useful with it. Remember? Do you believe me now?'

He flashed her a smile, then looked away.

'The other part was true, too. About her nasty-piece-of-work lover. Well, it wasn't as black-and-white as that, of course. Not at first. He was a big noise in the local territorial defence force; he'd got to a position of authority quite young and she respected him for that. Fair enough. But as the situation got worse it went to his head, like power does. His activities got increasingly irregular. But at first… There's no doubt he was charismatic and Zora was persuasive about being ready to defend her country's independence. All the more so after the Serbs declared their autonomous region and the violence started. And the refugees started coming, Croats from the Serb-held areas. She eventually had her house full of refugees from up country.

'And before long Lek had us trained up and ready to fight. I still can't believe how we got swept into it. No, I shouldn't keep saying "we". When I was telling Vinko he accused me of blaming his father. I don't – I've got no one to blame but myself. I mean, I believed in their cause, but war…?'

He fell silent, staring into the fire. She noticed he was biting his lower lip with a slight shake of his head, like he always did when she asked him something he wouldn't – or couldn't – talk about. Like the couple of times she'd ventured to ask him about his nightmares, or when he'd dismissed the scar on his belly as a routine operation that had gone wrong.

'You fought with them?'

He nodded. 'I fought,' he said slowly, 'and killed. The Homeland War, they call it. I'd gone with Ivan, chosen to live there, even if only for a while.' The fire reflected tiny pinpricks of flame in his eyes. 'The fight for their homeland, their independence, was mine, too.'

She wanted to ask more. But there was part of her didn't want to know. She couldn't help feeling that the Jay she felt close to had been snatched away from her. By whom, by what? His own past? Hadn't that always been there? *Think of the me you allowed into your life…*

She said his name as if to anchor herself. He looked round at her.

'I know, I know. It's hard. I've spent all these years trying to put it behind me. But…I started telling Vinko – it's about his dad, after all – though I only got so far.' He shook his head. 'It's also about me and you. I realised I wasn't being fair. I…I feel a lot for you and… Well, it's wrong to let us get too close to one another if I'm not being honest with you. Though you don't know how difficult it is to make myself talk about it.'

206

'I can imagine.'

He stood, moved to stand in front of the fire, looking at her. She felt the cold as he blocked out the heat.

'Thanks for trying,' he said. He ran his hand through his hair again and left it there half-covering his face. She wanted to stand, too, to reach out and touch him, but something in his manner stopped her.

'I'm getting round to Vinko, honestly, Polly.'

He broke the mood suddenly with a rueful smile, rubbing his arms through the sleeves of his jumper. 'But… can we get a hot drink first?'

She nodded and he went through to the kitchen. As she listened to the homely sound of him filling the kettle and rattling crockery, she imagined the courage it must be taking him to tell her the truth – assuming this was the truth. She'd known he was haunted by something, reassured herself that whatever it was didn't matter because he'd put it behind him. But now it wasn't behind him; it was here, between them. He'd killed people and destroyed their homes in a war. She told herself lots of people did, and got on with their lives and loves afterwards.

She followed him into the kitchen. As they waited for the kettle to boil he came over to her and put a hand hesitantly on her arm. She touched his cheek, thinking how awkward they'd become with one another, and as if she'd given him some tacit consent he took her in his arms and held her in silence. She returned his embrace, overwhelmed by the depth of emotion she sensed in him but still knew so little about. There was still a vague possibility that all this was in his imagination, a story woven from the reminiscences of people he'd met on the streets. She no longer knew whether she wanted stories or the truth.

Back in the living room, with two mugs of coffee, wisps of smoke from Jay's newly lit pipe escaped to explore the room as the main stream was drawn to the chimney.

'So are you going to tell me what that's got to do with now? Vinko?' she prompted, to stop him from closing off.

He looked round and his expression lit up as if pleasantly surprised she was in the room with him.

'I wanted you to know why he matters to me. Ivan saved my life. Seriously. Though at the time I hated him for it. Also seriously. And he was killed before I could make it up to him. So…Vinko's his son and my chance.'

He told her about his meeting with Vinko, their visit to the Pranjićs. She bit her lip but hoped she was keeping her expression impassive as Jay talked, confirming the extent of their involvement with people she'd only heard of as murder victims.

'So this money you're talking about – that was Zora's?'

'You got it. Remember I told you she'd got someone to bring it away? That was me.'

'You said it was someone else.'

'I'm sorry. I had to make it sound unreal, had to distance myself. Though it feels like it *was* someone else. But it happened, more or less like I said. I couldn't believe she'd trust me with something like that, but she did. I'd got so's I couldn't handle it. Everything I'd got myself involved in. It all felt so wrong. Things we did. *I* did. I couldn't go on.' He ran a hand though his hair. 'But deserting them would have been even worse. Zora knew how I was feeling – she always knew – and gave me a job to do, an excuse to leave. At great risk to herself, as I've learned recently. And so I did leave. I don't know much about finance, I was scared of the contacts she gave me and I daresay someone else could've done it better, but in the end I had a tidy amount in an account over here. It's also true that she told me if anything happened to her, and if…if Ivan died too, I was to keep it. And they *were* killed, and here I was, out of the way, safe… On my own. Feeling like I couldn't do anything for the blood on my hands.'

He held a hand up and stared at it as if expecting to see real dried-on blood clogging the lines in his skin. He drew on his pipe like an anaesthetic.

'So…I had this money and no one to give it back to. As I've told you before, I eventually borrowed it, put it down on the house I'd been renting since I got back to England. Zora had given me a letter. A kind of will. But I always intended to pay it off – the money and everything else – and I did. A bit at a time. Literally, and, when I'd failed once too many times to hold down a decent job, with this penance of a lifestyle.'

Her face must have betrayed her surprise; he laughed.

'You think it's romantic, don't you? Happy-go-lucky, raggle-taggle gypsies and all that. I won't deny it has its good points. But…' He shrugged. 'Anyway. A few years ago I finally satisfied myself I'd got it all paid back from the rents and whatever else, with what any impartial observer might call reasonable interest. And it sat there burning a hole in the bank account. The only person who could possibly be entitled to it, apart from me and I couldn't accept that, was Anja, Ivan's mum. Zora had said she wasn't to see a penny of it – there was enough hatred in *that* family to fuel a war, all right – but I spent ages trying and failing to think of alternatives and in the end, after a ton of soul-searching, rightly or wrongly, off I went to see Anja and Boris. Wrongly, as it turned out. A few months later – last weekend, in fact – I discovered that Ivan had a son.'

'You didn't know?'

'When I came back to this country I was in a right state. My best friend despised me. I hated myself, too. I drank him, all of them, out of mind. I don't remember much about that time so I guess it worked. I met some surprisingly kind people who one way or another stopped me from going too far down the road to self-destruction. I should have gone back, to find Ivan, or to make my peace with my father and sister, but I couldn't. I was scared of facing them, and I hated myself for that, too. I'm not proud of any of it. It was a couple of years at least before I got my act together enough to do anything sensible. I did go back to Croatia, after the war had ended. Didn't stay. Hardly anyone I knew was still around. There'd been an attack on Zora's place; she died soon after and Ivan was killed in action towards the end of the war. That was all I needed or wanted to know. I couldn't believe my friend was dead. Dead without me having a chance to make my peace with him.'

He turned from the fire to look at her, his face half lit by the warm glow of the flames.

'But I was supposed to be talking about Vinko, wasn't I? I didn't know about him until last week. And I gave his inheritance away.' He shook his head. 'And then, like an idiot, I went and told him I'd done so.'

'He must be pretty upset about it.'

Marilyn felt strangely detached, piecing it together as if it had nothing to do with her, or even Jay.

'I'm sure he is, though he doesn't show it. I think he trusts me. I suppose I should take comfort from that. God knows why he does, though – I can't pretend I know how to help him. I'm trying, but in truth I haven't a clue what to do next. Especially not now. I was going to meet him this coming weekend, go back to see his family, apologise

210

and beg them to take him in. But now... They're dead. Murdered? Tell me I was dreaming when you told me that; hallucinating, anything?'

'I wish I could.'

'Oh, to hell with it all!' He stood abruptly, walked through to the kitchen, came back with a whisky bottle and two glasses.

'Jay...'

'OK, so I just told you about boozing myself to destruction. Don't fret – that was years of it; this is a couple of drinks.'

He poured two glasses and handed her one. He downed half of his in one gulp.

'I knew he was in trouble – he told me – but this makes it ten times worse! And I haven't a fucking clue what to do about it!' He downed the rest of his whisky. She watched him in silence, fingers tightening around her own glass. 'I'm sorry, Polly,' he said more calmly. 'None of this is your fault. I shouldn't be shouting. I'm not shouting *at* you, love.'

'It's all right,' she said. She found his sudden apology reassuring despite herself. Dreading the reply, she asked, 'What trouble?'

He poured himself another whisky, took a more measured sip.

'Where to start? At first I just wanted to help him get his money, help him get his life together. That's where we went, to Winchester, to pick up Zora's papers, some kind of proof. But then I found out he's got no legal identity. His mother was a refugee at Zora's, that's how she met Ivan; after the war she left the country for Germany with nothing. She never even registered his birth because she was afraid they'd take him away, terrified of losing him. Can you imagine? That poor girl. I can't imagine the life she must have led, not only what she went through herself, but having to bring a little kid up like that, the only chance of medical care some backstreet quack, getting dragged down into a mire of prostitution and drugs… Anyway. Vinko seems… accepting. But what else can he do? What can I, what can anyone do? She's dead now. Gone. It's one more tragedy. So…' he sighed. 'So there I am, thinking we can go and find an immigration lawyer or whatever, but he won't. He's terrified. I eventually managed to coax out why.

'There's this guy, Novak; Vinko calls him his uncle. He's never explained how he's related, but there was a limit to the number of questions I could ask and there were more important ones. Novak found them, too late for his mother, as Vinko puts it. Offered to bring them away, but she was seriously ill – terminally ill, as it turned out – and Vinko had a job. So they stayed put. It turns out this "job" was with some kind of forger, and shortly after his mother died, the place got busted. Vinko was lucky he wasn't in work at the time, but it left him high and dry – and scared. He got back in touch with Novak who smuggled him over here. Not an ideal situation to be taking to the immigration authorities.

'So he's got a crappy bedsit and a no-questions-asked sweatshop job. Oh, and a paper round to add to the fun. No surprise, then, that he wants to put the past behind him and make something of himself. He's artistic, too – got talent as far as I can see. You'll relate to that. Well, it seems this Novak disappeared for a while, but he's back on the scene now. Vinko was getting messages while I was there. He's being dragged into something he doesn't want to do. Some deal, he says. He wouldn't tell me what but he swears he's told Novak to get stuffed. I just hope… Polly, why did you say the police had linked him with Anja and Boris?'

'The fingerprints – presumably from your visit. And he turned up at their old house looking for them.'

'Nothing more?'

She shook her head. 'Not at this stage.'

'Thank goodness. He says he'd decided to go and find them on impulse – I swear I believe him – after hearing me play. Makes sense – I learned some of those tunes from Zora and I daresay his mother would have done the same. You know, the day you…saw him.'

He looked at her warily. All he'd said made her deeply uneasy, but she remembered Vinko's brief smile and found she could empathise.

'I can see now why you were defensive earlier,' she said. 'There I was joking about getting his life story. I didn't know I was about to. I hope we can find a way to help him.'

'We?'

'Why not?'

He smiled, for what felt like the first time that evening.

'So what are you going to tell them?' she asked.

'Who?'

'The police wanted you to get in touch, remember.'

'Oh no. No chance. All I'd have to tell them is that I didn't even notice the guy you described in the crowd. And that I've never heard of Anja or Boris Pranjić.'

'Won't they trace you to them anyway?' She tried to keep the exasperation from her voice. 'If you gave them the money?'

He looked at her steadily. 'No,' he said quietly. 'I'm confident they won't.'

'But you can't lie! It's a serious case.'

'If I don't speak to them I won't lie.'

'And what am *I* supposed to say?'

'All right, I'll leave for a while. Disappear. Till it's over.

You haven't seen me. They can solve the sodding case without me or Vinko because I swear neither of us has anything to do with it.'

'But you've only just got back. You can't leave!'

He got up and shoved the poker into the fire, sending up a shower of sparks, before adding another log.

'What I can't do,' he told the flames, 'is go to the police. There's no way I could just rake up all that I've told you to… to *strangers*. And I'd lose Vinko. He'd never trust me again.'

He remained crouched before the hearth, head hanging. His back was like a wall. She moved to kneel beside him and put an arm round his shoulder. He collapsed into her embrace, burying his head on her shoulder. 'Can you understand that?'

'Of course,' she murmured. 'So what *are* you going to do?'

There was a long silence. He heaved a sigh. When it came there was a catch in his voice.

'I don't know. I just don't know.'

There is victory in the air as they hurry towards the rendezvous point by the barn. Shots fired into the air. Whooping and shouting. He feels on the outside. Lek's vengeful violence has left him cold. Ivan, walking ahead of him, turns and beckons through the slowly clearing smoke. He nods; increases his pace only slightly. A shot whines dangerously close to his head. Then another. Driven by terror, he is crouched tense and alert by a pile of rubble before he even realises. It shouldn't be happening. This village is won, isn't it? Through unnaturally clear air he sees an injured man across the street, lying almost motionless in a darkening pool of blood. Lost in his agony; there is no way…and he has no gun. Šojka looks up. Backing into the shadows behind the slumped figure, trainers stained by the man's blood, is a boy he recognises. The one he spared, sent running to safety, only a few moments ago. Nothing is fair.

The weapon looks too big for the boy and he seems scared of it. Probably not; they grow up with hunting rifles round here. His own gun ready but not raised, he holds the boy's gaze, unsure if he recognises him.

'Sjećaš li se me?'

The words come out wrong, but it's the contact that matters. The gun in the boy's grasp wavers. Or is it an echo of his own previous gesture? Escape while you can.

He stands slowly and takes a hesitant step forward.

'Give me that. I take you to find your family.' Understand me. Please understand me.

'You killed my father.'

The boy gestures with his head towards the small square.

'Not me.' It wasn't me. 'We can find your mother. Someone. Safety. Put that down and come to me.'

The boy continues to stare at him over the gun.

'Please.'

Recklessly, he relaxes his grip on his own weapon to hold out a hand. The boy's eyes are wary. He moves the muzzle of his gun imperceptibly – lowering it? A sign of trust?

A thunderous shot fills the air and the boy jerks sideways. He falls against the wall, blood running from the hole in his head, still clutching the stolen rifle.

Šojka stares, the aftershock holding him rigid.

Ivan runs up, grabs him in a manic embrace.

'Thank God you're all right!'

He continues to look, sickened, at the raw mess that was the boy he'd tried to save.

'I'm sorry, mate.' Ivan's voice is calmer now, deferential. 'Gets to me every time, too. But you can't dwell on it or you'd be a dead man yourself.'

Chapter 22

Hands shoved deep in his pockets, Vinko walked past the bus stop. Saving the fare wouldn't make much difference; he simply needed to keep moving. As soon as the hated building was out of sight he broke into a run. He sprinted blindly, simply to relieve the tension and feel the wind on his face, some instinct keeping him safe at road junctions and preventing him from mowing down passers-by.

He reached a small park and let himself go fully, charging across the grass. At a deserted children's play area he slowed and stopped, chest heaving. His head playing images of neat, well cared-for little kids filing into classrooms, their toddler brothers and sisters waiting impatiently for mothers to bring them here, he threw himself onto the flaking roundabout, kicked the ground violently hard and lay back watching the sky spin. His hands gripped the rails on either side, fighting the force that wanted to fling him outwards, dash him to the ground. The roundabout slowed and he struggled to kick the ground again, keep himself moving. Seeing as there was no one else to do it for him. One day he'd have his own, big enough to lie comfortably across, with a motor to keep it spinning. Yes, if ever he had a garden to put it in, he'd do that. As it was, the awkward shuffling and shoving soon outweighed the buzz. He heaved himself up and lit a cigarette, getting no pleasure or comfort beyond the satisfaction of a need.

Walking away, he tried again to phone Jay. Even though he knew there was no one at the other end laughing at him, no one had physically turned their back, the answer message sent a wave of anger through him. He glanced back at the playground. The stationary roundabout had no more release to offer. He paused, opened a blank text message, wondered where to begin and saved the blank to Drafts. Pointless, but wasn't everything? What did any of it matter? Why did it bother him? He never wanted that job anyway. It wasn't the job itself – it was that after phoning in sick for just three days they could simply turn round and tell him to piss off. That was how much he mattered. There were always plenty of others ready to do crap work for next to no money. He'd been reliable, done his best. It wasn't worth his best but he had his pride. He'd phoned in sick once before – genuinely sick, beginning to wonder what he'd do if it came to needing a doctor – and there hadn't been a problem. A whim. He simply didn't matter. Even Choudhury had found a boy to take his place.

He walked along streets he'd never seen before, totally lost and enjoying the feeling. He had nowhere he needed to go. No decent job to look for that wouldn't sooner or later involve a national insurance number, forms, references, whatever. He was weary of the black market, exploitation, risks, hiding. Jay hadn't got anywhere, for all his questions, all his show of concern. So he'd soon be out on the street. He should be looking for a squat instead of wandering aimlessly, getting angry with ghosts. He tried Jay's number again. Probably switched off so he could enjoy sweaty hours of fucking his woman undisturbed. He should have known, should have turned him in to Novak after all and at least got something out of it. What the hell had got into him? He thought of that train journey with embarrassment. Must still have been pissed from the night before. But it didn't bother him too much. After all, the past didn't matter; he hadn't spilled anything important. He had nothing important to spill.

Eventually he came to a main road and wormed his way onto a crowded bus, dodging the fare. He spent the journey to Keighley with half a mind alert for an inspector, the other half planning what he'd say when he arrived. He didn't need Jay this time. He wondered why he'd ever thought he did.

The long walk from the centre of the town was becoming familiar. Perhaps that meant something, though the little estate seemed no more welcoming than it had the first time. He made himself walk on. As he reached the cul-de-sac he was heading for, he stopped abruptly, heart thumping. He saw a white van, and a police car was parked near his grandparents' house. He was about to move on, annoyed at having to leave and wait till it was safe to come back, when he noticed the striped tape flapping in the breeze, guarding the neat garden. Two strangers talking on the pavement outside. An air of desolation from windows with curtains tightly drawn in broad daylight. Filled with panic and wild questions, he managed to rein himself in and walk on with an air of unsuspicious calm until he was out of sight. Then he was running again.

Back at the town centre the sight of the bus station and thoughts of Holdwick made him give Jay one more try. The mocking sound of the voicemail announcer hurt his ears. He went to a steamy café to get a coffee and gather his thoughts. The smell of cooking made his mouth water but he told himself he couldn't afford it. Someone had left a newspaper on the seat next to him; he felt as if everyone in the place was staring at him as he picked it up. It was no longer headline news, but in a corner of the front page was a small picture of the scene he'd just left behind. He fought with the flapping paper to get to the main report inside.

Reading as quickly as he could through the paragraph beneath a grainy photo of a smiling Boris and Anja, he registered *murder* and his own name. They were looking for him. He stared at the page. Who else but Jay would have connected his name with theirs? How many times had he told Vinko, *It would be for your own good*? What the hell good did he think this would do? Even if he'd dropped his name accidentally, whoever to, there was no excuse. Fumbling through a raw mix of sorrow, hatred and anger, he folded the paper roughly and made for the door, narrowly avoiding the waitress who was bringing his drink.

'Sorry. I must go. No more time for coffee.'

What good was a coffee without a smoke anyway?

On the way back to Bradford he came up with a plan of sorts. This place meant nothing to him. No one meant anything to him. He'd go and gather his things together, get some sleep and the next day head for London. More people there, a bigger chance of finding work, contacts to make, perhaps even a way of getting abroad. Going home. Real home. Whatever that meant. It wasn't much of a plan, but he didn't have a better one.

As he neared his street he looked resentfully at the shop, the bell over the door seeing off a woman with a bulging carrier in either hand. People coming and going on either side of the road, people with ordinary jobs to go to, ordinary lives. He walked on. A car slowed and came to a halt just behind him. He ignored it. A door banged, footsteps, a voice calling his name. He quickened his pace. So did the footsteps. A hand on his shoulder.

'Vinko, lad, wait on. Where've you been hiding?'

Despite the pleasure of hearing his own language he wasn't fooled by his uncle's false matiness. There was no genuine concern in that voice. He turned slowly to face him.

'None of your business. I told you I've had it with you. Fuck off and leave me alone.'

He turned away. Novak grabbed his arm.

'Not so fast. I want to talk to you – how about you come back with me?' He gestured to the car. 'Get in.'

Vinko refused to move.

'What's up? Been down the job centre, got yourself a better offer?'

It must have been Novak got him the sack.

'What is it to you?'

'You were supposed to be doing something for me, that's what. What was all that bollocks at the weekend anyway?'

He shrugged. 'Thought it was him but I was wrong.'

'You're lying.'

No denying it. Instead Vinko looked at him levelly. 'Lost patience, did you? Decided to pay them a visit yourself?'

Novak returned his stare. 'I don't know what you're talking about.'

'Whatever. Leave me out of this. I know about the man you're working for.'

'I work for myself.'

'You know who I mean. Lek.'

'Then you'll know he's a man you want on your side.' He paused, grip slackening slightly. Vinko pulled free, about to walk away, but Novak's next words held him. 'Your father would have told you the same. You know what a good friend he was to your father?'

Vinko shook his head. He didn't want to hear it.

'That's right. They were close. If it hadn't been for the war, if your dad was still alive now, he'd back me up. I don't know what you've been hearing but you're man enough to judge for yourself, aren't you? Ever since Lek heard I knew

220

Ivan's boy he's been eager to meet you. When he knows the situation you're in he'll want to see you right.'

Yeah, right. 'Why? What price?'

Novak shook his head sadly.

'You're bound to think like that. I'm partly to blame, I admit. Friendship, Vinko, that's why.' He stepped aside to let a man pulled by a German Shepherd walk past. 'Look, this isn't the place. I wanted to see you anyway – called at the factory yesterday to find you and couldn't believe they'd dumped you like that. I can sort you out with something else. Come back to my place and we can talk.'

Vinko glanced away towards his street. Perhaps his uncle hadn't ratted on him after all. Or perhaps he was lying. What did he care? He didn't want another dead-end job in this craphole city. He didn't want to get involved again with Novak, especially if he had anything to do with what had happened to his grandparents. And he didn't need another so-called friend of his father's. The last one had let him down. And yet… What was there to lose? He had nothing. If he didn't like what he heard, he could come back here, pack his stuff and still be away to London. Possibly even with money in his pocket.

'I can run you back later,' Novak said. 'No problem.'

Vinko got in the car.

Chapter 23

'You should have woken me.' Jay smiled as if the previous evening hadn't happened.

She watched him walk over to join her at the kitchen table, savouring an uncomplicated moment of simply being together.

'You were sleeping so peacefully. Eventually.' They exchanged a look. 'I thought you deserved a lie-in.'

'I'm surprised you think I deserve anything good. In the cold light of day.'

It was impossible to tell how serious he was. She got up to get him a coffee, kissing him warmly as she sat close beside him. 'Good enough to be going on with?'

He grinned. 'So what's the plan today?'

'I was going to ask you.'

'I thought we could sort the windows out. Plan what we're going to do with the rough bits of the walls; do a bit of pointing. Once we're sure it's weathertight we can start properly on the inside.'

'But what about—'

'Vinko and I agreed to meet at the weekend; he probably wouldn't thank me for turning up sooner. Not with the news I've got. Give him another couple of days' blissful ignorance.' He paused, sadness breaking through the façade. She took his hand and squeezed it. 'By which time I might actually have thought about what to suggest.' He reached for his coffee mug. 'In the meantime there's nothing like a bit of work to concentrate the mind. Let's just do our own stuff. Me and you. For a little while. That is… That is if it's all right with you?'

Pretending normality was tempting. The kind of strange normality Jay had come to mean to her. She couldn't deny that what he'd told her was deeply unsettling, but during a couple of long hours awake the previous night, as he slept apparently peacefully beside her, she'd found it actually made her feel closer to him. The fact that he'd put away his pretence. His veneer of larger-than-life unreality was fun, and attractive, but often frustrating. Now she thought she understood. Things were hardly going to be easy and she wondered what she was getting herself into, but nothing in life was straightforward, after all. She even realised she felt protective.

It was almost midday by the time they set off to choose the windows and pick up some other supplies. It felt good to be working on the barn again, to think her workshop was getting another stage nearer to completion. She enjoyed having Jay to discuss ideas with and when he suggested fitting a skylight in place of his temporary repair to the storm-damaged roof, mentally she added another on the other side. Imagining the space that much more bright and airy, on top of the prospect of having somewhere of her own to work in, almost dispelled the clouds they were both deliberately keeping at bay.

They were about halfway to Holdwick when Jay's phone buzzed. She glanced over.

'Missed calls. Vinko's been trying to get me. I forgot we were out of signal.'

'You get used to it.'

'Looks like he tried several times. I hope there isn't a problem.'

'Give him a call.'

223

It was strange to hear him leave a message in a language she didn't understand.

'Weird. He's always got his phone on him.'

'Didn't you say he'd be at work?'

That seemed to reassure him, and as they continued on to the builders' merchant his talk was all windows and helping her decide on the colour of paint for her newly-cleared spare room. Once there, he appeared to enjoy choosing with her, but she sensed he was becoming increasingly distracted.

'This isn't working, is it?' she said as they wheeled a trolley with cement and a large can of sunshine yellow out to the car, having arranged for the windows and skylights to be delivered the next day.

'What isn't?'

He lugged the supplies into the back of the car.

'Pretending nothing's happening.'

He stopped on his way round to the passenger seat and looked at her. 'I don't see what else we can do right now.'

'You could tell the police what you know.'

'I don't know anything that would make any difference.'

He got in and closed the door. She took her place behind the wheel. 'Wouldn't it be best in the long run? For Vinko? I mean, it might be difficult at first, but surely they'll help sort him out. Get him a social worker—'

'Get him a sentence in the company of worse types than the ones he's already mixed up with. He only just trusts me now. I want to talk to him first.'

She felt annoyed with him, and scared, but he was unmoveable and it seemed the only way would be to tell them herself. Which would mean betraying him. She set off wordlessly. He tried the number again, shook his head. As they passed a newsagent he suggested they stop to buy a

224

paper. He waited in the car; when she got back in he seemed as worried as she felt.

'This just came from Vinko. I haven't a clue what to make of it.'

He waved his phone in front of her with a two-word text message on the screen.

Ne vjer

'What does that mean?'

'It's incomplete, hard to tell. I think it must be "don't believe". Could be telling me not to, or "I don't believe", anyone doesn't believe. What's he playing at?'

'He could have pressed the wrong button. Or got interrupted. You'll probably get something else in a minute.'

'I hope so.' He shook his head. 'In the meantime, let's catch up on developments.'

He spread out the paper and they leaned together with the pages propped against the dashboard to read the piece about the murder. There was little beyond what she already knew. A neighbour had heard gunshots in the small hours. Two men seen running away. The police looking for the youth they'd just been talking about, to help them with their enquiries. Jay swore to himself and she looked across at him.

'Vesna Novak.'

She'd just seen the name herself. 'Their daughter, poor woman. You must know her.'

'Used to, 'course I did, but not by her married name. Novak. Same name as the guy Vinko was on about.'

He fell to staring at the photo of the couple heading the page. She followed his gaze. It felt strange to be confronted by an article like this one about someone with whom she had a connection, however vague. It made her sad she'd never have chance to meet them. The silence was broken

225

only by the slight rustling of the newspaper. Jay remained distant. She felt she had to say something.

'Could you talk to her? Do you think she'd know anything?'

'Know anything about what?' he snapped. 'I'm sure she knows her parents have been murdered. It's clear she doesn't know who by.'

'About your precious Vinko and her bloody husband!'

He stared at her. She'd gone too far. Shouldn't have shouted. But he wasn't the only one to be stressed by all this! He folded the newspaper roughly without taking his eyes off her. She was about to mutter something appeasing when he broke into a smile.

'I deserved that, didn't I?' He leaned over and kissed her hard. 'I'm sorry, Polly. You were right. I've got to stop running away.'

The knocking echoed loudly through the workshop and she felt a cold fear. She was still hesitating when the door opened and her hand reached out for a nearby cutting tool from the bench. The figure was momentarily silhouetted in the light of the doorway, but as soon as he strode in she recognised him. Only Matt. She released her grip, feeling slightly foolish.

'You OK? You look a bit tense.'

'I'm fine, thanks,' she said. 'Come in, sit down.'

He pulled over a chair and sat across the workbench from her. 'I've only just realised you're here – saw the light on. Your car isn't outside.'

'No.' She deliberately ignored his fishing and paused to enjoy the effect. 'What can I do for you?'

'I had the police round earlier.'

'Oh?' She laughed. 'What have you been up to?'

He scowled. 'I think you know what it's about. If not, you should.'

'Go on.'

He told her about the door-to-door enquiries among town-centre businesses and anyone who might have been on the marketplace two weeks ago, the day her purse was stolen. Looking for information about Vinko.

'They came to see me yesterday,' she said and told him about her purse. It felt like a confession as she explained it was probably her description that had made the link.

'That was you? You never told me you'd had anything nicked.'

She bristled. 'Sorry. I'll remember to give you a full report next time.'

'Only saying. By the way, did you catch up with your friend? Jay?'

'Yes, I got him. Thanks for passing his message on. Eventually.'

'Does he know anything?'

'Why should he?' But she remembered Matt saying he'd seen Jay meeting someone – Vinko, she knew now – last Saturday.

'So it wasn't this lad they're looking for that I saw him with?' She said nothing. 'I was worried you'd mind me mentioning you in connection with him, but if you've spoken to them yourself... So is there anything in it? Murderous intrigue or merely a casual fan-to-busker encounter?'

'Oh, stop being so melodramatic! Intrigue! I don't see why you even had to mention it. Jay bumped into an old friend, is all.'

'An old friend called Vinko? Whom the police want to talk to?'

'Just because they want to talk to him doesn't mean he had anything to do with it.'

'It *is* him? Christ, Lynnie, I was only winding you up. I suppose you've had Daniel Freeman, or whatever his name is, round for drinks too.'

'Never heard of him.'

'I'm sure you haven't. Your Jay probably has, though. Another one the police are looking for.'

'What's the connection?'

'They're hardly likely to tell me, are they? Just asked if I'd heard the name.'

'They never mentioned it to me.'

'Probably only just come to light.'

He was fiddling with a piece of paper, rolling it up one way, flattening it and rolling it the other. She wished he wouldn't.

'Oh, what have you got yourself involved in?'

'Whoa, steady. "Involved"? You're jumping to far too many conclusions.'

Matt shifted in his seat; leaned forward.

'Because you're not being straight with me?'

'Straight? I don't *have* to tell you anything, OK?'

Her phone rang. Jay. She glanced from the screen to Matt and turned it off. 'It'll wait,' she said, a silent apology going through her mind. She'd call him as soon as Matt had gone.

'So if you're being straight, tell me why you appear to be covering up for the little shit who stole your bag.'

'Purse. That was all. Only took the cash at that.' She shrugged. 'He needed the money, I suppose. I'm not judging till I know the details. That's one thing you used to like about me, remember? Anyway, I'm not covering up; I didn't know he was anything to do with Jay when I saw the police yesterday.'

'And today? I take it you've gone to them with all you know.'

'I'm leaving that to Jay. Seeing as he's the one who knows it.'

'Is that where he is now?'

She felt like telling him it was none of his business, but knew that was even more likely to make him stir. 'He's gone to talk to someone first.'

Matt laughed incredulously. 'Getting their story straight, hey?'

'Nothing of the sort.'

'You haven't lent him our jeep, have you?'

'*My* jeep. Hasn't been "ours" for months, remember. Why shouldn't I? You think I'll never see it again, is that it? It's fine. And as for the rest, I'll tell you when there's something worth you knowing. Until then it's... It's honestly nothing for you to worry about.'

He gave the scrap of paper another twist. 'But that's just it; I *am* worried. You look worried. I can tell.' She thought it was a pity she couldn't remember him showing such insight and concern when they'd been together. 'You're getting yourself dragged into trouble. You don't have to. I understand that he's your "friend" and you don't want to do wrong by him, but if he was a decent friend he wouldn't be putting you in this position. To my mind it'd be perfectly reasonable to ask him to leave until all this is sorted out. If you know nothing you don't have to cover anything up – or betray him, or however you see it. OK, so he's helping with your building work, but that needn't matter – you can stay here as long as you like. Sorry if I gave you the impression it was a problem. It isn't.'

He looked slightly embarrassed as his little speech came to an end. And so he should, she thought as the anger rose inside her.

'I thought you and Lucy seemed happy. Or is it just that you can't let go? I can't believe you'd stoop to such a blatant display of jealousy.'

'Jealousy? You probably don't want to hear this, Marilyn, but I still *care* about you. You've fallen for this guy. You're blinded.'

She rolled her eyes. 'And you know, do you? I've had enough! I appreciate your concern, but I can assure you I'm – we're – fine.' She stood up, waved a hand over the workbench. 'Now, I'm here because I've got stuff to do. Believe me, it's perfectly safe to leave me here on my own.'

After he left she stood for a long moment watching the door. She remembered Jay's call and immediately tried his number. A glance at her watch told her he'd be in the middle of his meeting with Vesna; he must have switched it off. She glanced at the door again. She recalled Matt saying he'd mentioned her to the police, and wondered how much he'd said. What if they wanted to see her again? She'd have to make the choice between lying or betrayal. Would it actually be such a betrayal? If they had nothing to hide, what was the big problem? Not for the first time, she wondered if Jay was as sure as he made out that Vinko wasn't involved. Perhaps he was the one who was blinded, by the memory of his oldest friend, and whatever else was going through his troubled mind.

She tensed as she heard the door to the main building bang. Footsteps. Heading up the stairs, presumably to the shop. She let out a sigh of relief. It was no good; she wasn't going to concentrate on anything. She phoned Sue who said she'd be delighted to see her that evening. Her friend's voice relaxed Marilyn immediately and she found herself saying more than she'd intended about what had been happening.

'You know, I think Matt's got a point.'

'Oh, not you as well!'

Marilyn wished she hadn't said too much before she'd gathered her thoughts properly.

'It's no secret that I was never Matt's biggest fan, Marilyn, but this time…well you've got to admit it all sounds a bit weird.'

'I'm not putting it very well, am I?' She stared at the unfinished design on the workbench in front of her. 'You can't judge till you've heard the full story.'

'OK, OK. Tell me all about it later. But I might not say what you want to hear. Perhaps I – and dare I say it, even Matt – perhaps we can see things more clearly. I haven't looked into your Jay's melting brown eyes, have I, fallen under the spell?'

'They're green, actually.'

They both laughed momentarily.

'Whatever; I think it'll do you good to get away. You're welcome to come over. Though I've got a busy night ahead. Unexpected party booked for dinner; they'll be arriving in a couple of hours. Listen, hope you don't mind me asking, but would you be OK to help out behind the bar for an hour or two? We can talk afterwards.'

'No problem.' A bit of normality. 'One more thing. Could you come and pick me up?'

'Don't tell me; he's gone off in your car.' She could imagine Sue's expression. 'Oh, of course I can. They can hold the fort here for as long as that'll take. Meet me on the square?'

As she tidied up ready to leave, Marilyn remembered what Jay had said that morning. Nothing like a bit of work to concentrate the mind. She wrote him a note with details of the pub and was about to tack it to the door when she hesitated, thinking of the prying eyes of Matt, the police or anyone else. She left it in a prominent place in the middle of the workbench, and made sure she left the door to the lobby unlocked. There were a couple of hours to go before Matt usually locked the main building, and in any case she intended ringing Jay again before long. Glad to be away, she walked over to the square to wait for Sue.

Chapter 24

Jay made himself slow down. She didn't have to lend him her car, after all, and he told himself to treat it with respect. He hoped she realised how grateful he was – about that and everything else. The way he'd lost his temper shamed him. Several times he'd got bogged down in his own concerns without a thought for what she must be feeling. He'd make it up to her. When things had settled down, he'd make it up to her. He wished she was with him now. She'd said she'd feel like a spare part, and it was probably a good thing he was on his own. Not just practically – talking on the phone to Vesna, a voice from the distant past, had made him feel strange and he'd inflicted enough strangeness on Polly recently.

They'd gone straight to the workshop from the builders' merchant, found Vesna's number in the phone book and reached her, as easily as that. She'd sounded surprised to hear him, and no wonder, but the accusation in her voice and in the things she'd said had saddened him. He told himself that someone going through what she must be experiencing would probably accuse anyone in sight. At least she'd come round enough to agree to see him, alone.

He'd set off immediately in the hope of missing the teatime traffic and found the tearoom, in a village on the outskirts of Bradford, with no problem. It was a similar kind of place to Polly's craft centre, in what looked like a collection of solid stone workers' cottages, except the feel of the area was more urban. He parked up and tried Vinko's number, still without success. He had about an hour to kill and set out to explore his surroundings. On one side of the main road some interesting-looking old streets led up the hill, and on the other a footpath headed down from the main road into a valley of scrubby fields bordered with dark drystone walls. He chose the solitude offered by the fields. A magnificent viaduct straddled the valley, beyond it glimpses of the outskirts of the city sprawling across its broad basin below in the clear autumn afternoon. The wind was keen on his face and in his hair and he pulled his jacket tight.

He hadn't been walking long when his phone rang. The ring tone, chosen with Vinko in a daft moment of closeness, was comforting and he was relieved to see the lad's name at last on the screen.

'Jay? This is Vinko. You must stop phoning me.'

The abruptness brought him up short.

'Sorry. I missed your calls this morning and thought—'

'It doesn't matter. It wasn't a good time to talk. I…I want to talk now.'

'Sure. Is something wrong?'

'Wrong? Why wrong? I'll see you tomorrow, all right? Tomorrow evening. Come to my place at eight o'clock.'

'OK. Though I was going to suggest—'

'No, you listen to me. I've got something I want to say.' He paused and Jay thought how hesitant and distant his voice sounded over the phone. 'I've changed my mind.'

'What d'you mean?'

'About…about you, Jay. I've had time to think. You lost my money and you gave me bad advice and no help to speak of. You didn't answer when I phoned. I can't trust you. Please leave me alone – but first,' the moment's pause seemed to last forever, 'first I want you to bring my money.

All that should be mine. That's why I want to meet tomorrow. Get the money and then come to my house.'

'You're kidding, aren't you? Listen, I was going to tell you when I saw you, but—'

'I know…I know what happened to my grandparents.'

The catch in his voice made Jay wonder if it was shock that was responsible for his sudden rejection. 'I'm sorry, Vinko, I really am. How did you find out?'

'I saw it in the newspaper. But that's not important to you. What's important here is we can't ask them about my money now. But remember, I know about your house. You can sell it, yes, but you can raise a loan on it now. Try to arrange it and bring the cash tomorrow.'

Jay's sympathy evaporated. 'Is that the only thing that matters to you? I'm not—'

'Shut up, Jay. You must give me my money. If you don't, I'll phone the police and tell them you went to my grandparents' house. I'll deny we were in Winchester.'

'For Chrissake Vinko, what's going on? Is someone with you?'

'No! Of course they're not! I trust no one. Like I don't trust you. I've got to look out for myself. Myself!'

His voice was rising and Jay thought it wasn't the first time that something he said had triggered pride expressed as anger in the lad. He took a deep breath. 'Look, I'll come and talk. Where are you?'

'Come tomorrow night – and bring my money. If you can't get it all, bring enough to show goodwill. Or I'll tell the police about you. And…and I'll visit Barton Mill.'

'Am I understanding you right?'

'Of course. You always understand me. Your woman can help me persuade you. So you'd be better off bringing my money tomorrow without that kind of persuasion, OK?'

He hesitated again. 'On your own – you know I've got a good view from my window. Don't bring anyone.'

'I can't believe—'

'Jay, please do this.' Vinko's voice dropped so he could hardly hear him. 'And don't keep phoning. I…I'll send you a message if I need to. Do what it says.'

He hung up abruptly leaving Jay looking at a blank screen. His hand was shaking. He knew Vinko had been disappointed that he had no magic wand to wave, and that he'd found it hard to trust him or anyone, but this about-face sickened him. Why should it, he thought irritably; what did he know about anyone? Just because he was into his forties didn't suddenly make him a good judge of character. Especially not kids; what had he ever had to do with kids? He felt a wave of hurt and betrayal, wondering how he'd allowed it to happen, how he'd believed a thieving little bastard brought up to a life of crime could suddenly change just because a figure from his father's past turned up and showed him friendship. He hated himself for still being such a stupid dreamer, for the fact that Ivan still meant anything at all to him.

Although he doubted Vinko was anywhere near Holdwick, he tried Polly's number. She wasn't talking to him either. He looked at his phone wondering what on earth the things had been invented for if everyone kept them switched off. His hand was in his pocket reaching for his pipe when the ringtone nagged him again. Still thinking of Polly, he answered it eagerly.

'Is that Jay Spinney?'

The unfamiliar male voice brought him up short.

'Who's that?'

'Detective Inspector John Abrahams of Keighley CID. Mr Spinney,' he paused, a question in his voice that Jay refused to answer, 'we're hoping you can help us in connection with an inquiry. We need to ask you a few questions. I'm sure you can understand it's not the sort of thing I want to talk about on the phone. Would it be convenient for you to come into the station, here in Keighley? Or we could arrange to meet – where can we find you at the moment?'

'I'll be glad to help but... You'll have to excuse me, the signal's really bad. If you could—'

He cut the call and stared at the phone. The crisp autumn air felt cruelly cold and bright. The stone wall running alongside the footpath seemed to conceal a multitude of threats, but at the same time guarded him from them. He switched the phone off completely before it could ring again – would he ever stop needing to run away? – and leaned back against the wall. The sharp stones dug into his back through his jacket, keeping him focussed. A cacophony of thoughts came and went like a badly-tuned radio station. But one thing was clear. Polly must have given them his number without even waiting for him to get back. Perhaps she believed she was acting in everyone's best interests, including his own. But without even hearing what he had to say? It hurt. It hurt that she didn't trust him, that he couldn't trust her. It hurt to feel alone, after he'd begun to think he wasn't.

He gazed up at the wide-open sky, washed-out blue with the occasional cloud. Not so different from himself, except his clouds were a red-tinged black. A plane was making its way to a destination he'd never know, leaving a sharp vapour trail. He suddenly saw hundreds, thousands of invisible trails criss-crossing the space. He got his phone out and stared at it. Could the police trace where he was from the stupid gadget? In a burst of pent-up anger and frustration, he threw it down and stamped it into the rough ground. He enjoyed the crunching beneath his boot. He'd never wanted one because he'd never had anyone to keep in touch with. Well, it seemed nothing had changed. He picked it up together with a couple of pieces of shattered screen and stuffed it in his pocket. He walked briskly back up the hill in an attempt to shake off the after-effects of the call. As he left the path and started up a narrow street he dropped the remains of the mobile down the nearest roadside drain. It made a satisfying splash as it hit the filthy water. Feeling strangely cleansed, he headed back towards the tearoom, trying to get himself back into a fit state to meet a woman he hadn't seen for years and who clearly didn't relish the thought of seeing him… Ready to talk with a show of conviction about something that was now pointless and a waste of her time.

Chapter 25

Jay got to the tearoom early. It felt like a homely place; safe. The atmosphere had a calming effect as soon as he stepped through the door. He quickly took in the other customers – two elderly ladies meeting over tea and scones; three young mothers with noisy toddlers – and established that Vesna hadn't arrived yet. After choosing a seat by the window he studied a couple of the watercolour views by local artists on the walls. Restless, he ran a comb through his windswept hair, trying to look nonchalant about it, even though the ladies, girls and children seemed unaware of his presence. In the elastic minutes spent staring out of the window at the cobbled courtyard, he wished he hadn't decided to wait before ordering a cup of tea. The waitress flashed him a look of sympathy as if he'd been stood up by a date.

He must have been distracted; Vesna was coming through the door before he saw any sign of her arrival. Jay knew her at once as she paused and scanned the room. This smart woman looked different from the girl he used to know, but he'd have recognised her even if he hadn't been expecting her. He waved and she walked over, smiling briefly. He was unnerved to see a fleeting resemblance to Vinko in her expression.

'You're early,' they said together, and both laughed nervously.

He stood to greet her and as he did so glanced over her shoulder, checking beyond the signs in the windows.

'I'm on my own,' she said, following his gaze. 'I trust you are?'

He spread his hands in a gesture of innocence and she shook her head.

'I don't know why I'm here. You try anything and I'll be straight on to the police.'

'Try anything? What do you think I'm going to try?' He felt weary of it all, and irritation flooded his voice. Not a good start. Try again. 'Though I don't blame you for being wary. Thank you for coming.'

As they sat down, he offered his condolences, which she quickly brushed aside.

'I don't think it's really hit me yet. I'm doing my best to keep it that way, at least until…you know, until the police find out who did it.'

She gave him a piercing look.

'Would I be here if I were guilty of anything?'

She laughed. 'You could be bluffing. I imagine that's something you're good at.'

He felt as if either straight denial or lighthearted response would be equally damning and they sat in an awkward silence until the waitress came to take their order. As they waited for their teas and scones, he found himself asking what she was doing these days. She had a son and a daughter, and worked as a receptionist and secretary. She had a few days' compassionate leave and the three of them were staying with a friend as she didn't feel safe at home; Jay had been lucky to catch her as she called back to the house to check the post. When he told her in return how he made a living, he found her nostalgia-tinged laugh irritating and cosy in equal measure.

'To tell you the truth I'd always assumed you'd be touring war zones as an aid worker for one of those relief agencies.'

She made him feel guilty that he wasn't.

'I thought about it,' he said half-truthfully, wondering what to add that didn't sound cowardly or heartless. Her reply surprised him.

'Actually, Jay, yours sounds like an interesting way of life. Very you.'

The waitress arrived with their order. As she left, Vesna gave him a smile that dissolved the years. 'You know I always had a soft spot for you?'

Taken aback by her directness, he didn't know whether to laugh or protest.

'There, I can say it now. I used to spend nights dreaming you'd both come back one day and you'd realise it wasn't just Ivan's kid sister who'd been under your nose all that time.' He felt a strange desire to apologise on behalf of his young self for never noticing a thing. Her expression hardened. 'Until I heard you were actually having an affair with my aunt.'

He stared at her. 'What?'

She brushed a lock of still-dark hair over her shoulder. 'Don't try and deny it. Ivan wrote to me once or twice. You know he was terrible at keeping secrets.'

He shrugged. 'You could hardly call it an affair.'

'No?'

'Young innocent loses virginity to attractive older woman? Of course I didn't see myself as a cliché at the time – it felt way more important.' He felt himself reddening. His ability to hide behind flippancy seemed to have deserted him. 'So Ivan kept in touch with you?'

'Not much, certainly not later on. He mentioned it when he did – in passing – because he was worried about you.'

'Really?'

She smiled. 'Especially as Zora was spoken for. *I* worried more that he seemed to idolise that guy – sounded like a bit of a gung-ho hard case from where I was sitting. But what could I do anyway? I'd probably got it all wrong and was overreacting.'

Jay shook his head. 'Trust your feminine instincts,' he said. 'We'd probably all be better off if Zora had.'

She smiled. 'You would say that, wouldn't you? I remember being totally unsurprised when I heard you'd left. I can't imagine Lek was the sort to let something like that go.'

He stirred his tea, disturbed by the way the conversation was going. 'What do you know about Lek?'

From her reaction he must have managed to sound normal. After the last few days he was getting practised at this. Vesna shook her head. 'Not much. Except my mother used to say he was the reason Zora turned bad.'

'You think she turned bad?'

'I didn't know her. It was, you know, received family wisdom. Ivan too. He was a nice boy, all set for a happy, successful life until she and then Lek got their claws into him. You know the sort of thing. They even said it about you, too, you know.'

'What, led astray or doing the leading?'

'The first, of course.' She looked away. 'Sorry, you must think I'm totally crass talking like this after… after what's happened. But, like I said before, I need to pretend it's happening to someone else right now.'

She paused, tears welling in her eyes, struggling to regain control.

'I understand. I know that feeling.'

'And, you know, just seeing you… Sorry if I'm saying all the wrong things. It's just…'

'Difficult. I know.' He reached across the table and put a hand gently on hers, waiting until the ghost of a smile returned. This had run away from him; he'd intended to start by telling her about Vinko. But now, after the phone call he'd just had, he had no idea how. 'Did you hear from Ivan after I left?'

'Only once. He mentioned you were on your way back. But you never turned up, did you? Till now. God, this feels weird. Anyway, a couple of years later we got a letter from a woman, Marta, who told us she was his wife, broke the news that he'd been killed. She said she was expecting his baby. Mum tried to trace her, but got nowhere. It broke her heart, on top of hearing of his death, to know she'd been cut off from such an important part of his life. Marta never wrote back. We heard more about what happened from Mihal – my ex, though of course he was nothing to do with me back then. We first met him when he came over to bring us the news. It had all sounded so exciting to begin with, the lives you'd made for yourselves there. I didn't care what Mum and Dad said; I'd always dreamed of joining you one day. But then there was the war and my big brother was killed.'

'And I wasn't. I couldn't help feeling I should have been there too. Sounds trite, I know, but it's true.'

He swallowed as he noticed the boy sitting quietly at a nearby table.

'You were the sensible one.'

He looked at her incredulously. 'You don't mean that – what about Zora?'

'Oh, all young men get infatuated. I mean you got out.' She waved a hand. 'Don't worry, I'm not going to ask. But I know enough from reading between the lines.'

'I'll just say – though I'm sure you know – it did my head in, the way Ivan and I parted.' He noticed he was stirring his tea again. As he gazed at the dwindling vortex in the middle of the cup he reminded himself this wasn't about him. 'Listen – Ivan's son. That's the main thing I wanted to tell you. I know him. Vinko.'

'Vinko? Isn't that the one the police are looking for? Up in the Dales somewhere?'

Jay nodded.

'He's Ivan's boy? Mihal never mentioned him.'

'Marta left for Germany before Vinko was born. Your Mihal probably didn't know anything about him.'

'You're sure it's him?'

'As sure as anyone could be under the circumstances.' He glanced up at her. 'Even more so looking at you. The resemblance is uncanny.'

'But what's he doing in the Dales?' Her face clouded. 'How on earth could he be involved in *this*?'

'I wish I could tell you he wasn't.'

He started to tell her about meeting Vinko, and their visit to her parents' house.

'How did you know about the money?' she interrupted.

'I was the one brought it to them, last year.'

'You?'

'It was Zora's money, but me who brought it.'

'My parents never said.'

'Boris wanted nothing to do with me. Your mum was more welcoming, but we still kept strictly to business. Hardly a happy reunion. I'm not surprised they didn't tell you.'

'Just a minute. The police traced the account the money came from. I can't remember the name, but it wasn't yours.'

'You could say that. Actually, Dan Freeman's the name I've lived by since I came back to England.'

She stared at him. 'What do you mean?'

'It was the name we used…when I was sorting things out

for Zora. And it stuck. You know me. Not bad at keeping up a pretence.'

'So what should I be calling you?' She looked at him quizzically, playing with a lock of her hair.

'What you've always called me – idiot, say?' He laughed. 'Good old bad old Jay. I had a change of heart recently, dragged Spinney back out of obscurity. Decided I needed to sort myself out. I thought I was doing quite well – I've even met a wonderful woman who seems pretty keen on me, too. Though that's another thing I could have got wrong. My past keeps insisting on catching up with me.'

He resolutely refused to look at the table from where he knew the boy was still watching him.

'Vinko, you mean?'

'Partly.' He shook himself mentally. 'Sorry, yes, I didn't finish, did I?'

The previous Saturday night and their trip to Winchester felt like a distant memory as he told her.

'He seemed genuine, as if he wanted friendship. Wary, yes, but that's understandable. Anyway, one thing I found out is that he's been mixed up in something – he wouldn't tell me what, but he referred to the guy he's involved with as Novak. So when I read your married name I put two and two together and thought I'd better find out what sort of man your ex is. I hope I'm not talking out of turn.'

'Not at all!' she said vehemently. 'It was never a happy marriage, and by the end…' she shuddered. 'What are you thinking? What's Vinko told you?'

'Nothing. But it sounds to me like Mihal knew or guessed about your folks' recent windfall, and he's using the lad to get his hands on it. If so, it went badly wrong.'

Vesna looked away, rummaged in her handbag and produced a tissue. Jay felt a pang of guilt.

'I'm sorry; perhaps we shouldn't be talking like this.'

'It's all right. I can't hide away.' She dabbed at her eyes. 'Why on earth did you take Vinko back there?'

'I had no idea he was involved in anything, and he *is* technically entitled to a share. He seemed vulnerable, alone. I'm stupid. How many reasons do you want?'

'Don't beat yourself up.' She gave him a brief smile then turned serious again. 'I had my suspicions but I just can't believe Mihal would go that far. Murder? *Mum*, for God's sake? What did he think he'd achieve?'

She sniffed and turned away again. Jay put a hand awkwardly on her arm as she wiped her eyes.

'Thanks. I'm fine now.' She smiled weakly. 'You must think *I'm* the one who's nuts, marrying a man like that.'

'I don't know him; who am I to judge? It must have seemed right at the time. Do you know what he's doing now?'

'I know where he lives. He comes – *used* to come; I wouldn't let him near now – he came to see the children about once a month. But, surprise, surprise, the police found his place empty and he hasn't been back since this happened. It looked like there'd been no one there for a while, either. He hasn't been at work for weeks, apparently. So I haven't a clue where he is. But I'm scared, Jay. I'm pretty sure that while the police are around he wouldn't dare come near, but even so…'

'Do you know any of his mates? Have you asked any of them where he might be?'

'You're the first person I've talked to about any of it. I've been leaving it to the police. What have you told them?'

'I haven't talked to them. I intend to, after I've been to meet Vinko tomorrow night.'

'You're seeing him tomorrow?'

'He called me. Just now.' He sipped his tea. It had gone cold. 'All pretence at friendship straight out the window; I couldn't believe the change.'

As he gave her an outline of the conversation he'd had, he felt a creeping unease.

'Do you think Mihal was behind that?' she asked, confirming his doubts.

'He insisted he was on his own. But… Shit, I could be so wrong here, but… He said something at the end about a message. I got this weird text a bit earlier. You might understand this, Vesi – what do you make of it?'

He searched in his pocket for his phone, realised what he'd done and before he could dwell on it took out his notebook instead.

'This was it. From Vinko's number.'

He wrote it out: *Ne vjer*

'That's all?' He nodded and she studied the words. '*Ne vjeruj* – don't believe? Jay, what if he knew he'd have to make that call and he's telling you not to believe it? Someone's making him do it?'

'Could be all kinds of things. He could be gloating: "I don't believe you're such a loser".'

She rolled her eyes. 'Do you have to be so paranoid? Why would he send half a message, unless he was trying to get you before…before the people that made him call you caught up with him?'

'What if he simply wanted to play games with me?'

'Would he? You've met him.'

'I haven't a clue. He was unpredictable – best mates one minute, unable to trust me the next. We've got to be careful. I suspect you simply don't want to believe your new-found nephew could be bad.'

'You should know – fancy yourself as a surrogate dad? Or cuddly uncle? Is that why you're denying him – scared of your own feelings?'

'Can we just stick to reality?' He hated to admit her words struck a chord. 'Anyway, I'm not going to know till I meet him tomorrow night, am I?'

'Surely you're not going to walk into that?'

He shrugged. 'I've got to. You might be right, he might be at risk. Even if he's not, if there are others involved, seeing Vinko could be the only way of getting to them. If anyone other than me turns up there, they'll know and they'll disappear. Until next time. They've waited till now; they'll wait longer. You want them at large?'

'The police could arrange for you to have cover at a safe distance.'

'That would mean talking to them. What if they don't believe a word I tell them? Keep me in for questioning or whatever? Vinko and anyone that might be with him are expecting *me* and I've got to go. He's threatened someone who doesn't deserve it. If I find anything else out tomorrow night, *then* I'll go to the police, believe me.'

'There might not be a "then", Jay. Where does he live, anyway?'

Jay forced a smile. 'Nice try.'

She shook her head. 'Do you honestly think you know better than the professionals?'

'No. But I don't trust *them* to know better than me, either. We can join our ignorant forces after tomorrow night. Or if I can find Vinko in the meantime.'

She sighed. 'It doesn't look like I could stop you without turning you in. But you will keep me posted?' She told him her mobile phone number and he jotted it down. 'What's yours?'

'I, um, don't have a phone anymore.' He felt himself reddening. 'I'll ring you.'

'What do you mean, "anymore"?'

'I had a brief flirt with carrying a mobile. But Vinko's wasn't the only call. My phone's been hot this afternoon – that detective got hold of me, too. I had this vision of them tracking me and trashed it. I always was impulsive, wasn't I?' He laughed unconvincingly. 'Didn't like having the thing anyway.'

'How come they've got your number?'

He stared out of the window, noticing a reflection of the boy behind him and trying to ignore it. 'Only two people know it. Vinko and Polly. It's hardly likely to be Vinko who told them.'

'Polly's your girlfriend, right?'

'I'd like to think so.'

'What do you mean by that?'

He watched the two elderly friends across the room rise and make their way to the door, then stared out of the window.

'You know, trust. Respect. She goes straight off to the police as soon as my back's turned. Is that how much I mean to her? Can I trust her?'

'You don't know what happened. She might be scared – I don't know how much you've told her, but I wouldn't blame her.'

'So *she* doesn't trust *me*. How does that make me feel?'

'Like someone who should find out what's happened before judging?'

'Ouch. You certainly know how to put me in my place.' He turned from the window.

'Sounds like you need it,' she insisted with a half-smile. 'Anyway, your love life's up to you. But if Vinko said he knows where she works, don't you think you'd better get back and check up on her?'

He shrugged. 'I intend to. Though I'm sure there's nothing to worry about yet. Imagine his situation, whether it's just him or he's with Mihal. If they touch her they've most likely lost their chance. They've got to wait and see what I do.'

'So where does that leave her? Polly?'

'It seems she's got the police on board, doesn't it?'

His words were sounding increasingly lame, even to his own ears. He realised he wanted nothing more than to be in Holdwick. 'Look, I'm sorry. I'm sure there's loads more we – I – should have said, but I guess I should be going.'

'Don't apologise. I'm the one suggested you went.' She looked at her watch. 'I've been trying to think how to get rid of you, to be honest. Got to pick the kids up soon, see?' He was relieved to see the sparkle in her eye and smiled back. She reached across the table and squeezed his hand. 'The circumstances could've been better, but it's been good to see you. Don't make it another twenty years. And keep me in touch with what happens – however you choose to do so.'

He smiled, noticing the boy's table was vacant, and got up to help her on with her coat. Not that she needed that kind of gesture, but it was an excuse to give her a hug, and she returned it. He watched her leave, feeling strangely reassured.

Chapter 26

The house felt empty even before it came into view. Like the workshop had before it. Jay had arrived late. He'd known Vinko wouldn't be at home but felt he had to try. So, after fighting the rush-hour traffic on his way out of the city, he'd got to the craft centre to find it locked up and Polly's workshop in darkness. Trying to convince himself she'd had an offer of a lift home, he came straight to Stoneleigh, but as he drove into the yard he saw there wasn't a single light cheering the windows in the early evening gloom. The barn door was slightly ajar and clacking in the wind. He entered the porch and tried the door. Locked. They'd never had reason for her to give him a key; the way he was feeling right now he doubted she would have anyway. And why should she? He went outside, checked under plant pots, in a few obvious niches in walls, the glove box of the car. Nothing. He knocked pointlessly. Perhaps he needed to hear the sound of his own knuckles on the solid wood, echoing through an empty house, to convince himself of her absence. Genghis appeared and greeted him with a loud meow. Gratefully, he bent to stroke the cat, who rubbed up against his legs before vanishing inside with a dismissive clack of the catflap.

He scanned the porch for a note, in vain. He sat in the car to wait, brooding, as the buffeting wind threw occasional showers at the windows. The weather meant the darkness had come early, the heavy blanket darkness of a clouded sky. She wouldn't come in this; he must have been right, she didn't trust him and was staying away. Whatever she thought of him, he was increasingly worried about her and felt a growing need to find his way in and get to the phone.

There was a torch in the glove box and he used it to do a circuit of the house in the rain, looking for open windows. When he tried the front door onto the garden, the grand-looking stone-porched entrance she hardly ever used, it opened so readily he almost fell in behind it. Of course! This was the door through which she'd taken her stuff out to the bonfire. He smiled at his own stupidity for not thinking of it sooner, and hers for leaving it unlocked.

He removed his boots and dripping coat and took them through to the kitchen to dry by the Rayburn. There was no note on the kitchen table either; he'd resigned himself to that before his eyes confirmed it. It felt strange to be here on his own, everything he looked at reminding him of Polly. She'd said more than once he should consider himself at home here, but he felt like a trespasser. He wondered what she'd say if she arrived back and found him here.

The kitchen was warm from the Rayburn and he pulled the blind down to keep out the weather and the outside world before picking up the phone. He found the Barton Mill number in the memory and stared at it for a few moments, steeling himself to ring them. He glanced through to the living room and sensed a familiar presence. He felt not so much fear as a weary resignation. It was no surprise that the boy was with him tonight, and he almost had to stop himself from greeting his persecutor out loud. He managed to ignore him and dialled the number. Waiting for them to reply, he longed for Polly to come back and interrupt him.

A friendly-sounding woman called Lucy answered and,

after he'd apologised for bothering her, told him no, she hadn't seen Marilyn that afternoon but Matt had. She offered to go down to the workshop and see if there was a message, ignoring an irritable voice asking her who was on the line. It seemed like an age, the sound of her footsteps on the stairs echoing spookily down the phone, before she breathlessly gave him the name and number of the Mason's Arms. As he jotted it down he heard a male voice muttering 'What did you tell him that for?' and the scuffling of the phone being taken from her.

'Matt here. Don't you think you've caused enough hassle?'

'Hassle?' He felt cold despite the warmth from the Rayburn. 'What's happened?'

'Isn't it about time *you* came clean on that? Nothing, yet, but no thanks to you. Why don't you just fuck off and leave her in peace? She's never been in trouble in her life and—'

'I don't have to listen to this.'

'I'm afraid you do. I'm on your case. Just think on.'

'Thanks for the advice. Nice talking to you.'

He cut off the call and stared at the wooden table top, fighting down his anger. The sound of Matt's voice reminded him of the only other conversation he'd had with the man, when he'd passed on his number. Jay found himself smiling as he realised there was someone else who could have given his number to the police. Relief at this combined with the discovery that Polly was safe at her friend's flooded through him. 'I'm on your case.' He could almost laugh. He rang the pub and eventually got to speak to her.

'Jay! I've been trying to get you. Why didn't you answer?'

'I lost my phone.'

'Lost it?'

253

'Long story.'

'Aren't they always?' She giggled and he could tell she'd had a drink. There were voices in the background. 'You got my message? Where are you now?'

'No to the first – I was a bit late back and they'd locked up at the craft centre. So I'm at home. Your place.'

'Why don't you come over? Sue's dying to meet you.'

'You wouldn't want me to. I'm not feeling sociable right now. How come you're there anyway?'

'I'm sorry, Jay.' Her voice sobered. 'I know I said I'd wait, but I just couldn't handle it, and— Matt came just after you left because the police had been to see him – don't worry, nothing serious, only door-to-door enquiries… But it's difficult enough as it is, and he just pushes my buttons. You know what he can be like – well, you don't, but—'

'I do. I've just spoken to him.'

'What? Why on earth…?'

'I was worried about you, so I phoned the Mill to see if they knew anything. That was how I got this number. Sorry, but I couldn't think what else to do.'

'What do you mean, worried?' He was glad to hear her moving to somewhere quiet. 'Was it something Vesna told you?'

'Partly.'

As he told her about Vinko's call he found it impossible to ignore the boy who was now sitting across from him at the kitchen table.

'That's awful,' she said. 'Did you have any idea he'd turn like that?'

'No, I…it came as a shock. And then, among other things, Vesna confirmed her ex could easily be Vinko's Novak.'

He forced himself to tell her the rest.

'So you're going to see him tomorrow? You must be out of your mind.'

He glanced over at the boy. If only she knew.

'I've got to. It might be the only way of finding out what's going on and…and if Vesna's right about that message of his – and I don't know if I believe her or just want to – Vinko might need my help.'

'Jay, this is serious. I really think you should tell the police.'

'Please don't. I've made my mind up and I'm too knackered to argue about it. Look, you enjoy your evening. I know this isn't easy for you either, I really do. I'm sure it's doing you good to get away. Shall I come and pick you up later? I haven't a clue where it is, but I'll find it.'

'You could…' She sounded apologetic.

'Stay over if you want to. I don't mind. We can talk in the morning. As long as I know you're OK.'

'I'll be there early. Try and stop you doing anything stupid. I…I don't want anything to happen to you.'

He glanced at the boy.

'Thanks.'

'Oh, Jay? I nearly forgot. It might be important – there was something else. When Matt was talking to the police they asked if he'd heard of someone; I wondered if you knew anything, whether it helped with this Novak business. What was it? Daniel Freeman.'

It was like a physical blow to hear her say the name out of the blue.

'Why were they asking?' It felt like trying to talk under water.

'They didn't say. In connection with the case.'

He stared as if hypnotised at his hand on the table.

'Jay?'

'Sorry. Um, yeah, I do. I know…I know of Dan.'

'You do?'

'I'll tell you tomorrow. But it's nothing to worry about. He's…he's no more connected to the case than I am.'

'You sure? You sound a bit weird.'

'No, I'm fine, honestly.' He made a real effort. 'Just knackered, that's all. I'll make sure I get some rest tonight so I'm up bright and early for you in the morning.'

'That settles it. I'd love to see you, but there's no way you should be driving over in that state. Can't wait, though. I'm missing you already.'

'Me too, Polly love, me too.'

She blew him a kiss down the phone and was gone. In her absence, or the absence of her voice, the wind at the window and the silence inside the house closed in on him. He thought he'd finally been straight with her, but there was always something else, wasn't there? Her reaction made him realise how scared he was of tomorrow evening's meeting. It would be so much easier if he could just go to the police. He looked across at the boy. Easier wasn't always right. Right wasn't always easy.

The catflap clacked and he jumped. As Genghis wrapped himself round his legs and he stroked the cat absently, Matt's words came back to him. Trite, maybe, but now *I'm on your case* was not something he could laugh at so easily. He needed time to think. What if there was a knock on the door now?

He hurried upstairs and packed his sleeping bag into his rucksack. He fed the cat, put on his half-dried boots and coat, switched out the lights and took a key from the rack on the wall. It was still windy but the rain had stopped and the sky was clear. Watched by the bright, unseeing eyes of the stars, he crossed the field behind the barn and found a

256

flat place where the trees began, just over the wall. He could see enough to know he was out of sight, but could keep an eye on the house if he moved a little.

It was darker in the trees, but he knew the boy was watching him as he pitched his tent. He knew the boy would want to share it tonight. He tried to ignore him, at least for a while, by smoking his pipe outside the tent. He paced up and down along a sheep track to keep warm. Unable to think or feel clearly, he shivered as a gust swept down the valley. For a moment he gave himself up to the elements, alone beneath the big sky, the wind stealing his thoughts as fast as he could produce them. The glittering blanket of distant stars made him feel insignificant. He liked to feel insignificant sometimes – if he didn't matter then neither did anything he'd done. If only he could stay out here, somewhere like this, forever. But whatever he did, he could never shake that nagging need to belong. The need that had caused him so much trouble. He could allow himself to belong here, surely?

It soon became too cold for common sense and he crawled into his sleeping bag beneath the canvas. Every mark was familiar to him, but that didn't make it home. He got out his book and reading light. Only a gesture; he hadn't a hope of concentrating. The boy was crouched just inside the tent flaps and it was going to be a long night.

He swallows again, coughs. He is tired of the taste of his own blood. It's only when there's something wrong you realise how strong is the reflex to swallow and how impossible it is to prevent it. With that thought he knows he won't drift back into welcome oblivion this time. He explores with his tongue. The gum where his tooth was is already healing, jellylike. There is another loose molar, too, hanging by a grisly thread. He can't leave it alone. It takes his mind off the other pains but the fresh taste of his own blood every time he moves his tongue irritates him more and more until he lifts the arm that he can move and with clumsy fingers grips and yanks. It doesn't come as easily as he'd expected and he almost gives up. His breathing makes his bruised ribs hurt as he finally holds it up between his fingers. It's hideous. He throws it across the room. He's momentarily forgotten his weakness and it lands only a few inches away, taunting him with its red and white ugliness. He turns to the wall.

Lek is telling him about the new currency. We don't have money now. Of course you don't, Šojka replies, you always did want to do things differently. You are learning, says the older man. Very differently. Who needs gold when we have teeth? Molars are the main unit, each molar worth ten incisors. And the canines, the canines are special, they are worth ten molars. Šojka almost laughs, thinking I'd give my eye teeth to be somewhere else right now. And our currency is particularly valuable, the big man is saying, because each piece is unique. Oh no, we don't mint them, we use the teeth of our enemies. They will come to understand one day how they helped to build a great nation. He gestures with a grimy hand over ranks of teeth set out on the table in front of him like a macabre mock-up of a battlefield.

Šojka looks away from the rows of stained ivory, rolls over and opens his eyes. One opens. He touches the puffy flesh around the other with his good hand. He is fairly sure it's only bruising, that the eye itself is sound. He can't think too hard about that now; the wrong answer would be too much.

He wants water, even though he knows it will taste of blood. Will it be Zora who comes? He remembers her touch as he drifted in and out of consciousness, how he wanted to feel the comfort, but when it came turned away, wishing only that she'd leave him in peace.

When he finally hears footsteps, when the door finally opens, it is Ivan. Šojka wonders if he can face this, but it is too late to fake sleep. Ivan is smiling hesitantly, as if he's embarrassed to smile when his friend is lying on a shabby mattress in the corner of a darkened room recovering from being beaten senseless. He goes over to the window and opens the sagging curtains.

Blinking in the welcome daylight, Šojka waits for Ivan to say something to stop him from thinking about Lek and teeth. Ivan helps him to sit up, gives him a drink of water and shows him a hip flask, his expression a question. Šojka nods and swishes the spirit around his mouth, remembering the floor of the truck and wondering how many more times will they play this one out? The rakija stings and like everything else it tastes of blood, but he feels better for it.

'I'm sorry,' Ivan says.

'Don't apologise. Not for this.' He waves a hand vaguely over his battered body. 'This was between me and Lek. You were nothing to do with that, at least.' His words sound strange as his jaw is stiff and his tongue swollen with the taste of his own blood.

'What, then?' Ivan sounds wary.

'I think you know.' He gulps again at the rakija, finds strength. 'That boy.'

'In Paševina? Fuck, he was about to mow you down!'

'No. He was about to drop the gun and let me lead him to safety. Till you ploughed in with all the shoot-first-ask-questions-later tactics you've learnt off Lek.'

'"Thanks, mate, thanks for saving my life!"' Ivan stands, almost knocking the old wooden chair over as he does so, and goes to the window. 'You really think you're better than us, don't you?'

259

He shakes his head, even though Ivan has his back to him.

'So why are you still here?'

'I won't be for long.'

Ivan turns. 'And what's that supposed to mean?'

'As soon as I'm well enough. I can't do this anymore.'

His friend's eyes are blazing. 'Have you forgotten what they're doing to us? Here? Vukovar? In Bosnia?'

'Of course not. I know why…why everything! But who's doing it? The ordinary villagers of Paševina?'

'Oh, for fuck's sake! The innocent ones were taken away to safety.'

'Away from their homes. Everything they've known. And it will be safe, won't it, where they've gone.'

'Of course it will. We don't—'

'We don't kill small boys for being in the wrong place.'

Ivan's fists are clenching and unclenching by his sides. 'I'll enjoy watching the news. "Peace finally achieved! No more bloodshed after mysterious foreign agent Šojka politely asks Milošević to stop." Get real!'

Their eyes meet and they almost laugh. But he shakes his head.

'Since when has reality been measured by Lek?'

'Do you think I like everything he does? Especially not now. You didn't deserve this. But overall…'

'Overall, bollocks. In his case "overall" means one Paševina after another.'

'You mean it, don't you? About leaving.'

He winces at the return of the bitterness to Ivan's voice.

'Ivan… You could come with me.' His friend stares at him in disbelief. 'This isn't you. You've changed. Why don't we both go home?'

'Because this is my home now. I thought it was yours, too. But no. You'd desert us.'

'It's not deserting.'

'What then?'

'I...I look around and I think, what are we doing here? What have I got myself into?'

Ivan laughs harshly. 'Ask Zora.'

It's like a final, underhand blow to the gut. He is aware again of the blood in his mouth, clogging his throat.

'Leave her out of it.' The words sound petulant as soon as he says them. But he hasn't the strength to try and explain. He can't even explain to himself.

'Isn't that what you should have done?' Ivan fires back.

His guilt turns to anger. 'Now who's being fucking self-righteous?'

Ivan glares at him. 'Perhaps Lek was right. Perhaps he's been right all along about you,' he says quietly, turning back to the window, away from the tension. When he speaks again his voice is almost apologetic. 'You're not thinking straight. I'll come back and see you again later. I—'

He strides out of the room. The dust motes dance in the wake of his friend's departure, giving Šojka no clues. He still has no idea whether it is more cowardly to leave or to stay.

Dawn brought relief in the form of daylight and calmer air. The only sound was the birds singing and an occasional thrumming of the guy ropes in the breeze. Jay crawled out and looked towards the house. There was a slight covering of frost on the jeep. He realised how hungry he was – he'd had nothing since the scones at the tearoom the previous afternoon – and slipped back to the house to help himself to bread, cheese and cake. While waiting for the kettle to boil he went to the kitchen sink and washed away the blurriness of a disturbed night.

All the time he was aware of a presence, in the trees, even

261

stronger in the house. As if the boy were claiming it, denying him the right to be there.

Go away, please, just leave me alone.

He was never sure whether he spoke out loud in those moments. He quickly made a sandwich, found a carrier and took his picnic and mug of coffee back out to the tent. He tried to concentrate on his breakfast, taking comfort from the food and the hot drink, to drive away the events of the previous night. He always thought of them as events, not dreams, not memories. Memories faded with time, didn't they? His tongue probed at the gap where the tooth had been. He still felt watched and wondered just what he had to do to free himself. He busied himself taking the tent down and packing up his bag. It was still early; he reckoned there was time for him to take everything back to the house. He was crossing the yard when he heard the phone ringing. Quickening his pace, he unlocked the door in time to hear a recording of Polly telling the caller she wasn't there.

Hi Marilyn, Lucy here. Can you ring me back as soon as you get chance, please?

Lucy. Barton Mill. He was relieved he hadn't reached it in time. A coward, perhaps, but relieved all the same. As he took his things up to the bedroom, he tried to calm himself. With Vesna's accusations of paranoia ringing in his mind he wondered if he shouldn't just light a fire and wait for Polly in comfort in the living room. But paranoid or not, she might not be the first to arrive. He rinsed the mug, saw to the cat and went back outside.

Walking briskly towards the patch where his tent had been, he caught a glimpse of a figure in the trees. The boy was still watching him and a smell of burning hung on the air. No effort of will could stop him looking back over his shoulder, half-expecting to see a column of smoke rising through the skeletal branches. He looked at his hands, glanced up again to where he'd seen the boy in the trees. Nothing but a movement of the leaves. As elusive as Vinko, he thought with a silent laugh, and realised the little bastard was even beginning to *look* like Vinko. A cold fear crept over him as he wondered how much of anything he'd done over the last few days was real. Had it all been an extended vision conjured up by some malicious part of his conscience, to show him what happened when you gave in, sought comfort in loving a woman?

He leaned against a tree, his breathing loud in his head, the bark rough beneath his fingers, and let reality settle back down around him like the airborne ash of a fire. The boy had gone. Of course – however much he wanted this to be a nightmare it didn't make it any less real. It was a lesson all right, but it was happening. It was almost enough to make him believe in a higher power, but that was just too scary to contemplate.

The sound of a car approaching up the track made him duck into the trees. It wasn't one he recognised. He couldn't make out much as he tried to stay concealed, but saw the driver was on his own. Looked a bit young for a detective, but why shouldn't he? Definitely too young for Novak. Most likely the police. Jay watched the car turn into the yard. Vindicated. *Looking for me? Sorry, mate, I'm on your case.* He smiled to himself, drew his jacket tighter and waited. The visitor knocked on the door, then went back to the car. He waited for it to start up and leave, but the man seemed prepared to wait. Whoever it was, Jay suddenly wished he had a way of warning Polly.

He made his way quietly down towards the barn, hoping to get down the track unseen and intercept her before she arrived. As he crept along the back of the barn he had a brief moment of doubt, remembering yesterday and wondering if she'd come at all. The thought had hardly passed when he heard a car pull up, women's voices and a door banging. He saw the newly-arrived car turn in a gateway and leave. From the corner of the barn he tried to attract Polly's attention, but she was already walking briskly up the yard, her attitude one of anger or irritation rather than fear. Her visitor called out to her and he felt a mixture of relief and annoyance as he recognised the voice.

Chapter 27

Cautiously, Vinko entered the building, hoping he'd got the right place. It was good to be in out of the wind; he couldn't remember ever feeling so cold. He was glad he had his jacket back, but it wasn't much use over a damp T-shirt. He eased his hands deeper into his pockets. They hurt. He concentrated on his surroundings to take his mind off the pain. There were three doors on the ground floor, to his right, and a staircase going up to the left. He heard a car pull up in the car park outside and stepped to the shadows next to the main entrance, checking for the reassuring presence of his knife. A man walked in without noticing him and made straight for the third door on the right. Not that one, then. A look at the signs on the wall in front of him indicated there was a shop upstairs. That seemed best. Most likely to be the place where he'd find what he was after and more public, more anonymous, if it wasn't.

He took a deep breath and started on the stairs. He managed to get about halfway up before he had to stop for a rest. Catching his breath sent sharp pains through his bruised ribs. He clung to the iron handrail to steady himself. It was cool, soothing. He rested both hands and his forehead on it for a moment.

The door at the top was closed, but a sliding wooden sign announced that the shop was open. There was a pane covered with signs and hangings. He peered through a tiny section of unobstructed glass and saw a large room full of the kind of stuff he admired but couldn't imagine ever owning. His mother would have loved to see this. He was thinking about her far too much recently. Hardly surprising, but he had to stop it.

A movement drew his eye to the counter. The person behind it was a woman. Good. She even looked a bit like his mother, too. How his mother might have looked if she'd had the chance to live and work in a place like this. But she hadn't and that was it. There was no sound on the stairs or in the lobby below him and he allowed himself a moment to gather his strength and rehearse what he was going to say. He still found the store of English words in his head could desert him when he needed them. When he was under stress.

He straightened his jacket and ran a hand over his hair before pushing the door open. A bell jangled harshly above his head. He glanced at the woman behind the counter, hoping he hadn't jumped visibly. The air was thick with a pleasant scent. He liked it but needed fresh air. Even though he was still so cold. He squared his shoulders and walked towards the counter, concentrating on not stumbling. That would be a disaster. He had to act normal. This had to go right or he was in trouble. He ran the conversation through his head one more time.

'Excuse me.'

It was a relief to get to the counter, to have something to lean on. He tried to look casual about it.

'How can I help?'

The woman was smiling. She seemed friendly but he could tell she was nervous. He'd already hesitated too long.

'I…' *tražim… suche* 'I look for my friend.'

She nodded slightly, eyebrows raised. He could smell that she'd been smoking recently and longed more than anything to ask her for a cigarette.

'Do you know where is Jay?'

266

That unsettled her. So he'd come to the right place.

'No, I'm afraid I don't.'

He wished he knew how to reassure her.

'Please, I hope you tell me? I make no trouble.'

She relaxed slightly.

'I think I know someone I can ask.'

Feeling slightly nauseous, he watched her looking in a book, picking a phone up. Hurry up, please get on with it... The room swayed around him and he gave in, allowing himself to slide down the front of the counter and let the floor take his weight. He made himself sit; it would be hard enough to explain that, let alone lying sprawled like some sad drunk. Why should I have to explain anything, he thought in a flash of anger. Jay will be here soon. He drew his knees up and rested his head, riding the pain, concentrating on staying alert. He heard the woman's voice behind him. Too briefly. The phone beeped off. It sounded like she'd left a message. He felt like swearing but held it in. He should call out to her, but didn't have the strength.

It seemed like an hour before she came round the counter, her steps hesitant. He looked up. It's OK I'm all right I'm OK. He saw the scissors in her hand and panicked; tried to back away.

'You gave me a fright there.'

He breathed more easily as she dropped them on the counter with a clatter that made the room sound ridiculously huge.

'I'm sorry. I... I don't feel good. You didn't phone someone?'

'No answer.'

He put a hand on the floor and struggled to get up. If only he wasn't so weak.

'You can't stay there.'

She reached out and he grasped her hand, gritting his teeth at the pain of her grip. He snatched his hand away as soon as he was standing and able to support himself against the counter. When she wasn't looking he pulled his sleeve down over the blisters. He didn't want her to start asking the wrong questions.

'You'd better come through to the back.'

She led him through to a storeroom and indicated a wooden chair by a sink. He sat gratefully. The air was cooler here. He breathed deeply, flinched as his ribs complained.

'What's wrong?'

'Nothing. I am tired. Do you have water? Please.'

He hated asking. She filled a mug from the sink. The harsh sound of the running tap made him brace himself against the memory. He savoured his next breath, remembering to keep it shallow. She passed him the mug and he drank greedily. It cleared his head a little. She offered him another; he shook his head.

'You have a cigarette, please?'

He really hated asking but his voice ran away from him. Not a good time for willpower. She pushed open a door that said Fire Exit and lit one for herself, too.

'Now, tell me who you are and why you're here.'

'Jay said of Barton Mill. I think you are his girlfriend.'

'She used to be here. That was who I tried phoning just now.'

He fought down the disappointment.

'So you are not she.'

The woman shook her head with a smile.

'I must find him,' he insisted.

'Why?'

He took a drag of the cigarette. How could he even begin?

'What's going on?' she said.

He exhaled and watched the swirling smoke get drawn to the door.

'You can trust me. I want to help you.' He was sure she wouldn't if she knew. 'Listen, we didn't get off to a very good start. I'm Lucy. You are?'

He smoked in silence. Why? Why did she need to know that?

'Vinko?'

The sound of his name made him look at her. 'How are you know this?'

'People are looking for you. You asked for Jay. I guessed. But I don't know anything more. You've got to tell me why you're here.'

'I do tell you.'

'Well there's no Jay here. So what now?'

Vinko stared at her in silence. She went over to a phone and stood with her hand hovering above it. 'I'm sorry, I can't let you stay unless you talk to me. If you don't you'll have to leave, or I'll …'

She nodded towards the phone.

'Please. I talk to you.'

Better her than anyone else. Till Jay got here. He was surprised to find the idea of talking was a relief. She put her fag out and closed the fire exit door. He crushed his own in the ashtray as she disappeared into the shop. He vaguely wondered again if he could trust her but he was past caring. He heard the distant sound of a key being turned. He stared at the floor, head supported in his hands, elbows on his knees.

'Your clothes are damp.'

She was back. He glanced up, his mind foggy as if he'd been asleep.

'*Nije važno.*' She frowned. Wrong words. '*Mach' nichts.* It doesn't…'

'Matter? Yes it does. Wait here, I'll get you something dry.'

'No!' He'd asked enough of her and he'd managed this long. 'It…it is right. You don't worry. I'm OK.'

She insisted and got him a blanket from a corner of the room. He was glad to feel the comforting weight as he dragged it round himself.

'So. You promised to tell me why you're here.'

How could he begin to tell her? What could he say? Let alone how. He grasped the blanket at his neck, savouring the warmth, and realised too late that his sleeve had slipped down. She was staring at his arm.

'All right, let's try again. How do you come to have wet gear? How did you get those?'

The pain had been a constant presence, but the attention made it worse. He eased his sleeve to cover the scabs. Though he knew the backs of his hands were still showing. Explain that.

'Oh, Jesus!' She rolled her eyes. 'Vinko, please! If you won't tell *me*, would you talk to the police?'

'No! I tell you.'

Lucy nodded, and he was sure her kindness was genuine. She offered him another cigarette and he began to talk.

Chapter 28

Marilyn's heart sank as she turned into the yard and saw Matt's car. He got out as she walked up.

'What are you doing here?' she demanded.

'I knew you were on your way back – I phoned you at Sue's and the cleaner told me I'd just missed you. I'm on my way up the dale to see a guy who does woodcarving, wants us to sell his stuff, and I thought I'd pop in.'

'Thanks, Matt,' she said with heavy irony, 'but I can look after myself.'

He gave her a look that suggested he wasn't so sure.

'Any chance of a quick coffee?'

'Matt, please…'

'We didn't part on the best of terms the other day. I wanted to apologise if I came across a bit heavy-handed.'

She thought of Jay waiting for her. Surely he'd have the sense to keep out of the way. A meeting between the two of them was the last thing she needed.

'Look, I accept your apology, but to be honest I came home to get a bit of space,' she said as she put her key in the lock and opened the door a little. 'No lurking terrorists, see? I'm fine.'

'But—'

'I thought you had an appointment.'

'I made sure I left time to spare.'

'You'll have to be early, then, won't you?'

She stood firm, blocking the doorway.

'I'm sorry, but Sue's right. I don't think you should be here on your own, Lynnie.'

'Hasn't it occurred to you I don't give a flying fuck what you think?'

He stared at her. She stopped herself from laughing nervously under the tension.

'Please will you stop wittering over me like an old woman? Get off and see your woodcarving bloke. I'll ring you if there's anything you need to know, all right?'

She stood firm and watched him leave. Once he was safely out of sight she went through to the living room and called Jay. Silence. Her pulse quickened. He'd sounded strange on the phone yesterday. She realised how worried she was about him and wished she'd come home after all. But they'd both been tired; she'd thought she was doing the right thing. She went quickly upstairs. He wasn't in the spare room. She pushed open the bedroom door, scared of what she might find. An empty, unused bed was one of the bad options, but not the worst. The rucksack was dumped on the floor, not in its usual corner. She hurried back downstairs and paused as she noticed a muddy footprint on the carpet. Jay always took his boots off. She tensed. The sound of footsteps hurrying across the yard made her grab the poker from the fireplace. She was standing in the kitchen doorway, wondering what on earth she thought she'd do with the fire iron in her hand if it came to it, when the outside door opened.

Jay looked at her for a moment, then broke into a smile. 'Going equipped these days? Wise move.'

'Sorry.' She put the poker down. 'There were footprints in there. It's not like you. I was nervous for a moment.'

'Sorry myself. Housetraining can take longer than you think. Fraught with ups and downs.'

His humour sounded forced, but his pleasure at seeing

her was real. She hardly had time to register the thought before they were in each other's arms. It was a relief to feel him against her.

'You smell of outdoors,' she said eventually. 'Fresh air. Have you been out long?'

'Long enough. I camped out.'

'Why on earth did you do that?'

'Some would call it paranoia. I call it common sense. And I didn't want to trespass.'

'Oh, Jay, I've told you to feel at home here. Don't you?'

'I was probably being silly.' He kissed her. 'Why was Matt here?'

'He just came to see if I'm OK, is all. He had to visit someone out this way, so he called by. I wish he wouldn't fuss. I mean, he didn't even think about me for months, and I certainly don't want anything to do with him, and…' She realised she was talking too much about the wrong things. 'Anyway, let's not talk about him now. Take your coat off and get the fire lit; I'll make a coffee.'

'Can we go for a walk?'

His worrying distracted air was back.

'Oh. Yes, if you want.'

'I'd rather make sure we don't get interrupted. Unwanted visitors.'

'I thought you said Vinko didn't know this place.'

'I don't think he does. And I'm sure he and his friends want the money too much to do anything stupid. But you never know. And you said yourself you might get a visit from the police. Oh hell, I'm sorry for this mess, Polly. All that's followed me here. It's not fair. On you.'

'Will you let *me* decide about that?'

The long silence was broken only by Jay snapping and unsnapping a press stud on his jacket.

'Let's go for that walk,' she said.

As she went to the coat pegs to get a warmer jacket, he said her name. She stopped and turned.

'You don't have to do this,' he said. 'I've told you before – I could just go; come back to you when it's all sorted out. If you still want me by then.'

Shaking her head, she turned back to the coat rack. It wasn't so much the actual situation they were in; his distance, unpredictability were what was unsettling her. She hesitated for a minute – *when this is all sorted out…think of the me you allowed into your life* – before grabbing a coat and winding a woollen scarf round her neck. She was smiling as she turned to face him.

'I've told Matt there's no way I want you to leave. And Sue. Don't you start.'

He nodded, managing to smile back, and she followed him out.

The vastness of the moors beyond the trees seemed almost as comforting as the gentle kiss he gave her before they walked the footpath out onto the tops. Whatever the practical reasons for coming out here, he looked less trapped with the big sky around them and the wind rustling in the coarse grass and dying heather.

'I should start with an apology,' he said suddenly. 'One thing I didn't tell you yesterday. The police called me. I didn't say anything, but that's what I meant by "lost" my phone. I smashed it. I'd just had that call from Vinko, you didn't answer when I tried to talk to you about it and I felt totally screwed up. No excuses, mind; it was a ridiculous thing to do. That's the kind of guy you're dealing with.'

'I'm sorry myself; Matt was there when you called. I intended to ring you straight back, but you must have got rid of yours by the time I did. I should have answered.'

274

He slowed his pace slightly and turned to look at her.

'That's not what I meant by apologising. I'm sorry, Polly, but I spent all yesterday afternoon thinking you'd gone to the cops behind my back. I was gutted that I couldn't trust you – what a hypocrite!'

'I honestly didn't—'

'Of course you didn't! But it took hearing Matt's voice last night to make me realise and see sense. What does that say about trust?'

The path had narrowed and she was walking behind him, unable to see his face.

'I'd like to think it says more about the state you were in. You didn't have to tell me now, but you have.'

'There's plenty more where that came from.'

'What?'

'Stuff I haven't told you yet.'

'Go on.'

Let him get it out of his system. She wondered what he was going to come out with next.

'You asked about Dan Freeman. He's me.'

She was beyond surprise.

'You lead a dual life? Mr Conventional Dan and Jay the free spirit?'

'Not exactly.' He stopped and turned to her. 'Jay the guy who used to hate himself and Dan the alter ego he wore after he ran away. Something like that.' He turned and started walking again. 'You seem to be taking it pretty calmly.'

'It depends who this Dan is. What he's done. Why do the police want to talk to him?'

'The bank account I transferred the Pranjics' money from was in that name. That's where it all started. It was the name Zora and I used to arrange things. I came to see

275

this Freeman as the one who had the guts to leave Jay Spinney and his mess of a life behind. Surprising how easy it was – practically.' He shrugged. 'I wasn't any happier. But he's still there – the house, the bank accounts were Dan Freeman's. I changed my name on everything else to go with it – anything official, he's the one.'

He'd got his wallet out and handed a bank card back to her without turning. She looked and passed it back, struck by the absurdity of such a transaction out on the empty moors.

'And you never know,' he continued, 'Like Vinko's, they could have picked up my prints from when we went to see Anja.'

'How would they have a record to match them to?'

Jay laughed. 'Anti-war demo in London, can you believe. Iraq. I suppose it's like reformed smokers or born-again anything, but there I was. It all got a bit OTT and the police were as heavy-handed as they usually are in those situations – but I suppose we would say that, wouldn't we? I got herded up with a van full of others, but they couldn't pin anything on me and after a sleepless night in the cells I was on my way with a caution, leaving behind a fingerprint record and a police file.'

'Is that all?'

'Well, if none of that's enough for you…' He shrugged. 'Just to be sure I'm getting it all out in the open, there were a few pub brawls, in the old "I'm a real bastard so I might as well behave like one" days before I got my act together. But I was never actually taken in for that.' He strode on, eyes on the ground ahead of him. 'I'm not proud of any of it and I'm sorry. Especially about the name. I've banged on enough about trust – I should've told you. But if it's any help, it's all part of it.'

'Part of what?'

'This. Me and you.' He stopped again and turned to face her. It was as if a barrier had dropped away. 'When I introduced myself to you – I can't believe I acted like that, just strolled in and made myself at home! But it was just after I'd decided I ought to make some changes in my life. Stop running away, can you believe – not done too well on that count so far, have I? Even so... When I met you, got talking to you, it just felt right. Like it was confirmation I was doing the right thing. You know, that was the first time in years – nearly twenty years – that I'd spoken my real name out loud. I heard myself saying "Jay Spinney" and it scared me, but...but I just kept going and... Didn't you think I was acting strangely?'

'I'd call it intriguing.'

He grinned. 'That's the kind of attitude that makes you special to me.'

'Does it have anything to do with why you've always called me Polly?'

'Because I think you're special?'

'No, silly – to match your sudden impulsive name change.'

'Not change. Reclaim.' He smiled again. 'Lost baggage reclaim. You know, it never occurred to me that Polly had anything to do with it. It just slipped out. Like I said at the time, I think it suits you. But if you don't like it, I'll—'

'Whatever gave you that impression? It's special. It's us.'

He hugged her and for a fleeting moment she thought he was going to kiss her, but he drew away and started walking on.

'I'm sorry. I shouldn't have allowed any of this to happen until you knew everything. I've not been fair on you, I know I haven't. But honestly, Polly, I thought...I thought I'd left it all way behind.'

'Left all what behind, Jay? Until I knew what? What exactly did you do?'

He glanced at her.

'I've told you, mostly. It's not *what*, so much as *why*. Or the absence of *why*.'

His pace quickened and she hurried to catch up with him. She reached for his arm. He pulled it away gently.

'Best not. Not yet.' He strode on. 'I killed people in someone else's war, that's what. I told you that. But... Listen, I'm not saying any war's right. But if you're involved because you believe in a cause, because you want to defend something or right the wrongs... Well, perhaps that's justification. What justification did I have?'

'Didn't you believe in the cause?'

He shrugged. 'Any belief I had was for all the wrong reasons. At first, yes. I'll allow myself that. I...I intended to make my home there. Looking back I realise I *wanted* to belong more than I actually did. And I suppose that blinded me. Yes, of course it was right. They wanted their independence, part of their own country had been taken over. They, we, wanted to win it back, safeguard it. But in time it became more than that. We got blinded; defence turned to aggression. We turned out to be just as bad as anyone else. We even had our own power-crazed maniac leader. Evil is too good a word for Lek.'

His pace quickened as if he were trying to walk away from his memories. 'But...he was Zora's lover and the rest of us were too scared to stand up to him. At least I was. Many of the others, there was no question of them even *wanting* to stand up to him; they had their cause and they admired him. I did too, for a while, if I'm honest. Even though, deep down, I knew that some things we were doing went too far. But I *made* myself believe it was right –

because of my friend, because of a woman I was infatuated with, because of a selfish desire to belong. I even had my own name for those times, too, Šojka. That's what you heard when I talked in my sleep. I should've told you right then, of course.'

He paused and she stopped alongside him, wondering how to respond. He held a hand up to silence her as he glanced around the moors, looking back down the hill towards the house, tiny among the trees in the distance.

'What's up?' she asked.

He shook his head as if getting rid of a fly.

'There's one more thing I haven't told you. I…I've got a travelling companion. I keep thinking I've managed to shake him off, but he's a persistent little bastard. He's around somewhere now.'

Marilyn shuddered at the thought there was someone with them.

'No need to worry, he's only a boy. Never does anyone any harm. Just follows me.' He laughed to himself. 'It does make sense – I think. I've never told anyone about him. I keep trying to give him what he wants and he keeps promising me he'll go away. Perhaps if I tell you now, Polly, he'll finally keep his promise and leave me alone?'

Shaking his head again, he sat down heavily on a tussock of grass. She glanced round, saw no one, and sat down beside him.

'Tell me, Jay.'

'This boy – I don't even know his name after all these years – he's from a village called Paševina. Not far from Zora's place. Lek's home village. Before the war, most of the people there just wanted to get on with their lives, like they do anywhere, but it was a mixed community like most in the area. When the war came there were plenty who immediately hated friends and neighbours, even family members, simply because they were Serb or Croat. It came under Serb control early on, and we were ambushed near there one time – I got injured.' He patted his side and she remembered the scar. 'Missed weeks of the fighting. When I got back on my feet I guess I was desperate to prove myself. I got my chance. Lek led a raid on Paševina, and even by his standards it was particularly vicious.

'I've said he was an evil bastard. And this was his revenge. It had been his home, once. It was personal. And what Lek did, we all did.

'Whatever I'd been involved in before, Paševina was different. We went in hell-bent on driving them out, destroying the place so they couldn't come back. *We*. Me included. I wish I could deny it. Until… It went beyond destruction, beyond brutality. Perhaps I'd just had time to think as I lay on my sickbed. There they were – the people I was supposed to be one of – in the centre of the village executing those they saw as the main troublemakers and there I was watching, a couple of streets away. The place going up in smoke round me like some vision of Hell. And Ivan… my best friend Ivan seemed *pleased* by it all. Like it was justice. I looked away; it was all I could do, look away as if it wasn't real. I saw this boy across the street, hiding behind a car, staring at me. Suddenly I was on his side. I let him go. We'd been told to kill or capture everyone we found. Under the guise of security – he might come back at us, might kill me, my comrades. Who could blame him? Everything I'd seen, he'd seen, and it was happening to his own family. Letting him go wasn't only dangerous; it was probably crueller than killing him. But I couldn't have done anything else.'

His fingers were twisting the ends of his scarf. He stared at his feet.

'You remember I said Ivan saved my life and I hated him for it? I didn't mean because I wished myself dead. I really did hate him for it. You see, that boy did have a go. He found a gun and threatened me with it. I've never been so scared in all my life. But I think I would have succeeded in talking him round, making him drop the gun so I could take him to safety.

'That was when Ivan shot him.' Jay closed his eyes. 'I swear I could see a look of betrayal on that boy's face.

'Who knows what would have happened? Perhaps Ivan was right. I'm sure now that he honestly believed I was in danger. But that's with hindsight. I didn't see it like that, not then. He'd changed; I didn't like the way he was going. I should've talked to him more. I've always regretted that I didn't – he might still be alive, Vinko might have had a father, if I had. Of course I might be talking self-important crap. He could've been killed anyway. But it doesn't stop you thinking and regretting.' He sighed. 'You know what? That wasn't the only time that boy came back at me. He won't leave me. I don't know now if he ever will.'

She followed his gaze down towards the sinister wind-whispering trees by her house. 'He's with you now?'

'You must think I'm talking gibberish. I'm not superstitious, really I'm not, but that boy… He's real. He's there.'

She sensed real fear, put her arm round his shoulders and hugged him to her. He rested his head on her.

'I keep thinking I can send him away. Last year, when I gave Anja and Boris Pranjić that money, I thought that was it. After all, I didn't have to do it.' He sat up straight and spread his arms. 'It was meant to be a great big gesture that would finally lay it all to rest. The boy promised to leave me alone. But then I met you. I dared to hope.' He made a darting movement with his hand. 'He was right back, as if that chance of happiness was too much.'

He stood abruptly. She watched his back for a moment as he strode down the hill, before hurrying to catch him up.

'Jay, you *have* got that chance. You've told me now. I'm still here, aren't I?'

She grabbed his arm. He slowed but didn't stop.

'I want to believe that you forgive me, you don't know how much, but... Oh, Polly, I'm so glad you keep on trying. One day...' He shook his head. 'But perhaps not. You don't need any of it.'

'Of course I do!' She pulled on his arm and was surprised how easily she managed to stop him. She drew him to her and kissed him and he responded passionately before drawing away.

'One day,' he said again and smiled, but set off purposefully towards the house.

This time there was no stopping him and he wouldn't be drawn to say another word. When they got back to the house he put the kettle on.

'Time for a coffee then I'd better make my way over to Bradford. Make sure I'm in plenty of time for my important meeting.'

The irony in his voice betrayed his unease.

'I've been thinking about that. You can't just take it on yourself. I could tell the police for you. Get you some back-up. I'll make sure—'

'No! Sorry. I don't know what I believe any more but if Vinko's in trouble... If whoever he's with got the slightest whiff of the police I hate to think what might happen to him. I've got to do as they say.' He paused, twisting his scarf. 'I'm probably being gullible, but I can't help it. I want to believe Vinko didn't mean it. I'm worried about him.'

The shrilling of the phone interrupted him. Marilyn sighed as she answered it.

'It's Lucy from Barton Mill here.'

'Oh, hi. Matt left a while back, I'm afraid. He was going up to see some guy—'

'No probs; it's not him I want to speak to. Vinko's here looking for your Jay.'

'Vinko?' She went cold. 'Lucy, are you all *right*?'

Jay came and stood by her. She put the phone on speaker so he could listen in.

'Yeah…yeah, sure.' She paused, then her next words came spilling out. 'He doesn't look like he'd hurt a fly and in any case he's in a really bad way. He's landed Jay in trouble but he had no choice and now he wants to find him and…and I think he should go to the police but he daren't and I can't just do it behind his back because the poor lad's in such a state. Can you come over? I feel out of my depth to be honest. Have you got Jay there? He's desperate to see him.'

'Are you sure it's not a trap? What do you mean "had no choice"?'

'He was forced to make some phone call, at gunpoint.'

'You mean when he spoke to Jay yesterday?'

'Yeah, that. He was rambling all over the place, but as far as I can gather, these two guys took him off to a house somewhere. They got him to talk – something about some money, you know? – by shoving his head under water till he half drowned – again and again – and he's really beating himself up that he even mentioned Jay, but – oh, Marilyn! There are these fag burns all over his hands and when they gave him his phone and said tell Jay, they stuck one on his knee and said that's where we'll shoot if you say a word wrong. They were at it again last night trying to find out

283

more, where you live and all that, but the poor lad claims he doesn't *know* any more. Makes me shudder to think! So, late on they went out and he managed to get out of the cupboard they'd locked him in – he seems well sharp even in the state he's in, even nicked the money for a taxi fare can you believe. He turned up at the shop first thing this morning looking for Jay.'

'Where is he now?'

'Upstairs in the flat. I told him to get some sleep, though whether he will or not... keeps going on about letting people down, but honestly, no one in their right mind could blame him. But I don't know what to do now. How soon can you get here?'

Marilyn glanced at Jay.

'We'll be straight over – twenty minutes at the outside, OK?'

She hung up and grabbed her car keys.

Chapter 29

'You don't believe her, do you?' Marilyn said without taking her eyes off the road.

'Not Lucy – Vinko,' Jay replied, on the defensive. 'Of course I want to believe him – but how do we know this isn't just another part of the act?'

He wanted so much to believe Vinko hadn't turned against him, whatever the implications.

'You only spoke to him on the phone. She's actually seen him.'

Jay shrugged. 'We'll find out soon enough. If he's lying, she's in trouble. If he's not, they both are. We've got to go either way.'

He looked across at her.

'I know it's a big ask, love, but if…if what he told Lucy is the truth, could we bring him back to Stoneleigh for a bit?'

'You're joking!'

'I mean it, Pol.'

She stared at the road ahead. 'Hasn't it gone far enough? Can't we just let the police deal with it?'

'I'm not saying we shouldn't, but…say we give him a break, talk to him first. *If* we decide to believe him. Lucy's going to call the cops straight away, I know. He might want to stay at Barton Mill, but if he doesn't… Just so he knows—'

'He can trust you.' She sighed. 'He'd better do a damn good job of convincing me he hasn't told those thugs where I live. Let's see what we find. I'm not promising anything.'

As they pulled into the car park, Jay paused before opening the car door.

'Are you sure about this, love? On second thoughts, you could always just drop me off. Come and collect me...us...' He shrugged. 'I don't want you following me into trouble.'

'Don't patronise me, Spinney.'

He grinned. 'It's for your own good, you know.'

The tension in the car eased a little as she smiled back. 'Shut up, let's go.'

As they made their way up to Matt and Lucy's shop they heard signs of life in the two other ground-floor units. There was a handwritten sign on the first-floor door.

Temporarily closed. Back by 11.
Sorry for any inconvenience. L ♥

'They must be up at the flat,' Polly said.

Jay nodded and followed her up the stairs. Like the floor below, there was only one door. She knocked and they heard indistinct sounds inside. He glanced at Polly and she took his hand as they waited. He squeezed it briefly and she knocked again. He thought he heard footsteps. No one answered. After a third try he raised an eyebrow; she looked worried but nodded and he tried the door, with mixed feelings when it gave.

'Let me go first,' he whispered.

As he pushed the door open slowly he heard a crash from a room to his left. The world seemed unnaturally bright and clear and he could hear his heart thumping in his ears. He gestured to Polly to wait by the door and stepped in. The boy from Paševina was standing by a window directly across the room, and Jay's heart skipped a beat as he saw it was wide open.

'Who's there?' he called in the direction of the noise he'd heard. There was a scuffle and he called again. 'Lucy? Vinko?'

The door of what looked like the bathroom was ajar and he heard footsteps. He wished he had something to defend himself with. Vinko appeared in the doorway clutching a flick knife. Jay grabbed a carved soapstone figure from the coffee table and looked back at Vinko, shocked by what he saw. There were dark shadows round his eyes and his hands were bandaged. One of the bandages had come loose and was trailing from his wrist. The lad's eyes looked wild.

'It...it's all right,' Vinko said, looking past him to Polly. 'I knock things over being...you know...clumsy. I'm sorry to hide. Lucy said you're coming. But you scared me.'

Jay nodded. 'You scared us too. She phoned and told us what you'd said.'

His voice sounded more suspicious than he'd intended and he felt bad about it. They stared at each other.

'It's true that I tell her. You believe me, please, Jay?'

Jay nodded, giving Vinko a brief smile as he realised he did. 'So where is she now – Lucy?'

Vinko frowned. 'The shop. She left so I can rest, she would phone you without to disturb me. She knows I'm OK and—'

'She's not there.' Jay swallowed, glanced at Polly.

Vinko shrugged. 'She said when there are no customers she will go to pharmacy to buy painkillers and...?' He paused, ran a hand over the bandage on his arm.

'Antiseptic?'

He nodded. 'Things like them. I think she will return here soon.'

Jay breathed a little more easily before giving Vinko a pointed look.

'Please will you put that down?'

Vinko glanced at the knife as if he'd forgotten he was grasping it, folded it and tucked it into the pocket of a pair of jeans that sagged baggily beneath an ill-fitting sweatshirt. Jay followed the movement with his eyes, unable to mask his disapproval.

'How do you come to have that thing?'

'I always have it. I taked it back for myself when I escaped yesterday night – this morning. I thought the knocking was someone else. It is...in the case of trouble.' He looked at the ornament in Jay's hand. 'But you, Jay. You put that down also. No stealing, yes?'

He grinned suddenly and before Jay knew it the lad was clutching him in a bear hug like his only friend in a hostile world.

'I took my phone back, too, and tried to call you. You didn't answer.' The familiarity caused him to slip back into Croatian. 'This was the only place I could think of to look for you. I'm sorry if I've caused any trouble.'

Jay muttered awkward words of reassurance, but Vinko pulled away.

'No. I mustn't be weak. I was weak yesterday, I was weak earlier when Lucy told me, "You must rest, Vinko, you're safe now." She must have been crazy to think I could sleep, but I was crazier because I *did* sleep.' He shook his head in disgust. 'I should have been alert, I shouldn't have slept. I was drowsy and confused when you—'

'Why don't you sit down?' They both looked round to where Polly was still waiting by the door, though she'd shut it behind her. She waved to the sofa where a crumpled blanket suggested Vinko had been sleeping. 'I don't know what you've been saying but you look done in. Sit down before you go any further.'

288

Vinko obeyed. She went over to the wide-open window, turned and gave him a questioning look.

'When I heard the knocking I think of the way to escape,' he said.

She leaned out, shook her head and closed the window.

'Jay, don't you think—'

'Let's give it a minute. Please, love?' He turned to Vinko, trying to smile. 'Vinko, this is Marilyn. Marilyn – Vinko.'

'I am pleased for knowing you,' he said. 'I think you hear bad things about me, but—'

'Don't worry about that.'

'Thank you. You sit down also, please.'

She smiled and sat on the other sofa. Jay positioned himself beside her, a protective arm around her.

'Who are they?' he asked.

'My uncle, Mihal Novak—' He looked away. 'I'm sorry, Jay. I really did tell him…when we were together. I say to him I don't want to… I must – I should…'

'Don't worry about me,' Polly said. 'Speak whatever language you like. Jay can explain to me.'

Vinko flashed her a grateful smile before turning back to Jay. 'I should have told you when you asked. I couldn't. I like you, how could I? He was asking all the time about my grandparents' money. I did want to meet them, honestly I did, for myself, but he kept on asking me to find out more. And,' he looked away, 'he wanted me to find you. And it was all for…for someone else.'

'Who?'

Vinko stared at the carpet. 'Lek.'

'Lek?' Jay felt the world drop away from him as he stared at Vinko in disbelief. The boy from Paševina was leaning insolently against the wall behind him, with an expression that said, 'It's your turn now.' 'I thought Lek was in prison.'

289

He looked at Polly to steady himself. Vinko followed his gaze.

'I'm sorry, he will tell you soon,' he said to her and turned back to Jay. 'He was. War crimes.'

'I heard,' said Jay. 'I confess I celebrated.'

'But he's out now. He said he managed to get his sentence reduced. So he says now he needs his money. It's his and he wants it for his retirement. He also said he thought you had a part in putting him away.'

Jay shook his head. 'I was never called as a witness. I suppose no one found me.'

'Well he thinks you did and he wants to see you. I didn't know anything about that when I went with Novak. Yesterday…yesterday morning I lost my job. Because we'd been away. I tried and tried to call you, Jay and I'm sorry, but I was convinced you didn't care. I'm not asking you to understand. But that's how it was. So Novak saw me and he told me Lek was a good friend of my dad's. They'd be good to me. I should have realised. I knew you didn't like that man.' He held up his bandaged hands. 'When Novak took me to that house, I knew he wasn't my dad's friend either.'

Jay was shaking his head. He was shocked at the betrayal but Vinko's obvious regret made him suppress it; he could deal with that later. He felt hardly able to force words out. 'I'm sorry, I didn't get your calls till later,' he said lamely.

Vinko turned to him, agitated. 'I didn't want to say what I did to you yesterday. I couldn't stand the things they were doing to me anymore; they made me tell them everything I know about you. I had to.' He looked away. 'I hoped you wouldn't believe I meant it. I tried to send you a message but they grabbed my phone. I tried.'

'I know you did. I'm sorry. I worked it out, but it was

too late by then. I went to your house but you weren't there. All I could do was wait till tonight.'

Vinko shuddered. 'I'm glad that's not happening.'

'Where are they now? How did you get here?'

'I don't know where they are. They told me yesterday evening they were off on some business. They were going to come back to that house this afternoon, to take me to my flat to meet you. They left me locked in a cupboard, but it was below the stairs and I smelled where the wood was rotten. I managed to break through.' His fingers found the trailing bandage and he wound it absently back round his hand. 'It took ages, and I was making such a noise. I was scared they were still there, tricking me, ready to beat me for escaping. But there was no one waiting. So I believe they really won't be back till this afternoon.' He glanced at Polly. 'You want to tell her?'

Jay hurriedly explained.

'Are you all right now?' she asked.

'Tired.' Vinko shrugged. 'Lucy cared after me. She helped with burns, she gave me food, she borrowed me dry clothes from her boyfriend. I will be OK.'

'She'll probably be back by now,' Jay said. 'We ought to go and tell her we're here. Take you home.' He glanced from Vinko to Polly. She frowned but nodded. 'We were thinking you could come back with us for a little while. Lucy can call the police here and—' He held a hand up to silence Vinko's protest. 'We can talk about it on the way. Come on.'

He made for the door, beckoning them to follow. The sign was still on the locked door of the shop.

'Do you know if there's a spare key at the flat, Polly? It'd be best if we wait for her here.'

'You have the credit card?' asked Vinko.

291

Jay swallowed his objection and handed him his card. He watched with grudging admiration as the lad forced the lock within seconds, and raised his eyebrows at Polly.

'There's a deadlock on the outside door to the building,' she said apologetically.

'First job for young Matt when all this is over – security review.'

They laughed nervously and he thought how they really shouldn't be laughing at a time like this. As they made their way towards the back of the shop, Vinko bent to pick up a pair of scissors lying with some scattered papers on the floor.

'Don't!' Jay's command halted him. 'Best not touch anything.'

Vinko stepped back. 'Lucy held that when she was feared of me.'

Jay nodded, trying to suppress the panic that threatened to engulf him. This shop felt like a scene from a dream. Despite the presence of Polly and Vinko, he felt alone.

No you're not. The boy sat on the counter, casually swinging his legs as he watched them. Jay was about to reach out and touch Polly for reassurance, when a knock at the door made him jump.

'Lucy?' A man's voice came through the thick wood.

'It's Paul from downstairs,' Polly said quietly.

Vinko had vanished into the storeroom by the time she opened the door to a tall man in an Aran sweater. 'Marilyn? What're you doing here? I heard footsteps on the stairs and assumed Lucy was back. D'you know where she's gone?'

She shrugged. 'She had to pop out to the shops. We happened to call round and I said we'd keep an eye on things till she gets back. Matt's gone to check out some woodcarving guy.'

'Uh huh, I saw him earlier.'

'I was just about to open up for them. This is my new boyfriend,' she added, indicating Jay.

Paul flashed Jay a look, nodded. 'Hi.' He turned back to Polly. 'I just came to see if your phone's working? Ours isn't getting a dial tone. *Nada.* Zilch.'

Jay was standing nearest to the phone and hoped the guy couldn't hear his heart thumping as he picked it up. It yielded a heavy silence. 'Yeah, this one too.' His voice sounded as if the dead phone had swallowed it.

Paul nodded. 'I'll look into it. Keep you posted.' He turned to go. 'Shall I leave the door open, then?'

Jay was relieved when Polly closed the door behind him, muttering something about a moment to familiarise herself as she hadn't been in charge there for a while.

'You'd best phone the police on your mobile,' Jay said as Vinko emerged from the storeroom.

'The door to outside stairs, it's not proper shut. I saw Lucy lock it when I was here before. Someone—'

He was interrupted by a ring tone. Jay watched him take his mobile from his pocket and listen. The little colour there was drained from Vinko's face.

'It's Lek,' he whispered, holding the phone out like a hand grenade with the pin pulled. 'He will talk with you.'

Jay took it, feeling the faint warmth left by Vinko's hand on the cold metal casing.

'Hello, Šojka Stranac.'

The distantly remembered voice added to the unreality of it all. Jay found it easy to pretend this was someone else's story, and that helped to keep his voice steady.

'Lek.'

'You don't sound enough friendly, Šojka. Young Ivan's boy, he thinks you don't want knowing your old friend. You must tell him he is wrong.'

'What do you want?'

He was glad Lek couldn't see him, fingers fiddling restlessly with the ends of his scarf and betraying his nerves.

'I think we should talk, my friend. See, I even speak your language now. We could have lessons…where I've been. I think you know. English is good for business, they say. And good for talking with people like you. You will help me, yes?'

'Just say what it is you want.'

'Vinko didn't already tell you? I want you to help me have my wife's money back.'

So he had married her. It meant nothing and it was someone else's story now. Jay glanced at Polly. Even with her worried expression he drew strength from her presence. 'I don't know what you expect me to do.'

'Don't play the games, Šojka. I had the long talk with Ivan's boy, you know? You stole my wife's money.'

'I stole nothing. She instructed me to look after it.'

'You say look after, I say stole. The important thing is, now you give it back.'

'I've already given it back.'

'To the wrong ones.'

'To Zora's family. She told me that if she died it was my decision what to do with it.'

'She told *me* before she sadly died to find you and have it back.'

'Even if I believed you, it's no longer mine to give.'

'You can find and give it. You must persuade Vesna.'

'What makes you think I know—'

'No games I said, Šojka! We know you are the family's friend. If you don't talk with her already, you can yet. Mihal, he can tell you where. You like to talk to the other man's wife, don't you, eh? But enough talking now. Go to the bank and you meet us soon. You bring enough of money to show me you will help, and we talk.'

Jay glanced from Polly to Vinko. 'Where will I find you?'

'You phone me after the bank, then I tell you. It is not far. We will have meeting-together soon, my friend. I will enjoy it. And Šojka? You come alone. Not with no one, not even with Ivan's little coward-son. We know you are at Bartonmill. We can see this and we will see if you bring someone.' Jay was just registering the fact that Lek was close enough to have seen them arrive, when he spoke again, 'And you come with no weapon. We have someone here who wants you to obey my asking.'

He heard shuffling and a woman's voice gasping indistinctly.

'For fuck's sake, Lek, don't—'

'Not yet I don't. Not when you do that I say. But why are you worried, Šojka? She says she is not your woman. Perhaps because you don't look after her good enough.'

Jay spoke over the unpleasant laughter. 'There's a bank on the square. I'll call you in a few minutes. Don't lay a fucking finger on her.'

He snapped the phone off and took a deep breath, trying to imagine the flow of air smoothing out the knot in the pit of his stomach. He still felt a dreamlike unreality as he gave Polly and Vinko a rapid account of what Lek had said.

'So, Vinko, can I borrow this?' He tapped the phone.

'Surely you're not *going*?' Polly said.

'Of course I am!' He brushed aside her obvious fear before it could infect him. 'Were you listening to a bloody word I said?' Her shocked expression made him realise how he'd sounded. 'I'm sorry, Polly love, this is stressing me out.' He tried to sound as apologetic as he felt. 'I've got to go; that girl's in serious danger.'

295

'But what are you going to do? Surely—'

'I'll think of something.' He slammed his hand down impatiently on the counter. 'I'll try and call you when I know where they are, but I've got to be careful. I might try and leave a sign.' He fingered his scarf and Polly nodded. 'If you don't hear from me in ten minutes, call the police anyway.'

He passed Vinko his phone back and shuffled impatiently as Vinko saved Lek's and Polly's numbers on it. He forced himself to take rather than snatch it from him as he began to enter the relevant numbers on Polly's.

'You can't be so stupid! I'm calling the police now,' she insisted as Vinko handed her phone back.

'Please don't. Give me chance to get there alone like he said.'

Jay was still trying to breathe steadily.

'Take this.' Vinko offered him the knife.

Jay frowned at it, shaking his head. 'No way. He said come unarmed.'

Vinko mimed putting it in his pocket. 'How will he know?'

'Oh, for fuck's sake! You want me to get done for carrying an offensive weapon on top of everything? They've got *guns*, right? Didn't do you any good, did it?' He realised he was shouting. First Polly, now Vinko. 'Shit, I'm sorry. I know you mean well.'

Vinko looked at him. That conspiratorial smile again. 'You perhaps need it for freeing Lucy, that is all.'

Jay tried to smile back. He had to admire the lad's quick thinking, but shook his head. 'I'll find a way. And, Vinko, don't try and follow. They might see you. Please.'

He looked at Polly, any idea of warning her to keep an eye on Vinko engulfed by his dread of leaving her. He wanted to reassure her, hold her, say goodbye properly, but the boy from Paševina was standing between them and Jay couldn't move. He could only hope his eyes spoke for him as he tore himself away and made for the fire door.

'Be careful,' she said as he started down the cast-iron fire escape stairs.

'I'll be back before any of us knows it,' he managed to say, fearing that neither Polly nor Vinko believed it any more than he did.

Chapter 30

Jay glanced over his shoulder, though he knew there was no one behind him at the cash machine. He forced himself to act deliberately and carefully as he stuffed the notes into his wallet, wishing the limit for withdrawals was higher. He hadn't dared enter the bank as he didn't trust himself not to give in and ask for help; to run away. Lek wanted to see him, alone; to attempt anything else was too much of a risk. Reminding himself that he'd be doing his best not to hand anything over to Lek, so the amount didn't matter anyway, he stepped aside from the machine and dialled.

'You took too long, Šojka.'

He felt the world jolt around him. 'But—'

Lek laughed softly. 'Nearly. You listen now.'

The pause felt endless. Someone else's story.

'Where do you want me to go?' he asked, hoping the edge to his voice sounded like confident impatience rather than desperation.

'You know where is Queen Street? You go to newspaper shop on the corner.'

This was completely the opposite direction from the one he would have expected, if his rapid assessment of all the buildings in sight from the fire escape had been correct.

'I'll call you back when I get there,' he said.

'No, Šojka! You stay with the phone. I don't want that you get lost.'

Jay could almost hear the other man's unpleasant grin and wondered how he'd been so naïve as to think Lek

298

wouldn't prevent him from telling anyone where he was going. He realised how much he'd been wanting Vinko to disobey and come after him. Hoping for Lucy's sake that the battery in Vinko's phone would last, he walked as quickly as he could around the edge of the busy Friday morning market, keeping out of sight of Mike Greene's stall. As he muttered responses to Lek's occasional prompts, he tried not to think how often he'd looked with disdain from his busker's vantage point at passers-by with phones clamped to their ears, playing their lives out ostentatiously in public. It was as if Lek knew his opinion and even now was thinking of new ways to humiliate him. He worked at his scarf with the hand that wasn't holding the phone, eventually freeing it and wiping the sweat from his forehead. The town centre was small, but Lek's tortuous route made the walk seem endless. The phone signal threatened to break up occasionally, filling him with cold fear every time. He was thinking painfully clearly, all his senses alert. The boy walked slightly ahead of him as if he, too, had a direct line to Lek. Jay ignored him. He kept glancing in the direction of Barton Mill, but despite its elevated position he never seemed to come to a point where the windows of the upper storeys were visible.

From the craft shop fire escape, Vinko watched Jay cross the market square. He kept in shadow, smoking a cigarette from the packet Lucy had given him, and scanned the buildings again; if Lek really had been watching them, it shouldn't be too hard to make out his vantage point. Jay had said he saw nothing, but Vinko prided himself on his long-distance vision. He suddenly caught a hint of movement, narrowed his eyes and concentrated further. He was certain the occasional soft flash like an erratic lighthouse beacon was the low autumn sun catching a pair of binoculars. It could have been his imagination, but he caught it again. It was a starting point.

'Come.'

He beckoned Marilyn over and they studied the buildings and streets between them and the movement Vinko had seen. Eventually satisfied he'd be able to find the place, he turned and went back into the shop.

'He will be moving now,' he said. She glanced unnecessarily at her watch and nodded. 'Perhaps we should phone him and not wait. In case he losed the number.'

'Jay? Do a stupid thing like that?'

She laughed nervously and he made himself smile back. He watched her make the call, remembering how Jay had left without even saying goodbye to her properly and wondering if he'd got it wrong – perhaps this wasn't the woman Jay loved, either.

'It's engaged.'

Her worried expression echoed Vinko's own fears. He suppressed them. They waited for a few seconds, then tried again. She shook her head.

'Then I go.'

'You can't!'

'I must.'

'I'm calling the police.'

'Please.' Vinko hurried to the shop door. 'You go to the man downstairs and talk about the phone if you are scared. After you give us time you call the police if you want. But please, some time!'

He ignored her protests and hurried down the stone stairs, hoping he'd got it right that the entrance onto the car park would be out of Lek's line of vision. He paused by the doorway to let a man pass.

'Morning.'

Vinko nodded and smiled but didn't reply, reluctant to let this man hear his accent.

'Hey, Matt!' The man Paul who'd come about the phones was standing in the door to his unit. The one called Matt paused. He looked about to move to let Vinko past when Paul said, 'I'm glad I caught you. Did you know Marilyn's at your place?'

'Marilyn?'

Paul shrugged. 'Seemed a bit weird. I went up a bit back – phones are off, I wanted to ask if yours was too – and the place was shut. I knocked and I couldn't believe—'

'Excuse me.' Vinko felt panic rising as he moved to get past.

'Just a minute.' Matt was staring at him with a frown, and Vinko realised this must be the boyfriend whose clothes Lucy had lent him.

'Excuse me.' He pushed past before Matt had time to react.

'Oy! What's going on?'

Without pausing to think, Vinko ran across the cobbled car park and slipped out onto the street, following the direction they'd planned from their vantage point. He didn't look back, but ran, slowing to a walk when he got too tired, hoping that Marilyn would be able to deal with Matt and, silently, apologising yet again….

It seemed like another day, another week, when Jay finally followed the harsh-voiced instructions to a passageway between a couple of two-storey, stone-built warehouse buildings typical of the little town. One bore a jumble of signs – Jay registered a graphic design office and a flaking board with a logo that meant nothing to him – and the

301

other looked empty. As he entered the passageway, hoping he was out of sight of the building's windows, he dropped his scarf and walked on. The sound of his echoing footsteps almost drowned out Lek's gloating voice and the short passage seemed to stretch before him like a tunnel. The dreamlike sensation had returned and he had to push each foot in front of the other to keep moving. It was almost a relief to reach a yard, neatly swept with a tub of flowers to one side, and a few weeds poking through the flags to the other. There was a gate across the yard ahead of him, presumably to the next street, an open door to the offices on his left and a couple of old but solid-looking doors to the building on his right. One or two of the windows were boarded up; the rest looked swathed in cobwebs. A tiny inner voice told him this was a mistake, to walk away while he still had the chance. He briefly considered ducking into the graphic design studio and calling for help, but he thought of Lucy and the way Vinko had been treated and knew he couldn't. He heard a lorry approach and the gate across the yard being opened. Lek swore down the phone.

'You wait there where I see you, Šojka.'

Jay stepped to one side and tried to look as if he were making a normal phone call.

Too exhausted to run, but making himself keep walking as quickly as possible, Vinko soon came to the end of the street Marilyn had told him to look for. He pretended to read the notices in the window of a corner shop as he scanned it. It was only short, one side lined with terraced houses, the other occupied by two smallish stone-built warehouse buildings. One of the warehouses looked empty and Vinko noticed a familiar scrap of fabric in the entrance to the passage between them. He saw no movement from the upper-floor windows but the sight of Jay's scarf and the knowledge that Lek was so close froze him with fear.

He recalled the way Matt had looked at him. It wouldn't be long before the police arrived. Goaded into action, he crossed the road and moved quickly towards the alleyway, keeping close in to the wall in the hope that a watcher from above would miss him. Vinko ducked into the passage and slowed. The sound of a lorry's engine running, with the occasional clattering and voices of a delivery being unloaded, drowned out the sound of his footsteps in the echoing space. Halfway down the passage he saw a cobweb-encrusted window with a broken pane and a door. The door was bolted; he peered in at the window. Scattered cans and cigarette ends, together with the charred stain of a bonfire against the wall, told him others had been here before him. It made him crave a cigarette himself, but he suppressed the feeling, annoyed by his own weakness. He eased the window open and climbed in, wishing his heart was thumping merely with the thrill of breaking into an illicit drinking den.

The interior door was ajar and he picked his way towards it, taking care not to trip and rattle the cans and bottles. The faint smell of old smoke and urine felt like a fog surrounding and concealing him as he peered through the door, gripping his knife and making the burns on his hand smart. An empty corridor led to a staircase. The sound of the lorry was more distant now and as he paused, listening, he heard the distant murmur of a voice from upstairs. The sound of his tormentor threatened to immobilise him again and he had to force himself to move slowly on. Action caused his terror to settle into a simmering anger. The hulking shape of a cupboard against a wall between him and the staircase offered a scant sanctuary should anyone appear. He crept past an open door, which revealed a huge dingy room, and his heart leapt as he saw Novak waiting by a door to the courtyard. Crouching in the shadow beside the cupboard, he paused. When it came again, Lek's voice was still distant but Vinko had tuned in and could catch the words.

'You stay waiting. If they ask you something you make the excuse and go, you stay talking to me and you come back when I say. Remember, Šojka – you mess with me, I mess with her.'

Vinko shuddered. He heard footsteps on the floor above and shrank back into the shadow. Once he was satisfied Lek wasn't coming down, he crept silently but swiftly up the steps, keeping a wary eye on the top. The staircase was dark and he kept close to the side in deepest shadow, heading for the relatively bright light of the room on the first floor. He paused before approaching the open entrance, the wall between the stairwell and the room concealing his presence but blocking his view. The fear that Lek might have turned from the window and was now waiting just around the corner grew until he could almost smell the man's sour breath. But he had no choice, and peered into the room, his blade cold comfort in his aching hand. He scanned the room ahead of him in a split second. A row of windows ran down each side of the wide room; Lek was silhouetted against one to the left, his back to Vinko and his attention outside. The window was open and sound of the lorry loud, but the room was empty – no chance of a hiding place. Terror gripped Vinko as he saw no sign of Lucy. She wasn't here, this was a trap, and he'd walked into it. Was he too late to stop Jay walking into it too? He almost shouted out – anything to distract Lek, somehow let Jay know. He was about to open his mouth when he noticed the glazed door to a room on his right, above the ground-floor corridor. Lek spoke into the phone again; Vinko didn't hear the words as he took the opportunity to dart for the room.

She was there, tied to a chair and gagged. Vinko was momentarily glad of the gag as without it she'd probably have betrayed his presence in the seconds before she registered who he was. He worked at the ropes with the knife and freed her, a hand on her arm compelling her to stay where she was and stay quiet after he removed the gag. As rapidly as he could, he indicated with hands and fingers the escape route, hoping the intensity of his gaze would force her to obey when he gave her the signal. Trying to stay hidden, he peered out through the glazed door into the warehouse. Lek was still by the window, the phone still at his ear, the air now menacingly silent. The lorry must have gone. After a tense pause, Lek spoke.

'Good. Tie him and bring him up here to me.'

His attention was still out of the window, and Vinko hoped with all his heart that Marilyn had already sent help. No time to waste on fruitless thoughts; he nudged Lucy and indicated with his eyes for her to leave. She'd been immobile for a while and her movements were painfully stiff at first. He waited by the office door, ready to distract Lek's attention away from her, dreading the moment when he'd have to. The distance to the top of the stairs stretched before them, impossibly vast. She ran silently, but too slowly. Vinko wanted to breathe but couldn't. She was almost at the top of the stairs when Lek noticed the movement. As his gaze darted from Lucy to the office, he fixed Vinko with cold eyes and raised his pistol.

Jay's senses were heightened, taking him to a place beyond fear. A place he remembered. With the cold reality of a gun to his head, at first he didn't resist, waiting for an opportunity as the man who'd been Vesna's husband began to bind his hands. He must have had the cord in a loop ready and was working single-handed. Trying to judge the best moment to break free from the grip of a man with a gun, Jay followed the man's every clumsy move, but the pressure of the weapon never slackened. The man's muttered insults betrayed his fear, a fear that made him all the more dangerous. The rope was pulled tighter round Jay's wrists – he had to act soon or admit defeat. He was tensing, ready to risk jerking free, when a shot cracked out.

He remembered that moment of blissful unawareness before the pain kicked in. But this time, though the pressure against his temple had gone, no agony rushed in to fill the absence. A split second later he was thinking clearly enough to realise the shot had come from elsewhere, magnified by the empty building. He jerked up with his shoulder and knocked the gun from Novak's hand. As it clattered to the floor he realised with relief that he'd recovered from the paralysis of shock momentarily faster than his adversary. He pulled his hands apart, ignoring the rope burn as a minor irritation, and bent to grab the gun a second before the other man snapped out of it and lunged towards him. Jay swung round and struck him hard on the side of the head with the butt, clumsy but effective.

As the man sprawled behind him, Jay paused, trying to decide which way to go. There was a loading door at the far end of the room and a smaller door to his right. The sound of someone clattering wildly down stairs on the far side of that one caused panic to rush in and fill his mind in place of the pain he'd been anticipating a moment before. His overriding thought was that he was too late. Lek had fired. The bastard had probably never intended to spare

306

Lucy. The thought made Jay feel sick, but he forced himself to suppress it, along with jumbled questions about why Lek hadn't waited for the chance to gloat as he forced Jay to witness the girl's torment.

He snapped his focus back; whatever had happened, Lek was on his way down. Jay checked Novak's pistol as he moved quickly to the door, familiarising himself with a model he didn't know. He had no time to do anything but hope. The footsteps drew level with the door and Jay braced himself. He saw the fleeting image of a figure running past, caught a momentary snapshot of a young woman's face as she passed. Too surprised to question how or why, he reached the door and looked after her down the corridor. From a room at the end to his right he heard the jarring rattle of a can being kicked, and a scrabbling which suggested she was making her escape.

He was about to follow her when he heard the sounds of a struggle in the room above. He'd been an idiot to assume there were only two of them. Before he could beat his own retreat he heard a curse in a language and a voice he recognised, and the new wave of fear that coursed through him was sharper, more real, than anything he'd felt all morning.

Vinko.

As he rushed up the stairs, wondering how on earth Vinko came to be there, he saw the boy from Paševina looking into the upstairs room. Jay ignored him, readied the gun and peered round the door at the top.

A movement to his left drew his attention. Lek was waiting for him. He had Vinko held against the wall. The lad struggled ineffectually, his arms pinned behind him, a large dark stain spreading across his sweatshirt from a nasty-looking gash in his neck. Vinko's knife lay on the floor, out of reach, the blade glistening with blood. Lek's pistol touched the side of his head and he froze.

Jay forced himself to look away from Vinko's scared eyes to stare at Lek. He appeared older, much older, but the cold eyes were the same and he was still strong. Strong enough to hold Vinko in his weakened state.

'I'm here as you asked.' Jay's voice was hoarse. He spoke in Croatian – someone else's story. 'Let him go.'

Lek barked a laugh. Didn't move. 'Why, Šojka?' he replied in the same language. 'This is why we're here.'

Jay steadied the gun in his hand, trying to aim at Lek while missing Vinko. Lek tightened his grip roughly.

'My reactions are fast, remember, Šojka? You shoot and I shoot.' He gave Vinko a slight shove and more blood oozed from his neck.

'Let him go. I've got the money. Take it and I'll give you more. Soon – tomorrow. Whatever you ask for. Don't—'

'It's not about the money.'

'But—'

'I got you here. That's what it's about.' He stared at Jay, holding him motionless. Out of the corner of his eye Jay saw the boy from Paševina, watching. 'You took *her*. You turned Ivan against me. You took my freedom— *No!* Don't argue. This is my time. Now it's your turn to lose something.' He shoved Vinko and the lad's yelp of pain was like a knife to Jay's old wound.

'This won't bring anything back! Let him go, Lek, for fuck's sake. He's nothing to do with it!'

'He's everything.' Lek's expression was impassive. He shook Vinko with each phrase. 'He's a worthless, lying little bastard. Like his father. But he matters to *you*.'

Jay stared at Lek, and past him to the boy from Paševina. The boy gave the tiniest nod. Deal. Jay spread his arms, bracing himself against what was to come. 'So it's me you want.'

'No, Jay, don't!' Vinko protested and Lek twisted his arms cruelly. Three pairs of eyes held Jay. Vinko's scared but defiant, Lek's cold, victorious; the boy's merely curious.

'Go on.' Jay tightened the grip on the gun in his outstretched hand, ready to swing it round as soon as Lek shifted his attention from Vinko. 'Take me. What are you waiting for?'

Lek laughed again. 'Oh, no. Not so simple, Šojka. I could have you. Easy. But dead men don't feel guilt. Dead men don't suffer.'

The two men stared at one another, each waiting for the other to waver. Jay despaired. As soon as he moved, or as soon as Lek had enough of his game, Vinko would die or get seriously hurt. He knew Lek could do it. His arms began to tremble and ache but he held himself steady, terrified that any movement would be the other man's cue. The cold air of the warehouse grew thick and heavy. He was aware of vague sounds from outside, but none of it mattered. Help seemed impossible. Without taking his eyes from Lek he was aware of the boy. He longed for him to intervene; knew that was impossible, too.

Lek smiled slowly. 'Ready for this, Šojka?'

The silence that followed was sliced by a shrill sound from the phone lying on the window ledge behind Lek. He ignored it but the instant the tension was broken, Lek's attention faltering briefly, Jay brought the gun round with nothing to lose, aimed just enough to miss Vinko, and fired. He was aware of two shots but in a frozen moment had no idea who had reacted first. He vaguely heard Lek's gun clatter to the floor as, sick to his heart, he watched Vinko, his hair sticky with blood, sink to his knees.

Before Jay could react, the lad shoved away, leaving the older man clutching his shoulder, lunged for his knife and plunged it into Lek before stumbling a few paces and sinking down again, his strength spent. Lek fell to the floor behind him.

Hardly aware of what he was doing, Jay grabbed Lek's gun and threw it and the one he was holding as hard as he could across the room, out of reach. He knelt by Vinko, tearing his own shirt off to staunch his wounds. He realised with relief that the stickiness in his hair was not the lad's own blood and fought down panic as he pressed the fabric to his neck, not knowing whether he was doing any good or causing more damage. In his helplessness the years melted and he wondered when it would ever end.

'It's OK, Vinko, it's all right.'

'All right? It fucking *hurts*.' His voice was small and he tried to smile but his attention was wavering. 'But thanks. I'm sorry, I tried...'

His eyes fluttered closed.

'Shhh. Stay still. Stay awake. We're safe, it's going to be all right.'

He willed Vinko to believe him, though he didn't know himself if he was speaking the truth this time. He couldn't look away but sensed the boy from Paševina had gone and hoped that was a good sign. Footsteps rang through the building and Jay called out that it was safe; heard himself shouting for help, an ambulance, as he felt Vinko getting weaker. Hushed voices grew louder, and with relief like a soft drop of rain in the desert of his fear, he heard Polly's among them.

'So that was you?'

Polly nodded and squeezed his hand as they watched the

medics carry the stretcher towards the waiting ambulance. Jay tried to shrug off the cumbersome shock blanket and follow. She held him, told him to stay where he was, sitting on the dirty floor against the wall. He was shaking.

'He's in the best place. You can't do anything more right now.'

'I want to go with him. I'll answer all the questions they want, but later. Just—'

'You'll be following all right – you're in shock yourself, Jay. Let go for a few moments. Give yourself a chance.'

He relaxed slightly under her touch and shrugged, stared in the direction of the ambulance.

'Tell me, what was he doing here? What were *you* doing here?'

She glanced around, clearly as conscious as he was of the police activity around them. He was certain someone was listening to her words. Let them. They had nothing to hide now.

'You didn't imagine that either Vinko or I would just let you go like that? As soon as we realised you weren't going to call us, he was off. I couldn't have stopped him if I'd wanted to.'

'I bet you hardly tried.'

'Well, it seems he met Matt on the way out. You know, if it hadn't been for Matt I might not have come. I mean, I can understand he was upset, of course, but… I'd phoned the police, the minute Vinko left. And then there was Matt, ranting and raving as if it was all my fault. I couldn't take any more of him. I ran here – Vinko and I had worked out the most likely building while we were waiting for you. And I saw your scarf. Just before I literally bumped into Lucy. She told me how Vinko freed her and she'd seen you. Well, she thought you were one of *them*, but she doesn't know you.'

'An easy mistake to make.'

'But I do. You know when it's a crisis, you do things without thinking? I was sure it was you. No way could I just stand there, but I had no idea what to do either. I got her to tell me the way she'd come and by the time I got to the bottom of those stairs I saw sense and stopped, realised how stupid I was being. What use could I be? I'd only put myself, you, in more danger. I heard you and *him*. I couldn't understand either of you, but I could hear Vinko was distressed and then the silence obviously meant some kind of stand-off. Vinko had given me those numbers and...and I had some mad notion that I could distract Lek; even if I couldn't talk him round, at least give you some time. Oh, Jay.' She squeezed his hand, close to tears. 'I'm sorry, I could have killed Vinko.'

'But you didn't. You saved us.' He glanced in the direction Vinko had been taken. 'I hope.'

Chapter 31

The interview room was the same as the one she'd spent much of the previous day in – it may even have been the same one – and Jay looked alone, sitting at the bare, graffiti'd table. He was staring into space, fiddling with the collar of the regulation overalls. Marilyn recognised the gesture, remembering the way he twisted his scarf in his fingers. He turned and his expression brightened as the duty officer showed her in. She smiled back. He looked weary. She hesitated inside the door, watching him stand, glancing at the policeman by her side and unsure of the protocol.

'Is it OK for us to have some privacy?'

The officer nodded. 'We're just outside.'

Oblivious to the door shutting behind her, she found herself in Jay's arms, revelling in the feel and familiar smell of him.

'I'm so glad you've come,' he murmured.

'I'd have stayed with you if they'd let me.'

'I know.'

'You shouldn't be here! It's not fair. You're worn out.'

'There's a man dead. And a lot more for me to be complicit in.'

'They can deal with that later! You're not going anywhere, can't they see that?'

'Obviously not. And do you blame them, honestly?'

She responded by kissing him, trying to forget their surroundings. He held her as if they'd never be parted again.

313

They drew apart and sat close, holding one another's hands tightly.

'How's Vinko?' he asked. 'They've told me he's OK, but nothing more. "It's you we're here to talk about," was all the reply I got. I've been going out of my mind. I'm desperate to see him.'

'He'll be fine. That wound's more superficial than it looked; it was the loss of blood, on top of him being so exhausted, that was the danger.'

'Apparently Vesna's being a star.'

'The proverbial protective tigress.' Marilyn had warmed to Vesna, touched by the fondness she already felt for a nephew she'd only just met. 'She's got her solicitor looking after his case. And she's hijacking both the hospital systems and the police investigation to establish definitively that he's Ivan's son. She'll have him an identity before he's in a fit state to know what to do with it. Apparently her home's his, as soon as he's able to go there and for as long as he wants it. She told me she's not only pressing for leniency for his part, but she'll have them on their knees apologising to him.'

'What for?' he asked with a smile.

'She'll find something.' She turned serious. 'She says she's got to stop *him* apologising.'

'He should know—'

'You saw what he was like when we met – was it only yesterday morning? He really feels he betrayed you and that's why Lek got to you, why all this happened. He even blames himself for his grandparents' murder.'

Jay looked down at their intertwined hands.

'Will you be seeing him? If I can't go, tell him from me – I really mean this, Polly – he's got to stop talking like that. No more guilt. Tell him not to let Lek win.'

314

His head was bowed, his face hidden.

'Look at me, Jay.'

He raised his eyes slowly.

'Try telling yourself the same thing.'

'But I've been such an idiot! If I'd listened to you, if we'd gone to the police when you said… Are *you* in trouble?'

'Nothing serious.' Conspiracy to pervert the course of justice in Boris and Anja's murder case. She'd been angry and frustrated with him, of course she had. She'd revealed details of his life, and regretted it. When she'd told them how he'd known Lek years ago and knew what the man was capable of, she'd meant to make it obvious he'd acted in self-defence. But apparently, knowing what the man was capable of gave Jay the perfect motive for wanting to kill him. She'd said little more, and looking at him now, his expression almost as haunted as when he'd told her about Paševina and all that led up to it, she was glad. 'They haven't charged you yet?'

He shook his head with a sigh. 'I think they'll accept that Lek's death was self-defence on both my part and Vinko's. We shouldn't have been there, we were both carrying offensive weapons, but… I don't need to tell you.' He drew away from her and leaned on the table, his head in his hands. 'It was only this morning they finally dropped the talk of…of Anja and Boris's murder. Direct involvement, anyway. Mihal Novak came round overnight, apparently, and confessed. Of course it was he and Lek who broke in, intending to do no more than threaten them, so he claims. They must have got frustrated that Vinko wasn't doing more, about getting information from his grandparents or finding me. It seems Boris had a gun under the bed and Mihal panicked. I don't know whether Lek shot Anja to get rid of a witness or some warped revenge because she was

Zora's sister. Neither would surprise me. But at least Mihal had the decency to confirm that Vinko knew nothing about it at the time. And I certainly didn't.'

Marilyn shuddered. 'It took his confession? They didn't believe *you*?'

'Probably just wanted to make me sweat. I'm the sort of guy they'll want to pin as much as possible on.' He looked round at her. 'I'm so sorry for putting you through all this, Polly.'

'It's not your fault.'

'How can you say that? I've let you down and I'm sorry.'

She tried to take his hand. He pulled away, sat up straight.

'Please. Don't get any more attached than you already are. I don't deserve you. And you certainly don't deserve me. In the opposite sense.'

'I don't blame you for anything.'

He looked at her steadily. 'Don't you see how selfish I've been?'

'I know what you've been through.'

'There you are. Me.'

'You were trying to protect Vinko. And there was Lucy and—'

'And a chance literally to lay my ghosts to rest. Sod how it affects anyone else.' He shook his head. 'I find someone who matters to me – *two* people who matter to me – and it's still all about myself. The boy from Paševina was there – he hasn't been near me since with his horrors and his nightmares. Even during a sleepless night in this place. Perhaps I've done something right at last.' He ran a hand through his hair. 'But there we were with Vinko about to get his brains blown out and a little part of me could actually feel *pleased* to hear Lek claim I turned Ivan against him. See? Me, me, me.'

He stood up and turned away.

'I can live with that if you can.'

He turned back to her. 'Please, don't make any daft promises. Give yourself time to think. I'm not worth it.'

'You said it yourself, Jay. Don't let him win.'

'This isn't a fairy story, Polly.' He laughed. 'I know, you're thinking "You're a fine one to talk about fairy stories, Jay Spinney." It's true, I am. And that's why I don't trust happy endings.'

'It won't work,' she said.

'What?'

'Stop trying to make it easy for me.' He raised an eyebrow. 'Easy to walk away.'

'You think that's what I want?'

She shook her head. 'No. But you've been saying it all along. "Just say the word and I'll disappear and leave you in peace." Well, I won't make it that easy for you to run away again.'

He tried to smile, then shook his head. 'How long have we known each other? I've messed up your life enough even in that brief time.'

'You'd do just that if you rejected me now. Come back here.'

She motioned to the plastic chair. He stayed where he was.

'Be realistic,' he said.

'I am. Listen. We're trying to get you out of here. I've already given them my address as yours. Vesna would be prepared to put up bail money if it were needed.'

'Thank you. It means a lot. But there's no chance of bail.'

'You don't know that. I could be driving you home in a couple of days. Or sooner. They haven't charged you yet. But whatever happens, I'll be here.'

His expression made her feel as if her words were nothing but irrational childish optimism.

'Sit down, Jay.'

He perched uneasily on the hard plastic chair, looking fearful and vulnerable. She touched his arm and his sudden smile filled her with relief.

'You must be mad,' he said as he took her hand. 'But whatever you decide, haven't you got work to be doing? Go on, prove I'm not messing up your life.'

'In good time. I can hardly go back to Matt's at the moment, can I?'

'Then it's up to me to get out of here and help you sort that building out, right?'

As they held each other, she wondered momentarily why she'd been so quick to dismiss his suggestion of walking away. There was no question. She was inextricably involved in his story now, and he'd claimed his part in hers.

Chapter 32

Jay becomes aware of someone in the grey cell, looks up and sees the boy standing watching him. A wave of anger, betrayal, hurt rushes through him and he simply looks back, knowing shouting will do no good. He takes the stupid flimsy slippers he's been issued with and throws them in anger. The boy doesn't flinch. Jay thinks of Polly, hoping that by strength of will he can make the boy go. It doesn't work. His anger subsides, to be replaced by an overwhelming sadness and defeat.

'I should have known,' he says. 'You told me before that you don't keep your promises. I should have listened.'

The boy shakes his head, smiling, and beckons for Jay to follow. His smile fades, but for that brief moment it had seemed warm, almost genuine. He has never smiled before. Jay is unsettled.

As he walks down the rutted lane to Paševina, his anger returns. This is so unfair. He should refuse to go, but he can't. He has tried to resist before. No effort of will can keep him away. It is rare that he is aware of reality this far along the road, but it makes no difference to the fear. The deep dread feels the same as always. He comes to the first outlying house and refuses to look. His eyes firmly on the dusty surface of the road a few paces ahead, he keeps walking. This is a mistake. He glances back. The walls are still pockmarked with the scars of war and in need of paint, but the roof is whole. The blazing sun reflects off glass in the windows and the garden looks tended. It jars. He is on guard, stares at the road ahead then suddenly turns back, as if he can trick the house into its accustomed dereliction. It remains stubbornly inhabited. He tries to smother the optimism. This is a trick.

As he enters the village, the first thing he notices is people. No one is immediately visible out on the street, but he senses everyday activity. The houses and buildings here, too, are coming back to life. There are plenty of gaps where the damage was too great or the owners have not returned, and side alleys are still rubble-strewn and broken, but there is an undeniable sense of hope. He passes the building where Šojka once watched the boy die. He stops and looks round. This is where the boy usually vanishes, leaving him alone with his fears. He walks away more slowly this time, turning to smile at Jay again, a smile that lights up his face. He walks calmly into a nearby house.

Jay has no desire to follow him into a stranger's home, nor has he been invited, so he walks on to the square, where a small group sits talking over coffees outside a café. He sees a man about his own age walking purposefully by. Two young women with babies, talking. The buildings, the tables and chairs in front of the café, even the monument on the square, are real, undamaged. He wonders at the normality of the scene as he waits for the people to stop and stare. One or two of them watch him, but there is no menace, merely the curiosity of ordinary people wondering what a stranger is doing in their village. They do not form a hostile crowd, do not surge towards him to take their revenge.

Not yet. He wants to smile at what he sees. He wants to feel happiness that things are finally as they should be. But he can't trust it. He quickens his pace, eager to leave them to the business of getting on with their lives before he can make a wrong move to spoil it. He hurries away from the square, down a different road from the one he came down, but it's all right, he knows his way around. His spine tingles with the feeling of being watched, the anticipation of worse.

As he walks he sees now what he wasn't ready to notice as he approached – the fields are also being coaxed back to life. A crop is being harvested. The sound of sheep bells reaches him on the wind. A couple of farm workers pause to look at him, then go back to their work. The road winds through the scrubby, undulating landscape until the village is out of sight. He thinks he recognises the woods ahead where they were ambushed, and realises he has taken the wrong road. His scar itches with the faint memory of pain. But when he tries to turn it is like swimming against a strong current. He yields and continues walking. In any case, he can't face the thought of seeing the people in the fields again. They have their hardships, far too many, but they are working together. He knows the people on the square have suffered, but those who have returned – and he still feels his share of the guilt for those who have not – are rebuilding their community. He pauses as if to adjust a heavy load on his shoulders, and continues down the road. Alone.

It is around here that he always sees Zora. This time there is no sign of her and he is disappointed – he had been looking forward to telling her he's free now. But he's here, so how can he be free? Up ahead he sees a woman talking to a man and his heart jumps.

Polly shouldn't be here. He doesn't want to bring her here, doesn't want her to have to see any of this. But wasn't it wrong to keep it from her? He loves her and can't help smiling as he approaches. Ivan has a bottle and three small glasses. He pours, they raise them, and down the rakija in one. Ivan claps him on the shoulder and thanks him, though he doesn't say what for, and walks away, leaving him alone with Polly. She takes him by the hand and leads him to a patch of shade beneath a tree. They sit in silence for a few moments watching the hot sun mottled by the swaying leaves, then she says, 'You will come home, won't you? However long it takes. I'll be there, waiting for you.'

He wants to say, I will, of course I will, but the words don't come out. It doesn't matter; they are comfortable in each other's silence. He leans his head on her shoulder and dozes in the warm shade. When he opens his eyes she is no longer there. He knows which way she has gone and starts to follow, preparing to face whatever is lurking in the trees. As he becomes aware of the sounds of war, the smell of diesel and gunfire, he remembers something he once said: you don't stop feeling fear; you simply get used to it. And he walks towards it. That's the way forward and he won't go back to the village.

This time it is different. He knows she will be waiting. He remembers her face as she told him that, back in the dismal interview room, and he knows she meant it. He winces as he recalls telling her not to make silly promises – he fears it will take a long time and he needs her to help him face it. He breaks into a run, bracing himself against the terror that crouches, ready to pounce, in the trees. His tension begins to lessen as he realises the woods are quiet, the only sounds the cicadas and the rustling of a light breeze in the leaves, the only smell the herby scent of grass beneath his feet.

But he carries on running because he has to get home.

Alison Layland is a writer and translator. Raised in Newark and Bradford, she lives in mid-Wales with her husband and two teenage children. She studied Anglo-Saxon, Norse and Celtic at Cambridge University, and after a brief spell as a taxi driver worked for several years as a chartered surveyor before returning to her first love – languages. She was Welsh Learner of the Year in 1999, and in 2001 won first place at the National Eisteddfod with a short story written in Welsh. She translates for various publishers and agencies from German, French and Welsh – works of creative fiction and specialist information texts – and has been teaching herself Croatian while writing her first novel, *Someone Else's Conflict*.

For further news and information see www.alayland.uk

ABOUT HONNO

Honno Welsh Women's Press was set up in 1986 by a group of women who felt strongly that women in Wales needed wider opportunities to see their writing in print and to become involved in the publishing process. Our aim is to develop the writing talents of women in Wales, give them new and exciting opportunities to see their work published and often to give them their first 'break' as a writer. Honno is registered as a community co-operative. Any profit that Honno makes is invested in the publishing programme. Women from Wales and around the world have expressed their support for Honno. Each supporter has a vote at the Annual General Meeting. For more information and to buy our publications, please write to Honno at the address below, or visit our website: www.honno.co.uk

Honno, 14 Creative Units, Aberystwyth Arts Centre
Aberystwyth, Ceredigion SY23 3GL

Honno Friends

We are very grateful for the support of the Honno Friends: Jane Aaron, Annette Ecuyere, Audrey Jones, Gwyneth Tyson Roberts, Beryl Roberts, Jenny Sabine.

For more information on how you can become a Honno Friend, see: http://www.honno.co.uk/friends.php